Praise for Angelina M. Lopez and *Lush Money*

"The romance burns slow and hot throughout. Fans of fake-relationship romances will delight in this fresh spin on the trope."
—*Publishers Weekly*

"*Lush Money* is a gorgeous story full of heat and feels—and tons of sexy, royal fun!"
—*USA TODAY* bestselling author Sierra Simone

"[W]hat Lopez offers is almost a publishing magic trick in itself. She delivers that escapist fantasy in spades... But then she digs into the wounds and hard work underneath that fantasy, exposing the truth that a happily ever after in the context of reality is all the more rewarding."
—*Entertainment Weekly*

"A sexy, emotional and pitch-perfect romance... A novel that subverts classic romance tropes in an extremely satisfying way."
—*NPR*

"*Lush Money* was nothing I expected and everything I needed."
—*USA TODAY* bestselling author Naima Simone

"Lopez successfully flips the gender switch on the wealthy CEO trope while at the same time incorporating a generous dash of fairy-tale glitz and glam into the captivating storyline of her marvelous debut. And when these elements are combined with engaging characters and an abundance of boldly sensual, vividly rendered love scenes, you have everything fans of sexy contemporary romance could ever crave."
—*Booklist* (starred review)

"This is Lopez's debut and from just this one book, she's easily in my top five writers if you want some grade-A dirty talk and hot sexual situations."
—*Smart Bitches, Trashy Books*

**Also available from Angelina M. Lopez
and Carina Press**

Hate Crush

And look for book three in Angelina's Filthy Rich series,
coming in 2021!

LUSH MONEY

ANGELINA M. LOPEZ

carina
press

Recycling programs
for this product may
not exist in your area.

ISBN-13: 978-1-335-92179-6

Lush Money

First published in 2019. This edition published in 2021.

Copyright © 2019 by Angelina M. Lopez

This edition published by arrangement with Harlequin Books S.A.

For questions and comments about the quality of this book, please contact us at CustomerService@Harlequin.com.

Carina Press
22 Adelaide St. West, 40th Floor
Toronto, Ontario M5H 4E3, Canada
www.CarinaPress.com

Printed in U.S.A.

To Peter, who always believed

LUSH MONEY

January: Night One

Mateo Ferdinand Juan Carlos de Esperanza y Santos—the "Golden Prince," the only son of King Felipe, and heir to the tiny principality of Monte del Vino Real in northwestern Spain—had dirt under his fingernails, a twig of *Tempranillo FOS 02* in his back pocket, and a burning desire to wipe the mud of his muck boots on the white carpet where he waited. But he didn't. Under the watchful gaze of the executive assistant, who stared with disapproving eyes from his standing desk, Mateo kept his boots tipped back on the well-worn heels and his white-knuckled fists jammed into the pits of his UC Davis t-shirt. Staying completely still and deep breathing while he sat on the white couch was the only way he kept himself from storming away from this lunacy.

What the fuck had his father gotten him into?

A breathy *ding* sighed from the assistant's laptop. He granted Mateo the tiniest of smiles. "You may go in now," he said, hustling to the chrome-and-glass doors and pulling one open with a flourish. The assistant didn't seem to mind the dirt so much now as his eyes traveled—lingeringly—over Mateo's dusty jeans and t-shirt.

Mateo felt his *niñera* give him a mental smack upside the head when he kept his baseball cap on as he entered the office. But he was no more willing to take his cap off now than he'd been willing to change his clothes when the town car showed up at his lab, his ears ringing with his father's screams about why Mateo couldn't refuse.

The frosted-glass door closed behind him, enclosing him in a sky-high corner office as regal as any throne room. The floor-to-ceiling windows showed off Coit Tower to the west, the Bay Bridge to the east, and the darkening hills of San Francisco in between. The twinkling lights of the city flicked on like discovered jewels in the gathering night, adornment for this white office with its pale woods, faux fur pillows, and acrylic side tables. This office at the top of the fifty-five-floor Medina Building was opulent, self-assured. Feminine.

And empty.

He'd walked in the Rose Garden with the U.S. President, shaken the hand of Britain's queen, and kneeled in the dirt with the finest winemakers in Burgundy, but he stood in the middle of this empty palatial office like a jackass, not knowing where to sit or how to stand or who to yell at to make this *situación idiota* go away.

A door hidden in the pale wood wall opened. A woman walked out, drying her hands.

Dear God, no.

She nodded at him, her jowls wriggling as she tossed her paper towel back into the bathroom. "Take a seat, *Príncipe* Mateo. I'll prepare Roxanne to speak with you."

Of course. Of course Roxanne Medina, founder and CEO of Medina Now Enterprises, wasn't a sixty-year-old woman with a thick waist in medical scrubs. But "prepare" Roxanne to...

Ah.

The nurse leaned across the delicate, Japanese-style desk and opened a laptop perched on the edge. She pushed a button and a woman came into view on the screen. Or at least, the top of a woman's head came into view. The woman was staring down through black-framed glasses, writing something on a pad of paper. A sunny, tropical day loomed outside the balcony door behind her.

Inwardly laughing at the farce of this situation, Mateo took a seat in a leather chair facing the screen. Apparently, Roxanne Medina couldn't be bothered to meet the man she wanted to marry in person.

Two minutes later, he was no longer laughing. She hadn't looked at him. She just kept scribbling, giving him nothing to look at but the palm tree swaying behind her and the part in her dark, shiny hair.

He glanced at the nurse. She stared back, blank-eyed. He'd already cleared his throat twice.

Fuck this. "Excuse me," he began.

"Helen, it sounds like the prince may have a bit of a dry throat." Roxanne Medina spoke, finally, without raising her eyes from her document. "Could you get him a glass of water?"

"Of course, ma'am."

As the nurse headed to a decanter, Mateo said, "I don't need water. I'm trying to find out..."

Roxanne Medina raised one delicate finger to the screen. Without looking up. Continuing to write. Without a word or a sound, Roxanne Medina shushed him, and Mateo—top of his field, head of his lab, a goddamned *príncipe*—he let her, out of shock and awe that another human being would treat him this way.

He *never* treated people this way.

He moved to stand, to storm out, when a water glass appeared in front of his face and a hair was tugged from his head.

"Ow!" he yelled as he turned to glare at the granite-faced nurse holding a strand of his light brown hair.

"Fantastic, I see the tests have begun."

Mateo turned back to the screen and pushed the water glass

out of his way so he could see the woman who finally deigned to speak to him.

"Tests?"

She was beautiful. Of course she was beautiful. When you have billions of dollars at your disposal, you can look any way you want. Roxanne Medina was sky-blue eyed, high-breasted and lush-lipped, with long and lustrous black hair. On the pixelated screen, he couldn't tell how much of her was real or fake. He doubted even her stylist could remember what was Botoxed, extended, and implanted.

Still, she was striking. Mateo closed his mouth with a snap.

Her slow, sensual smile let him know she'd seen him do it.

Mateo glowered as Roxanne Medina slipped her delicate black reading glasses up on her head and aimed those searing blue eyes at him. "These tests are just a formality. We've tested your father and sister and there were no genetic surprises."

"Great," he deadpanned. "Why are you testing me?"

Her sleek eyebrows quirked. "Didn't your father explain this already?" A tiny gold cross hung in the V of her ivory silk top. "We're testing for anything that might make the Golden Prince a less-than-ideal specimen to impregnate me."

Madre de Dios. His father hadn't been delusional. This woman really wanted to buy herself a prince and a royal baby. The king had introduced him to some morally deficient people in his life, but this woman... His shock was punctuated by a needle sliding into his bicep.

"*¡Joder!*" Mateo yelled, turning to see a needle sticking out of him, just under his t-shirt sleeve. "Stop doing that!"

"Hold still," the devil's handmaiden said emotionlessly, as if stealing someone's blood for unwanted tests was an everyday task for her.

Rather than risk a needle breaking off in his arm, he did

stay still. But he glared at the screen. "I haven't agreed to any of this. The only reason I'm here is to tell you 'no.'"

"The king promised..."

"My father makes a lot of promises. Only one of us is fool enough to believe them."

She took the glasses off entirely, sending that hair swirling around her neck, and slowly settled back into her chair. The gold cross hid once again between blouse and pale skin. She stared at him the way he stared at the underside of grape leaves to determine their needs.

Finally, she said, "Forgive me. We've started on different pages. I thought you were on board." Her voice, Mateo noticed, was throaty with a touch of scratch to it. He wondered if that was jet lag from her tropical location. Or did she sound like that all the time? "I run a multinational corporation; sometimes I rush to the finish line and forget my 'pleases' and 'thank yous.' Helen, say you're sorry."

"I'm sorry," Helen said immediately. As she pulled the plunger and dragged Mateo's blood into the vial.

Gritting his teeth, he glared at the screen. "What self-respecting person would have a kid with a stranger for money?"

"A practical one with a kingdom on the line," Roxanne Medina said methodically. "My money can buy you time. That's what you need to right your sinking ship, correct? You need more time to develop the *Tempranillo Vino Real*?"

Mateo's blood turned cold; he wondered if Nurse Ratched could see it freezing as she pulled it out of him. He stayed quiet and raised his chin as the nurse put a Band-Aid on his arm.

"This deal can give you the time you need," the billionaire said, her voice beckoning. "My money can keep your people solvent until you get those vines planted."

She sat there, a stranger in a tropical villa, declaring herself the savior of the kingdom it was Mateo's responsibility to save.

For centuries, the people of Monte del Vino Real, a plateau hidden among the Picos de Europa in northernmost Spain, made their fortunes from the lush wines produced from their cool-climate Tempranillo vines. But in recent years, mismanagement, climate change, the world's focus on French and California wines, and his parents' devotion to their royal lifestyle instead of ruling had devalued their grapes. The world thought the Monte was "sleepy." What they didn't know was that his kingdom was nearly destitute.

Mateo was growing a new variety of Tempranillo vine in his UC Davis greenhouse lab whose hardiness and impeccable flavor of the grapes it produced would save the fortunes of the Monte del Vino Real. His new-and-improved vine or "clone"—he'd called it the *Tempranillo Vino Real* for his people—just needed a couple more years of development. To buy that time, he'd cobbled together enough loans to keep credit flowing to his growers and business owners and his community teetering on the edge of financial ruin instead of free-falling over. He'd also instituted security measures in his lab so that the vine wouldn't be stolen by competitors.

But Roxanne Medina was telling him that all of his efforts—the favors he'd called in to keep the Monte's poverty a secret, the expensive security cameras, the pat downs of grad students he knew and trusted—were useless. This woman he'd never met had sniffed out his secrets and staked a claim.

"What does or doesn't happen to my kingdom has nothing to do with you," he said, angry at a computer screen.

She put down her glasses and clasped slender, delicate hands in front of her. "This doesn't have to be difficult," she insisted. "All I want is three nights a month from you."

He scoffed. "And my hand in marriage."

"Yes," she agreed. "The king has produced more than enough royal bastards for the Monte, don't you think?"

The king. His father. The man whose limitless desire to be seen as a wealthy international playboy emptied the kingdom's coffers. The ruler who weekly dreamt up get-rich-quick schemes that—without Mateo's constant monitoring and intervention—would have sacrificed the Monte's land, people, and thousand-year legacy to his greed.

It was Mateo's fault for being surprised that his father would sell his son and grandchild to the highest bidder.

"I'm just asking for three nights a month for a year," Roxanne Medina continued. "At the end of that year, I'll 'divorce' you—" her air quotes cast in stark relief what a mockery this "marriage" would be "—and provide you with the settlement I outlined with your father. Regardless of the success of your vine, your people will be taken care of and you will never have to consider turning your kingdom into an American amusement park."

That was another highly secretive deal that Roxanne Medina wasn't supposed to know about: An American resort company wanted to purchase half the Monte and develop it as a playland for rich Americans to live out their royal fantasies. But her source for that info was easy; his father daily threatened repercussions if Mateo didn't sign the papers for the deal.

In the three months since Mateo had stormed out of that meeting, leaving his father and the American resort group furious, his IT guy had noticed a sharp rise in hacking attempts against his lab's computers. And there'd been two attempted break-ins on his apartment, according to his security company.

Billionaire Roxanne Medina might be the preferable devil. At least she was upfront about her snooping and spying.

But have a kid with her? His heir? A child that, until an hour ago, had only been a distant, flat someday, like marriage and death? "So I'm supposed to make a kid with you and then—what—just hand him over?"

"Didn't the king tell you...? Of course, you'll get to see her. A child needs two parents." The adamancy of her raspy voice had Mateo focusing on the screen. The billionaire clutched her fingers in front of the laptop, her blue eyes focused on him. "We'll have joint custody. We won't need to see each other again, but your daughter, you can have as much or as little access to her as you'd like."

She pushed her long black hair behind her shoulders as she leaned closer to the screen, and Mateo once again saw that tiny, gold cross against her skin.

"Your IQ is 152, mine is 138, and neither of us have chronic illnesses in our families. We can create an exceptional child and give her safety, security, and a fairy-tale life free of hardship. I wouldn't share this responsibility with just anyone; I've done my homework on you. I know you'll make a good father."

Mateo had been trained in manipulation his whole life. His mother cried and raged, and then hugged and petted him. His father bought him a Labrador puppy and then forced Mateo to lie about the man's whereabouts for a weekend. Looking a person in the eye and speaking a compliment from the heart were simple tricks in a master manipulator's bag.

And yet, there was something that beckoned about the child she described. He'd always wanted to be a better everything than his own father.

The nurse sat a contract and pen in front of Mateo. He stared at the rose gold Mont Blanc.

"I know this is unorthodox," she continued. "But it benefits us both. You get breathing room for your work and financial security for your people. I get a legitimate child who knows her father without...well, without the hassles of everything else." She paused. "You understand the emotional toll of an unhappy marriage better than most."

Mateo wanted to bristle but he simply didn't have the energy. His parents' affairs and blowups had been filling the pages of the tabloids since before he was born. The billionaire hadn't needed to use her elite gang of spies to gather that intel. But she did remind him of his own few-and-far-between thoughts on matrimony. Namely, that it was a state he didn't want to enter.

If he never married, then when would he have an heir?

Mateo pulled back from his navel gazing to focus on her. She was watching him. Mateo saw her eyes travel slowly over the screen, taking him in, and he felt like a voyeur and exhibitionist at the same time.

She bit her full bottom lip and then gave him a smile of promise. "To put it frankly, *Príncipe*, your position and poverty aren't the only reasons I selected you. You're...a fascinating man. And we're both busy, dedicated to our work, and not getting as much sex as we'd like. I'm looking forward to those three nights a month."

"Sex" coming out of her lush mouth in that velvety voice had Mateo's libido sitting up and taking notice. That's right. He'd be having sex with this tempting creature on the screen.

She tilted her head, sending all that thick black hair to one side and exposing her pale neck. "I've had some thoughts about those nights in bed."

The instant, searing image of her arched neck while he buried his hand in her hair had Mateo tearing his eyes away. He looked out on the city. *Jesus*. She was right, it had been too long. And he didn't need his little brain casting a vote right now.

She made it sound so simple.

Her money gave him more than the three years of financial ledge-clinging that he'd scraped together on his own, a timeline that had already caused sleepless nights. The only way Mateo could have the *Tempranillo Vino Real* planted and profitable in three years is if everything went perfectly—no problems with development, no bad growing seasons. Mother Nature could not give him that guarantee. Her deal also prevented his father from taking more drastic measures. The chance for a quiet phone and an inbox free of plans like the one to capture the Monte's principal irrigation source and bottle it into "Royal Water" with the king's face on the label was almost reason enough to sign the contract.

Mateo refused to list "regular sex with a gorgeous woman who looked at him like a lollipop" in the plus column. He wasn't led around by his cock like his father.

And that child; his far-off, mythical heir? The *príncipes y princesas* of the Monte del Vino Real had been marrying for profit long before Roxanne Medina invented it. He didn't know what kind of mother she would be, but he would learn in the course of the year together. And if they discovered in that year they weren't compatible…surely she would cancel the arrangement. After the initial shock, she'd seemed reasonable.

Gripping on to his higher ideals and shaky rationalizations, he picked up the pen and signed.

The nurse plunked an empty plastic cup with a lid down on the desk.

"What the…?" Mateo said with horror.

"Just the final test," Roxanne Medina said cheerily from the screen. "Don't worry. Helen left a couple of magazines in the bathroom. Just leave the cup in there when you're finished and she'll retrieve it."

Any hopes for a reasonable future swirled down the drain. Roxanne Medina expected him to get himself off in a cup while this gargoyle of a woman waited outside the door.

He stood and white-knuckled the cup, turned away from the desk. Fuck it. At least his people were safe. An hour earlier, his hands in the dirt, he'd thought he could save his kingdom with hard work and noble intentions. But he'd fall on his sword for them if he had to.

Or stroke it.

He had one last question for the woman who held his life in her slim-fingered hand. "Why?" he asked, his back to the screen, the question coming from the depths of his chest. "Really, why?"

"Why what?"

"Why me."

"Because you're perfect." He could hear the glee in her rich voice. "And I always demand perfection."

January: Night Two

The next night, Mateo once again waited in an opulent room with one of Roxanne Medina's minions, once again in jeans, t-shirt, and ball cap. He'd thrown on a blazer, but otherwise opted for comfort for what he assumed would be a first date.

Fuming as he checked his watch—she was forty-five minutes late—he glared at the attorney shuffling papers at the desk of the boudoir-styled hotel suite and congratulated himself for not dressing up for this worst-first-date-of-his-life humiliation.

He'd worked all day to convince himself he could normalize their insane arrangement. He figured he'd pick her up at the Fairmont Hotel at the room number she'd sent, they'd go to dinner, and there, like rational adults, they'd discuss the details of two strangers wedding and bedding. He would take the first steps in getting to know this woman who wanted to be the mother of his child.

Instead, when Mateo knocked on the door of the Fairmont's honeymoon suite, a salt-and-pepper-haired African-American man opened it. William LaPierre, Roxanne's general counsel, had introduced himself, asked Mateo to sign more documents, and now seemed content to wait. As he sat on the arm of a luxurious purple velvet couch, Mateo's temper percolated. Now that he was on Roxanne Medina's payroll, she must expect him to wait, too.

"Why is she doing this?" Mateo asked, jiggling his leg as he stared at the attorney. "Sir?" The older man looked at him, not unfriendly, through silver-rimmed glasses.

"Why does she want this marriage? A kid? With someone she doesn't know? Why doesn't she just go to a sperm bank?"

The attorney smiled with more compassion than Mateo thought was possible from a Medina Now employee. "That seems like a question for Ms. Medina, don't you think?"

"*Por supuesto.* And I'd be asking it if she were here," Mateo said. "But she isn't and you are. Give me something."

William leaned back in the leather desk chair, clasping his fingers over his well-fed belly. Finally, he asked, "Do you know much about her?"

Mateo rolled his shoulders, irritated. "I know what Google knows."

Hours' worth of Googling during the sleepless hours last night had given him an understanding of Roxanne Medina's "brand." Article after article spoke about her childhood spent in poverty, the tiny Kansas hometown where she was from, the absent Mexican father, the single mother. Her fortunes changed when she won a full ride to Princeton. Over and over again, Mateo found the story of how the twenty-one-year-old woman had walked from the lawn of Nassau Hall, where she'd just graduated, to barge into an investor's meeting five blocks away. With diploma in hand, she'd bullied the roomful of men into helping her buy a failing online fitness-wear company.

He knew she'd "bullied" them because it was the word he read repeatedly, like so many of the matching adjectives from different writers in different publications. It seems the now twenty-nine-year-old Roxanne Medina—they were the same age—had found a way to circumvent the First Amendment and control every drop of information about her. He knew the next detail in her story by heart because he'd read the identical sentence so many times: "Roxanne Medina began her meteoric rise when she sold Heart and Sole Fit Wear for twenty times the purchase price the same week she received her MBA from Harvard."

"So you know her father abandoned her and her mother?" William asked.

Mateo scoffed. "Sure, it's in every story written about her."

"Then you might understand why she wants her child to know their father. A sperm donor would be anathema to Ms. Medina."

Mateo pushed angrily off the couch arm. "*¡Joder!* So I'm supposed to share a kid with someone who has daddy *and* control issues? That's stable."

The attorney shook his head as if he were disappointed in Mateo. "Her 'control issues' have empowered her to see this company through the worst of financial times without laying off a soul. Her 'control issues' allowed her to take on her entire board when they protested her bringing on a black ex-priest with a night school law degree as corporate counsel."

Mateo looked at the man closely and then rolled his eyes. "I'm seeking sympathy from her number one fan."

"Who's my number one fan?" asked a raspy voice from the dark hallway leading into the sitting area.

She had snuck in like a cat.

"I am, Ms. Medina," William LaPierre said cheerily.

Roxanne Medina stepped into the warm light. "Damn right." She looked at Mateo, a large cashmere shawl wrapped snugly around her. "Wow." She approached him as she untucked the shawl at her neck. "You truly are the Golden Prince, aren't you?"

That stupid moniker. He'd been stuck with it since he was seventeen, when paparazzi had taken pictures of him on the beach in the Maldives. The complexion, the light brown eyes, the blond he got in his hair every summer, the stature and shoulders—they were nothing more than a lucky combination of DNA, "gifts" from his parents, no more useful than the quick temper he'd inherited from his father and the addict's need for flan he got from his mother. He used his looks when they were effective tools and ignored them the rest of the time.

But if he was the Golden Prince, she was sexy Snow White. Lustrous black hair hung in a soft wave down her back, and pale, perfect skin revealed itself as she slowly unwrapped. Her blue eyes—just like the sky—stroked over him. She had the audacity to bite into her full, juicy, apple-red lower lip as her eyes traveled over his body. He gritted his teeth as she pulled the final layer of her cream shawl away like Salome's veils, revealing an emerald-green silk dress that clung to her lush body as closely as Mateo would have liked to.

She was flawless—perfect skin, round hips, full breasts, long lashes, and direct, encompassing eyes. Under any other circumstances, he would have done everything in his power to get this stunning, accomplished woman in his bed.

She extended a slim hand that glowed with creamy luminescence. Mateo took it, enjoying its silky feel.

"*Príncipe*," she purred, her smile wide and luscious. "You and I should have no problem making a beautiful little princess."

Mateo got lost in that soft, throaty voice. Like velvet with tiny hooks in it, soothing and scratching across his skin. But when he thought of her actual words—his *child*, with this rampaging stranger—his arousal died on the vine.

"Ms. Medina." He nodded. He let go of her hand. "You're late."

"Am I?" the woman mused as she hung her shawl on the back of a chair and fussed in her expensive handbag. "I'm sorry,

Príncipe." Her perfect Spanish lilt when she said his title had the hairs rising on the back of his neck.

But he remembered her apology from the night before: *Forgive me. We've started on different pages*. Roxanne Medina handed out *sorrys* like tips, effortless dollar bills from a billionaire.

Mateo hung his thumbs in the front pockets of his jeans. "Don't let it happen again."

He saw a quick narrowing of her eyes when she turned to focus on him before she relaxed, flicking that thick hair over a shoulder and sitting on the edge of the desk. The move pulled the dress higher and showed a naked, toned leg that shined like satin. She swung it lazily. "I'm glad you're eager," she said, disarming him with steamy blue eyes that laughed at him. "We'll wrap up with William and I'll make it up to you. I'm told the beds at the Fairmont are very comfortable."

"Roxanne," the attorney admonished.

Roxanne Medina leaned back on a delicate hand, looking over her shoulder to roll her eyes at him. "I forget how much of a prude you can be, William." She looked at Mateo. "Did he tell you he used to be a priest?"

Mateo stared at her. "We're starting tonight?"

"Of course," she said, without even looking at him. She nodded at William. "Let's get to it."

"Fine," William grumbled. He looked down at a piece of paper on the desk, and then looked up at Roxanne. "Do you?"

"You betcha." She winked, and then reached across the desk to take a fountain pen from William's hand and sign the paper. William pushed the paper close to Mateo and held the pen out to him. "And do you?"

Mateo, with a genius IQ, a PhD from Cornell, and his name on the door of one of the most well-respected viticulture labs in the world, struggled to keep up. "Do I what?"

"Are you willing to enter into an agreement of marriage with Roxanne Medina?"

Now? They were getting married now? He opened his mouth to protest, to express shocked astonishment, to tell her that she was as *loca* as a... But he glanced at Roxanne Medina, and the satisfied expression on her face as she swung that sky-high heel had him clamping his mouth shut and swallowing his disbelief.

She'd had him spinning since the second she'd walked into the room. No, since the second he'd been foolish enough to pick up his phone without looking at the caller ID yesterday. Mateo knew what she wanted and knew what he would get in return. His attorney had looked over the documents during an early-morning phone call and had complimented the agreement for its cold clarity; Mateo had seen her clean bill of health before he'd even shaken her hand. This wasn't a marriage; this was a business arrangement. And he didn't need to behave like some outraged groom. He was an Esperanza, a descendant of kings, and the only hope for the Monte del Vino Real. He would stop spinning and stand tall now.

He leaned one hand on the desk and held the other out to William, forcing the man to place the pen in his hand while he met his gaze. Mateo bent down and scratched his signature onto the document.

"*Sí*, I do."

"Then by the power vested in me by the state of California, you are now husband and wife." William's words were surprisingly solemn. The attorney signed the document, blew on it to dry the expensive ink, and then placed it and the other papers in his briefcase, without looking up.

Mateo turned his back on them and walked to the window. Here, in the honeymoon suite of the Fairmont, high atop a San Francisco hill, he could stare down at the lights of the

Transamerica building and the glowing ships leaving the Bay. He hovered above thousands of people who would never sell their heir in a business arrangement.

He'd never been more ashamed in his whole life.

From behind him, he heard murmured conversation, the shuffle of feet, and the opening and closing of the suite door.

And then he heard her say: "We might as well get the next part over with."

In no way should getting sex "over with" punch him with desire. He blamed his father. He blamed the nights in his lab and his ignored twenty-nine-year-old libido. He turned on her slowly.

"What about dinner?" he asked, gripping on to the educated, cultured man that he was. Looking at her voluptuous body in that dress made base male lust flood his gut.

She crossed her arms under her breasts. Her cleavage was deep and soft, the delicate cross tickling at the top of it. "I have an early meeting."

He scoffed out loud.

She raised her chin, daring him to argue. Her bloodred nails, gripping her arms, would rake like talons over his skin.

Fuck it. "Fine," he said, jerking his cap at the hallway. "Bedroom."

Those eyes daggered him before she said, "No. Sit on the couch."

His body's reaction to that command, in her throaty voice, made him hate himself even more. The last thing he needed was to start panting every time this billionaire cracked her whip. He just wanted to get the fucking night over with.

He stalked to the deep purple velvet couch and threw himself on it, keeping his cap brim low as her legs came into view. He watched her sullenly from beneath his brim as she slipped out of her heels and placed the shoes side-by-side, like good little soldiers. Then her knees wiggled as she pulled a scrap of cream silk down them. She stepped out of her panties, folded them, and then placed them on the couch near Mateo's hand.

He knocked back his head and met her eyes as she reached for his button fly.

"Are you going to help at all?" she huffed as she worked to open his jeans.

"You've got it under control," he said through gritted teeth as she found the opening in his boxers and pulled him out. He was semi-erect but not hard enough to be of use to her. "You've got your hand on everything you want from me."

A smile blossomed on her lips. "Not everything," she said as she stroked softly up his length. And then, for the hundredth time since he'd met her, Roxanne Medina shocked him: she leaned over and surrounded the tip of his cock with her hot mouth. He swallowed his gasp as he looked down at her bent over him, her round ass in green silk in the air and her thick black hair dripping over his legs and her mouth, oh God, those lush lips, smoothing down his cock. He could feel their pillow; trace the lick of her tongue. She engulfed him, took him whole, then pulled up, sucking, sucking, sucking the entire long length of him.

"Gah," Mateo choked as she reached the tip again, his fingers clawing into the velvet couch. He was as hard as a fucking rock.

He popped out of her mouth. "Excellent," she purred as she straightened, and then she was climbing on top of him, straddling him as green silk pulled up her thighs, and then, holy fuck, hot satiny skin was surrounding him and then... wet. So much wet and warmth.

He slid into Roxanne Medina and it was like heaven in hell.

"Fuck," he gasped as she spread her thighs to take him in deep, those amazing soft breasts pushing against his chest, the succulent offering of them in green silk all he could see with his ball cap still on. Through her expensive perfume, he could smell her. Roses. Hothouse roses covered in steam. She pulled away, a tight slick slide, and then began to pump. Fuck, he could see her hips working him, feel her sweetness gripping him. He turned his head to the side and squeezed his eyes closed, grabbed on to the couch cushions. Bit his lip. Hard, she was taking him. So fucking hard and demanding. It was worse and so, so much better with his eyes closed, the press of her breasts, the squeeze of her pussy, her fingernails biting into his biceps.

And then she moaned. Raspy and breathy against the day-old scruff on his jaw. Hot into the shell of his ear. A throaty, low sound of uncontrolled pleasure from this woman who ruled with an iron fist.

Mateo was lost.

He gritted his teeth against the excruciating orgasm that punched him in the lower back like a fist. But she was relentless. She was pitiless. She pumped and fucked and worked him, making him come and come and come. The pleasure was unbearable, like it came from the floor, from the walls, from every bed in the hotel, like every orgasm ever suffered at the Fairmont was flowing into his toes from where they were curled against the carpet.

"Enough," Mateo panted when he could, grabbing her thighs, finally touching her, holding her down against him. "Stop."

This time, finally, for the first time in the twenty-four hours that he'd been intertwined with her, she did stop. She leaned close against him, resting. Mateo could feel her soft, hot pants against his neck, her quick, exhausted breaths against his chest. He was wreathed in the smell of warm rose petals. She squeezed him once more, gently, and Mateo shuddered against her like a fourteen-year-old boy. But she soothed him, sliding her lips along his jaw, against the lobe of his ear. Mateo still held her slippery, silk-covered thighs. It was almost an embrace.

"We're going to get along just fine," she whispered into his ear. She slowly rose up on her knees and sighed as Mateo slipped out of her. His hands slid from the fabric to bare leg, silkier than the dress.

She stood. Leaned down to pick up her shoes. Mateo picked her folded panties off the couch, intending to hand them to her, but she turned away. He watched her cross the room through half-closed eyes; she swayed like Cleopatra in that dress. She picked up her handbag and slid her shawl over her shoulder.

And then she walked past Mateo without looking at him once.

Mateo sat on the purple velvet couch, his spent body unable to protest, her silk panties crushed in his hand, his wet cock lying exposed outside of his button fly, as he heard the door click closed behind her.

January: Night Three

Mateo found himself the next night where he could be found most nights: knees in the dirt of his greenhouse lab on the edge of the University of California, Davis campus. With a cool, starless night pressing against the greenhouse glass and the soothing smell of moist soil and green growth in his nose, Mateo was doing what he normally did: giving love to his grapevine, the *Tempranillo Vino Real*. His days were busy providing one-of-a-kind vine clones and disease-free planting material to prestigious vineyards around the world, so night was usually his only time to work on the vine that would save the Monte del Vino Real.

But the sudden bang on the outermost door of the Esperanza Certified Vineyard Material building highlighted how the location and activity were the only things "usual" about this night.

Taking a deep breath of calm, Mateo continued his tiny cut into the 420A rootstock planted in the soil. He blew away the cut-off wood, revealing a perfect V, and reached into his box of precious budwood to grab a stick of *Tempranillo Vino Real*. With steady hands, he began to slice the base of the stick into a matching V.

Quick, hard bangs against the door made him jump, made him slice the wicked-sharp grafting knife into his thumb.

"*Joder*," Mateo swore, sucking on the cut. He grabbed the

grafting tape meant for his vine and wrapped it around his thumb. He shook it hard, trying to shake away the pain. He hadn't cut himself in years.

Roxanne Medina had him fumbling like a new hand in the field.

When his phone had started buzzing like crazy that evening, he'd ignored it for an hour, the vibration a taunt in his pants before he finally snatched it out and turned it off. He'd retreated to his lab, searching for the comfort and validation he'd always found at this world-renowned mecca for viticulturists, a castle that he'd built with his own two hands.

The frustrated rattle of the outside door against its lock was like the clawing of his worst tendencies against its walls.

Mateo refocused on his work with gritted-teeth resolution. He carefully sliced off the end of the Tempranillo budwood until it was a protruding V. When he slid the budwood into the cut of the rootstock, the Vs matched perfectly, like sliding a piece into a puzzle. Mateo sucked in a breath of contentment as he wrapped a piece of grafting tape around the joined pieces of grapevine, ensuring the Tempranillo vine would merge with the pest-resistant rootstock. His field crew would have teased him mercilessly about how long it took him to graft one vine. His vineyard manager could do it in seven seconds, and he was one of the slow ones. But this was Mateo's love, the one thing in his life he could control. He liked to bask in it.

He slid forward on his knee to the next vine, dragging his budwood box with him as he ground dirt into his jeans.

A tap sounded on the glass of the greenhouse, just at the end of the row he was kneeling in. "My assistant assured me you received my email about where we were meeting tonight." While muffled, the sexy rasp of Roxanne Medina's voice could still be heard through the glass.

Mateo focused every muscle on keeping his head down, his eyes on the cut he was making.

"*¿Príncipe?*"

The knife bit satisfyingly into the plant like butter.

"Mateo?"

The V was a perfect slant, smooth, without snags.

"*¿Mi esposo?*"

Mateo's head shot up and he glared through the glass. "Don't," he warned her.

God, it was hilarious, that she would call him "my husband" while she stood out there dressed in white, his ghostly bride against the black night. She was wearing a long, filmy white skirt that covered her toes and a top that rose high on the neck but exposed her arms and midriff. Her black hair was piled on top of her head. All that silky, exposed skin was probably freezing. His jaw tensed at the unwanted considerations of how he could warm it.

She pressed the pads of her fingers against the glass and cocked her head. "Look. Maybe I was a bit abrupt last night."

"Maybe?" Mateo threw his knife into the budwood box. The last thing he needed was to slice off a finger because of this woman. "Three days ago, I don't know who you are. Two days ago, you shove your way into my life and declare yourself my wife, mother of my kid, and savior of my kingdom. And last night... *¡Joder!*" he swore, shaking his hand.

She'd treated him like he was a stud in her stable. And, *Jesucristo*, he had neighed.

His parents' dramatics and affairs had put him through some stomach-churning humiliations growing up. If he hadn't loved his sister and the people of the Monte del Vino Real, he would have spent his summers and breaks on the grounds of the Massachusetts boarding school where he got his education. The day he turned eighteen and gained control of some of his trust, he commissioned his own mountain home in the Monte, determined to limit the number of his times his parents could shame him.

He'd never offered himself up for humiliation. Not until last night.

"I'm sorry for—"

"No," Mateo cut her off. He'd had enough of her worthless apologies. Roxanne Medina preferred to ask forgiveness instead of permission. He tilted his face up so she could see his eyes under the ball cap. "I want. A divorce."

She didn't even blink. "But what about your kingdom?"

"If you're our only hope, then burn it down now. Regardless, I'm not fucking you again."

Wide awake last night, he'd tortured himself with how eagerly he'd consented to Roxanne Medina's demands. He'd handed her a wedding vow, a promise of a kid, and his cock on a couch without a whimper of protest. While salivating. Had his mind really agreed so readily because of the money she offered, the time to develop his vines, the security for his people? With her contract came the promise of having his father off his back and a thicker financial security blanket than the threadbare one he'd woven together on his own.

Or had his mind simply squeezed its eyes shut and allowed his body to have what it wanted? It had been so easy to lie back and let a gorgeous woman suck and fuck him, get the orgasm he craved and give her what she wanted in return for the millions she would shower down on him. He literally hadn't lifted a finger.

His stomach rolled at the thought that his father, at twenty-nine, would have thought the deal was a wish–come–true.

"There isn't some girlfriend the king doesn't know about, is there?"

Mateo shook his head in amazement and breathed through

his disgust. She truly didn't get it. Once again he reached for his knife and a stick of budwood.

"A boyfriend?"

He let out a grunt. "If I say yes, will you leave me alone?"

"It's difficult to talk to you through this glass." The glass was the only thing protecting her from his hands. Whether he'd stroke her or strangle her, he wasn't sure. But it was the tiniest salve to Mateo's howling ego to hear the frustration in her voice.

"Then stop talking," he said, loud enough so she could hear him clearly while he took a perfect slice out of the stick. "Just send me divorce papers."

The first slice on the opposite side of the stick was wobbly—Mateo took a deep calming breath—but the next one created a nice insertion V. He matched it to the rootstock, grabbed his grafting tape, and wrapped a neat bandage around the joined vines.

Roxanne Medina's silence was disconcerting. He glanced up when he moved to the next vine.

She was gone.

He rolled his head on his shoulders, tilted his cap back to scrub at the front of his hair, and then rubbed at his crotch, repositioned the semi he'd had since she first rattled the door.

He was a better man than his father. He wouldn't stoop to creating a child within this chaos. He'd...figure something else out, increase his focus on the *Vino Real*'s development while juggling the other, profitable ventures of his lab, avoid the inevitable screaming phone calls from the king, visit the Monte soon to calm the growing concerns there, step up his cyber and personal security to head off whatever the American resort group tried to pull...

Mateo looked down the row at all the rootstock that still needed grafting and felt his shoulders sag with exhaustion.

He straightened his cap and sat back on his feet. It could wait until tomorrow. Two nights without sleep were catching up with him. Tomorrow was a new day.

"Ah, this is better."

Mateo swung around on one knee, shock ripping through him as Roxanne Medina strolled into his highly secure lab.

She glanced around the greenhouse as she rubbed her naked arms, the motion making her breasts surge against that top, calling attention to the Venus curve of her waist and the pristine skin of her revealed torso. "It was chilly out there," she said, smiling angelically, as if a conversation about the weather would distract him from the fact that she'd broken into his lab.

She was here. Inside the glass. Reachable. Touchable. Fuckable.

Mateo snapped. "What the *fuck*?" He surged to his feet. "How did you get in here?!" He charged down the row toward her, his muck boots digging into the soil. "You don't belong here." He moved faster as he neared the end of the row and saw her grin finally wobble, saw her float back a step in that gauzy skirt. "I don't *want* you here."

Want, want, want, want...

This was his lab, his home, the sum of every valuable thing he'd ever done with his life. It was the cornerstone of his reputation and the padded cell for his sanity. And this woman, this stranger, picked its locks and rooted out its secrets whenever she had the urge. She invaded it like its bolts and codes were mist, easily blown away by those lush, red lips.

"I just wanted to..." She gasped, her blue eyes widening when he wrapped his dirty hands around her satiny arms. The instant bolt of lust at the feel of her, the distinct wild rose scent of her, made him enraged. Mateo raised her up on her toes.

"We're done talking about what you want," he seethed, stepping her back against one of his silver lab tables. That wide mouth fell open. Her skin was flushed and fine. "What I want (*want, want, want*) is a little fucking respect. Stop thinking you can shove me around with your money and your employees and your velvet-lined pussy." Bad words. Just the memory of her squeeze on him... Her flesh in his hands made him hungrier. He felt a predator's desire to eat her whole.

"Mateo, I'm sorry I..." she said in that sexy goddamned voice. He ignored her meaningless words as she put her hands on his chest and stroked them up to his shoulders.

Her skin was cool. But those hands? They were burning. They singed him through his thin t-shirt.

Mateo groaned, "Fuck you," the instant before he lifted her against him and slammed his mouth down on hers. Her juicy, temptress lips fell open at the thrust of his tongue and he was inside her, punishing and devouring her, searching for that thing that made Roxanne Medina his worst nightmare. His hottest wet dream. "Fuck your useless apologies."

She dug her fingers into his nape and dragged him closer. "Goddammit," he cursed. "I'm going to fuck you."

Her moan against his mouth made him desperate to hurt and to please.

He slid his hands down her arms to pull her closer to him, and when he did, he saw the trail of black dirt on her skin. He pushed her back, held her against the table as he looked down at her once-pristine white outfit. CEO Roxanne Medina was now smeared in the dirt of his vines.

She'd bribed his father. Corralled him into a wedding vow. Fucked him into submission. But Mateo Esperanza, prince and future ruler of one of the world's great wine-producing regions, had power here, too. He could leave his mark on her as well.

"But we're doing it my way," he said. His words made

her tense, made those lusty eyes widen. He swooped his arm around her naked waist and pulled her close against him.

"What's the matter, *Princesa*?" he said, smiling menacingly into her face. He could feel her warm bursts of breath against his cheek. "You came to your stud. Let me do my job." He spun her around, the gold bangles on her wrists clanging against the steel top of the table. He pulled her back against him, iron arms wrapped around her chest and waist. "Here I'm not a prince," he growled, hot into her tender ear, made oh-so-accessible by her pulled-up hair. "I work in the dirt. And I like to fuck dirty."

He marred her skirt as he raised it up, left contrails of dirt up her pale silken leg as he reached for the core of her. She was soft, yielding ass against his jeans-covered cock, and wet, wet heat in his palm. He bit down on her earlobe to stifle his groan.

"Your little clit is so slippery," he whispered into her ear. "Tell me you want this."

"Yes," she gasped, nodding so tendrils of black shook against her neck as Mateo felt more moisture drip into his hands. He filed away the knowledge that she liked filthy talk as he made quick work of his button fly and continued to thrum at her. She was leaning forward, holding her weight against her hands and panting as he fluffed up her no-longer-white skirt to find her, to find the silken curve of her ass and then...wet and wet and wet.

Want.

The low throaty moan trembling through her body made him bite his lip. He pulled her back against him, took her defenseless bud of flesh between two focused fingers as he began to pump inside her. "Do you like this?" he said low into the exposed shell of her ear. "Or this?" He laughed cruelly at her guttural groan. "Oh, *Princesa*, your eager clit makes you so easy. What I could do to you if I liked you. All the ways I could make you come."

She was already fluttering around him and he crossed his arm over her to grab on to her shoulder, to leave his handprint on that delicate skin, to begin to pound into her hard as his finger relentlessly fondled her. Her skirt frothed between them and she cried out at every up stroke. "So wet," he jeered at her between gritted teeth. "So easy." A warm pulse of moisture rained down on him. "So...so...so fucking tight and soft and warm."

She broke beneath him, hands squeaking up the table as if looking for something to grab on to as she came, and Mateo gripped his eyes shut—he couldn't watch her orgasm—and mentally listed every vine clone he ever learned as the velvet-lined pussy he'd sneered at squeezed and pulsed and stroked his bellowing cock.

He didn't come.

He staggered back from her, out of her, away from the earthy perfume of her arousal, his vines, and sweet, hot roses. He wiped her moisture on his jeans leg and—with a silent hiss—carefully buttoned himself away.

She didn't move, was still bent over and stretched out on his cold silver lab table, her pale skin and filmy clothes marked by his dirt and fingers and teeth. She was still gasping from her pleasure, looking like a virgin sacrifice after the dragon revealed he had a few tricks up his sleeve. When her skirts shifted and Mateo realized she was widening her legs—an invitation—he glued his eyes to the exit door.

"That's quite a pussy you have there, *mi reina*," he said, making sure none of the strain of his begging cock could be heard in his voice. "I might enjoy it if I could stand you."

He made it to the exit without running. He made the ten-minute drive home before succumbing to the hardest—and quickest—self-induced orgasm of his life. But even with self-loathing seeping into his system, Mateo felt that he had done what was necessary to show Roxanne Medina that he was not the prince she wanted. He was not a docile and easily manipulated man. This monstrous mistake could still be undone. The confidence of that had Mateo yielding to much-needed sleep.

Until, eyes popping open, he realized his misstep.

"Mi reina," he'd called her.

My queen.

February: Night One

Roxanne Medina tapped the note card against her bottom lip as she tapped the red sole of her Louboutin against the marble elevator floor and watched the elevator numbers descend.

The prince was being difficult. Again. Even after her heartfelt apology. She counted her small blessings. At least he was somewhere in the jewel box of a boutique hotel where they were supposed to meet.

I'm at the bar, said the note stuck in their suite door, scrawled in a slashing, masculine print. Roxanne was strategically on time, so the prince had shown up early to make his stand.

A smile grew on her face beneath the note card. Roxanne loved a challenge. But after a lifetime of them, the battles had grown...less fulfilling recently. Maybe life was just simpler after you'd earned a billion.

Not that running Medina Now Enterprises and maintaining its stock as a "bull-with-a-bullet" was simple. Neither was choosing new women-run companies to invest in and help prosper. Or keeping her thousands of employees on three continents—she had headquarters in San Francisco, Madrid, and Hong Kong—happy. Or maintaining her carefully cultivated image. Or ensuring that her charitable interests were properly overseen. Or managing her mother.

But nothing she'd tried, not sex or competitive kickboxing or setting her sights on a South American expansion, had filled the void that began as a pinprick and seemed to widen by the day. She refused to call it loneliness. Nothing until, from the tinted window of a town car, she'd seen a woman holding a toddler's hands as the tiny girl figured her way up some steps.

That, she'd thought instantly. Just as she made every other decision in her life. *I want that.*

She didn't want a husband or a relationship and all of their attached complications. And she didn't want a test-tube baby—she'd turned the lack of a father in her own life into an advantage, concocting a delicious modern fairy tale that hid the ugly reality. But her baby girl wouldn't have to do that. Wouldn't have to make up who she was or where she came from. Wouldn't have to dream of some hero-on-horseback father saving her from her life. Wouldn't have to fend off the jeers and hair-pulling because of who her mother was. If her money couldn't create a perfect life for her baby girl, then what value did it have?

Now all Roxanne had to do was hang on to her prince.

She had misstepped with him; with a month of distance, she could acknowledge that. Her first critical mistake was believing that he'd come to her office ready to sign. She'd assumed that—as an intellectual, a busy scientist with so much on the line—he'd see the merits of the arrangement and wouldn't worry about the moral dilemmas. But, as she'd observed him on the security camera hidden in the waiting room, she'd been surprised by his muddy boots and the size of his biceps. She'd been shocked by the angry, passionate "no" in his eyes.

Her second critical mistake was abandoning the finesse she'd learned convincing wary female business owners that she was a partner who wouldn't screw them. Instead, when he'd challenged her with his eyes and temper and staggering good looks in the hotel room, she'd reacted like she'd learned on the playground: push him down, kick him in the balls, and run away.

That last night, the prince pushed back.

The note card fell from her lips to drag absently across her shoulder as she thought about that night, about the warmth of the greenhouse, about how he towered over her when he pushed her against the table. And then bent her over it. For all of his insults, he'd worked like a yeoman to blow her mind. As the drag of the card against her shoulder made a *scritching* sound, Roxanne realized what she was doing: it was where he'd held her as he pounded into her, as the other hand had pleasured her with the touch of a hummingbird wing. Roxanne felt a flush of heat over the pale skin that she so strategically kept out of the sun.

She hastily opened her pink leather clutch and shoved the card inside.

She would institute some kind of détente tonight. Maintain the upper hand while allowing him to feel a measure of control. It was why she'd sent him the apology after their last meeting; the man did have his pride and she had mauled it, if she took a step back and looked at it objectively. She would point out the benefits of the arrangement to the both of them and appeal to his reasoning instead of shoving him around, as he'd accused her of.

And he'd better listen to reason. Because even if she had to chain him to a bed and store him away for her personal use three nights a month, she was going to have her prince. With her money and his blue blood, there would be nothing denied her child.

No humiliation, ever, that her daughter would have to overcome.

The elevator bell dinged. The doors slid open to reveal the

lobby, dripping in red leather and crystal chandeliers, and the darkly lit bar across the way.

Her shell-pink heels clicked against the black-and-white-checkered marble. As she crossed the threshold into the bar's darkness, she raised her sunglasses onto her head, pushing back her unbound hair to look around. Yes, the whole sunglasses-at-night thing was a little ridiculous, but as the only female self-made billionaire under thirty, she was known and recognizable. And she didn't want to be photographed with her prince until she was ready.

She looked around for a baseball cap. He'd worn a "Real Madrid" cap the first evening. A fraying "Russian River Valley Winegrowers" cap the other two. She looked for a man in jeans in the elegant bar of dark wood and rich leather. She'd dressed down to accommodate him, worn a v-necked, black, silk jumpsuit and a pale pink blazer and loose hair. Casual. Unthreatening. Ignore the four-inch heels.

If he hadn't been staring at her, she would have looked right past him. A couple, a lady by herself, a party of four, a gorgeous male, another couple, two girlfriends… Only the gorgeous man's insistent eyes on her had her going back for another peek.

Her red sole slipped on the marble when she realized she was married to the gorgeous man. She looked behind her, acted like…something on the floor. Then she plastered an assured smile on her face and walked toward him.

He was breathtaking. All shoulders and endless height in a beautiful, rich blue Italian suit as he stood at a high, round table. The glowing whiteness of his open-collared shirt set off the golden tone of his skin; a fine, navy-blue scarf hung over his lapels, an accessory only a Spanish man could make look casual and necessary. His light brown hair, streaked with blond, overlong and pushed back, touched his collar. His eyebrows, she noticed for the first time, were dark and thick and heavy. They highlighted the bright eyes, such a bizarre amalgam of caramel and bronze and sunset, that watched her warily. Like she was an approaching bomb. It was the first time she'd seen him, his face, his hair, his skin, those scowling dark brows, without the shadow of his ball cap. The first time she'd seen him in all of his oft-photographed, Golden Prince glory.

The paparazzi pictures and reports from her investigators had assured her that the Golden Prince was a handsome, kind, and passive man who liked to bury himself in work rather than stand up to his father. He had an outstanding professional reputation, few personal attachments in the U.S., and casual lovers every few months.

Nothing in those reports had prepared her for this tall, wide-shouldered, hard-handed man with soft, sulky lips. Nothing had readied her for the defiance in his eyes, a defiance that stoked an unwise need to bring him to heel.

Finesse...she breathed to herself before she took her time slipping her sunglasses off her head, shaking her hair down her back, and putting her clutch and sunglasses on the small table. The prince continued to stand, but Roxanne eased into the tall, leather club chair.

"Nice wine," she said, nodding at the '09 Kosta Browne Pinot Noir.

"It's for me."

Hell. She bit her lips against a challenging smile. "You needed a whole bottle of wine to face me?"

Those eyes narrowed and a fine slash of a line appeared between his dark, lickable brows. "I didn't know how long I'd have to wait."

"Oh, I didn't want to waste a second," she said, unable to keep from poking the bear.

Those muscles he built in a field stiffened beneath his suit as a waiter placed another wineglass on the table and poured for Roxanne.

As Roxanne wrapped her fingers around the goblet, the prince asked, "Should you be drinking that?"

She looked at him quizzically before she caught the gist. "Ah… No, I'm not pregnant." She tipped the glass at him and then took a sip.

"Good," he said. "Then I want to amend the contract."

She choked down the wine with a cough. "That's adorable."

"Fine." He raised his glass and finished off the wine in two large gulps, the liquid pulsing in his strong, golden neck. He put the glass back down with a crack. "I've already paid for the bottle. *Hasta nunca.*"

Damn her mouth. He moved fast for a tall guy, quickly instituting his "see you never." He was already two strides away before Roxanne slipped out of her seat and caught his hand. The feel of it again, its strength, calluses, and heat, was electric. It took two of her hands—hands that had never seemed small—to constrain it.

"Did you get my letter?" she asked.

The tension in the hand she gripped, his eyes that watched her, told her that he would have ripped himself away if they weren't in public. "I got it."

"I meant every word," she said, drawing him in by his outstretched arm. She pulled his hand toward her as she continued to look into his face. "I'm sorry for the way I treated you at the Fairmont."

The back of his hand lightly brushed the silk of her jumpsuit.

"You didn't deserve that," she said, up into his face. He shadowed her, cast a hazy shelter of dark and warmth. This close, she could finally smell him again. He carried the smell of bright, sharp things growing and warm earth. She recognized that pheromones were at work here, and she'd selected perfectly. His smell, the way it made her chemicals dance, was why she'd been willing—eager—to put her mouth on this stranger the first night they met.

"I never should have made you feel...un-princely," she continued, voice made weak by the dancing chemicals. "And that last night... I never should have convinced that campus security guard to let me in."

His dark brows crinkled. "Is that how you did it?"

She nodded while gently, carefully, brushing her jumper against his knuckles again. "Don't blame him. He recognized me. When you have as much money as I do, people assume that they can let you into Fort Knox and you won't steal anything."

He shook his head, as if trying to clear the fog from it, without taking his eyes off of her. "Your convenient apology still doesn't make this arrangement sane."

"Maybe. But it is beneficial. To both of us. And there does seem to be some connection, don't you think?" She took a tiny step closer and let the back of his hand rest against her stomach, let him feel the shiver that touched her. "Some chemistry that has nothing to do with the papers we signed?"

His hand turned over. Hidden in the shadows of her open blazer and his swaying scarf, his big, hot hand smoothed over the silk, rubbed slowly down her trembling stomach. His eyes drifted down to her lips, which suddenly felt plump and tender and needy.

"*Vale,*" he said. And pushed her back a step, away from him and against her seat. "Then let's talk."

He moved back to his side of the table, sat down and poured himself another glass of wine. While Roxanne stood there, ass propped against the seat, still feeling the promise of that dominating hand traveling down her stomach.

"Talk?" she finally echoed back.

"*Sí. Nos hablamos.*" His big hand gestured at her. "That's the amendment I want. I talk to you and you talk to me. One night of the three, we go on a date. We get to know each other. Like normal people before they get married." He leaned back in his seat, scarf dripping down his white shirt. "And no sex that night. I want it stated in the contract."

Roxanne put both hands on the table and stared at him, trying to see into his well-shaped skull. Where had this come from? She was used to tears and outbursts and hugs during contract negotiations. But not full left turns. Her skill as a negotiator was always being able to outthink her opponent by seeing his objections, options, and addendums before he did. But the prince had blindsided her with his fully developed, from-out-of-nowhere and completely unnecessary contract amendment.

She tried to be conciliatory. "Well, I guess we can add a fourth night…"

The prince was already shaking his head "no."

Her stare turned into a glare. "But our nights are already limited to the peak of my ovulation cycle," she said. He was a genius. He could be reasoned with. "If we take one of the nights away, we're cutting the chances of getting pregnant by a third."

He smirked. "It's gonna drop lower if I won't do you at all." Words from her genius.

She could feel that dangerous bubbling just under her ribs. Anger. Frustration. And a flutter of panic. She didn't *want* to get to know him. That was the whole point of this contract. She just wanted her baby. She pinched her lower lip, realized she was doing it, and then pressed both hands flat against the table. She'd already tried sincerity.

Now, she'd try a different tactic.

While keeping her eyes on him, she slid out of her pink jacket, revealing her naked pale shoulders and the curves of her breasts in the deep V of her jumpsuit. She tilted her head and watched his eyes flicker to the black hair that fell over her shoulder. She reached across the table and stroked the back of his bronzed hand with a nail. "I want you, *Príncipe*," she said, low and throaty. "As often as I can get you. Isn't that every man's fantasy? Three nights a month of no-strings-attached sex with a woman who will do anything to make you come?"

She was thrilled when his fingers let go of the glass to entwine with hers, to pull her gently and slowly toward him across the table. But the heated eyes coming toward her weren't filled with passion. They were blazing—flames growing higher with every millimeter that shrank between them—with anger.

"Before we take another step, you need to erase everything you assumed about me." His words were gravelly with anger, deep and distinct, tinged with the Spanish accent she rarely heard. "I am not my father. I don't care about fame. I don't care about wealth. I don't care about the mind-numbing squeeze of your cunt." The word flew at her like a bullet as his eyes burned her. "I care about my people. I care about my vines. And I care about *my* kid. I need to know more about his mother than her favorite sexual positions. So you're going to talk to me. You're going to let me get to know you. And then maybe, just maybe, I'll be able to tolerate giving you the baby you want and getting the money I need."

He let go of her fingers and Roxanne jerked her hand away. She fought to hide the galloping in her chest as she settled back against her seat.

Everything she wanted *Príncipe* Mateo to know about billionaire Roxanne Medina was on the internet; all other information was hidden for a reason. And if she wanted to talk to a man, she had plenty to choose from: her attorney, her assistant, her bodyguard, and her priest. She was dripping in men to talk to and certainly didn't need to add a prince to her speed dial. His "amendment" directly contradicted everything she was trying to achieve with her contract—a born-in-wedlock baby with a reliable father without all the emotional mess and fuss.

As he stared at her stonily from across the table, Roxanne finally accepted that this prince wasn't going to be as passive as she'd hoped.

Fine, she decided, willing herself to adapt as quickly as she adapted to other antagonists across the bargaining table. She would talk to the prince. She would tell him exactly what she wanted. She would manage their one-day-a-month "talks" with the same precision that she managed everything else in her life. In the end, she would still have her fairy-tale baby. And the *príncipe* would return to his lab or his kingdom or wherever the hell he wanted with the same perfectly crafted image of Roxanne Medina that she'd crafted for the rest of the world.

"Okay," she conceded, raising her chin. "We'll talk."

Those golden eyes took her in, assessed her. Slowly, he nodded. Then he stood up, buttoning the single button of his coat as if getting ready to leave.

Frustrated, she said, "But I thought we were going to talk."

His eyes narrowed with a smirk as he walked around the table toward her. He tipped up her chin with a hot fingertip and searched her eyes. "You really think I'm going to trust your word, *Princesa*?" She could feel the warm puffs of his words against her lips. "Send the amended contract to my attorney. Tomorrow we'll talk." He nodded. "And since

I'm feeling generous and you've already used up one night of your three, we'll also do…whatever else you want to do. *After* we talk."

His quick kiss was a surprise, barely a brush of skin and wine-spiced breath. Still it made her lips tingle. Still it made her gasp a quick intake of breath. He heard her and rewarded her with his first real smile as he straightened.

His smile was glorious, a slow reveal of blinding white teeth and a dimple in his right cheek and laugh lines that pointed to eyes that seemed to glow just for her. His smile made her not care that he was laughing at her, that he'd palmed some of the power for himself and that he was gloating. His smile was beautiful, transforming her sullen, angry prince into a man who obviously felt joy enough to get laugh lines, a man who probably spent a lot of time smiling when she wasn't around.

He turned his back on her and Roxanne watched his broad, tall silhouette leave, hands in his pockets, head probably already back in his greenhouse.

His smile—and the man himself, Roxanne was starting to realize—was very, very, very dangerous.

February: Night Two
Part One

The next evening, Roxanne stood on a North Beach sidewalk busy with San Franciscans heading home and stared at a large, neon-orange finger pointing at the "restaurant" where she was supposed to meet the prince. The Golden Boy Pizza sign flashed against the dark. Roxanne checked the address on her phone. He'd conveniently forgotten to include the name of the restaurant in his email, but, yep, she was at the right address.

Goddamn him.

The dive bar was about half the width of her office. The window displayed slabs of pizza, and a mix of punk rock and happy-hour shouting vibrated out of the place. When two dudes with thick beards and lip rings opened the door, the smell of pepperoni, pot, and grease wafted out.

Roxanne grimaced at the thought of her clothing choice. Her dress beneath her coat was a light black wool that hugged her breasts and hips, that ended in an asymmetrical peak over one knee while revealing the other, that displayed her cleavage but lifted in a stiff collar around her neck. Her lips, the tiny belt at her waist, and her towering heels were all a blood-rich red.

When she'd seen his email, she'd recognized the address as being in the heart of North Beach. She'd assumed he made reservations at one of the neighborhood's renowned trattorias, some linen-clothed and candlelit place where they'd drink Brunello and he'd try to worm his way into her head. She'd dressed for war.

But the prince had changed the battlefield. She was going to stick out like a diamond-encrusted thumb in this pizza shack.

Roxanne straightened her shoulders and cut through the tide of people to get to the door. She'd eaten in places that would melt the prince's silver spoon and had worn the wrong wardrobe until she'd made her first million. She opened the jangling door to a blast of punk rock and greasy air, and squeezed in among the hipsters and punks. The prince was going to have to do a lot more than this to push her off her game.

Like, perhaps, sit at the bar and give his glorious smile to a tattooed and purple-haired bartender serving up her own impressive cleavage, her dark skin and great breasts stunning in a white tank top as she leaned over the bar toward him. Roxanne stopped short. He was wearing a damn baseball cap again. But the overhead fluorescents were bright enough to catch the gleam in his eyes as the bartender stroked his arm.

He'd never given that happy gleam to Roxanne.

A guy with gray in his chest-long beard bumped into her. Foam from his full beer splattered her neck, coat, and *décolletage*. "Sorry, ma'am."

A man at least ten years her elder had just called her "ma'am." She said nothing. Just closed her eyes and took deep breaths as she counted to three. When she opened them, both the prince and the bartender were staring at her.

She stomped over to them, beer dripping into her cleavage.

"Charming place," she spat as the prince, bemused, held paper napkins out to her. She snatched them out of his hand and patted at her skin and coat.

"It's the best pizza in the city."

"And so intimate." She threw the napkins on the bar. "A wonderful place for conversation."

"It's cozy."

"Sure." She raised her voice over the Dead Kennedys shouting about the superiority of California. "You can hear a pin drop."

She turned her irritated gaze on the bartender who glared, the woman's muscular, Maori-tattooed arms crossed over her monumental chest.

"Yes?" Roxanne prompted.

The woman raised her lip in a snarl. "You want something?"

"Do you have wine?"

"Yeah." And that was it for the description of the Golden Boy Pizza wine list.

Roxanne grabbed on to her composure like a life vest in a flailing ocean. "I'll have a beer."

As the bartender stalked off, the prince murmured, "Good choice."

She lifted a finger. Not yet. She winced as she set her $2,000 handbag on the dirty floor and then slid out of her coat. The press of bodies made it six hundred degrees. She laid her coat over the cracked, red-pleather barstool next to him and clambered on. The bartender slammed a beer in front of her, and Roxanne wiped the rim with a napkin before she took a deep, soothing drink. The beer was lukewarm. She promised herself she would buy the building and shut down the restaurant the instant she'd gotten what she'd come for.

Speaking of....

She centered the beer bottle in front of her. "*Príncipe*, I assumed you were intelligent enough to read all of the documents you signed. Or, at least, hire attorneys who were." She turned her chin to look at him and saw his bemusement fading. "Our contract states that you're required to practice a certain level of sexual restraint during our marriage. You've already been tested and given a clean bill of health. I'd hate to have to test you every night we're together. It would be so inconvenient for Helen."

The smile on those soft, sulky lips became narrow and brittle. He turned from her, shaking his head, and stared at his beer in his hand. "I thought I could do this," he said, his deep voice reaching her under the blare of crowd and music. "I can't do this. You think I'm your whore. Why would you let a whore father your child?"

He took a long drink of his beer and then sat it carefully on the bar. He rose from the stool. There was nothing angry or dejected in his movements. He was simply finished.

Finished with her. Wait. "I—I don't think you're a whore," she stuttered.

"A man led by money and pussy. Yes you do." He pulled his wallet out of his back pocket. "I don't cheat. I've never cheated. I would never cheat." His looked at her with pity as he tossed cash on the bar. "If you can't understand that about me, there's no reason for us to continue."

Of course he wouldn't cheat. Within moments of reading about his scientific expertise and quiet lifestyle, she'd known he was cut from a different cloth than his greedy, womanizing father. The king had settled two paternity cases out of court and was infamously known for stowing away the queen's best friend so he could secretly screw her during the honeymoon voyage across the Mediterranean. Just last year, the sixty-four-year-old man had been photographed with an Italian porn star in his lap. The king had sent it to Roxanne as proof of Esperanza virility.

Mateo de Esperanza wouldn't cheat because he'd been mortified by it his entire life. He'd already told her, *"I'm not my father."*

But in the first moments of her campaign to break down his resistance with a carefully curated version of herself, that's exactly what she'd accused him of. Of being just like his father.

"Wait, wait, I'm sorry," she said as he turned away, a second from wedging those wide shoulders into the crowd and getting lost in it.

"You say that a lot," he threw back at her.

"But I mean it this time. You wanted to set me back on my heels. Congrats, it worked! You knew I wouldn't be expecting this place; I'm totally overdressed. And you're wearing that stupid baseball cap again."

Roxanne was babbling. She wanted to jam both hands over her mouth. But her prince had stopped. He turned his head, his cap shadowing everything but his ski-slope nose and those lips.

"What's wrong with my baseball cap?"

"And on top of that..." Relief made her continue babbling, almost shouting to make sure he heard her over the music. "You bring me to a place where you've obviously slept with the bartender. I was jealous, okay. So, I'm sorry."

She'd known victory—over a conference table, in the ring, looking down on classmates who were certain they were better than her as she gave the valedictorian speech—but nothing compared to the win of having him turn around and study her. He crossed his arms, showing off those thick biceps in his faded concert t-shirt. She could feel his eyes assessing her, his dark brows drawn together as he searched her for bullshit.

Finally, he said, "You know, *Princesa*, this is the first time I believe you." He stepped closer and looked down at her, forcing her to tilt her head up. "When we're together," he drawled, "we're going to have to find something better for you to do with that mouth than insult me."

His brim shadowed his eyes. But she could feel his gaze on her lips. Heat slid over her like slow-melting butter as moved to sit back on his barstool.

"This really is the best pizza in San Francisco," he said quietly. She turned around to face the bar again as he nodded at the beautiful bartender. "And I've never slept with Leah. I wouldn't bring you here if I had."

"But she wants to," Roxanne said, dragging her thumb over her beer label.

He stayed quiet. Then he murmured, "I'm glad you overdressed."

She looked down at herself, at the cleavage, the knee, the red shoes, and turned to eye him with a begrudging huff of a laugh. "I can't tell if you're making fun of me with that cap on." Tonight it was a black SF Giants cap. "Take it off and I might believe you."

"I can't. I had to come straight from work. I hope your expensive suite has a shower."

She leveled her eyes at him. "I'm overdressed. You can be greasy."

"How about this?" He grabbed the brim of his hat and twisted it around to the back, then smoothed his tawny hair behind his ears. He turned to face her with his hands wide. "Is this better?"

It was fabulous. Without the shadow of his brim or the camouflage of his hair, his gorgeous face was fully exposed to her for the first time. The diner lights reflected off his high, hard cheekbones, the dark stubble on the sharp lines of his jaw and chin. His lips were pressed together, his smile wary, but his eyes seemed to watch her with the tiniest measure of hope. She was close enough to see that a ring of dark mahogany brown, the same color as his eyebrows, circled his golden irises and was the reason his eyes stood out so spectacularly. He'd shifted around his hat for her. He'd just, for the first time, done something to please her.

Roxanne felt like she was teetering back on the heels of her cruel, red shoes.

She needed to regain control of this interaction. Or, at least, control of herself. She had nine years of sexual experience under her belt, the last five of them vast and rich and exotic. But she felt as awkward and tongue-tied as when she'd gotten her first kiss from her freshman year RA.

When paper plates full of pizza were thrown onto the bar in front of her, Roxanne had never been happier to see a woman who despised her. She stared astonished at the quantity of pizza squares while the bartender asked the prince, and only the prince, if he wanted another beer.

"Is all this for us?" she asked, the tempting scents of tomato, garlic, and cheese reminding her that she'd skipped lunch again.

He reached an arm across her—his arm was tanned, and the hair on it sparkled blond—and grabbed for a paper plate, its slice covered in spinach and tomatoes, the cheese at the edges crisped to a char. "I wasn't sure what you liked," he said as he sank his teeth into the slice and got a smear of tomato sauce on his upper lip. He held the plate and the slice in the same big hand and motioned with it. "That one is gluten free, that one is vegan, that one is paleo…"

The warm glow building just under her ribs, where her fury and fortitude and pride also made themselves known, was uncomfortable. "And that one?" she asked, pointing to a slice groaning with ingredients in the middle.

"That's the Golden Boy Supreme," he said, smiling at her cautiously. "It's got everything you could want."

She cocked her jaw at him. And appreciated his grin when she grabbed the plate and took a bite.

"So you eat meat?" he asked, settling into his slice.

She nodded and covered her lips as she chewed. "You?"

"Vegetarian."

She looked down at the gobs of crumbled sausage and round slices of pepperoni burnt at the edges. "Do you mind?"

His grin kicked up. "Not in the least."

She took another bite and resisted moaning at the combination of smoky meat, garlic sauce, and butter-rich, focaccia-like crust. But she had inadvertently closed her eyes. When she opened them, he was watching her, amused.

She covered her mouth again as a huff of a laugh escaped her. "Okay, yes, it's good. But don't think the irony of the Golden Prince bringing me to Golden Boy Pizza has escaped me."

He wiped the sauce from his lip with a thumb and then picked up his beer. "It wouldn't be any fun if it had," he said, holding the bottle up to her.

They were eating pizza. Verbal chess seemed unnecessary during pizza eating. So she allowed him the point, picked up her beer bottle, and clinked it against his. "*Salud,*" she said. They both drank deeply.

"*¿Hablas español?*" he asked when he put his beer down.

"*Sí,*" she answered. "*Y francés y chino.*"

His eyebrows rose. "*¿Chino? Dime algo.*"

"*What would you like me to say?*" Roxanne began immediately in Chinese. "*Would you like me to validate your choice of pizza? Would you like me to tell you that this night is going so differently than I'd planned? Would you like me to describe how mesmerized you look as you watch my lips?*"

Roxanne was accustomed to the request, accustomed to how novel people found fluent Mandarin coming from her mouth. But the prince watched the soft curves and stretches of her lips like they were casting spells. Like her mouth was capable of magic.

When she finished, his eyes flicked up to hers for only a second before he returned his attention back to his pizza and took a huge bite. But that second was more than enough. The hungry fire of his look lit her up. It was a look that should have been reserved for red rooms and tight leather and explicit, hard-core acts. That it was a look he'd given her here, in a bright-lit pizza shack, when she smelled of beer and could feel the gleam of garlic and grease on her skin, seemed very wrong. Seemed dangerous.

"Why those languages?" he asked around the big bite, as if the moment had never happened.

Roxanne took a steadying drink of her warm beer. "They were useful. And easy."

"Sure." He shrugged. "Learning an entirely new alphabet and phonetic structure is easy. Did you learn Spanish from your father?"

Roxanne barely prevented herself from banging down her beer. She was *not* talking about family. But after years of manipulating the press, she knew that an emotional uptick to any question meant the question would be pursued. So she said, calmly, "No. My Mexican side is mostly theoretical. I never knew the man or his heritage."

He turned on his barstool, the remaining quarter of pizza still in his hand. "What about this?" Without any warning, a hot finger flicked across her chest to lift up her cross.

She was suddenly leashed by the small, rose-gold chain and pendant that her father figure had given her for her Confirmation. She'd worn it ever since. She couldn't let the prince see how irritated she was that he dared touch it.

"What about it?" she asked, working to hold on to her temper.

"Aren't you afraid of bursting into flames?" When she looked up into his face, when she saw that he was good-naturedly teasing, unaware of the raw spots he was rubbing, she had no reservations about smacking his hand away.

"Believe it or not," she said as she took another bite of pizza. "I'm a practicing Catholic."

"And that has nothing to do with your father?"

How did he... But, no, the prince wasn't asking about Father Juan, the only parent-like person she'd ever known, the man who'd helped her feel pride instead of shame about being half Mexican in an all-white town.

"What would my absent father have to do with the religion I practice?" she asked.

"Well, my people brought Catholicism to your people's shores."

Roxanne rolled her eyes dramatically and threw her pizza back on the plate. "Oh God, is that what we're going to discuss during these 'talks?'" she drawled, wiping the grease off her hands. "'*My people conquered your people.*' The last thing we need to bring into this marriage is who vanquished whom."

She was choosing subject-changing sarcasm and expected sarcasm in return. But the prince folded his arms in front of his now-empty plate and considered her thoughtfully.

"We're married," he rumbled, that little line appearing between his dark brows. "We're married, you're going to have my kid, and I just learned that you're a meat-eater, that you speak four languages, and that you go to church."

He rested his chin on his bicep, unfairly calling attention to the bulk and muscle of it, while his eyes caught hers. "We're married and I haven't even kissed you yet."

She suddenly felt breathless. She covered it with a huge, alluring smile. "Yes, you really have."

She didn't change his course. "No," he said, his eyes steady. "That wasn't a kiss. That was punishment. I need to give you a proper first kiss."

She looked down to scrub at the grease that was no longer present on her hands. "A kiss is a kiss," she said. "There is no reason to overemphasize it."

The warmth of him suddenly crowded her as he slid his arms along the bar toward her, into her space. Stunningly, through the thick scents of butter and beer and pepperoni, she could still smell him, could smell that beckoning clean spice of his.

"*Venga, belleza*," he murmured, close to her ear. "There's a reason you picked me over a million impoverished blue bloods who would cry to have you. Let me give you your fairy tale. Don't you want your first kiss from your prince?"

February: Night Two
Part Two

Her heart was racing, her head was muzzy.

This was ridiculous.

She straightened the spine that had built a billion-dollar corporation and turned to face him squarely. "You know exactly what I want from you, *Príncipe*, and it isn't found in children's fairy tales." He hadn't moved his chin off his bicep, so she spoke down at him, clearly, so he could hear every word. "What I want from you is raw and wet and has nothing to do with first kisses. In fact..." She made a show of looking at the diner clock on the wall. "It's time for you to stand and deliver. We've wasted enough of the evening on your get-to-know-you chitchat. Why don't you say goodbye to your little friend? I'll be outside."

She rose from her seat, leisurely, picked up her coat to fold it precisely over her arm, and bent over slowly to pick up her handbag. The audible groans behind her let her know that others had caught the show.

But as she made her way to the door, taking her time, the crowd now parting in front of her, she was troubled that the one person she hadn't drawn a reaction from was the prince. In fact, that bemused smile hadn't wavered from his lips during her speech.

The cool San Francisco night air was jarring as she stepped

out into it. The sidewalk now was relatively empty. She slid her coat on and let the bracing chill wipe away the scents of pizza, the blare of punk rock, and the heat of mind-fogging temptation.

She felt like herself again, mostly, when the prince opened the door a few minutes later.

"I've called the car," she said. "It should be here in a couple of—"

"Let's walk," he interrupted, his hands in an olive-green coat, a black scarf doubled around his neck. The pizzeria door sealed shut, and the night suddenly seemed very quiet. "The hotel is only a couple of blocks."

Roxanne thought of her towering red shoes without breaking eye contact. The prince, whose baseball cap was still on backward, raised a dark, challenging eyebrow.

Without a word, Roxanne lifted her chin and began to march past him, toward the hotel.

He caught her arm. "Other way. I know a shortcut."

He swung her around and then slid her arm through the crook of his, making it rest there against the unyielding strength. She barely kept herself from tugging away.

The chill air of this February weeknight had chased most San Franciscans indoors, and the raucous streets of North Beach were relatively quiet as they walked, him moving at a pace that implied they had all the time in the world. He turned off the main drag and up into the residential streets, buildings tucked tight together to keep from toppling down the steep street. She needed to hang on to him a bit to keep her heels from succumbing to gravity. His arm carried her weight like it was nothing.

When he began to turn into a dark alleyway, she tugged him to a stop.

"It's the shortcut," he explained.

"Are you sure this isn't where you're going to dump my body?" she asked, trying to see into the gloom.

"Is there a death benefit in that contract?" he drawled, grinning.

"Very purposefully no."

"Then I say no also."

He tugged her lightly to get her started. A few steps into the alley, she realized that it widened, that the concrete became last-century brick, and that residents had taken advantage of the unexpected space by creating quaint patios behind their homes, bistro tables and flower boxes and tiny white lights turning the alley into a pretty, urban courtyard. It was dimly lit and invisible from the main street.

Roxanne refused to be enchanted by it.

"I find it interesting," the prince rumbled quietly while her heels tapped against the brick, "that an offer to kiss you offends you more than me violating you in my lab. Why is that?"

She forced ennui into her voice while her heart rate picked up. "Do we have to discuss this again?"

"No," he shot out. That arm that had been supporting her suddenly swung her toward him. Big, hot hands framed her face and her vision was instantly filled with gorgeous, determined prince, his eyes licking over her lips.

Roxanne jerked out of his hands, pulled back two steps. "What are you doing?"

"Not discussing it," he said, his eyes hungry as he moved toward her. His hand slid up her jaw before she was able to stumble back from his reach again.

"Stop it," she demanded as his relentless walk told her he had no plans to stop. "You're being ridiculous."

"Maybe," he said. "Perhaps you don't need a first kiss. But I do."

Roxanne's heel hit a riser and she almost toppled back before he caught her, caught her and lifted her up on the step and pressed her back against the cool wall of the sheltered doorway. The dim lights of the courtyard were just able to catch the fire in his eyes.

"We may be all out of order and fucked up," he said as his fingers caught her behind her neck and his thumb tilted her chin up. "But if there's to be a child from this, I need something that doesn't make me ashamed every time I look at him." His eyes hungrily roamed her face. "Something that makes it okay for me to want you this much."

The kiss—the kiss she expected to be devouring and erotically painful—was a sweet, tingling slide of skin against skin, a rub of that sulky mouth across hers. It filled the dark doorway with sparks. He did it again, the slide, a press at the corner of her mouth, and Roxanne felt her mouth slacken, giving him access to every millimeter of flesh. He kissed her top lip like he was soothing it, like he felt sorry for it. The bite into her bottom lip was tender, just a taste.

She lifted her face to let him have more.

He rumbled—he was happy, she'd made him happy—and the kisses continued, warm, lingering, while he tilted her head to get to every spot, while he made a destination of sweet kisses instead of a signpost raced quickly past, while she began to kiss as well, eager to trace the shape and smoothness of that mouth that absolutely killed her.

He was a treat she couldn't resist. She licked at his bottom lip with her tongue.

"Aw, *mi reina*," he groaned as his free arm wrapped around her waist, lifting her up on her toes and against him. "*Bésame*."

And she did kiss him, touched him with her tongue, stroked inside his mouth, while he continued to hold her face in one calloused hand, controlling her movements as if giving her free rein would be more than he could handle. When she

Lush Money

stroked across his tongue, when she shivered in his embrace at the sensation, he broke. He pushed her up against the wall with his long, strong body, planted his hands against the wall on either side of her head, and took her mouth, making her feel like she was an endless well of pleasure and he was searching for every last drop.

His position, caging her, protecting her, gave her access to his body, and as she was rawly kissed by her prince, as she was wrapped in the outdoor spice of him in their tiny doorway, she stroked him for the first time. Her trembling hands spread wide to encase the brawn of his biceps and shoulders, to stroke down into the muscles of his back, the act made into a wondrous, horrible tease by the fact that his strength and warmth could be felt even through the canvas of his coat. Were she truly his queen, she would chain him naked to her throne. She would burn a million in cash right now for a touch of his hot skin. She buried her hands into his back pockets, digging into his rock-hard ass to press his rock-hard front between her legs as she sucked his tongue.

"Fuck," her prince groaned against her mouth, his hand dropping to his zipper. "I can't wait."

"Don't," she begged, hands pulling him closer. "Don't wait."

But there was a wait, an awful, trembling one as he bit at her chin and fumbled with his fly and Roxanne resisted writhing against him, and then he was kissing her again, devouring her again, and wrapping big hands around her thighs and lifting her up and propping her against the wall and sliding his hand up to shove the thong of her panties to the side and then…he was there. He was heat and velvet-covered steel sliding into her tight, wet warmth. He was enormous strength, hands and shoulders holding her effortlessly and soft lips asking if she was okay. And he was golden eyes, bright in the dimness, watching as her body eagerly accepted him. Watching as her mouth—the mouth that said she didn't want to kiss him—fell open in overwhelmed pleasure.

Roxanne was struck by a thought: Anything she tried to hide from him to protect herself, Mateo could easily see in the dark.

"Wait," she gasped. "Wait."

And he did. Gripping her flesh, Mateo stopped, dropped his forehead to her shoulder. His breath was harsh and velvety against her neck.

Oh God, he felt good. Big. Hard. Overwhelming.

Roxanne clenched him with her thighs and circled her hips and gave herself now what she'd regret later.

His chuckle was helpless as he lifted her higher and began to thrust. "*Gracias, mi reina.* I don't want to be…in violation of…our contract."

There was no more talk of waiting—and no more words—as the billionaire and her prince became two elemental beings of sensation in the dark alley of a San Francisco night.

February: Night Three

From: Bouchon, Brandon
To: Esperanza, Mateo
Subject: Cancellation

Príncipe Mateo Esperanza,
   I regret to inform you that Ms. Medina must cancel your appointment for this evening. I will contact you soon to schedule your March appointment with her.

Brandon Bouchon, Assistant to Roxanne Medina, CEO and President, Medina Now Enterprises

From: Esperanza, Mateo
To: Bouchon, Brandon
Subject: Your boss is a coward

Brandon, inform Ms. Medina that unless she would like me to share graphic details of our "appointments" with her assistant, I expect to receive all communications directly from her from this point on. As her husband, I'm not interested in speaking through an intermediary.
   Also make sure to tell her that she's chickenshit.
   Dr. Mateo Ferdinand Juan Carlos de Esperanza y Santos,

Ph.D., founder and head viticulturist, Esperanza Certified Vineyard Material, University of California, Davis

From: Medina, Roxanne
To: Esperanza, Mateo
Subject: You're a child

I'm sorry that this is unclear and I have to explain this to you.

1. Never abuse my assistant

2. If you have "shit" to throw, you can wait until we're behind a door.

3. Do not use the word "husband" with the uninformed. There will be a stampede when the world finds out.

From: Esperanza, Mateo
To: Medina, Roxanne
Subject: What I would do to you behind a door...

Darling wife, I would have been happy to take up my grievances with you had I been given a chance. Instead, you have your assistant make and cancel "appointments" with me as if I'm your masseuse or hair stylist. I didn't volunteer for this place in your bed; you will not treat me like your cock-on-demand. Twenty minutes at a sperm bank would be more pleasurable and leave me with more dignity than this shit.

From: Medina, Roxanne
To: Esperanza, Mateo
Subject:

You're right. I'm sorry. And I mean it.

I will still need Brandon to handle some logistics. But in the future, I will communicate with you directly.

From: Esperanza, Mateo
To: Medina, Roxanne
Subject:

Wow. Shocking. You made a concession without contacting the attorneys.
    Why did you really cancel tonight?

From: Medina, Roxanne
To: Esperanza, Mateo
Subject:

What do you mean why did I "really" cancel? I'm swamped. I have a meeting with my VPs in five minutes.
    If it's any consolation, since you seem so distraught about it, my VPs will be here late so they won't be getting any nookie tonight either.

From: Esperanza, Mateo
To: Medina, Roxanne
Subject: :-(

Am I disappointed I won't be inside you tonight? Weirdly, yes. You're not as intolerable as you made yourself out to be when we first met. And there's something that happens when I get close to you, when I smell you and get a glimpse of that mouth and those eyes. That thing that happens, I don't hate it.
    But I don't think you like it. I think it made you lightheaded

last night, when I was taking you up against the bricks and had to cover your mouth so you wouldn't wake the neighbors. I have your teeth marks in my palm. I was going to make you kiss them better tonight.

Another first for us to explore.

Maybe you have a meeting. Maybe you don't.

But it is vastly gratifying to realize that, even with my signature on your papers and your leash around my neck, you're not as in control of this thing as you'd like to be.

From: Medina, Roxanne
To: Esperanza, Mateo
Subject: Wedding announcement

When would you like to announce our marriage? Would next week work for you?

From: Esperanza, Mateo
To: Medina, Roxanne
Subject: RE: Wedding announcement

No, next week does not work.

I truly am "swamped." My crew and I have been working around the clock to gather the scion wood to fill our vineyard orders. Vineyards use this wood to grow new vines; they must be collected and sent now while they're still dormant, before the spring months. My crew and I have been working 16-hour days as it is. I don't have a spare moment to handle the media circus that will accompany our wedding announcement.

I am sorry that I outed you to your assistant. I assumed he knew.

★ ★ ★

From: Medina, Roxanne
To: Esperanza, Mateo
Subject: I know what scion wood is

You'll be pruning in March, managing the growing season through the summer, and harvesting in September.

I would prefer to announce our wedding before our daughter is born.

From: Esperanza, Mateo
To: Medina, Roxanne
Subject: April?

I understand. Things will slow down in April. I will have copious amounts of time to play whatever role you'd like me to play then. The world will have never seen such a devoted husband.

Why do you keep insisting the baby is going to be a girl?

From: Medina, Roxanne
To: Esperanza, Mateo
Subject: RE: April?

I'm not sure April will work for me. I have to consider my calendar. My obviously far-less-important, non-vineyard calendar.

I have to run now. My imaginary VPs are waiting for me in my conference room in the clouds where we will have a pretend meeting about whether we must close an Iowa factory and put 625 make-believe people out of work.

It's been real. See you in March.

★ ★ ★

From: Esperanza, Mateo
To: Medina, Roxanne
Subject: Sorry

Perhaps I was a little hasty in assuming your motives for canceling.

Please don't make any announcements until we speak again.

From: Esperanza, Mateo
To: Medina, Roxanne
Subject: Please get back to me

Could you give me a call? I'm concerned how we left things last night in our last email.

From: Esperanza, Mateo
To: Medina, Roxanne
Subject: I will beg if that's what it takes

I've left a couple of messages with your assistant. It's galling that he won't give me your number. If he did, I would plead on my knees.

Please don't make an announcement before I see you again. Resist, and I will be the picture of obsequiousness. I will be the lap dog you've always wanted.

In all seriousness, please don't. I can barely get a spare hour to eat and sleep right now.

Mateo

March: Night One
Part One

Mateo sat in the backseat of the Escalade, staring blindly out of the tinted windows at the Bay Bridge blurring by and white-knuckling his buzzing phone in his hand. He'd looked at the ID; he knew who it was. He was already on his way to deal with the billionaire, so he might as well face the other nightmare in his life. Continuing to ignore the king's calls would only inspire the man to thrash harder with his scepter.

It wasn't as if his father could call Mateo something worse than what he thought about himself.

He answered. "*Díme.*"

"You're a disgrace," his father barked in a clear, unaccented English. "You're letting that woman make a joke out of you and the Monte. All you had to do was keep her happy tickling her *pepita* until you stuck a baby in her; you're not man enough to do even that."

While little that King Felipe Miguel de Esperanza y Santos said bruised Mateo anymore, the man could always be counted on to give it the old sporting try.

"Yeah, I'm a disgrace," he said quietly in gritted-teeth Spanish. His eyes flashed to the driver, whose aviator lenses were pointed at the road as he expertly negotiated the last of San Francisco's rush-hour traffic in the middle of the three-car security caravan. The man may or may not speak Spanish. But since Mateo didn't have Roxanne Medina's linguistic skills to lean on, he figured he would at least try to make his secrets a challenge to learn. "It's disgraceful that I agreed to this deal you two dreamed up. The Monte became a joke the second I let you tie its future to one of your fucked-up schemes."

"Listen to yourself. Always the victim. A king does what he must to take care of his people. This is how you've taken care of them: *'Beggar Prince Wins the Lottery.' 'Billionaire Saves Impoverished Kingdom.'*" The king's voice dripped malice as he read some of the choice headlines that had appeared about Mateo over the last three weeks. "This one's a favorite: *'Billionaire Gives New Gleam to Golden Prince.'*"

Mateo closed his eyes against the burn of anger and humiliation as his father continued to read in his deep, barrel-chested voice: "*The príncipe reportedly proposed to her from the top of the Castillo del Monte's medieval tower that overlooks the storied vineyards. 'I have little to offer,' the príncipe whispered on bent knee. 'Only my hand, my kingdom, and my heart. None are worthy of you.'*"

"I know what it says," Mateo growled. His father was loving this. The man finally had an opportunity to get back at his sanctimonious, high-and-mighty, holier-than-thou son.

"She says you two were married in a secret ceremony in St. Tropez. Does that chilly bitch ever leave her office? No one goes to St. Tropez."

Sixty-four years and the seventy extra pounds of living a dissolute life full of drinking, food, and women hadn't slowed his father's anxious need to be invited to the latest casino opening or hottest nightclub or biggest party. Sharing a stage with the worst of the rich-and-selfish filled his father with haughty power the way taking care of his people never could. The rumor that his son was married in the "been there, done that" luxury of St. Tropez probably struck him deeper than any of the other horror stories being sold to the press over the last three weeks.

She'd done it. CEO and head demon Roxanne Medina had gathered her minions and unleashed her hellfire in a barrage of marriage announcements that painted Mateo as a sick-in-love boy toy, the Monte as a kingdom on the brink of financial disaster, and the billionaire as their only hope. She'd succeeded where his father had failed: she'd reached into the life Mateo had built for himself in California, the walled-off world he'd established away from the king's manipulations, and made him a fool. More injuriously, she'd undermined the three years of financial tightrope he'd provided for his people to teeter on; now creditors were banging on the posts and they were going to start plummeting over.

All because Mateo had teased her in an email. All because Mateo had wanted to get to know her, to give her a kiss, to make this thing between them controllable and respectful, if not noble.

All because Mateo couldn't keep his hands off of her.

If he'd walked away that first fucking night in her office, if he'd resisted and controlled his mindless impulse that slobbered at the thought of orgasms with her, he never would have been jarred awake at 4 a.m. three weeks ago by a phone call from *El Mundo*. The reporter asked if he planned on quitting his work as a "laborer" in order to stay by his new bride's side. The barrage of phone calls didn't end until he'd thrown the phone against the wall. His home line was now disconnected.

A worthier man would have just said "no," he thought as the Escalade's hard turn made him jerk against the seat belt. They'd crossed the bridge and were now in downtown San Francisco. The three-car caravan had to do more maneuvering to avoid the vehicles tailing them.

As he'd dreaded, the press and its horrible derivatives, the paparazzi, found and pounced on him at his home, at his lab, and even into his fields where ravenous photographers had trampled a row of prime Cabernet vines that he'd nurtured for five years. Had the police not shown up quickly, he would have done murder. He was always a little touchy this time of year, with all of the cold coffee and food truck burritos and lost sleep as he raced from field to field, overseeing his many crews gathering the scion wood that would fill the lab's many orders. But the fact that his overworked days and exhausted nights were accompanied by this deliberate, vindictive, humiliating madness had him vibrating with pent-up anger.

Anger that was going to find its outlet once he got his hands around Roxanne Medina's neck tonight.

"You don't like your deal with the devil?" Mateo said, grunting as another hard turn had him jolting against the car door. "Give her a call. I'm sure she'll make any changes you ask for. She's flexible that way."

His father scoffed his disgust. "You make jokes. I wouldn't have been forced into this deal if you'd simply signed the papers from the Americans."

"*Joder,*" Mateo growled. The king constantly nurtured Mateo's weariness, disgust, and unending awe that his own father could be such a self-involved asshole. "This again?! I wasn't going to give away half our land and displace half of our people just so you could keep filling your closet with Prada. Those families have been growing grapes on that land since Queen Isabella gave it to us."

"Some of them could have continued to grow," the man protested.

"Sure. Like the fucking robots at Disneyworld. Without pride or profit."

Mateo had been struck by the gall of the American firm, CML Resorts Incorporated, when they'd approached him and his father about selling half the Monte to build a royalty-themed resort and amusement park.

"*Your way of life is dying*," said the smug CEO of the firm, a blond and clinch-jawed Princeton grad near Mateo's age named Easton Fuller. "*But there's no reason we all can't profit from it.*"

In a conference room in Madrid, Fuller and his CML execs had shown them mock-ups of the resort. The Royal Buffet Hall would have parked itself on the Monte's only primary school. The Ducal Manor—timeshare condos for the upper middle class—would have been built on the Monte's most fertile vineyard. Fuller had highlighted vineyards he wanted to keep in production and tenants he'd like to keep on, and his lackeys had carried in a rack of "uniforms" the tenants would wear when tourists were driven past in horse-drawn carriages.

Mateo had thought—naively, stupidly—this one time he and his father were surely going to join forces to throw the assholes out of Spain. Instead, his father had stroked his $200 Brioni tie and called the idea "intriguing," his father's word when he wanted to appear hard-nosed but was actually salivating over the money. Fortunately, the rules in the charter signed by Queen Isabella stated that no part of the Monte could be sold without the consent of both the king and his heir. Without Mateo's signature, the deal was a no-go.

Easton Fuller had smiled a smile full of shark-like teeth and recommended that Mateo rethink his answer. There'd been more threat in that purred statement than in the king's months of screams.

"What kind of pride are you giving our people now?" his father said, his voice dripping with scorn. "The whole world is laughing at them. That bitch has everyone convinced that one of the greatest wine-growing regions doesn't have two Euros to rub together."

Mateo was shaking his head at his father's obstinacy—the state of the Monte's finances were largely the man's fault—when he again banged into the car door. A beat-up car had thrown itself into the Escalade's path and barely avoided being T-boned before Mateo's excellent driver swerved away.

"If the Monte had more than two euros to rub together, I wouldn't be married to a stranger," Mateo growled as he watched a telephoto lens emerge from the car's back window and begin shooting.

"I'll tell you this," his father said. "If that little cunt was under me, she'd be too busy thinking about the size of my cock to worry about the size of my bank account."

"*¡Cállate viejo!*" Mateo erupted, seeing red. "You keep your filthy mouth shut!" His father's obsession with a few inches of flesh had twisted the lives of everyone around him. "That's my *wife* you're talking about, the wife you forced on me. She's my problem now, so you don't think about her, you don't talk about her, you don't even fucking breathe in her direction."

Instead of lashing back, his father purred, "She doesn't have to be your problem."

His lazy tone concerned Mateo the way none of the rest of this call had. "What?"

"Easton Fuller gave me a call. CML Resorts is still interested. And with the extra publicity you've given the Monte, they're willing to double their offer."

"What about the contract with Roxanne?"

"It covers one year." His father's tone implied he'd never talked to anyone as stupid as Mateo. "With the bigger offer, you can walk away now and pay her breach-of-contract penalty and still have plenty left over. But, if you don't get her pregnant…"

Mateo scowled sightlessly at the lights of the bodegas, stores, and restaurants of San Francisco's Mission District racing by.

Stopping for red lights had become a thing of the past. "What are you saying?"

"All the contract asks for is a 'good faith' effort to fuck—oh, excuse me, *Príncipe*—make love to her for a year. If she doesn't get pregnant, that's her fault. We can have her money and CML's money."

"So you want me to..."

"Fake it. Beat off before you see her. Squirt lotion into the woman, I don't care. Just don't come in her. Women fake it all the time."

Mateo realized he was rubbing the band of burnished gold on his left ring finger. The ring had been courier delivered that morning. He'd thrown it into the trash, and then had to dig it out when the car arrived, fantasizing of ramming it down her throat.

All Mateo had asked of his father was time. The king knew about his work on the *Tempranillo Vino Real*, knew how close Mateo was, knew how hard Mateo had worked to find the money to buy that time. Instead, his father had unleashed on him...all of this.

And Mateo hadn't been smart enough or strong enough to avoid it.

The ring was heavy as he clenched his fist in his lap. "You're out of your fucking mind if you think I'd agree to that," he said tonelessly in English. At this point, he didn't care who knew how sordid his life had become.

His father released a litany of screaming curses in rapid and colorful Spanish.

Ignoring him, Mateo saw a news van, now parked, that they'd barely avoided hitting a minute earlier. A cameraman and reporter were scurrying out of it. He turned to look through the front window of the Escalade. He bit back a crazy laugh.

This wild ride through the city had been useless. Mateo might as well have been driven in one of CML Resort's horse-drawn carriages with a sign flashing "Idiot Prince" above it. He could have waved to the crowds. He could have thrown candy.

The press and paparazzi knew exactly where he and Roxanne were having their quiet, intimate dinner.

"I have to go." He interrupted his father as he tapped his driver on the shoulder and pointed at the front of the restaurant, where a crowd and cameras jostled on the sidewalk. He wasn't going to waste another second trying to outmaneuver them. He wanted to get this night over with.

"You go, *mi hijo*," his father jeered at him. The king hadn't called him "my son" in years. "But know this: Queen Isabella's charter might not be as ironclad as you think. Get control of this situation. If you don't, I will."

March: Night One
Part Two

Roxanne adjusted the monstrous five-carat white diamond on her ring finger as the noise outside went up an octave, the crowd rattled the restaurant's front window, and a police bullhorn shouted for everyone to make a lane. She gave a winsome smile to the ring for the benefit of the diners who watched her; the center diamond was wreathed in half-carat champagne diamonds to represent the earth, and the rose-gold band was entwined with emeralds to represent vines. In reality she wanted to rip it off. It was too heavy, too jagged, and it made her finger sweat.

Or perhaps that was simply her guilt. She'd gone too far this time.

She never should have called for an emergency meeting earlier that night to discuss the fate of the Iowa factory; one of her VPs was still angry that he'd missed his anniversary dinner with his husband. And she never should have woken the head of her PR department in the middle of the night to recite the first press release about her marriage to the *príncipe*. The prince had been correct in his assumptions—she'd canceled their last date in February because she'd been unsettled by their previous night together.

If she'd just met the prince as planned, just let him touch her again, she might right now be pregnant. Except for an occasional dinner to legitimize their marriage and wave at the crowd, she might right now be free of him.

Instead, she forced a smile for the benefit of the cameras and patrons in this $100 per-entree, free-range, locavore, Michelin-starred restaurant as an angry giant burst through the doors on a wave of crowd shouts. The giant wore a sateen, slate-gray suit that poured over his body like water, a tan that hadn't been there the last time she'd seen him, dark eye circles that hadn't been there either, and a fury that should have been familiar but was still intimidating.

Roxanne lifted her chin as his eyes homed in on her like sword points.

What was done was done. He had a kingdom he needed to save. She had a fairy tale to create. They were imperative to each other; the prince, for all of his grousing, had to understand that. She would apologize for the chaos she'd caused and make amends, and then they would do what was necessary, what they'd agreed upon, to ensure they each got what they needed.

Roxanne pushed back her seat, knocked a light cashmere shawl off her shoulders and stood. She heard the collective inhale as the restaurant goers caught a look at her dress as she strolled toward her husband. The gold dress, held up by two tiny straps near her neck, was gathered at the waist and ended mid-thigh. It would have been relatively simple if not for the hundreds of pearl-and-gold-colored sequins sewn to it; their weight made the dress cling and caress. Her back was naked except for the sheet of her hair and a thin line of gold cord that connected the straps to the rest of the dress, her deep cleavage bared to him except for her rose-gold cross.

If it was possible, the dress only made the *príncipe* angrier.

But if the world was going to think this were real, if the power of her money and his royalty had any chance of creating an immaculate life for their daughter, it had to start now, with the wall of cameras pointed through the restaurant window to capture the first glimpses of the "Golden Couple." For all of the make-believe she'd already injected into the world press, the fairy tale truly began at this moment.

Reaching him, she ignored his furious, furrowed brow that warned her off and wrapped both hands around his rigid biceps, leaning into him.

"*Mi esposo,*" she murmured, as if they were truly married, as if work and circumstances really had separated them and this was her first opportunity to touch his warm, strong body in weeks. Her heart didn't seem to know this was make believe; it beat faster against the clinging V of her dress as she caught the woodsy scent of him, as those fiery eyes seared her with anger and then, as if he couldn't help himself, stroked over her suddenly tender lips. She had a visceral memory of cool bricks against her back and his hot mouth devouring her as he pulsed inside her.

That hot mouth, those sulky, pleasure-giving lips, filled her vision as the prince slowly leaned down. He was so big. She could feel his hard arm muscles shift under the sleekness of his suit. She squeezed, just a little, and then held on. This was going to be good.

He gave a quick, perfunctory kiss to her forehead. The shutters of a hundred cameras could be heard going off outside the window.

"I'm starving," he said. He pulled out of her hold so fast she stumbled and had to take a step in her delicate gold heels to right herself. He was already around her. His big hand smacked her ass, lightly but audibly, as he passed. "Let's eat."

The cameras sounded like a stampede of bugs crawling across the glass.

Roxanne didn't let a millisecond pass before she raised her

face to their round blank eyes and smiled. Warm and wide. She turned around, straightened her shoulders, and walked calmly through the dimly lit restaurant as conversation returned to the room. She felt the speculative eye of every dinner guest. Her "husband" was already seated at their table, draping a linen napkin over his lap while he read the menu, forcing a waiter to hustle over to pull out her chair. She settled into her own seat, strategically facing the cameras, smack dab in the middle of the restaurant, and picked up her own menu.

With the cameras capturing her every breath, Roxanne let her eyes skim over the menu while her blood boiled.

Remember, her inner voice chanted to calm herself. *Remember, remember. He can make you a fool.* She slowly filled her lower belly with air and, just as slowly, pushed it out again. *Remember. Only you can make yourself weak.*

She'd misstepped with him...several times. Now she had to add the uncomfortable weight of guilt to her own frustrations. She needed to clear the air. She needed to make it right.

Only by prostrating herself could she regain the upper hand.

She glanced over her menu at him. He'd left dark scruff on his jaw and chin, giving him a savage air in his Armani suit. He hadn't had a cut since she'd seen him last. His hair curled blond where it touched his white collar. The candlelight caught at the shadows under his eyes.

She placed her menu perpendicular to her fork and picked up her wineglass, steepling it between her fingers so that it hid some of her face from the cameras.

"Well, that was an inauspicious beginning for the Golden Couple," she murmured from behind the glass.

"Hmmm," the prince said without raising his eyes from the menu. "I guess we don't have pictures of your mouth around my cock. Or me jacking it into a cup. Those'll be missed from the scrapbook." His deep, low voice was placid with apathy.

Roxanne felt the annoying prickle of frustration at the back of her throat. She dragged her teeth across her lower lip and lowered her glass to the table. And then plastered on a smile. "Look," she said through her grin. "I wanted to wait until we had some privacy, but…what I did was wrong. So wrong. I shouldn't have announced the marriage without your consent and I shouldn't have created such an exaggerated tale about…"

"My growers became garbage collectors last week," he said, his eyes focused on the dinner courses.

What? "Why?"

"The Monte has a contract with a garbage collecting service. We're behind in our payments, but I'd convinced the owner that we'd catch up soon. When your stories broke, the garbage trucks stopped showing up. No word. No warning. The man won't return my calls." His eyes continued to read over the menu. "So, last week, I asked some of my more loyal growers to collect the town's trash and haul it away. They're the only people I could mobilize quickly who had trucks. So you can apologize to the men and women who heeded the call and moved mountains of trash when they needed to be working in their fields." He looked for all the world like he was completely at ease. Only Roxanne could see his white-knuckled grip on the thick, linen card stock. "But don't apologize to me for spreading your lies. You wanted my degradation. You got it."

The corset of guilt that had been tightening since she'd sent out the press releases cut off her air.

Brains and bravado were her only resources when she started making her way in the world. But she realized quickly that she had something others lacked when she sat in class next to disdainful Ivy Leaguers with no empathy for the 99 percent or made decisions next to corporate bigwigs who cared more for their portfolio than their employees. She had good intentions. Yes, she wanted power and money. Yes, she wanted to control her destiny and never again be at the whim of another. She'd been able to acquire those things by helping—rather than harming—those around her, by assisting female entrepreneurs and helping them make their businesses the best they could be.

Roxanne had stopped asking permission long ago because she'd earned the right to demand what she wanted. Even when she'd made this deal with the prince, she'd truly believed it would benefit him.

But only blind, antagonistic anger had gone into conjuring those press releases. He'd made her crave something in that alley that she didn't want from him or any man. Passion was fine. But not tenderness. Not vulnerability. She was punishing him because he was stronger than she was. He could admit that he craved to touch her even when that craving made him weak.

Roxanne was using her wealth, power, and influence to punish a man—not a prince or a scientist or her contractual husband—but a man who was just trying to hold his world together.

She would never be able to make this right while the eyes of the world watched.

She signaled the staff. The waiter, sommelier, and manager hustled over as the prince's shoulders tensed in his jacket. "My handsome *príncipe* would like a little privacy before we dine," she said, giving a secret smile to the female manager. "Is there a room where he and I could…chat?"

The excellently trained staff didn't even blink. "Of course," the woman responded. "Come with me."

The waiter pulled out Roxanne's seat as the prince rose, eyeing her suspiciously. She circled the table toward him and nestled her hand into the crook of his arm. Together, they followed the manager out of the dining room and down a low-lit hallway. Roxanne felt the diners' eyes on her ass and the menacing anger of the prince all over her skin.

The manager unlocked a door and flipped on some lights with a murmur about it being an extra room for large parties. Right now, the room's gold-flecked wallpaper and elaborate chandelier were only decoration for the dining tables, high-top bar tables, and accompanying chairs crammed into it, spare alleys of space running between the furniture. The wise manager closed the door without a glance back.

The instant she did, the prince pulled his arm out of her hold like she was toxic. "I'm not fucking you," he said as he strode between a row of chairs and away from her.

In the closed off, slightly musty room, she could smell him; smell the wild, earthy spice of him. He walked like a caged lion through the aisles of the furniture, all of his rage in the shoulders of that sleek, expensive suit. "I don't expect you to," she said, letting her fingers rest on the gold cross. "I need to apologize for what I've done and letting this get so out of…"

He shoved into a chair as he turned, making it screech along the tile. "Stop it," he said, glaring at her. "You give out apologies like junk mail and they're just as worthless."

Roxanne raised her chin and swallowed her pride. "I can make this right," she continued, fingering the cross. "I'll pay off the Monte's outstanding debts now; we don't have to wait until I'm pregnant."

He laughed an ugly groan up to the sparkling chandelier. "After this, you think I'll trust anything from you? I don't want your money. I don't want your body. I just want out." His big hands curled at his sides. "Tell the press you're divorcing me because…because I can't get it up. Or whatever, I don't fucking care. Just think of this as a failed experiment and walk away."

She slapped her hands helplessly at her sides. "I understand why you hate me. But you know you can't walk away. Without my money, the Monte will be destroyed."

His dark eyebrows creased in disbelief as he shook his head at her. "*Jesucristo*, can you get over your savior complex? Yeah, it'll be tough but we can manage it. I've still got three years of reserves to draw on."

His words, his confidence, hit her ears like an off note. She narrowed her eyes at him. "Three years? You barely have a few months."

"Because of you." Thunder gathered on his brow as he pushed a barstool out of his way to get an aisle closer to her. "Because of the lies you told. You've made it harder for my people to get credit, but we can keep our heads above water until my vines start producing."

Roxanne raked her fingernails through her hair. Frustrating and mule-fucking-stubborn the prince might be. But he wasn't an idiot. His continued insistence that he had more time didn't fit with the facts that Roxanne knew. That he should have known.

"How much time do you think you have before the Monte starts defaulting on its loans?" she asked.

"Why would I tell you?"

She watched his face closely. "You have fourteen months, tops."

When the prince just smiled menacingly as he shoved between chairs to get closer to her, Roxanne knew something was very, very wrong. "Pulling scary numbers out of your fine *culo* is not going to make me…"

Only a row of high-top bar tables separated them now, and Roxanne put her hands on the closest, making sure it was squarely in his path before she delivered the blow he didn't deserve. "I'm not lying. Fourteen months, tops, before the Monte del Vino Real is bankrupt. I'll send my auditor's re-

ports over. Have them checked by an independent accountant."
The prince truly didn't know, and Roxanne realized why he
was being so obtuse. He'd been kept in the dark. "*Don't* send
them to your treasurer."

His own hands came up to grip the table edge as he sneered
at her. "Stop it! You want me jumping at my own fucking
shadow. You're not going to play me..."

She saw his big hands, his angry, white knuckles choked
by that gold band as they gripped the table—and something
ridiculous made her reach for them, made her try to soothe
them with her palm. "Mateo, listen..."

The bar table flew from between them and landed with a
deafening clatter against other furniture. Roxanne stumbled
back and then kicked off her heels, jumping into a defensive
stance as Mateo grabbed for her. "You'll stop at nothing," he
roared. "Touch me, suck me, lie to me to get what you..."

Roxanne kicked out her foot and swept the prince's legs
out from under him, landing him neatly and with a thun-
derous crash on the tile floor space he'd created when he'd
thrown the table. While he gasped for the air that had been
knocked out of him, Roxanne jumped on him and straddled
his chest, balancing the bulk of her weight on her knees to
pin his shoulders down.

She leaned over him. "I've never lied to you. I even called
an unnecessary meeting last month to ensure it. And I'm not
lying now. Your financial situation is the main reason I chose
you to be my husband." As she spoke, her black hair cascaded
around them. "I had my pick of impoverished aristocrats. And
not one of them needed my money as urgently as you. Do you
honestly think I would propose this crazy deal to someone
who wasn't desperate enough to agree to it?"

In the shadow of her hair, the prince's eyes clenched as
he took huge breaths through his teeth, moving her up and

down. "I assumed you knew the razor's edge your kingdom is on." His body vibrated with resistance. "This was a business deal, Mateo. Disregarding my recent bad behavior, I'm actually not aiming to torment you. I want a baby, now. You need my money, now. I thought you knew that."

Some of her hair was about to slip into his eyes and she flicked it away, brushing his broad forehead. His skin was warm and smooth. "You don't like my apologies so I'll stop offering them. Instead I'll make you a promise. I promise to make this right. I promise to rectify the damage I've done to your reputation and the Monte's reputation. And I promise to stop…being such a pain in your ass."

His body was as stiff as marble beneath her. But he opened his eyes, golden fire joining her in the cavern of her hair.

She tensed, readying for whatever happened next.

"Now I know you're lying," he said, guttural and low. "You're still going to be a pain in my ass." She felt his shoulders jerk beneath her. "Get off."

Roxanne shifted off of him, moved her butt to the dusty tile in her $3,000 Chanel dress. But she kept a leg slung over his torso, not holding him down but just…there. And he let her. He didn't sit up. His hand settled on her bare knee.

Now that she was aware of it, she could feel that warm gold band every time he touched her.

"I have no reason to trust you," he said, staring up at the ceiling.

"I know." But she could see that royal brain of his working. She could imagine the square pegs of various financial details suddenly sliding neatly into their holes. But when his head lolled to the side, when his eyes caught hers, it wasn't finances he asked about.

"Why did you call that unnecessary meeting last month?"

She stiffened under his gaze. But she didn't look away. She

knew what he wanted, he wanted the truth. He wanted her to reveal herself. He wanted something that would make her as vulnerable as he was, laid out on a dusty floor, embarrassing secrets exposed.

It was the only way he would trust the other truths coming out of her mouth.

She swallowed through a tight throat and thought of her daughter. "The way we were together in that alley was too..." She looked at him. But he wasn't going to save her from this. "Just too. I assumed having sex with the Golden Prince was going to be all show and no substance."

A hint of a smirk settled over his features. "I gave you too much substance?" Then the smirk fell away. "I want to see those reports tonight."

Apparently, he was satisfied with her pound of flesh. She nodded, relieved he let her off the hook so easily. "I'll have them couriered over the instant you're home."

"Our treasurer has been doctoring the books?"

"He must be. He answers to your father. Your parents' spending actually went up after the offer from CML Resorts."

When the prince closed his eyes this time, his forehead creased with pain.

"*Príncipe*..."

"Call me by my name."

"Mateo..." She wondered if he knew he was stroking her knee with his thumb. She wondered if it felt as good to his thumb as it did to her knee. "None of this is your fault."

"Stop." He opened his eyes and pushed her leg off of him. "Let's go finish dinner." When he pushed himself up and stood, she was looking up and up and up at a dusty mountain of a man in a gleaming suit. She had enough respect for the fight to understand that she had held him down because he'd allowed it.

He took a half-hearted swipe at his suit pants and then extended his hand to her. She hesitated only a moment before she took it. "We don't have to go back in there," she said. Tonight, the fairy tale could wait.

"We do," he said as he lifted her to her feet. "*Eres mi salvador y única esperanza.*"

His bitter smile as he called her his "savior and only hope" changed when he caught the gleam of her giant wedding ring. He brought her hand up to his face, straightened the heavy diamond, and surprised her by kissing it, his mouth warming the icy jewels. His golden gaze traveled up her arm and touched her hair, her eyes, the sheen of her lips, like it was the first time he'd seen her that night, before his gaze wandered over her bare shoulders and down, down into the V of her cleavage.

His low voice, when it came, felt like it traced the same path over her skin. "Unless you want to stay here and do what everyone already assumes we're doing?"

Standing next to the raw heat of him, she was tempted. For a moment. Staying in that room would further her own ends. But the prince was wounded; she couldn't take advantage of him while he was bleeding. Looking into the shadows in his eyes, misery he wanted to forget for a few minutes while he thrust inside of her, Roxanne felt nothing but regret for the blows she'd struck against him.

Surprised by her own tumble of emotion, Roxanne looked away from him. "No... I... The contract..."

"Right." His voice was raw and self-deprecating. He straightened his coat, held out an elbow for her to take, and then motioned to the door with a sarcastic flourish. "Then let's go put on a show. Let's show them how a prince earns his millions."

March: Night Two

Roxanne stood in the fluorescent-lit lobby of the Medina Building's underground garage, quickly scanning an update on the Monte's creditors from her assistant while she chatted with her bodyguard. Henry was a blond-and-burly Texan and a fierce Cowboys fan. With her 49ers skybox and the bad taste in her mouth left by those Dallas Cowboys cheerleader posters of her youth, Roxanne could not let that pass.

"But you can see the fear in your quarterback's eyes," she said, looking up from her phone to tease him. "That's why he screwed up that snap during the wildcard game. He was afraid the ball was going to hit him."

Henry chuckled, crossing his mammoth arms over his tight black knit shirt, the silver clutch he held looking like a coin purse in his huge hand. "The 49ers ended the season with a losing record. You want to talk about playing scared. Every single one of their starters is shaking in their boots."

"Hey, those starters got us to the playoffs."

"Which they lost."

"Sure, but when was the last time the Cowboys even saw…" Roxanne stopped talking when the ex-Marine put his finger to his ear and snapped to, dropping all pretense of ease. He tilted his thick neck to talk into the mic at his shoulder. "Yep. The garage is clear. Send him on down."

Henry handed her the clutch, which he'd been holding

while she checked her email. "Your husband is on his way, Ms. Medina." Roxanne took a longer glance at him before returning her eyes to her phone to finish her email scan. She wondered how he could say "your husband" with a straight face. As head of her security, Henry was one of a handful of employees who helped coordinate her life outside of the office. He knew where she went and with whom. He knew there'd been no romantic trips to northern Spain, no wedding in St. Tropez. She paid those employees generously for their discretion and knew that they would jump in front of a bus for her—it was in their makeup, showed in the Myers-Briggs and other personality tests she required of her closest employees. She'd spent holidays with them, had been invited into their homes and met their families.

And she knew not one of them could be trusted.

That was the human condition. Given the right levers and stresses, any person could turn on you. So she paid her employees well, treated them better, and looked forward to the day her baby—her daughter—would stand by her side not because of bribes and bonuses, but because standing by her side was a pleasant place to be.

With the reminder that she would be working on producing that daughter tonight, fingers of sensation tip-tapped up Roxanne's spine. She opened her clutch to throw her phone into it and noticed her mirror. She hesitated before she pulled it out quickly, turned slightly away from Henry, and opened the compact to check her lips, hoping the bold, glistening red hadn't smudged. The casual waves of dark hair trailing over her shoulders still looked smooth and glossy.

"You look gorgeous," her bodyguard said behind her, voice full of humor.

"Shut up, Henry," Roxanne said. She snapped the compact closed, put it in her clutch, and then straightened herself to her full five-foot-four inches, five-foot-seven with the heels. She raised her chin to add another inch.

Just in time to watch a faded blue pickup truck straight out of the '70s come rattling around the corner. It was covered in road dust and bug smears, and Roxanne was shocked when, instead of calling for backup, Henry moved to the lobby door and opened it for her. The death rattle of the truck echoed louder in the underground garage as it pulled up to the curb.

Henry grinned at her as he held the door open. "I'm pretty sure this is your ride."

With a percussive crack of the driver's door, the prince's head and shoulders appeared above the truck's roof. Roxanne walked out into the garage slowly as the prince walked around to the passenger side, his eyes unreadable under his worn ball cap. He pulled the truck door open for her, a weld of duct tape across the top of the door apparently keeping the window in its frame.

"What are you driving?" Roxanne asked at the same moment he asked, "What are you wearing?"

Roxanne glanced down at her off-the-shoulder gray wrap sweater, multilayered chiffon skirt that floated around her waist to her knees, sheer black stockings, and demure patent leather heels before looking back at him. "What? It's a skirt."

"That's not a skirt. That's a dust bunny." The prince's fashion selection for the evening was a beat-up canvas coat, old khakis, and dusty Blundstones. "Don't you own a pair of jeans?"

Roxanne cocked her hip. "If I'd known we were heading to the rodeo, I'd have dressed differently."

His grip on the truck door tightened. "The truck belongs to one of my guys. It was the only way I could sneak away from the paparazzi."

Roxanne sighed and eyed the interior of the truck. It, too,

had some duct tape repairs. But at least it looked clean. If the prince wanted her to pay penance for unleashing the world press on them, she'd better start writing those checks now. She looked back at her bodyguard and nodded. "Thank you, Henry."

Henry's cool gaze took in the prince before he nodded back at her. "Have a good evening, ma'am."

Roxanne took a step up and settled herself into the big roomy cab that smelled of pine and tool oil while the prince closed the door with a little more force than necessary.

He got in on his side and they drove up the levels of the parking garage without speaking a word.

Near the exit, he said, "Duck down." Roxanne slumped down on the vinyl seat but stayed high enough to see that, as they exited onto the city street, even the late hour and soupy fog hadn't chased away a few determined paparazzi. Their collars raised against the damp cold, they barely glanced up from their phones as the truck passed them on the street. She imagined that even the most desperate celebrities wouldn't stoop to riding in vehicles with rust decorating the fenders.

Roxanne glanced at the prince, who'd kept his head low and his shoulders hunched high as he'd driven past the photographers. "You were right. This car is good camouflage."

He relaxed his shoulders and tilted his cap farther back on his head, revealing shadows of exhaustion that were almost purple. Then he turned right on the nearly empty downtown street, when their hotel was two blocks to the left.

"But the St. Francis is—"

"I can't go there," the prince cut her off. "Not right away. I need to fucking breathe." He looked at her, chin raised, and she could see the pride he was swallowing. "Do you mind if we drive around?"

When they'd returned to their table last night, he'd played

the part of the fairy-tale prince, the perfect, attentive gentleman as he held her seat for her and asked about her work and
kept her wineglass full. Roxanne would have been as thrilled
as the press and other diners, all who were snapping pictures,
if the bleakness in his eyes hadn't hollowed her out a bit. Seeing the prince ask her permission now, knowing that he'd accepted the bitter truth that she was the only person who could
save him, should have made her relieved. He was finally ame-
nable to the logical plan she'd drawn up.

She'd only wanted him to bend. Not to break.

She shook her head and lowered her eyes. "No, I don't
mind." She looked out her window, the thick fog making the
downtown buildings barely discernible as they drove up California Street. A shiver caught her unexpectedly.

The prince cranked on the heat without a word, the blower
filling the cab with noise and warmth.

After a few minutes of silent driving, he asked, "Who was
that guy? Back at the garage."

Roxanne turned to look at him. Both work-hardened hands
were resting on top of the steering wheel, and the gold of his
wedding band caught the gleam of the traffic light he was
focused on. He'd shaved and she realized, from this vantage
point, she could see the sharp angle of his jaw and cheekbone.
She could see the muscle ticking where they met.

"That's Henry. He's head of my security team."

"Oh." That muscle continued vibrating as the light turned
green and the prince took a left on Masonic. The streets were
quiet and the lights of the urban townhomes they passed were
soft blobs of light in the fog.

"I don't sleep with my staff," she said, glancing at the ring
again. She was surprised he'd worn it. "If that's what you're
wondering."

A humorless smirk bent his lips. "I'm proof that that isn't true," he said, low and bitter, without taking his eyes off the road.

"Ours is a trade agreement," she said calmly. "You have a product I want. I am paying you for it. We meet as equals."

The prince rolled his eyes and slumped against the door-frame, leaving one arm resting on top of the wheel. "*Princesa*, I've never come to anyone more hat-in-hand. At least that meathead can protect you. The only thing I've got for you is what every man who lays eyes on you is desperate to give."

Roxanne felt a warmth bloom just under her gold cross that had nothing to do with the ancient heater. "Henry isn't a meathead."

"Then maybe you *should* be fucking him."

"I wouldn't—"

"I know." He tilted his head to look at her, and his shadowed eyes under his cap, his dark, furrowed eyebrows, let her know that none of his disgust was for her. "I know you wouldn't."

He turned back to the road. "But maybe you should be. I imagine his 'product' is far superior to mine. I'm the idiot who allowed his kingdom to be robbed right under his nose."

Roxanne looked down at her lap, squeezed her fingers around her silver clutch in the cloud of her skirt. The bleakness on his face was hard to look at.

"How far were your numbers off?" she asked quietly.

"Farther off than I thought possible," he said, voice hollow. "Thank you for the..." She heard him swallow and shift away from her. "Payments. There were creditors on that list I didn't know about. Brandon writes a very succinct report; maybe your assistant wants to run my kingdom. He'd do a better job than me and the king."

It was like he'd pulled off a layer of skin and now sat next to her raw and exposed. She'd seen him furious and she'd seen him cocksure. And at times, she'd not seen *him* at all, only a tool to achieve her goal. But right now, with his self-disgust stripping him naked and vulnerable, Roxanne saw an echo of herself, a shadow of what she felt when a business venture failed or when she had to tell a female business owner that her losses had surpassed even Roxanne's ability to save her. She imagined that if she looked in the mirror when terror of failure startled her awake, she would look very much like the prince right now. For the first time, Roxanne—a poor girl from Kansas who made an empire out of nothing—felt a kinship with this Spanish man born into royalty.

He stared blankly out the window, his jaw stiff, as they headed up into the San Francisco hills, passing million-dollar homes crushed together on the slopes.

"What happened to you could have happened to anyone," she said as the yellow light from the dash glinted off his face. "Do you know how many corporate tycoons invested in Bernie Madoff's scam?"

Those sulky lips pulled back in a grimace. "I wasn't fooled by a friend of a friend's financial advisor. I was lied to by our treasurer, a man I've known and trusted my whole life. Worse, I was lied to by my father, a man I don't trust. I should have checked the facts." He punctuated "facts" with a punch to the steering wheel.

Then he gripped the wheel like it was his father's throat.

"I should have known better. I should have *been* better. My whole life…" He swallowed like he was choking on the words. "I've lived my whole life declaring I was going to be better than the king. I did well in school and stayed away from my parents' excesses and…fuck, just figured I was some superior fucking creature who was going to swoop into the Monte and save it just in time. But in the end…" He shook his head, shoulders weighted down in pain. "I'm just as worthless as my father. And, just like during the reign of my father, the innocents will suffer most for it. Your baby, our child, will be the one left to clean up the mess."

The truck snapped to a hard stop. Roxanne slapped her hands against the dash and glanced out the windshield. Her mouth fell open.

Through the glass, a wide view of the city spread before her. They were above the fog but could look down on the city encased in it, lights glowing inside its soft billowy cotton. The Transamerica building mightily poked up its triangle peak, and a bright full moon hung above the Bay Bridge.

She looked at the prince. "Where—"

He jerked his thumb over his left shoulder. Behind him, she could see the red legs of Sutro Tower, a gigantic radio tower that was both a landmark and an eyesore for San Franciscans. She'd never thought of coming up here. They were in an empty parking lot, surrounded by trees and dark. She wondered how many others who looked on this radio tower every day had missed the opportunity to look out from it, to take in this spectacular view.

The prince turned off the truck, leaving them in a silence that was dense after the roar of the heater and the rattle of the muffler. The light of the full moon cast a pale blue light inside the cab.

"If someone scattered diamonds in your skirt, it would look like that," the prince said quietly, his head lowered but his ball cap nodding at the view.

It was an affecting way to describe what they were looking at. Or he was giving her shit.

Setting her clutch on the seat, Roxanne leaned toward him and plucked the ball cap off his head.

The prince's hair tumbled into his face, releasing the clean, woody smell of his shampoo. Slowly he raised his hand to brush it back, and then he lifted his head to look at her. The misery was still there, in that dent between his dark brows. But his eyes also glowed with what he wanted to do to forget his misery, if only for the evening.

Roxanne swallowed. And then pushed the cap against his canvas coat.

"If you keep wearing these to our dates, I'll—"

His hands came up to capture her hands against his chest. "Rob me blind? Beggar my people? Get in line," he smirked.

She pulled her hands away from him. "I'll be annoyed."

He tossed the cap to the floor. "Well, you'd better get used to them. I've got a good reason to hide my face."

The beautiful view and the extra degree of heat in his eyes hadn't made Roxanne forget his gut-wrenching tirade. The prince truly wanted to make the Monte a better place for his people. For their daughter. And he believed that he had failed his life's mission. She couldn't imagine, after all of the work, all of the focus, what that must feel like. *"I've lived my whole life declaring I was going to be better than the king."* Hadn't she, in her own way, said the same thing to herself? Never out loud. Never to another living soul. But hadn't she also said she was going to be a better person, a better mother, than her mother? Hadn't so much of what she'd accomplished been about getting far away from that woman in her run-down rooms with run-down men?

If she discovered that all the work, somehow, had been for nothing; that she was still going to end up a victim to her mother's whims and inflict those same mistakes on her daughter? Well, she'd probably stick a gun in her mouth.

"You won't need to hide your face when you realize how lucky you are," she said, clasping her hands together and settling them in the puff of her skirt. "Righting sinking ships happens to be one of your wife's specialties. We'll get the kingdom's financial affairs in order."

Paying off the most insistent creditors had been effortless. Garbage would once again be collected in the Monte. The bulk of the money would still have to wait until Roxanne was pregnant or the year was up, whichever came first. She wasn't a fool. Still, there was plenty she could do that didn't involve cash. She was excited to roll up her sleeves and attack the books.

She pulled her thoughts away from her daydreams—she was a nerdy bookkeeper at heart—to find that he'd settled back against the door to watch her. She realized that she'd just called herself his wife.

"All of this is for the sake of our daughter, of course," she said quickly.

"Of course," he responded. Was he mocking her? "It's a perfect story, how mommy saved daddy." His soft voice took away the bitterness of his words. "Why do you keep insisting it's going to be a girl?"

She felt the flush along her chest, exposed by the low wrap of her off-the-shoulder sweater. "Because I'm going to have a daughter." She kept her head lifted and eyes on him. "Don't you believe in the power of positive thinking?"

"I believed I could build a better kingdom for my heir and look how that turned out." While shadows darkened his eyes, his grin grew teasing. "You know this is one area, my beautiful billionaire, where your money won't buy you what you want."

"I know. But I'm still going to have a daughter." She tilted her head, felt her hair slip across shoulders that were growing cool.

What could she tell him? That she'd never considered the possibility of having a son? That would sound delusional. And she wouldn't tell him—no matter how nakedly honest he'd been with her—that only to a *daughter* could she give the child-hood denied herself. That she wanted a friend and compan-ion, a girl who could one day inherit her company the way his heir would inherit his kingdom. That sometimes, in her tower above so many, she was a little lonely.

She shivered, as much from the raw truth at the tip of her tongue as from the rapidly growing cold in the cab. Instantly, he zipped down his coat, leaned forward to pull it off his arms, and scooted forward to wrap it around her.

Roxanne leaned her head forward as he closed the gap at the front of the coat, leaving her completely surrounded in the spicy green smell of him. He wore a plain white t-shirt that pulled across wide shoulders and showed off a hard chest. He was as close to naked as she'd ever seen him.

"*Gracias, Príncipe,*" she murmured.

His warm hand settled on her nape, under her hair. "Don't call me that. Not tonight." Slowly, he pulled her hair out from the collar of his coat, and then brought it over her shoulder, his fingers trailing through it as he spoke. "In fact, don't ever call me that again. Use my name. I'm your husband." She could feel her hair catching in his calluses as he gently raked his fingers through it, creating sensitive prickles on her scalp. "Tonight, I'm just a man who brought his wife to a make-out spot so he could try some new 'firsts' with her. Use my name."

As her hair slipped from his fingers onto her shoulder, Rox-anne turned to look at him over its long black fall. "You're never *just* a man. *Príncipe.*"

In the flare of his perfect nose and the gleam of his white teeth, Roxanne knew he'd caught the gauntlet she'd just thrown down.

The prince was a good man. He didn't deserve what hap-pened to him. She'd come prepared to play, to seduce and distract him out of his despair, if only for a couple of hours.

She owed him that much. She could revel in the heat they'd discovered together, tease and touch him on her terms, while firmly keeping control.

She returned her gaze demurely back to her lap as the prince moved closer to her, the old springs of the truck seat squeaking. He tucked her hair behind her ear, and then leaned down to it. "And you, *belleza*? Are you never anything but a billionaire and captain of industry?" His low voice, rumbling directly into her ear, dripped straight down to the core of her. "Are you never just a woman, demanding her pleasure in a stranger's doorway. Are you never just... Roxanne?"

Her teeth bit into her lower lip as she heard her name cross his. He'd never said her name before, although she had, at times, said his. In moments of weakness. She resisted making this another one of those moments as his deep voice encased her name in velvet, made it something exotic and sensual with the whisper of his Spanish accent. "Roxanne... Roxanne." His big hand dipped under the mass of her skirts and found her knee, traced delicate circles on the sensitive inside through her stocking. "It tastes good. My spouse's name. You should try it."

"Okay," she said, breathlessly. Those circles were making her crazy. "I'll try it." She raised her head and looked at him, licking her top lip. A long lick, making it shine, as if the heat between them had evaporated all its moisture. She dragged her teeth across her bottom lip and then opened her mouth, inhaling as his eyes focused on her lush lips.

"Roxanne," she said, long and breathy.

His blunt nails scraped halfway up her thigh, the unapologetic sensation making her legs jolt apart. His glare turned calculating. "My sweet Roxanne, you obviously need some help. I know how easily you lose your mind when I touch you. Here."

And as effortlessly as if she were his baseball cap, Mateo lifted her up and pulled her over him, forcing her to straddle him as her skirt billowed over his lap and his coat fell off her shoulders. His big hands engulfed her jaw, the furnace of their heat surrounding her face as his fingers stroked her nape. "Now focus." He held her inches from his face, her eyes flooded by him, her body controlled by him. He was thick and hard in his worn, soft khakis. She gripped his strong wrists for something to hang on to. "Ma-te-o," he said, those soft lips taunting her. "Mateo."

He was so fucking gorgeous. She licked her lips for real this time—all the moisture had left them—and when he watched the journey of her tongue, the taunt in his eyes turned into something hotter. "Let's try this," he rumbled. And he pulled her mouth to him. "Mateo," he said, stroking his name against her lips, breathing his name into her mouth.

She could taste his name on her tongue. She couldn't... She tilted her head and pressed her lips against his. For a spare second, he closed his eyes and kissed her back.

Then his hands clenched on her jaw as he jerked her head away. "Uh, uh, uh. Mateo," he demanded. But he was no more immune than she as he pulled her mouth slowly back to him, his eyes losing their fight to keep their domineering gleam. He kissed her, cradling her face as he tasted her lips and then licked into her mouth. That pleasure of a whole month ago came roaring back as he tilted her head to taste every corner, and Roxanne dropped her hands to grip his t-shirt, welcoming him inside her as she tilted her hips to nestle him closer. She spread her hands wide to caress his chest. When she bit at his tongue and then licked to soothe it, his groan drowned out her gasp of pleasure. God, she loved the way he tasted.

With a ferocious suck on her lower lip, he pulled her away

again. His fiery eyes burned into her. "Mateo," he said, shaking her head slightly with his powerful hands. "Say it."

Roxanne rolled her hips against the thickness of him, clawed her nails down his torso. "*Príncipe*," she groaned.

Never had she seen excitement and fury war so determinedly on someone's face. His expression made her pussy squeeze like he was already inside her. And then his eyes narrowed.

"*Princesa*, you're fucking with a tyrant," he growled. "Do you know what my forefathers did to young women who wouldn't give them what they wanted?"

He picked her up and dumped her ass on the seat. Then he slithered to his knees on the floor of the truck, the bigger-is-better styling of the inside giving him lots of room to move around and get his hands on her knees. His hands began pushing up the chiffon froth of her skirt as his wide torso shoved her legs apart.

Suddenly, Roxanne understood what he intended.

"Wait, wait," she gasped, trying to get a handhold on the slippery seat to pull herself up with one hand while pushing down her skirt with the other. She'd teased him and played with him to help him forget. He was a good man. But there on his knees, he was the devil. And this desperate, jittery thing happening inside her felt nothing like play.

"Wait," she said again. Mateo just grabbed her around her stockinged knees and dragged her closer to him.

He leaned over her, a menace of heat and power. "No, there won't be any waiting," he said, eyes capturing her as he relentlessly began to pull up the chiffon squeezed between them. "You're my wife and I want to know what you taste like. I want a taste of heaven to balance the hell you put me through this month. I want you all over my mouth and down my throat." The eroticism of his angelically sculpted face promising such filthy pleasure stabbed her between her shoulder blades, made her want to writhe against him. "When you come, I want my name on your lips. Just like your pleasure is going to be glistening on mine."

Both of them inhaled when his hot hand touched skin at the top of her thigh. His eyes looked into hers for a beat. Then he reared back.

"Holy fuck," he groaned as he looked down at her. Roxanne gritted her eyes closed against the awe on his face. The lingerie she'd chosen was the favor to him. The way to help him forget. She imagined slowly revealing it to him in the privacy of their hotel room, slowly letting him see the thigh-high stockings and black garters with their bloodred rosettes under her ballerina froth. She imagined slowly slipping off the barely there panties before climbing on top of him. She imagined being in control.

But all control was ripped from her when he shoved her thighs wide and pressed those soft, sulky lips to her core. She groaned as he nuzzled in then licked, rubbing the lace of her panties against her clit. She felt him let go of the skirt at her waist. "Get this fucking thing..." he mumbled against her, and then, with a rip and a tug, he tore the ribbon of her panties at her hip.

She felt satin tickle between her thighs. And then... "Oh fuck. Yes." And Mateo was there, fingers separating her and mouth kissing her and tongue tasting and licking and then flicking so hard. Roxanne would have snapped her thighs closed at the unendurable lurch of pleasure if Mateo's strong shoulders weren't holding them so commandingly apart. Roxanne opened her eyes on a gasp, looked down. And couldn't see anything over the ridiculous bank of her skirt.

Mateo lifted her thigh and tilted his head so he could push his tongue inside of her.

"Oh God," Roxanne choked out, gripping the seat and

arching her back to get him farther in. He growled his approval, adding vibration to the tongue lunging inside of her like it couldn't get deep enough, like there was a sweetness he was still relentlessly searching for. His unrestrained mouth fucking—without modesty or mercy—whipped her into a frenzy.

But she wanted to see him. She wanted to see Mateo's gorgeous golden face between her thighs.

She tried to get her hands under, knocked her clutch off the seat as she settled for her elbows and looked down over the length of her body, over the mound of her skirt. Eyes catching her, Mateo took a final taste before easing her thigh back down and spreading it wide, her torn panty trailing lazily across the seat.

Without taking his eyes off of her, he wiped his chin on the shoulder of his white T-shirt.

"What is it, Roxanne?" he said, keeping her eyes trapped as he slowly leaned down again, his big workman's fingers separating her neatly trimmed lips. "Do you want to watch?" That sulky mouth pursed to give her swollen, begging clit a soft, slow kiss. "Do you want me to stop?" His tongue came out to tease her, to make her throb slowly. "Do you want me, Roxanne, to keep licking this pretty..." His lips brushed over her, delivering a hot puff of air. "Little..." He did it again. "Pussy?" And again.

All while his rough Spanish accent sent sensation over her skin and his golden eyes stayed on her.

With deliberate intent, his tongue reached out and he began to flick at her. Imprisoned by his gaze, Roxanne resisted letting her head fall back between her shoulder blades. But she couldn't resist spreading her thighs. She couldn't resist pushing closer to his face.

He raised his lip in a snarl. "Say my name," he demanded

before his full lips surrounded her and he began to suck, his tongue working in tandem with his lips.

She couldn't breathe, much less talk.

"Say my name, Roxanne." His finger stroked down and then pushed inside. One finger, pulsing and pulsing into her while his tongue snapped at her. Until it was two. "Say Mateo or I swear to God I'll stop."

"Nonononononononono," Roxanne sobbed, her hips rolling against him as he sucked.

"Then say it." His fingers twisted until… Roxanne, lurched, head jolting up and abs tightening as he touched some spot inside of her, some delicate trigger that had never been touched before. It made her feel like screaming. "Who am I?" His mouth took her relentlessly between his words. "Who's the father of your baby?" His arm moved like a jackhammer as he fucked her with his fingers. "Who's your husband?" His lips were raised back in a grimace as his tongue whipped at her. "Who's the man you're going to be dreaming about after you say goodbye?"

The orgasm tore through Roxanne's body like a tidal wave.

"Mateo," she screamed as she bolted upright, thighs shaking as she tried to claw away from the unendurable pleasure. But he kept her locked to his mouth, kept feasting on her. "Mateo, Mateo, oh my God, Mateo."

And then her words were stolen from her by a squeal of the truck door and a flash of blinding light and the horrifying sound of a rapid-fire camera taking endless pictures. Pictures of the Golden Prince's face pressed between Roxanne Medina's legs that could potentially be sold for thousands.

And seen by millions.

March: Night Three

Mateo held Roxanne Medina's slender, fine-boned hand in his, their fingers entwined, and brought it up to his lips. Her hand lotion—or maybe it was just her—made him think of the boudoirs of his teenage fantasies, rooms tempting with candlelight and incense and satin-clad women who commanded with a smile. He smoothed his lips over the fine skin before he kissed it, enjoying the tensile strength of her bones under all of that delicateness, while he stared into Caribbean-blue eyes that swallowed him whole.

"Would you be able to keep your hands off this woman if you were married to her?" he asked, loud enough for the bank of microphones in front of him to catch every lust-drenched word.

He fought to keep from blinking as flashes exploded like strobe lights all around them. He could see Roxanne's thick, black lashes twitching as she fought to do the same.

As soon as the dance party died down, Roxanne leaned close to the microphones without taking her eyes off of him. "We understand we had no presumption of privacy, doing what we were doing, in a public park, but..." She let her eyes flutter away from him demurely, let her teeth bite into that lush lip she'd painted a shell pink. She smiled shyly and sweetly into the cameras. "We hope everyone can understand that a couple, newly married, can sometimes…forget themselves. No matter who they are."

Jesus Christ, she was brilliant. It had been her idea to veer the "sex in public" hysteria that the press had flown with into a "two crazy kids in love" story. Now, during this midevening press conference in the lobby of the Medina Building, she was using the standard misogynistic fantasy about women—a lady in the parlor and a whore in the bedroom—to her advantage. The delicate pleats on her knee-length, dove-gray skirt, the little lace collar on her matching short-sleeved sweater, and the ponytail that curled like a comma between her shoulder blades all suggested a woman too innocent to like and chase sex, to demand it whenever and however she needed it.

That skirt had been up around her waist as she'd ridden him hard in an empty office five minutes before the press conference. There was too much damage control to do to get a hotel room, she'd insisted. There'd been little pleasure in the act for either of them.

Or at least, probably not for her. Although she'd been wet and he'd been hard and there'd been this spine-melting hitch in her throat when he'd pinched her nipple through her sweater…. Stripped of pride, resources, and alternatives, Mateo saw little reason to deny the orgasms she wanted from him. She truly was his only hope.

Roxanne's attorney, William LaPierre, stood just to the left of Roxanne and pointed at one of the dozens of hands waving in the seated rows. A crop of photographers sat on the floor in front of the podium and the blank eyes of video cameras stared from the back of the room.

A mousy man in wire-rimmed glasses cleared his throat. "What do you think about the photographer getting eight million for that photo?"

Roxanne's small smile turned to Mateo, and with their entwined hands pressed against his chest, she adjusted her weight to lean against him slightly. Wanting her man. Depending on him. Mateo fought the urge to smirk. "We would have paid him nine million," he said, shrugging at the reporter and earning a laugh from the audience.

Roxanne had actually planned on offering the man ten million when they found him, ten million with a promise of calling in "alternative methods" to convince him if he didn't accept. Mateo shuddered to think what those alternative methods were. But while Roxanne's unlimited resources and Mateo's extensive experience with the paparazzi had allowed them to track who was bidding on the photo, they hadn't found the source by the time the shot premiered in the morning print version of a British tabloid and, an hour later, was viewable online throughout the world.

The photographer had only gotten two useful shots before Mateo had flung his coat over them, shielding them both. And while the photo didn't reveal anything pornographic, the overwhelmed pleasure on her face, that full, open mouth and anguished squeeze of her eyes and thrown-back tilt of her head, was enough to stiffen the cock of every man walking. Mateo personally wanted to punch every one of them in the teeth. The photo didn't show his face, but the adamant squeeze of his fingers into the bunch of her skirts, keeping her attached to his mouth, spoke volumes.

She'd been delicious on his tongue. He'd still be at it now if he hadn't had to extricate himself to chase the photographer, whose dash to a quiet-as-a-mouse Prius hadn't been hampered by a roaring erection.

"Don't you mean *she* would have paid nine million?" the mousy man interrupted Mateo's thoughts with a scoff. "There's no 'we'? It all would have been Roxanne's money, right? I mean, your kingdom doesn't have some secret stash of cash, does it?"

Mateo's life—and therefore his kingdom—had become the farce he'd dreaded and worked his whole life to avoid. The Monte now looked like a penniless backwater whose prince hid between his wife's thighs. Maybe it was the lack of sleep that kept him from caring. Or maybe it was Roxanne, who leaned close to the microphones and closed the conversation with a simple word.

"We," she said distinctly. She looked at William. He pointed at another raised hand.

The billionaire was doing what she'd promised, circling the wagons and making sure Mateo and the Monte del Vino Real were in its protective enclosure. For the first time in his life—another first—Mateo wasn't bearing the burden of the Monte alone. The contract, which days before had been a sword in his side, now staunched his wounds. The worst had happened. He had no other options. He had no recourse but to shag the stellar Roxanne Medina on a regular basis.

"Ms. Medina, whose bright idea was it to go up there, yours or his?" a smarmy younger reporter asked. "Because you can say 'we' all you want, but the stories coming out for the last month make it pretty clear who wears the pants in the marriage."

Mateo stiffened and glared at the reporter. But Roxanne squeezed his arm and stayed as pristinely unruffled as the swaying pleats on her skirt. "I understand a salacious motive will make this story more interesting, but it just doesn't exist. My husband wanted to show me a beautiful view of the city." She let go of his hand to raise her hand to the side of her mouth and leaned comically close to the microphones. "I don't know if you've noticed, but he's a pretty big guy. There's not a lot I can force him to do."

A voice from the back of the room called out, "We heard his 'size' is why you married him," and the laughter that rolled through the crowd was ugly. Mateo suddenly realized that maybe the reporters weren't buying their story as well as he'd thought. William's chest puffed up and he stepped forward, about to end the press conference.

A petite brunette woman stood up and raised her pencil, an impatient scowl on her face. "Ms. Medina, there is a rumor circulating that you are paying *Príncipe* Mateo for sex. Do you have a comment?"

Mateo felt his jaw harden and worked to keep it relaxed. Fuck. *That* was the one revelation that could make their world implode. If the contract was ever revealed, Mateo would be known as a man who sold himself and his child. Roxanne... Roxanne might be hailed by some as a feminist hero, but it would be difficult to explain the contract as rational decision-making to the stockholders of her publicly owned and traded company. And their child—the perfect princess Roxanne wanted—would always carry the stigma of being bought and sold.

For the first time in their relationship, the powerful, manipulative, and sexy as hell billionaire had no response. She blinked, opened her mouth, and then closed it. She looked vulnerable. She looked young.

Mateo was going to destroy his father.

But his smile was slow and easy as he slid his hand around her waist to bring her close to him and let all of his Golden Prince shine for the cameras. "In what crazy, upside-down universe would this woman have to pay for sex?" The crowd gave a titter that let him know the women, and some of the men, had felt the glow.

But the brunette reporter was unaffected, her pencil still in the air. "You have to admit that there is an imbalance to your relationship. *Príncipe* Mateo, you bring very little to the table."

Mateo forced himself to chuckle as Roxanne held herself imperceptibly away from him. "Well, that's not pulling any punches. True, the Monte del Vino Real is not as prosperous as I would like, but I plan to make improvements soon that will..."

The reporter interrupted him. "Is the king aware of your plans? We understand that he's been ensconced with his bishop all day and is refusing to comment. Have you spoken to him?"

Right, ensconced with his bishop. The king honored only one deity: Money. But Mateo now knew why his day had been eerily free of screaming phone calls. The king had been making his own calls, spreading his own rumors about the reality of Mateo's marriage. He'd suggested just enough to humiliate Mateo without jeopardizing the terms of the agreement. The man was no fool; he still wanted Roxanne's money.

"I have not spoken to my father. He understands foolish mistakes," he said darkly.

"*Príncipe*, do you feel your marriage is one of them? So far, all it has done is highlight your weaknesses."

"Okay that's enough," William jumped in, waving an arm. "Thank you all for coming."

As the room exploded with shouted questions and clicking flashes, Roxanne turned away from him. Mateo realized he was clenching the fabric at her hip, and he let go a bare second before the press noticed, before a photo caught Mateo literally clinging to his wife's skirt.

Jesus.

He followed her off the dais surrounded by a gauntlet of security—he scowled at the way her good-looking bodyguard took a place at her side—and down a hall to a small yet elegant lounge where Roxanne's private retinue waited. "Everybody out!" Roxanne commanded her assistant and nurse as she entered the room, her tiny gray heels clicking on the marble like a fancy-footed general. Mateo followed her and grabbed a sparkling water out of an ice bucket, twisting off the cap and flinging it into a trash bin as her bodyguard leaned down to murmur something in her ear. Roxanne nodded and touched his mammoth forearm appreciatively. Helen, the nurse of Mateo's nightmares, shot a glare of promised torture at Mateo before the bodyguard ushered her out and clicked the door closed behind all of them.

Roxanne swung on Mateo, her blue eyes flashing and her dark ponytail flying like a banner signaling an approaching army. "Did you do it?"

"Do what?" he asked, taking a glug of the crystal-cold water.

"Did you leak our arrangement to the press?"

Mateo barely swallowed before he choked. "*Coño.* Are you kidding me?" He slammed down the bottle. "Of course not."

But the accusation in her throaty voice made it clear she'd already made up her mind.

"You've resisted this arrangement from the start."

"Of course I did. Any sane person would. If you'd continued humiliating me with your made-up courtship stories, maybe I would have told someone."

She reared back. "So you considered it?"

"I've also considered strangling you," Mateo said, glowering at her. "Yet so far I've restrained myself."

Goddammit. After last evening's date and their all-night effort to find the photographer and the unified front they'd presented to the press, he thought they'd made some progress toward…camaraderie. But now he watched her mouth drop open in dawning horror. "Did you arrange that whole event with the photographer?" she accused. "Is that why you took me up there? Is that why you did...that to me?"

He'd done "that" to her because he couldn't stop himself, because he'd wanted to know if reality was as good as his sweat-soaked dreams. Reality was better. But perhaps a primal part had sought to make her as vulnerable as he was, had wanted her helpless with him, if only for the moments that his mouth played between her strong and velvety thighs.

He raised his hands up, unable to stop the hurt mixing with anger in her blue eyes. "Why would I arrange a public scene like that? What possible advantage would there be to me? You heard what they said out there. They're saying I'm your kept boy!"

She held that gorgeous body tall. But she slid her arms over the delicate cashmere of her sweater and wrapped them around her waist. "Maybe humiliating me has more value than saving your kingdom. Maybe you'd risk the Monte to be rid of me."

When she'd displayed power over his kingdom and future, Mateo had pushed back. Mateo, it seemed, had power over her body. She was making him pay for her vulnerability.

"Fuck!" The tie he'd worn for the press conference felt like it was choking him. He dug his fingers into it, wrenched it off, and hurled it across the room. Unbuttoning his top button, he whirled back on her. "Last night, in that truck, that was just you and me. You weren't the powerful billionaire with a sex kink, and I wasn't the penniless prince with nothing to his name but a big cock. That was just us, just Mateo and Roxanne. I, Mateo, took you, Roxanne, up there because...the hotel rooms make me feel like a prostitute. And I wanted to show you my favorite spot in the city. And...because I need you, and you need me, and it would be nice if I got along with the woman who's going to save my kingdom and bear my child."

One arm still crossed her waist, but she'd raised her other hand to her lip. She petted and pinched that full lip he liked to suck on, her eyes full of doubt. He took a cautious step closer, looked down at her.

"I haven't forgotten the way you were in the truck with me last night." Roxanne stiffened at the reminder and Mateo continued quickly. "*Before* I made love to you. You were *nice* to me. You listened to me grumble and moan, and you made me feel calm. You offered me help. Roxanne, if you believe nothing else, believe I wouldn't fuck over the *one person* who's offered to help me dig out of this mess."

He'd told her things last night he'd never told anyone. About his lifelong ambition to be superior to his father. About the certainty that he would fail. The contract gave him breathing room, a safe space to tell secrets to a temporary wife who didn't care about his weaknesses and failures. She only wanted two things from him: his cock and then his absence. He was happy to give her both.

Her fingers dropped from her lower lip. Her pretty blue eyes had rain clouds in them as she looked up at him. "I have no reason to trust you," she said, echoing his words of two nights ago when, against all odds, Mateo had given her his trust.

There was a light tap on the door. If it was that He-Man bodyguard... "Not now," Mateo shouted.

A chime on the smartphone her assistant had left on the counter drew Roxanne's attention. She walked over to it, picked it up, read the message with a frown. "You're going to want to open the door, *Prínc...*" She blinked. And then looked up at him. "...Mateo."

Those goddamn lips around his name. Roxanne Medina held every single card: she'd paid off his most demanding creditors, she promised a future for his kingdom, she held his personal reputation in her hands. And yet, she made him feel like he had power here, too.

He lowered his eyes and grinned at her. He was pretty sure they could handle whatever was on the other side of that door.

He strolled over and opened it without taking his eyes off of her.

Until he had to grab a fighting, spitting, she-devil around the waist as she launched herself through the door and at his wife.

"You bitch!" the girl yelled, folded over at the waist as she tried to escape the belt of his arms. "I'll claw your eyes out for what you've done to my brother!"

Mateo grunted as he tried to keep a handle on the lithe girl who could always slip out of his hold, no matter how small she'd been and no matter what rule she was breaking. "Roxanne Medina," he called over his sister's cursing. "Meet La Princesa Sofia Maria Isabel de Esperanza y Santos. My baby sister."

Roxanne raised a sleek eyebrow in amazement, still safely across the room. "Nice to meet you?" she hazarded.

Sofia fought her way out of hair that scissors only glanced at to growl in response. "You make my brother look like a fool, you bring worry and fear to the Monte, you show off a picture of the best man I know down on his knees." Holding her back was like trying to hang on to a willow branch in a storm. "You'll be meeting my fists!"

Roxanne just raised her hands. "It's okay, guys. We've got this."

Mateo glanced behind him to see her entire security crew crowding the doorway. He-Man looked like he planned on folding Mateo's little sister into a cube. "That's right," Mateo said, catching his foot on the door. "We've got this." He kicked it shut and then grabbed his sister by the belt loop of her skinny jeans.

"*¡Para!*" he demanded, swinging her around to face him. "What are you doing here?"

Sofia's dark eyes flashed wide as she looked up at him. "What am *I* doing here? What are *you* doing here? Why are you standing in front of those cameras with her *como un bufón*? Why are you letting her spread all those *mentiras*? *¿Por qué no me has llamado? ¿Por qué no hablas conmigo?*"

His sister, five years his junior, had spent her formative years at a Catholic boarding school in Santiago de Compostela with nuns determined to save her unrepentant soul. Spanish—and colorful Spanish curses—flowed through her accent and words more naturally than they did through his. Her texts let him know that she'd known about the contract, but never thought he'd agree to it. He'd only replied with a promise to tell her more "soon." Her bewilderment about his abandonment— *Why haven't you called me back? Why won't you talk to me?*— seemed much worse in the language they used as children.

He felt stripped of words. "I...uh... I needed to get a better handle on..."

Roxanne spoke up from the other side of the room. "It's my fault," she called. "I've not treated your brother with the respect he deserved. If you haven't heard from him, it's because I put him in an uncomfortable position."

Sofia whipped a malicious glare at Roxanne. "He doesn't need you to speak for him," she spat.

Roxanne raised her hands in a surrender position while Mateo shook his head at trying to get a word in edgewise around two strong, quick-witted women. He took his sister gently by the elbow and turned her toward him.

"What she says is true. I regretted signing the contract, and we had some differences to work out. I wanted to get things under control before we spoke."

There was so much hurt on his little sister's face. "So you let three months go by?" she said in a low but outraged Spanish. "Stop trying to solve everything by yourself. Talk to me. Be my brother. I'm tired of you hiding here."

Behind his sister, Roxanne was studying the light fixtures. Mateo leaned toward Sofia. "She speaks Spanish," he informed her in English.

Sofia rolled her eyes. "Of course she does."

"And she is trying to make things right. I trust her."

That's when he noticed the tears in Sofia's dark doe eyes. "You trust her but not me? You trust her but not your people? We're all ready and waiting to help. But you…you don't ask for our thoughts or our input. You act as though the only way you can stand us is when we're 2000 miles away."

"*Basta*, Sofia," he breathed. His distance had *never* been about her or the Monte.

"And you," Sofia said, flicking away the moisture from her lashes as she turned on Roxanne. "My brother won't be of any use to you if the king has anything to say about it."

Mateo had to blink before he could process Sofia's words. "What?"

His sister shrugged her narrow shoulders in her tan leather blazer, shifting effortlessly from an enraged banshee to a lithe and careless socialite, showing the blink-and-you'll-miss-it mood changes that were the special providence of Spanish women. "That's why I'm here. I overheard the king on the phone." She swayed away from both of them, toward the display of refreshments, and grabbed a Diet Coke. "He told the person on the other end that you'd humiliated him for the last time." She popped the Coke and sat on the arm of a sofa. "He said he had a way to make sure you never became king."

And with that bombshell dropped, his sister took a long, long drink.

During the harvest season in the Monte del Vino Real, Mateo would drive to the vineyards in the middle of the night, when the air was cool and the grapes had settled, to check the sugar levels and determine whether the fruit was ready to be picked. He'd known some of the happiest moments of his life on those nights, there in the dark with only his flashlight for light, the leaves of the vines stroking his cheeks, and the tang of fertile soil rich in his nose. But the land where his ancestors had chosen to build their empire was proud and didn't give its gifts effortlessly. Winds from the Bay of Biscay would find their way through the Picos de Europa and come barreling through the vines, piercing Mateo where he stood and shaking his almost-ripe grapes to the ground.

Standing in this technological fortress, Mateo could feel the battering of that proud, pointless wind.

"Can he do that?" Roxanne's question was soft as she walked up to him.

Mateo looked at her. There was something about tracing his eyes over her high cheekbones and smooth, delicate skin that soothed him. He realized, as he looked down at her, that her skin wasn't as creamy pale as he once thought. She had an olive undertone, more Latina than he'd originally realized. And there, right there at her hairline in the shine of the lights, was her hair slightly lighter there? More chestnut than black?

"Of course not," his sister snapped, tossing her tawny hair over her shoulder and bringing Mateo out of his musings. "The king only wishes he were all-powerful. If any of his wild schemes had succeeded, he'd have oil pumps in the middle of the village and an international chain of King of the Monte dance clubs."

Slowly, Mateo shook his head. "It's different this time. You know that. That's why you came."

Sofia narrowed her eyes and took a defiant drink of her soda.

Mateo folded his hands over his heart. "*Y mil gracias.*" That seething twenty-something softened in an instant to the baby sister he adored. "The CML Resort deal has emboldened him. He was probably on the phone with that donkey's ass of a CEO, Easton Fuller."

King Felipe was playing a very dangerous game. He wanted Roxanne's money, so he was being cautious about sabotaging their relationship. He wanted CML's money, so he was promising something that was improbable.

But not impossible. Negative public sentiment was the first uneasy step in getting a prince deposed and, while Roxanne had unwittingly laid the groundwork with her hasty press releases, his father had fanned the flames by whispering rumors that the all-mighty Golden Prince was a gigolo to a billionaire. Mateo needed to make amends to the people of the Monte. Soon.

But before he could go to the Monte, he needed to solidify his relationship with Roxanne. It was almost ludicrous, this shimmering panic in his gut that this woman he despised two days ago might leave, might decide that his Golden sperm wasn't worth the hassle. He was no better than his father; he needed her money.

The possibilities of a bankrupt Monte del Vino Real and a destitute citizenry were why his palms were sweaty. They had nothing to do with the thought of never touching Roxanne Medina again.

Knowing how Roxanne liked his body, Mateo slid out of his suit jacket and hung it on a nearby chair, and then slid his hands into his pants pockets as he bit his lower lip. He knew

Roxanne liked his lips, too. "So we need to satisfy a suspicious press that our marriage is real and get in front of whatever bullshit my father is brewing up." He shrugged his big shoulders. "We're going to have to spend more time together."

Roxanne's blue eyes flared. "What?"

He leveled his Golden Prince gaze on her. "We're going to need to make this love affair look real."

"*¡Qué asco!*" his sister cried, leaping off the sofa arm in disgust. "With her?"

He turned and walked toward his wife, taking in the stiffening of her body and the mutinous thrust of her jaw as he drew closer. He lifted her hand, which she would have tugged away if his sister hadn't been there, and enfolded it and her ostrich egg of a ring against his chest.

"Roxanne. *Mi esposa.*" The storm didn't soften in her eyes. "It seems we're going to have to make your fairy tale come true."

April: Interlude

Mateo leaned back against a six-hundred-year-old stone wall, his phone in his hands, as the sun slipped just above the snow-capped Pico Viajadora and began to warm the vendors setting up in the Monte del Vino Real's plaza. April mornings in the Monte always began cold, warming up to the daytime temperatures that would encourage the vines to flower then set into the hard, green nodules that would become Tempranillo fruit. Mateo nodded to a passing vendor; the man gave him a quick bow and a *"Buenos dias, Alteza,"* but ducked away from further conversation.

Mateo shook out his chilled hands, his burnished gold ring catching the morning light, before setting his thumbs on his smartphone's keyboard. He stared at the blinking cursor.

It was 9 p.m. in San Francisco, a good time to write Roxanne if he wanted a quick response. He didn't need a quick response. He didn't need to contact her at all. But after the last week of evening strolls and long dinners and cuddling close during ballet or opera performances, making sure to smile and stare longingly into each other's eyes for the benefit of their paparazzi entourage, he'd become…accustomed to her presence. Her smell. Her under-her-breath smart-ass retorts as she gazed at him like he was the most glorious thing ever born. It was nice being looked at that way, even if it was only playacting for the hundreds of cameras and cell phones trained on them whenever they were out. It was nice looking back, especially when—in private—she dropped the act and rolled up her sleeves, shoved on those little black reading glasses to attack the documents spread out on her conference room table, working with Mateo to get a handle on years of financial mismanagement by the king and his advisors.

Her sincere desire to help the Monte gave him a convenient excuse to contact her now, just a couple days since he left her in San Francisco.

He huddled into his worn canvas coat, shifted on a wall that was the last crumbling remains of fortifications that once encircled the village, and typed, *Need some help.* He pressed send before he could chicken out.

The decadent odor of fresh-baked *sobaos*—butter, lemon, and a dash of rum—filled Mateo's nose as a lanky twelve-year-old boy lugged past a basket filled with the breakfast cakes.

"Helping your mamá, Fernando?" Mateo asked in Spanish.

The boy stopped and blanched. "I'm… I'm Álvaro, your highness," the boy stuttered, his arms quivering. "Fernando is my brother."

Inwardly, Mateo cursed. But he gave the boy a smile. "Of course. I'm sorry. Don't let me interrupt your work." As the boy staggered away, Mateo realized it had been three or four years since he'd seen Fernando. Fernando was probably preparing to leave the Monte for college or work, destined to never return like so many of their best and brightest young people. Mateo's infrequent visits hadn't paused the Monte in amber, stopping its changes. His kingdom had kept moving forward; Mateo just hadn't been paying attention.

His phone buzzed, almost leaping out of Mateo's hand. He

caught it, tilted it to read the message in the growing morning light.

K. What do you need?

She'd said "K." Not "maybe." Not "why?" Just "K." Yes.

Still can't get a lead on the guy the King is trotting all over
the Monte. And mystery surveyors have made themselves
scarce, too. Any chance you can get your investigators to
find out if Easton Fuller has close ties to a dark-haired man
named Roman?

Mateo had eked out all the time he could pantomiming a
happily wedded couple with Roxanne before the daily phone
calls from his sister—she'd returned home as his spy—reached
a crescendo of panic. Surveyors had been popping up on the
Monte's vineyards and taking measurements before they could
be chased off with hoes and pruning shears. The king had been
showing a dark-haired American around the Monte, introducing him to villagers who said that while the man was more
pleasant than the usual people his father brought around, he
left them no clue to who he was, what he was doing there,
or what he wanted.

Mateo pressed send before he could re-read the text. Asking her for help made sense, right? He'd had no luck discovering what his father or CML Resorts was up to. It wasn't a
totally transparent reason to write her. Was it?

Her response was immediate.

Good thought. I'll see what I can find out.

Shit. Now what?

Thank you, he typed back.

Lame.

Fortunately, the reply dots began to bubble. No prob. How's it going?

He found himself grinning underneath the worn-out brim of his Giants baseball cap. He took in the marketplace hustle growing around the tortured statue of San Vicente de Zaragoza, the patron saint of wine and the Monte, as vendors set up stands for produce and vegetables, for hanging meats like *jamón* and *chorizo*, for the pungent *queso picon* made from the milk of mountain-shepherded goats, for handwoven baskets and locally created bagpipes, and most importantly, for the heavy bottles of local wine. He took in the laughing and the backslapping and the chiding owners gave each other. And then he took in the circle of timeworn granite the vendors maintained around him, like hot lava that they couldn't cross. During his high school and college days, when he was home more often, he would have been yelled at by some gray-haired citizen to get off his lazy *culo* and carry something.

His grin slid away.

Fine. Feels like the calm before the storm, like all the bad guys are lying low until I leave. They probably think my stay is temporary. He glanced up at the bubble of isolation around him. Everyone seems to think my stay here is temporary.

He watched the response dots throb as the sun warmed the wall at his back. He unzipped his canvas coat and let the rising Spanish sun in. He imagined his *Tempranillo Vino Real* doing the same, unfurling to let the sun feed it and nurture it. He imagined his people turning their faces toward him like a plant did toward the light.

After several minutes, the response dots died away. Mateo continued to stare at the screen. It pulsed with her silence.

Mateo had other questions he could ask her: *When are you coming? Are you pregnant?* He had other things he wanted to know about her: *What were you like when you were little? Why do you try to hide your Mexican heritage? Does your back ever feel like it's breaking under the weight of your responsibilities? Do you like to dance? Do you know how much seeing you in your reading glasses turns me on?*

It had been a tactical error when he'd suggested one late night that they didn't need to wait a month to have sex. He'd been sitting shoulder to shoulder with her, wreathed in her rose scent as they stared into a laptop screen. She'd looked at him absently, her startling blue eyes blinking through those black frames, before she returned her gaze to the numbers on the screen. "Why would we have sex if I can't get pregnant?" she murmured as she highlighted another miscalculation from his treasurer.

Her response that night, like the empty screen now, implied that the conversation was over.

A mighty crash jolted Mateo's attention away from the phone. The lid of an *olla ferroviaria* rolled toward him, hit his work boot, then spun on the granite with a pleasing harmonic ring.

He looked up and saw an older man in his sixties doing his best to hold up one side of a table collapsing under the weight of the portable cooking pots. Mateo stuck his phone in his jeans pocket as he rushed to his side.

"*Damela, señor,*" he said, and the man shuffled over as Mateo took a corner, lifting the table to steady the squat cookers trying to slide off of it.

"I got it," Mateo told the man in Spanish as he shuffled his hands to the middle of the table, saw that a bent leg on the cheap card table was to blame. "Find something to prop this up."

"*Gracias, Alteza,*" the man said, but Mateo didn't really need any of this "your highness" crap when his shoulders were yelling from the weight of the clay inserts and metal cookers. The *olla ferroviarias* were an invention of resourceful railway men who wanted hot stews on long, cold hauls through the mountains.

The man kneeled down and began to hurriedly stack nearby boxes under the table. "This used to be Julio's stand," Mateo grunted to the bald spot at the back of the man's head.

"*Sí,*" the man said, continuing to stack boxes. "He's my brother-in-law. I took it over when he caught the cancer."

"I'm sorry," Mateo said.

"Don't be," the man shrugged, pulling up the heavy shoulders of his cardigan. "He was an asshole."

Mateo bit back a huff. Julio had been kind of an asshole, always complaining about his location on the outskirts of the market and trying to overcharge tourists.

"I took the stand over three years ago," the man said, his head still down as he began to work on a second tower of boxes. Mateo was going to feel this tomorrow. "I've been waiting to meet you."

Hands occupied as they were, Mateo couldn't protect himself from the metaphorical gut punch. "Yeah, sorry..."

The man withdrew his hands from the boxes and then signaled for Mateo to let go of the table. The tower of boxes held the weight and they both breathed a sigh of relief. The man stood on creaky knees and stuck his hand out to Mateo. "I'm glad you're here now," he said with a kind smile. "My name is Ricardo."

Mateo shook it, glad to be let off the hook so easily.

"*Príncipe,* I have some ideas. I tried to talk to your father but..." Ricardo shrugged again. In that shrug, Mateo could see all the ways his family had let their people down.

But as he and Ricardo began to restack lids on the table and Ricardo explained that he'd run a successful marketing firm in Barcelona for thirty years, that he was climbing the walls trying to "relax and retire" in the Monte, that he could create a website for the market and a marketing plan that would bring tourists and their dollars to the Monte, Mateo realized that not all hope was lost. As one of the women who used to yell at him brought him a cool drink and Álvaro returned with a *sobao*, still warm and crumbly, he thought—just maybe—he could still lead his people out of the wrack and ruin his family had created.

Mateo ate the cake and took notes on his phone and felt the closing of a circle when Roxanne's response popped up on his screen.

Sorry. Had to take a call.

Your absence made your people distrustful. But your intentions and desires for them are pure—you made ME believe that and I don't trust anyone's intentions. Show them that good stuff inside of you. Let them see your hopes. They'll come around.

Dummy.

Mateo smiled and texted Roxanne back with one thumb while he continued to listen to Ricardo's plans for the Monte and felt the sun's heat, soft and warm, on his neck.

One Week After That...

Mateo grinned, slumped down in his truck, his knee up on the dashboard, as he read Roxanne's fourth enumerated reason why it was his fault that they hadn't gotten pregnant.

#4 Jeans-waaaaaaay too tight.

The way I look in my jeans is why you wanted me to get you pregnant in the first place.

Sure. That was then. Now I want you in loose pants. Baggy. Let the boys breathe.

"The boys" have got too much breathing room. For all your promises of a non-stop sex marathon, we've actually only been doing it once a month. The boys are starting to ossify.

He grinned at the silence on her end of the line after their rapid-fire back-and-forth. He wrote: Gotcha.

Their texts over the last week had slipped from daily status updates to several-times-a-day conversations. When he'd texted her this morning to ask her if she was pregnant, he hadn't truly wondered, of course she would let him know, but he'd been strangely preoccupied until she'd answered. If she was pregnant, he wouldn't have a reason to touch her again.

When he read her answer—No because #1-your golden sperm apparently thinks it's too good for my lowly midwestern eggs—he'd just pulled up to the vineyard where they were testing the *Tempranillo Vino Real* in Monte soil. He'd chuckled out loud and sent his sister out of the truck to talk to the vineyard manager who was waiting for them.

With the afternoon sun turning the vines gold, he got Roxanne's next volley: #5 too much talk, not enough action.

Oh no, lady. I volunteered to give you all the action you can handle. He paused a second, and then typed out an idea that had been knocking around in his brain. How bout this: You have sex with me just because we want to, and I'll give up my night of conversation so you can have your third night of oh-so-sexy ovulation sex.

He pressed send before he could rethink it. It made sense: even surrounded by a phalanx of photographers and bodyguards, or elbow-deep in financial documents, they'd been getting to know each other, sharing anecdotes through fake smiles, comparing observations while staring at spreadsheets. And these text exchanges felt more unguarded than any of their true life interactions. It felt silly to continue insisting on a no-sex night so they could "talk."

But instinct warned him that it would be unwise to concede too much ground to the indomitable Roxanne Medina without her own concession. He was willing to let her know that he enjoyed spending time with her—in and out of bed—outside of their prescribed three days. She had to let him know that she wanted him for more than just his sperm.

Mateo peered at his phone, the heat growing in the truck as he waited for a response.

His driver-side door swung open.

"*Coño* Mateo, Carmen Louisa is waiting for you," his sister Sofia said.

"I'll be there in a moment," he said absently as he watched for the dots on his phone to bubble.

"*Venga ahora*. Fall in love with that woman later."

Mateo's leg crashed to the floorboard. With her hair in a long braid down her back, Sofia looked like her twelve-year-old self barging into his room to bug him.

"What? I'm not—"

"Whatever. You stare into that phone like a lovestruck boy. Which is…sick and sad but I'm not responsible for your taste. *Pero venga*." And with that bombshell, his sister turned and stalked back into the rows.

He'd apologized to Sofia for making her feel ignored and, during the last month, she'd been his ear on the ground and second in command. She'd taken a sabbatical from her apprenticeship to a winemaker in Rioja and Mateo was grateful to have his wild child of a sister beside him as he rebuilt his relationship with his people and endured the family meals. Not that there had been many of them; his parents were devoted to their out-of-the-Monte social lives. But there had been a couple for show with international guests whose names appeared on the front pages of the tabloids. They were as uncomfortable as his father could make them. Only Sofia made them bearable.

But now—for her to say that he was *in love* with Roxanne?

His phone buzzed in his hand.

#6-Aggressively pursuing me for my hot bod during times when said hot bod is less likely to get pregnant.

Mateo's impulse was to type back: Chicken.

He wanted to push against the boundaries they'd set. He wanted her to acknowledge him as more than her baby daddy. And in that—the *more*—he could see a bit of what his sister was referring to. He wasn't in love, definitely not. But he might be in something. Roxanne Medina was a gorgeous, powerful woman who wanted to have sex with him while helping him save his kingdom. A man would have to be dead to not be in *something* with her.

So, instead, he wrote back: As much as I would love to continue to discuss your hot bod and all the ways I've failed it, I gotta go talk to my vineyard manager.

He sent the message. Maybe it was time to back off all the texting. Her boundaries—three days a month, sex only for conception—weren't budging. He'd be an idiot to blink first against a woman who was so well-armed. Yeah, back off a little bit. It was the right thing to do, he thought, as his thumbs typed out: Talk later?

Shit.

He stepped out of the truck and determinedly stuck his phone into his back pocket before he stretched out his kinks. He took off his baseball cap and shook out his hair before putting it back on. He squinted his eyes against the afternoon sun and got a good look at how his vines were doing.

Only when his phone buzzed did he realize he'd been doing all of that with his breath held. He let out a long exhale as he eased his phone from his back pocket.

Sure. I'd like to hear how the vine is doing. And you've never failed me. Not once.

With his heart thundering, Mateo made his way into his vines.

One Week After That...

Mateo slammed the ancient wooden door of his childhood bedroom and then, remembering, stopped short to glare at the king-sized bed. The replacement for his twin bed had been a bribe, like everything else his father offered, a negotiation tactic to get Mateo to accept an engagement to a thirty-something Egyptian heiress when he'd only been seventeen.

Mateo had discovered the king-sized bed the same moment he'd discovered the heiress, naked, on top of it. A virgin, Mateo had been embarrassed by his stubbornly hard cock, her bored porno-flick come-ons, his father's willingness to throw him to the fucking wolves. He'd shoved her and her clothes out of the room and slept wrapped in a comforter on the cold terracotta floor.

If his sister hadn't been in residence, Mateo would never have stayed in this six-hundred-year-old castle that was supposed to be his heritage.

The Castillo del Monte had been part of Queen Isabella's largesse; she'd deployed two celebrated Arab craftsmen to build it. With its intricate brick edifice, forty-meter-high tower, crenellated parapets, arched doorways, and mosaic-tiled ceilings, the Castillo was recognized as one of the best-preserved medieval castles in Spain. Infected by his parents' presence, however, it had never felt like home.

Mateo wrestled out of his tight suit jacket, threw it across the room, and pulled his phone out of his back pocket before he sat down on the cursed bed.

He typed: I fucked up. Again.

Only Sofia's calming presence and his dedication to the Monte had gotten Mateo through the last three weeks of dinners with the wealthy and powerful who'd ignored his parents before Mateo's marriage. He gritted his teeth through multi-course meals while he was side-eyed and asked pointed questions about his wife, her billions, and, once the drinks were flowing, if the picture in the truck was a publicity stunt. For the Monte, he withstood it. For Roxanne, he breathed and smiled, gave the relaxed answer her PR people had crafted so they had time to restore Roxanne's reputation for her investors and the Monte's reputation for the world.

But tonight he let it get to him. When the slimy chairman of a German ski resort had asked about the picture, Mateo's father had roared, red-faced and sweaty with wine, "Of course it's not real! The Kings of the Monte never kneel. He makes that bitch get down on her knees and—"

Mateo had wrapped his fist in the king's tie and choked off his words. "You shut your mouth, old man," he'd growled into his father's gaping face. Then he'd shoved him back into his seat and stalked out of the room.

The vibration of Roxanne's instant incoming message soothed him like little else could. What happened?

I just threatened my father in front of the ambassador to Luxembourg, the heads of a couple of ski resorts, and a Greek shipping magnate, Mateo typed as he toed out of his shoes.

I'm sure he deserved it. What did he say?

Nope. Not going there.

K. Were you defending my honor?

Mateo gave a begrudging smile to the lime-lit screen. A gentleman never tells.

They'd texted every day this week, long conversations that Mateo wrote from bed while Roxanne had her lunch or she texted with a glass of wine in hand while Mateo had coffee in his.

Her text dots oscillated on his screen. He'd begun to think of them—during their early-morning, late-afternoon, middle-of-the-night text conversations—as her thought bubbles, the visual version of her figuring out what to say to him. Was she as cautious as he was? Did she, sometimes, throw caution to the wind like he did and text the truth, the emotion closest to her heart? Did she wonder, too, what he was thinking? What he was feeling?

You know, your father no more deserves you as a son than I do as a sperm donor. You're a good man, Mateo. I trust whatever you did was justified. When I get there, I'll help make it all better.

Jesus. When Roxanne Medina, billionaire, giantess, his once worst enemy, said shit like that, it sent a bloom of warmth from his chest straight down the center of his body. He crawled backward up the bed and stretched out, his cock pulsing with want for her.

When exactly will you be getting here?

I'll start ovulating in four days.

Mateo huffed at the phone, relaxing into his mattress. *Ooh baby. Stop with the sexy talk.* He stretched out his legs, arching the evening's tension out of his toes. His cock was a hard, happy friend stretched down his pant leg.

I've got something that wants to be made all better right now.

Sounds like a personal problem.

No, it's definitely a you problem. Mateo typed rapidly into his phone. You, making me wait to touch you while you say kind things and tease me and flirt with me and make me feel better. You, transforming from a woman who only wanted to take from me to a woman who gives and gives and gives. You with your goddamned time restrictions when you've made me realize that inside that jaw-dropping body is a wicked-smart brain and giant, generous heart. Fuck you, Roxanne. I'm definitely having a you problem.

He pressed send before his brain could catch up with his pounding heart.

God love her, she didn't make him wait long for a reply: I might be able to be there in three days.

Something with wings took off in his chest. Make it two and I promise to make it worth your while.

I'm a billionaire married to a hot prince. Not sure what else you could offer me.

Mateo grinned wickedly as he began to text back with his left thumb, his wedding ring helping to hold his phone steady, while his right hand undid his belt.

Oh, belleza. Let me count the ways...

His location and the night's event were forgotten as Mateo began to type, in heat-soaked detail, what he was going to do to his wife when she landed on Spanish soil.

April: Day One

Four days later, Roxanne clicked through the final articles Brandon had compiled for her as her Dassault Falcon 8X—the newest plane in the Dassault fleet—began its descent toward the Monte del Vino Real's tiny runway. Her excellent pilot Priscilla effortlessly handled the steep approach angle through the Picos de Europa, and Roxanne's espresso barely shimmered in its porcelain cup. Having already showered and gotten herself ready in her bedroom suite at the rear of the plane, she relaxed into the white leather recliner and sipped her coffee in her sun-bright luxury jet, enjoying these final minutes of peace as she scanned the last article, looking for any mention of their sex photo or deprecating comments about Mateo's position in their marriage.

She hummed with satisfaction when she didn't find any. It seemed their full-court playacting to the media over the last month was working—of eighteen articles printed about them this week, only three mentioned the photo and four questioned the veracity of their marriage. Through leaks, intermediaries, press releases, and interviews, Roxanne and Mateo were bamboozling the world into believing they were giddily-in-love newlyweds. This *New York Times* article even did a wonderful job of highlighting Mateo's many accomplishments and his dedication to the Monte, written just as Roxanne had dictated them to the writer.

Roxanne coughed suddenly, covering her mouth to avoid getting espresso all over the bronze silk of her dress. There, at the bottom of the article, was a quote she didn't remember giving to the writer:

"If I couldn't see or feel, I'd still be attracted to him."

They'd pulled it out, highlighted it in big font so the words couldn't be missed. Anchored it below a photo of her and Mateo, in San Francisco, at a charity ball as they chatted with the hosts, him with his tuxedoed arm around her and her giving him—a look. A look that Roxanne, who was the master of her own face, who knew exactly how to communicate with it, had never seen before.

She remembered, barely, chatting with the writer for a couple of minutes after she'd thought the interview was over. She remembered liking the aspiring female writer. And she remembered the writer mentioning Mateo's killer good looks.

If I couldn't see or feel, I'd still be attracted to him.

She snapped her laptop closed as the plane touched down and pulled her necklace from her dress to touch her cross. Maybe Mateo hadn't seen the article.

Of course he had. It was *The New York Times*.

As the plane began to slow, the roar of the engine was replaced with the increasing roar of a crowd. Priscilla clicked on the intercom to let her know that Henry, who'd arrived the day before, had okayed Roxanne's disembarkment and that they would be pulling up to stairs and a roped-off crowd of about three hundred people. Roxanne felt her first shiver of nerves. Glancing around the elegant leather-and-chrome interior of her plane, she caught Helen's eye. Helen had been a flight attendant and former Army nurse when she'd met her, an astonishing flight attendant who'd kept her coworkers and two hundred passengers calm when their plane had been forced to take extra laps around the San Diego airport because of stubborn landing gear. They'd eventually landed safely and Roxanne, who'd observed Helen from her coach seat, began an immediate campaign to convince the woman to join her eventual empire.

From the jump seat, the fiercely loyal Helen gave her a wink. Roxanne returned a trembly thumbs-up.

In here, this was her kingdom: transportation she'd paid for and staff she supported and luxuries, the designer silk dress and the Tiffany earrings, she'd earned through sweat equity.

But out there, that was *his* kingdom. And in her impulsive and still regrettable announcements about their marriage, she'd humiliated him and undermined the Monte. She was working hard to make amends now. But she wasn't sure what reception she was going to get when she stepped off the plane.

When she met his people. When she met, for the time being, *her* people. When she met the people who would call her daughter *Princesa*. The rising hum of the crowd as the plane settled to a stop made this future she'd planned and schemed for terrifying real.

With her view blocked by the closed windows, she undid her seat belt and stood to shake out her dress. It was a dark bronze silk at the top, gathered at her waist with a belt, and falling away in lighter gold-cream pleats to mid-calf. She wore delicate heels that cinched at her ankle, a gold bangle at her wrist, and simple pearl earrings exposed by her braid, styled softly to the side so that it flowed over her left breast.

She'd called in her personal stylist and hair/makeup person for this moment. And then sent them scurrying away. How did an essentially orphaned Mexican-American urchin from Kansas dress to meet the subjects of her husband's European kingdom? What could she wear that said, "Hey, I know I screwed you and your prince over, but I'm totally cool and I hope you don't hate me or my daughter who will one day rule you."

Helen stood by the plane's interior door and looked at Roxanne. Straightening her constantly lolling "wedding" ring and sweeping her hand down her braid, Roxanne gave Helen a nod and then took a deep, steadying breath. Helen took hold of the disarming handle with both hands, pulled, and then shoved the door open.

What she wanted most of all, she realized as the blinding Spanish sun poured into the plane, was for Mateo to think she looked pretty.

The sharp rise of crowd noise hit her like a plank. She worked hard not to wince against it. Stuffing every fear and nerve and hesitation down deep, Roxanne stepped out onto the top of the stairs with a fixed smile on her face.

A wave of cheers rose up to greet her as if she'd just scored a goal for Real Madrid. Her smile softened and grew. So did the whistles. She raised a hand and gave a wave. "*¡Viva Señora! ¡Viva la multimillionaria!*" the people of the Monte del Vino Real shouted as Roxanne's eyes adjusted to the sun and she saw them, packed in close against the velvet ropes, waving signs and blown-up photos.

The backdrop behind them—Roxanne's first glimpse of this fairy-tale kingdom—was breathtaking. The lush, leafy rows of the Monte's vineyards came up almost to the runway. In the distance, Roxanne could see the red terracotta rooftops of the town proper. The Castillo del Monte, the medieval castle with its tall tower and fortress walls that would be her daughter's part-time home, stood on a hillside above the town. And looming above it all was the jagged Pico Viajadora, a member of the Picos de Europa, snow-covered peaks that sheltered the Monte, transforming the secret valley into a land whose thin layer of soil soaked up the sun and encouraged grapes to grow.

The best sight of all, however, was the man coming up the

stairs to greet her. His smile was as dazzling as the sunlight. His eyes were as steady as the mountains, and he looked at her like they, together, shared its secrets. He reached for her when he stepped onto the platform, and she let him, found her hands reaching for his shoulders, like a toddler reaching for her parent, but there was nothing childlike in how he slid one hand around her waist and the other around her nape and pressed her against his body for a full, consuming, month-long wait of a kiss.

The crowd went crazy.

He tipped his forehead against hers, panting against her lips, before sliding his mouth to her exposed ear. "Welcome to my home, Roxanne."

Her nails clenched into his suit jacket.

With his hand still around her waist, Mateo swung around to face the crowd and wave. Roxanne joined him, drawing on the poise she'd practiced facing down smirking CEOs and racing through screaming paparazzi and speaking in front of a thousand stockholders to manage this gobsmacking situation—waving with a kind, warm, and not-freaking-out smile at her husband's cheering subjects while being wrapped in his hot prince arm.

How in the holy flying fuck did she get here?

It's the sentiment she spoke in the ear of Mateo's sister when the princess—who'd been waiting halfway down the stairs with a plastered-on smile—joined them up on the platform. Sofia snorted before she remembered that she hated Roxanne, gathered herself, and turned to join them in waving at the crowd.

Roxanne knew that only Sofia's love for her brother was keeping the girl from pushing Roxanne off the platform.

"The king and queen send their apologies," Sofia shouted as she waved.

"I bet they do," Roxanne said. She glanced at Mateo, who didn't react except for a tic in his strong jaw. Skipping their new daughter-in-law's big reveal was a slight, an effective one if they were trying to distance themselves from Mateo. It was more proof that they were actively working to displace him.

If the enthusiasm of the crowd was any indication, their plan wasn't working.

Sofia led the way down the stairs. "But you're to appear in the throne room at 8 p.m.," she called behind her. "My parents had it remodeled this year; you'll love it."

"Can't wait," Roxanne said as Mateo slid his arm through hers and escorted her down. At the bottom, Sofia stationed herself on Roxanne's open side and strolled next to her as they walked the red carpet to a waiting limousine, declaring her allegiance. It was a vote for her brother, not Roxanne, but Roxanne still appreciated the sentiment. When Mateo opened the limo door and Sofia slid in, Roxanne stooped down to tell her so.

But Sofia halted her with a palm in the doorway. "*Tía rica*, get your own ride." Puzzled, Roxanne looked at Mateo, who only grinned as he motioned her out of the doorway. Roxanne stepped back, allowed him to close the door. The limo smoothly slid away.

A dusty white truck was parked behind it.

If Roxanne thought the loudest the crowd was going to get was when they kissed, she was mistaken. The people of the Monte erupted in cheers, whistles, and no small amount of catcalls. "*¡Planta las vides!*" they shouted. "*¡Las viñas son vida!*"

Without dropping her smile, Roxanne narrowed her eyes. "Why do I get the impression that *planta las vides* isn't referring to planting the vines?"

Mateo shrugged as he escorted her toward the truck. His body, in an elegant dark gray suit, felt sure and firm brushing against hers. "I have no idea," he said, his innocence belied by the tilt in his grin. "I'm taking you on a tour of the vineyards."

He opened the door for her and held her hand to help her hop inside. It was no horse-drawn carriage, but the truck was immaculately clean and a strangely appealing accessory of the gorgeous, sun-stroked European prince who walked around the front of it. When he stepped up into the driver's side and started the truck, Roxanne rolled down her window and rested her arm on the door. How surreal that she was driving away with her prince in the same vehicle that was ubiquitous in the small Kansas farming community where she'd grown up? The same vehicle that Father Juan had driven—he'd had a rattling orange Ford 100—when they'd brought Communion to people who couldn't make it out of the house.

As the truck began to move, Roxanne tilted out a hand and waved a thank-you and goodbye to the people of the Monte. The crowd cheered and waved back.

As they passed out of the airport gate, Roxanne checked her sideview mirror before rolling up the window and leaning back in her seat. "There are no photographers following us," she said.

Mateo kept his eyes on the road. "The Monte is a pain in the ass to get to without a private plane." He glanced into his rearview. "We also told the international press that you were coming later in the day."

Roxanne quirked an eyebrow at him, knowing how important positive world opinion was to Mateo's goals.

"This was for them, my people," he said, gripping the steering wheel. "I didn't want to share you with the fucking paparazzi."

"Oh," Roxanne said, turning to look out her window, wishing she'd left it open, wanting a little breeze to cool her as her stupid, stupid body flooded with heat.

Remembering what was at stake—his reputation, her reputation, the Monte's future, her daughter's entire life—had made it easy to maintain her parameters with him when they'd been surrounded by observers or shut away in her office. Even when her body had leapt at his suggestion that they have sex when she was less likely to get pregnant, at the realization that he was as vibrantly attracted to her as she was to him, she'd kept her head on straight. It would serve neither of them to let this get emotional.

But then she'd let her thumbs get away from her.

Mateo had been so far away, and the texted words—once he'd opened the door for them, once he reached out to her and told her he needed them—came so easy. While in her mile-high office or luxury condo, she'd given him advice that he'd listened to, she'd teased him and poked at him, she'd offered him insight just to...just to bolster him. Or to make him laugh at the end of a trying day. She liked that she could make him laugh. She owed it to him, to fix the damage she'd caused. So that he could build a strong kingdom for their daughter.

She might have even told him, lying in bed with a half-empty bottle of wine, about her dressing room fantasy. The one about the mirrors and the handsome stranger and the tight skirt shoved up to her waist. She might have even texted those messages one handed.

The words had seemed so...impermanent, just a letter on a button that sent a black mark to a faraway screen. The words were like bubbles, something that would float away and pop, leaving nothing behind but a delightful moment.

But the words now felt like lead links to a very, very, very bad idea. The words, coming back to her now as she inhaled the earthy spice of him and shimmered at his nearness, made her want to fling herself out of the truck and hide herself in the vine rows racing by.

When she realized she was holding her own breath to listen to the quiet huffs of his, she spoke just to have something to fill the cab.

"What vineyard are we seeing first?"

She jerked against her seat belt as the truck took a sudden left onto a dirt road between vine rows. Mateo slowed to a crawl, preventing dust from coating the baby grapes and leaf canopy, but when Roxanne glanced at him, she noticed the hard grip he had on the steering wheel as he glared out the windshield. He didn't look at her—hadn't looked at her for the entire drive, she realized—and didn't speak as they were surrounded by an ocean of green. A hundred yards in, Mateo took a right and pulled the truck up to a small rock-walled cabin with a terracotta roof and powdery green doors and shutters. The shutters were open wide to the breeze. Vines grew up the porch columns and created dappled shading over the hammock and rustic picnic table on the patio.

The truck was barely in park before Mateo was out his door and pulling Roxanne from the vehicle.

"Mateo, what're we—" She almost stumbled on her delicate high heels as Mateo pulled her by her hand, but he turned, caught her, then swung her up into his arms, her pleated, bronze skirt fanning down his legs like a matador's cape. She gasped, clenching her hands around his hot-to-the-touch neck as he muttered, "Uneven ground," still without looking at her. In a few powerful strides, he was up on the patio, his back against the intricately carved wooden door, and pushing inside.

Roxanne barely got a glimpse of the interior of the one-room cabin—a heavy iron bed frame, a basin, an ancient armoire—before he slid her to her feet, buried both hands in her hair, and wholly took her mouth, his tongue tasting and stroking and plundering like he'd been starving and she was his only sustenance in eons. Mateo banged them both back against a hip-high bureau. Roxanne gasped, ripping her mouth away, lightheaded as all her blood felt like it was rushing to the surface. "What are you doing?"

"Can't wait. Can't think," he growled, taking advantage of her turned head by attacking her neck, by sucking her earlobe into his mouth and making it feel absolutely filthy. He began to pull up the silk of her skirt. "Need you." Moaning, Roxanne clenched her nails into his biceps, into the $3,000 suit jacket that did nothing to hide the animal.

"Fucking silk," Mateo groaned as his fingers stroked hard up her naked legs. "Can't tell the difference between you and the dress." When his fingers brushed against the lace of her panties, he reared back, gripping her skirt at her waist. The way he stared in the half-light of the small room, the way he licked those full, gorgeous lips, made Roxanne's thighs tense and rub together. He slid to his knees on the stone floor. "*Hola cariño*," he whispered, like he was having an actual conversation with her pussy as he lifted her leg and hooked it over his shoulder. "You always look so pretty for me." And with only that for preamble, he shoved the crotch of her bronze, lacy panties to the side and sucked her into his mouth. Tongue and teeth and lips set to hard, devouring work as he lifted her, got one ass cheek up onto the bureau, to aim where she was most wet and open against his mouth. The words coming out of Roxanne were wrecked nonsense as she supported her weight back on her hands and rolled her hips, helpless to the pleasure.

He fucked her hard with his tongue, getting his jaw into it, before biting into her thigh. "The taste of you gets me so hard," he growled against her skin. He dropped her leg to his side as he swooped to standing, towering over her, lips shiny with her, his suit pants open and his thick, long, gorgeous cock—the friend she'd barely gotten to taste or stroke or know in any meaningful way—already ready for her, hard and angry red from where he'd stroked it as he ate her. She reached for it with desperate hands, and he let her as he wiped his face on his shoulder. But he slammed her back against the bureau as her hands stroked its length, ripped her panties down her legs until they were hanging off one ankle, and cupped her ass in his hands as he raised her to him and then—all unceasing power—pushed inside of her.

The way was warm and wet and sweet.

"Fuck," Mateo groaned, slamming into her like a declaration. Roxanne hunched against his chest at the pleasure. "Fuck, fuck, fuck." He pulsed into her, fast and hard, his fingers digging into her ass, until he slid one hand away to grab the mirror behind Roxanne, a mirror she didn't even know was there, and used it to gain more leverage. His huge body shadowed her, dominated her, and she clutched at him, her legs wild, to draw him closer. When he grabbed her ass to lift her, Roxanne gave a half-shriek at the deep, G-spot-stroking punch. He turned, took a long stride, then collapsed with her on the bed, the ancient springs squealing. He was on her, over her, his big body overwhelming her with heat and strength and Roxanne would have closed her eyes at the pleasure if it wasn't for Mateo's beautiful hungry face looking down at her, eyes glowing with lust, white teeth bared, so much gorgeous demand that she wanted to wrap herself around him and hold him close.

It was too much.

With her heart beating a terrorized rabbit pace in her chest, she wriggled out from under him and to her side, facing away, and he let her. But when he pulled her back against him, when he locked her thigh over his bent leg and shoved effortlessly back inside of her, caging her against his body while he turned her chin up for the deepest of kisses, she panicked that this might even be worse.

All conscious thoughts of worse or better scattered as he thrust inside her like he couldn't get deep enough. Roxanne tilted back her hips, wanting him deeper. Unheeded cries began to burst from her throat as Mateo fucked her like he was trying to tattoo himself on her skin. The iron headboard twanged against the wall; Mateo gripped the sheet, popping it off the mattress as he ground against her, the fingers of his free hand rubbing her slit while he whispered filthy, reverent words into her skin.

Roxanne started to come. White heat tore her like a blinding rocket launch and her mouth fell wide, no sound able to come out as her body shrieked into orgasm. She was coming, trapped and coming as Mateo pounded, deep and fast, gritting against the convulsions of her pussy around him, and Roxanne realized he wasn't slowing down, he wasn't stopping, and her body spasmed against the mangled bedcovers, and Mateo, when he saw her trying to escape the unending orgasm, he started to laugh, his golden eyes wild as he kept her head tilted up to him. He started to laugh and laugh, and he jerked and she knew it was happening to him, too, this impossible orgasm, and he was still laughing and coming and holding her thigh open and fucking, fucking, fucking into her until every crevice of her body was singing and screaming and begging with the pleasure he was giving it, his laughter—his joy and satisfaction at this whirlwind they'd created together—ringing in her ears.

Roxanne came out of the doze she'd collapsed into at the feel of Mateo unbuckling her heels and slipping them and her panties off her feet. She was on her back, sprawled across the bed, and facing the open window. Through it, she could see green grape vines hanging off the portico and a slice of rich blue sky. A hawk shrieked in the distance, a welcome predator to keep away the rodents and small birds that would feast on the vines' fruit and roots.

The springs of the old mattress squeaked as Mateo settled back on the bed. He didn't touch her.

"You looked like a queen when you got off the plane." His voice was deep and rich in the quiet room. "Thank you."

"You're welcome," she said softly, trailing a finger through her now loose hair as she continued to gaze out the window. Her skirt, she realized, had been pulled down to cover her thighs.

"I'm sorry I couldn't wait." His breathing was so heavy it could have lulled her right back to sleep. "You deserve better."

She smiled to herself as she twirled the strand of hair around her finger. "I don't think I can survive anything better," she said.

The mattress shifted as if the weight of his anxiety floated away. Then Mateo chuckled softly and slid a hand across her stomach. "You're so beautiful," he murmured, closer, his breath brushing her neck. "I was afraid I was going to throw you down on the tarmac."

"What about the contract?" she asked, seeing the vine leaves flutter in the breeze, feeling the same cooling touch against her skin. Her brain was slow but not so sluggish that it didn't process the meaning of having sex on their first day together. Was Mateo willing to forgo their day of chitchat? She hadn't— and wouldn't—agree to having sex outside of their contractual three days a month. She'd been clear about that.

"I'll keep my hands off you tomorrow." His hands gripped into her waist. "Somehow."

She was too sated, too floating, to argue with him right now.

"How long are you staying?" he asked.

She wondered if she'd ever seen a sky this blue before. "A

week." She wondered how sluggish his brain was. Did he process the meaning of that decision?

The old mattress complained as Mateo hooked his arm around her waist to pull her to him and snuggle her against his long, warm, engulfing body. "Good," he said, forcing Roxanne to close her eyes against the blue sky as her world became the soft, consuming touch of his lips against her neck.

April: Night One
Part One

Roxanne pulled the eyeliner pencil away from her face and said a quick prayer for patience as Sofia lolled on a nearby settee in a fluffy cocktail dress and continued to list in exacting detail every woman that Mateo ever dated.

"And then there was Victoria in college. She was *una rubia.* Did I tell you that Mateo always preferred blondes?"

Roxanne gritted her teeth in the vanity mirror. "You've mentioned it."

"Victoria was studying to be a doctor. She works with Doctors Without Borders now. Can you imagine living in a hut, saving people's lives, sacrificing yourself for others?" Sofia bobbed her Manolo on the end of her toe as she spoke. "Mateo always said she was *la mujer perfecta.*"

Roxanne put down the pencil before she stabbed herself in the eye with it. "She couldn't have been that perfect since they're no longer together."

"I think he wore her out," Sofia said smugly. "Couldn't keep his hands off of her. I'd stay at the other end of el Castillo when they were visiting. Their screams and groans, I was afraid the castle walls were going to come tumbling..."

"It makes no difference to me who your brother has dated," Roxanne said, smiling poison at Sofia in the oval vanity mirror. "He could have screwed every woman between here and

Madrid. I don't care. That's why we have this little arrangement—so we can have a kid *without* sharing messy personal details."

Mateo brought her to this six-hundred-year-old castle, introduced her to the kind chatelaine and her five-person staff, and then led her to one of the guest suites so she could shower and change. She'd come out of the bathroom to the welcome sight of her makeup kit and gown, delivered by her own staff, and the unwelcome sight of Sofia lounging in the bedroom. Roxanne had already dried and arranged her hair, so couldn't even depend on the roar of the hair dryer to give her a break.

Meeting the king and queen was going to be hard enough without Sofia winding her up.

"Did he tell you about his vineyard manager?" Sofia asked, her darkly lined eyes lasering in on Roxanne in the mirror. "The woman who's overseeing the *Tempranillo Vino Real* here in the Monte? He used to screw her all the time. And they've been spending *muchísimo* time together since he's been home."

Shit. That one landed. Roxanne began applying her blush.

"She's older than he is," Sofia continued. "And so beautiful. I'm not certain, but I think she helped him lose his virginity. He spent the whole summer after he turned eighteen at her house next door. He'd come home with the dumbest grins on his face."

Twin talons of arousal and jealousy clawed through her. She could imagine a sun-kissed eighteen-year-old Mateo, stretched out on a woman's bed, shivering as the woman made love to him. As his now-vineyard manager made love to him.

Roxanne let none of her irritation show on her face and smiled into the mirror. "I've seen that grin on his face," she said, letting her eyes simmer. "There was one time that I was on top of him and…"

Sofia sat up, her stiletto dropping to the floor. "*Que asco. ¡Cállate!*"

"What's wrong?" Roxanne said, whipping around to face her, her silk robe slithering against the brocade of the stool. "I thought we were discussing your brother's sex life. I figured you'd like to hear some of my stories."

"You're disgusting," Sofia sneered.

"And you're a pain in my ass," Roxanne shot back. "Why are you in here? What do you want from me?"

The girl glowered at Roxanne. "I want you to let my brother out of the contract."

"You know I can't do that," Roxanne said, trying to reach through her irritation to her empathy. Sofia was five years younger and even through the princess's tough-girl look— she'd wrapped up her hair in a high messy bun and wore a strapless black-and-white cocktail dress that highlighted the bloodred "The Queen is Dead" tattoo down her forearm— Roxanne could see her vulnerability. Sofia was truly worried about her brother.

"You don't like me and I haven't given you much reason to," Roxanne said, trying to breathe calm into her words. "But I've apologized to your brother and I'm sincerely trying to make things better. Mateo believes me. I wish you would, too. As soon as I'm pregnant, I will be out of your hair. You'll never have to see me again."

If anything, her words only made the princess angrier.

"That's the problem!" Sofia said, standing and kicking off the stiletto that made her lopsided. "Don't you see that the last thing my brother needs is a wife and child without any strings attached?"

Roxanne looked up at Sofia, nonplussed and a little impressed by her fury.

"You know he doesn't come home anymore," Sofia said.

"He's trying to avoid your father—"

"No." Sofia dismissed her with a wave of a hand. "That's what he tells himself. But it's more than that. He ignores the needs of his people. He avoids...*su familia*." Since Mateo seemed to have almost no involvement with his mother, the only *familia* Sofia could be referring to was herself. "He still thinks I'm a rebellious sixteen-year-old."

Roxanne heard the ache in the girl's words. "Your brother admires you very much." And he did. There'd been undisguised pride as Mateo told Roxanne about his baby sister, about how Princesa Sofia had been a special thorn in her parents' royal sides, smoking in her convent school at ten, eschewing princess wear for oversized jeans and white tank tops as a young teen, and getting a tattoo of the Smiths album title "The Queen Is Dead" scrawled across her forearm for her eighteenth birthday. Roxanne had wondered how that same girl had graduated with a degree in enology from the University of Bordeaux and was apprenticing for a winemaker in Rioja. She realized now that there might have been some gaps in Mateo's storytelling that had allowed Roxanne to believe Sofia had partied her way into a role that required exhausting work, scientific precision, and deep academic study.

His wild child of a sister had become a focused twenty-four-year-old woman without Mateo realizing it.

"He isolates himself in California," Sofia continued, her hands moving wildly. "He would rather deal with hard, brown sticks than people. He is kind, funny, intelligent, gorgeous... and yet he hasn't had a girlfriend since Cornell. I don't know why he keeps himself so—" Sofia wrapped her arms around her tightly bound waist. "...*obstruido*. I don't know what he's so afraid of."

Seeing the weariness hanging off those lovely, caramel-colored shoulders, Roxanne wondered how much Mateo's absence had forced Sofia into the role of intermediary and caretaker. Sofia was asking for her help to unlock the puzzle of Mateo. It was a task that Roxanne absolutely did not want.

"He's busy…" she said ineffectually.

Sofia scoffed and slapped one hand against her thigh. "Yes, too busy to notice his people, his sister, and the billions of women who would kill to have a man like him. Too busy to be a real prince, find a real wife, and enjoy the real love that he deserves. You smacked at his sense of nobility with this contract, but truly, I think he loves it. He stays separate and alone and still gets an heir and a wife. You're giving him what he wants and nothing that he needs."

Roxanne was flabbergasted by the idea that Mateo could unwittingly be getting out of this arrangement exactly what she wanted out of it: a child with no emotional entanglement. He'd been so disgusted by her proposal, so adamant about his higher ideals. Part of her had admired him for simply being a better person than she was, for acknowledging the impact her plan would have on a future human being, their child. But to think that he actually wanted to avoid the same unwanted emotions that she was working to avoid made him her compatriot. Put him on the same lower, selfish, realistic level that she was on.

It was another tie that connected a Spanish prince with a rural girl who'd counted on free school lunch for her daily meal.

"I'm alone. I'm isolated," Roxanne said, standing. "Most people dedicated to their career are. What about you? I imagine if you had a man and a huge collection of friends you wouldn't have spent the last month dreaming of ways to ambush me."

Sofia huffed. "I'm not…"

Roxanne waved her off. "I know. I'm kidding." As Sofia

settled down, Roxanne had a glimpse of how much fun you could have messing with a younger sibling.

"It's true, I don't have much of a social life," Sofia said, drawing herself up like the *princesa* she was. "The best wine apprenticeships are competitive, and you must dedicate yourself to the learning entirely if you want the best winemakers to accept and recommend you."

"So you probably have never been in love either."

Roxanne instantly regretted the throwaway statement when she saw the shock of pain blanch the woman's face. Sofia pressed her hand to her stomach and looked away.

"Oh God," Roxanne opened her mouth, but didn't know what to say other than, "I'm sorry."

"For what?" Sofia demanded, her face still turned away. And then, Roxanne knew she should be shot on the spot. The young woman raised her hand to her face, as if wiping away tears.

She couldn't leave her just standing there. "Oh God," Roxanne said again, rushing to her sister-in-law. Yes, Sofia was her sister-in-law. "I'm an idiot. I'm so sorry." She touched Sofia's shoulder.

The woman wiped again and then turned to face Roxanne. "No, I'm the idiot. *Mierda*." Her dark eyes were misty pools as she cursed. "It was so long ago. I can't believe I'm crying. I can't believe I'm crying in front of you!"

Roxanne smiled miserably, still hanging on to Sofia's shoulder. "I'm good at bringing out sadness in people."

Sofia's scoffing laugh still carried traces of tears in it. But at least it was a laugh.

"Do…do you want to talk about it?" Roxanne asked, not believing she was speaking those words to a woman she would have gladly punched minutes earlier.

"Not at all," Sofia pronounced. She pulled Roxanne's hand

off her shoulder and squeezed it, looking into her eyes. "And please don't tell my brother about this. It happened so long ago, before I started college. He doesn't know…and doesn't need to!"

Roxanne squeezed her hand back. "Okay, I won't." She hesitated. And then realized, again like a lightning bolt, that she would have a connection, even if tenuous, to this woman for the rest of her life. "But I'm here if you need to talk. I'm your sister-in-law now."

"*Dios mío.* That's right." Sofia's curse was softened by the fact that she hadn't let go of Roxanne's hand. She continued to look at Roxanne, as if the tears had cleared something from her eyes. "Maybe my brother isn't the only one who should be looking for something more than a contract in their life?"

Roxanne pulled back, now feeling a little trapped by Sofia's slender hand. "Because you've just given 'falling in love' such a ringing endorsement." She laughed hollowly.

Sofia patted the back of her hand before letting it go, before crossing her arms again and studying Roxanne like she was a glass of wine whose varietal she couldn't figure out.

"*Sí*, love sucked for me," she said finally. "But nobody's better suited for a *por siempre amor* than my brother."

Sofia stepped back into her sky-high shoes and turned on her heel, leaving the room and abandoning Roxanne with half-done makeup and unwanted thoughts about Mateo's "forever love."

A half hour later, Roxanne walked on the arm of her princely husband into a room designed à la Versailles. The room was ridiculous, with its weighty crystal chandeliers and gold-leafed Rococo side tables and red-velvet-lined walls and golden lions snarling at her from each side of a raised platform.

Mateo had explained, when he'd taken her on a brief tour

of the castle that evening, that two wings had been closed to save on costs. But what she'd seen of the Castillo del Monte had been updated, the Moorish influences of arched door-ways, ornate black iron light fixtures, and mosaic tiles blended effectively with warm rugs and modern furniture. She imag-ined that they had the welcoming staff they had met earlier to thank.

Because the two people on the raised platform, sitting on red-velvet and gold-leafed thrones, were definitely respon-sible for the monstrosity of this room. Roxanne had once bumped into Britain's prince and his wife at a hors d'oeuvres table during a Wimbledon match. They'd chatted about sail-ing as they'd escorted her to their box, where his mother had quizzed Roxanne about female entrepreneurship in London. They'd all been lovely.

King Felipe and Queen Valentina, minor royalty from a tiny principality, were the worst.

Standing in front of them, Roxanne curtsied low as Mateo bowed next to her. She watched him out of the corner of her eye, wanting to send a lifeline out to him, a wink and a nudge that said, "Are they kidding with this?"

But as they straightened and Mateo introduced his parents using the long formality of their names, Roxanne saw that he found nothing about this situation humorous. He was angry and humiliated; he'd been stiff-jawed when he'd picked her up outside the door of the bedroom and warned her what to expect. Roxanne had tried to tell him then, was trying to tell him now with her small smile and relaxed body posture that she didn't mind. She'd spent her *life* having people look down at her, since kindergarten when Becky Turner had warned all of the kids not to play with her because her mommy was an H-O-R. She was years past caring about their ostentatious display; knew the curtsy they forced on her spoke volumes more about the insecure king and queen than Roxanne. If only she could find a way to communicate her ease to Mateo.

But he was distant in his dark gray suit, as cold and humorless as a statue of a classical god.

Roxanne heard the echo of Sofia's words: *I don't know what he's so afraid of.* Shoulders back, she looked King Felipe square in the eye. *Bring it*, she thought.

"At last, we meet in the flesh," said the king, who'd positioned himself so he could literally look down at her. She could see traces of Mateo in the man's heavy, dark brows and the cleft in his chin. But the whispers of a once-handsome man were overshadowed by the gut stretching his shirt front, the over-tanned hue of his skin, the unnatural tautness around his eyes, and the gel slicking back his dyed black hair. That he said the word "flesh" while working his gaze down her body didn't help his cause either.

Roxanne merely nodded. "It's an honor, your majesty."

"That's a lovely dress," Queen Valentina said without lowering her nose. Like the king, the queen had made it difficult to see any natural beauty through everything she'd tucked, pulled, injected, and altered. Her hair was a shining frost and her breasts in her body-hugging sheath were as high and round as a prom queen's. "Last year Gaultier?"

Roxanne looked down and shook out the creamy, floor-length chiffon. "Theallet." She smiled at the queen. "Custom."

"Well, it's fine for tonight's gathering," the queen sniffed. "But you'll need to wear something more appropriate when we present you." Mateo had informed her that a banquet would be held in her honor in three days. "People already assume so many unsavory things about you."

Roxanne didn't let her spine move a millimeter. "Oh?"

Mateo's father waved a thick hand. "Don't misunderstand my wife," he said. "We're thrilled you're as beautiful in real life as you are in pictures. When someone has to purchase a husband, you're never sure what you're going to get."

Without looking at him, Roxanne quickly put a constraining hand on Mateo's shoulder. "I see the gloves are off," she said.

Queen Valentina narrowed her eyes at her. "We thought some plain speaking would be best before we join our dinner guests. My husband made an arrangement with you in good faith and you've dragged his name through the mud."

The ludicrous, self-centeredness...as if the son they'd sold off wasn't worth mentioning. "I've apologized to Mateo and I've put the full weight of my influence behind improving the image and fortunes of the Monte." She clasped her hands at her waist and took in both the king and queen. "Some of the rumors about the legitimacy of our marriage have been so persistent, though, it's almost as if someone doesn't *want* the image of the Monte to improve." Roxanne smiled with teeth. "But don't worry, my investigators will find the source of the rumors. And I'll shut him up; those with big mouths usually have such small...everything else, don't you think, *Alteza*?"

The king's skin turned florid with temper. "I wonder who bends over who at night," he sneered.

Mateo pivoted on a heel, startling Roxanne. With his back to his parents, he offered her an arm, which she gingerly took, and then walked with her at a steady pace out of the room. "That's right, Mateo," his father called, smugness echoing off the room's high wood beams. "Inform our guests the king and queen will join them soon."

Mateo closed the heavy door behind them and slipped his arm free of hers, burying his hands in his pants pockets as he stood in the doorway.

Roxanne wanted to smack herself. "I'm sorry," she murmured. The last thing he needed was her sinking as low as his parents.

"You have nothing to be sorry for," he said. He looked straight ahead, a bit of pomade keeping his waves off his forehead, staring at the ancestral portraits that lined the low-lit hallway. He spoke without emotion. "I'm ashamed they're a part of me."

Oh. That. Shame about your origins. She knew *that* shame better than anyone. "Mateo, you're not responsible for—"

He stepped away from her and motioned down the hallway. "We should join the dinner guests in the drawing room," he said tightly. "It's not fair to leave Sofia alone with those jackals."

Roxanne nodded and once again slipped her arm through his. But rather than the warm strength he'd pressed up against her side when he'd met her at the airport, Mateo was now stiff and formal, keeping inches away from her. Roxanne wasn't offended; she was surprised. Surprised that he let his incompetent and morally deficient father get to him, sad that that gross man could make Mateo wall up his humor and brilliance and inherent lust for life. For the first time, Roxanne fully understood how Mateo had created such a gulf between himself and his beloved Monte.

As they walked on centuries-old terracotta, Mateo gave the impression of a man who wished himself very, very far away.

April: Night One
Part Two

Hours later, they were quiet as they entered Mateo's hilltop home. At least, they were quiet until Mateo, in the dark of the entryway, cracked his shin against something. "God fucking dammit!" Mateo yelled in both Spanish and English, hopping around on one foot and cursing until he reached a wall to slap on the overhead light.

Roxanne's suitcases, stacked by her staff in the entryway, had been the culprit. "Oh God, sorry," Roxanne said, throwing her clutch on a side table and sliding out of her wrap. "Helen wasn't sure where to put my things. Can I get you some ice?"

"That gorgon is here?!" Mateo said, still hopping and cursing. "Did you bring your centerfold bodyguard, too? Are they going to jump out and mug me just to make the night more perfect?" He sank down on her stack of suitcases and leaned over to rub his shin.

Roxanne looked down at his golden head. "My staff is staying in town," she said quietly. "Please don't call them names. They're working hard for both of us."

"Then why didn't they put everything in my bedroom?" he groused. "Where in the hell else would it go?"

Roxanne stayed quiet as she watched him. The dinner had been legitimately horrible, a multicourse barrage of barely concealed insults, inflated name dropping, and exaggerated tales of the king and queen's success and social standing in front of Sofia and a few of the king and queen's closest "friends," tittering hangers-on and sycophants. They were intentionally trying to make Roxanne flee, as if a few not-remotely-clever insults could do that. She and Mateo had stomached through it, like crawling through the mud of a military exercise. The only time Mateo had raised his voice was when they were leaving, when he'd argued with his sister about staying at the castle—he'd wanted her to come back to his house with them. But Sofia had insisted he and Roxanne needed time alone.

Roxanne wished she'd come, too.

"*Joder,*" Mateo said under his breath. He let up on his shin and shoved to standing. "Which suitcase do you need now? I'll carry everything else in tomorrow when I'm less hobbled." He looked drawn and exhausted in his perfectly tailored suit.

"Mateo," Roxanne sighed.

"What?" he barked.

She met his tired, stormy eyes. "I think it's best if I sleep in my own room while I'm here."

He stared at her for a full tension-building ten seconds before exploding. "Jesus fucking Christ!" he yelled. "This again?"

"Mateo…" she attempted.

"I'm sick and tired of this power play. Can't we fuck like normal people? I want you. You want me." He stomped around. "So why does this have to be so fucking complicated?"

"Mateo, you need to stop…"

"Stop what!"

Roxanne finally let her voice raise. "Stop yelling at me!" she replied.

"I'm not—" Mateo shouted at the top of his lungs. Then he swallowed. "Yelling."

He slumped back down to the suitcases. "Sorry."

She twined her fingers together to keep from stroking them through his hair. "You're forgiven. It's been a rough night."

He sighed heavily in agreement as he stared at his boots. "Got any booze?"

He motioned with his elegant fingers toward a doorway without looking up.

Roxanne ventured forward into the next dark room, slid her hands over a cool, limestone wall until she felt switches, and slowly slid them up. She stood agog as a massive room with a peaked cathedral ceiling and a nighttime vision of the Monte was revealed. The two-story wall that fronted his great room was glass; in the bright blue moonlight she could see a few glowing lights of the town and the snow-capped peaks of the mountain. She imagined the view was spectacular during the day. An image came to her of a tawny haired little girl running out of her bedroom to see that spectacular morning view.

Roxanne would never get to see the look on her daughter's face as she watched the sun come up over her kingdom. She rubbed at a sudden pang under her breastbone.

Must be something she ate.

Roxanne forcefully pushed the image away and stepped farther into the room. She noted the doorway into a modern-looking kitchen on the left, a hallway on the right, the sunken pit of comfy couches and chairs, the raised dining-table-and-chairs dais with a gorgeous metal sunburst chandelier. She headed to a sideboard and its collection of liquor and wine bottles. She grabbed two cut-crystal glasses, poured several fingers of good bourbon into each of them, and then walked down the gleaming hardwood steps into the living room pit in the center of the room. She slipped off her heels and slid onto the leather couch, tucking her feet under her and pulling a cashmere throw from the back of the couch around her.

She heard the tap of Mateo's boots as he joined her in the room. From her nest, she held one of the glasses out to him.

His eyes took her in as he slowly walked down the steps toward her. "For someone who doesn't want to sleep in my bed, you sure do make yourself at home," he said as he took the glass and settled on the leather next to her.

Roxanne shrugged. "I like your place."

"Yeah?" he leaned back against the sofa as he looked around. "I do, too." He took a sip of the bourbon as he let his shoulders relax.

"When did you buy it?" she asked, sipping her own drink.

"Built it. I had it built the moment I got my hands on my trust fund," he said, leaning forward to shrug out of his suit jacket before settling back. Roxanne admired the pull of his fitted shirt over his defined shoulders. He loosened his tie around his neck. "An architect who grew up in the Monte helped me design it. Not that..." Mateo looked down at his drink. "He doesn't live in the Monte anymore."

"What's your favorite thing about it?"

Mateo turned his head to peer at her from under the wave of his hair.

"What do you like about the house?" She refused to let him slide back into his moroseness.

He sipped as he considered. Then he lowered his glass. "The light. The view. The shower pressure. There's a goat path winding through the thick woods just out my study window and it reminds me how impenetrable the Monte once was, how protected it was from the rest of the world. I like the wood floors—they're so much warmer than stone. I like..." He swallowed as he looked at his glass. "I like that it's an example of how the Monte can evolve, how we can use the talents of our people to celebrate what we've been given and create something new."

Roxanne stroked the glass across her lower lip. "Once the vineyards have been invigorated, I imagine your architect friend can find lots of work here building houses."

Mateo said nothing as he sipped his drink. Sitting this still and close to him, Roxanne could smell the warm sun and green earth of him.

"I'm sorry for that shit show at the castle," he said, looking out at the night.

"Me, too," Roxanne murmured, apologizing for her part in antagonizing his parents. "It's a wonder you and your sister turned out as sane as you did."

He gave a laugh without humor and his heavy, expressive brows crinkled in pain. "Oh, *belleza*, that was easy. Our parents were such a glorious fucking example of what we didn't want to be. We have negative polarity; my father goes right and I go left. What he wants is what I despise; the more he shouts, the quieter I get." He looked down at his glass. "Any decency I have is just my own desperate attempt to prove that I am the polar opposite of my father."

Roxanne knew the way it stripped one bare to reveal the horrible truths about your parents. She understood the shame of it, the way an injured child always felt responsible, regardless of the amount of therapy, for a parent's deficiencies. The child always believed, deep down inside, that she must have done *something* to cause a parent to be so monstrous.

But the last thing Mateo needed right now was pity. She remembered the words of his sister: *He isolates himself in California... He ignores the needs of his people.* "That negative polarity thing... Do you ever worry your father has driven you too far away?"

He looked at her, those brows quirked.

"I mean, you do live in *California*." She took a slow sip of her drink and swallowed. "I guess you could move to the southern hemisphere if you wanted even more distance."

"My lab is there," he said defensively.

"Oh, right, and there's no way you could have set up a viticulture lab in Spain."

"Not with the resources and talent that UC Davis—" He smacked his crystal glass down on a wood-topped coffee table and turned to face her. "What the fuck, Roxanne?"

He didn't need this now, not after the night he'd endured. She knew that. But if not now, when he barely held on to his kingdom, then when? If not her, the temporary wife he seemed to trust, then who?

She set her glass next to his and folded her hands in her lap. "Have you ever considered that in your efforts to distance yourself from your father, you've also distanced yourself from the Monte?"

His beautiful eyes narrowed on her. "I give this valley my heart," he said, jabbing his finger at the window. "My blood."

"I know you do," she spoke slowly and soothingly. "Sometimes, as a caretaker, what you're caring for doesn't need all that. What it needs is your time. Your attention. When you were young, how much more valuable would it have been if your father had spent time with you rather than showing you off at press conferences?"

He shot to standing, tall and angry over her. "No. You don't get to do this. You don't get to refuse my bed and then burrow into me as if you care about the outcome. You're either my wife or you're not."

She untucked her feet from beneath her and stood as well. On bare feet, she felt so much smaller than him. She took his white-knuckled fist into her hands.

"I'm not your wife. Not really." She grabbed on when he tried to drag his hand away. "But I am your friend."

Arrested, he stared down at her.

"Mateo, do you believe that I care about the Monte?" He nodded. "Do you believe that I care about you?" She saw the tension in his stubborn jaw. Then, slowly, he nodded again. "I like you and I respect you. That's why I want my own bedroom. Things have become…" She felt her speech stutter on her lips as she looked up into his beautiful face, felt the full weight of his undivided attention. "They've become muddled this month. And we have so much on the line: the child I want, the kingdom you need to save. We can help each other; right now we both trust that we *want* to help each other. But if this becomes romantic… One of us is going to hurt the other person. One of us is going to hurt. And then what do we do? We have so much at stake."

At some point, she didn't know when, her clasp on his fist had become their fingers entwined, their palms locked. He stared, down and into her, and she stared right back, into the man with the golden skin and horrible parents and big brain and tendency to mope and willingness to laugh. She didn't see a prince. She just saw Mateo.

Her Mateo. And because it was so unfamiliar, Roxanne Medina had no idea that it was at that moment she tumbled head over heels in love with him.

Mateo continued to look down at her as his thumb gently stroked over the back of her hand. "This has to be the first time a wife has implored her husband *not* to be romantic."

Roxanne smirked as they lowered their joined hands, keeping their fingers entwined. "Certainly in Spain."

"So friends?" he asked. They were so close she could see that intriguing dark ring around his irises.

"Friends with benefits."

"A kid and enough money to save a kingdom," Mateo teased with a slow smile. "We're rife with benefits."

"Oh," Roxanne said a little breathlessly. Standing this close to him, that smile did something to her insides. "I was just talking about the really hot sex."

His move closer to her was almost imperceptible, but Roxanne felt it in her bones, sensed it in her blood. "So tomorrow will be our day of conversation," he murmured.

"That's right." Her lips tingled, like she could feel his eyes tracing over them. "We need to get everything back in order."

"But tonight?"

His big hands stroked up her naked arms, tickled like feathers.

Roxanne felt out of breath and lost for words. "I... I guess..." She licked her dry lips, felt the blaze of his eyes at the motion. "If we're only working on getting pregnant two days a month, we should probably work extra hard." She looked into his glorious eyes like they were the only thing that could save her. "Shouldn't we?"

Mateo nodded, said nothing, and swept her up—mouth, body, and heart—to claim her on his couch.

April: Day Two
Part One

Mateo drove his black Audi Q7 through winding village streets that he'd driven through a million times: over the stone bridge from which villagers poured wine into the stream to satisfy the ghostly hermetic monks who haunted the mountain caves, beneath the balcony of Restaurant Martín—the site of a million love affairs and heartbreaks—and its flower boxes weeping scarlet red geraniums, past the bodegas of Familia Pascual, San Sebastian, and El Gato con El Queso, wineries run by stubborn old fucks who refused to make anything better than cheap jug wine with Monte grapes, leaving great Tempranillo winemaking to those outside of the Monte.

"Why do they do that?" Roxanne asked as she looked out her window, the audience of one for Mateo's tour.

Her distraction allowed him to linger over her, over her midnight hair loose down her back, her ivory peasant-top threatening to reveal a shoulder, her naked lips that pursed as she watched century-old granite buildings streak by. When she'd come out of her bedroom this morning in jeans and easy makeup and asked, "Is this okay for today?" he'd wanted to shove her back into the room and lock them both in.

Instead, he'd told her she looked "nice." Placid words from a "friend" who was doing all he could to control his excitement about showing her his kingdom and showing her off to his people.

Mateo focused his eyes back on the cobblestone streets and his mind back on the issue of Monte del Vino Real winemaking. "Why are they stubborn old fucks? Because the lazy way of doing things has kept them rich enough," he told her, turning into the village plaza and slowing down to look for a parking space. "They claim that the Monte has also been known for its wine*growing*, not its wine*making*. I'd like to improve our wine quality, but I can only tackle one million problems at a time."

She turned to face him, that gleaming shoulder finally popping free. "Not a million and one?" she smirked. "Wimp."

He grinned back at her, and then turned to realize he'd just passed two available parking spots. He set his jaw and began another slow circle around the plaza, past the fountain of San Vicente de Zaragoza, the Monte's patron saint who was tortured with iron hooks and left to die on shards of broken pottery.

He wondered if that felt as bad as trying to remain calm and collegial with a woman he wanted to chain spread eagle to his bed.

She was right; things had become muddled over the last month. The contract had drawn out strict boundary lines, but in his campaign to equalize and normalize their relationship, Mateo had smudged them. Not always to his benefit. Roxanne Medina was now letting him see behind her armor and, Jesus, it was fucking killing him.

She'd been a jack-booted Amazon when he'd met her in January, a warrior who regularly kicked him in the balls. That it was the same woman who turned to him yesterday while she waved at his people, who looked to him for comfort and reassurance while nerves blazed in her eyes, tied him in fucking knots. When she'd curled onto his couch, accepted the horror of his parentage with a tilt of those luscious lips, and then offered him tenderness and insight and the soothing absolution of her body...

Do you believe me that I care about you?

Mateo needed to stop his father and finish developing the *Tempranillo Vino Real* and re-energize his people and prove he was worthy of his kingdom and he didn't...hadn't...couldn't imagine a future where billionaire Roxanne Medina fit into that long term. Not that she'd implied that she wanted "long term." But if they kept blindly skipping down this path, compelled by their bodies and their shared concerns and mutual intellects and just this...fascination...she was right: *One of us is going to hurt.*

Mateo didn't want to hurt her. And he had no need, time, or energy for a spouse. No more than Roxanne did. The terms of the contract served them both well. He would let it do its work, let it set the appropriate limits, and count down the seconds until the contract allowed him to touch her again.

Friends, he reminded himself as he pulled into a parking space and smelled her, like rain-dewed roses, in his car and all over his skin.

Friends, his mind groaned as he saw a beauty mark on her collarbone he'd never noticed, never kissed. He'd never seen her fully naked. There still were so many firsts for them to explore.

He turned off the car and cleared his throat. "So, we're here to meet my *niñera*. She's going to be...effusive about you and me and the marriage. And I'm gonna have to play along or she'll smack me upside the head. If I didn't bring you to meet her, I'd never hear the end of it, but in light of our 'friends' conversation, you need a heads-up."

Roxanne's smile had grown as he'd stammered. "We're meeting your nanny?"

"Yep."

"Will she show me naked bath-time pictures of you?"

"Almost certainly."

Roxanne kept that soft amused smile as she slipped on her cross-body bag, and Mateo resisted the urge to wrap his hand around her neck and lick her lips, tickle them at the corner until she opened to him. Before last night's conversation, he would have.

Blind, stupid, stumbling…

Mateo got out of the car and waited for Roxanne in front of it, rather than opening her door for her and touching her as she got out. He motioned toward the door of the sandwich shop, a glass door within centuries-old stone and masonry, and followed her to it, focusedly not watching her heavenly, heart-shaped ass in tight jeans.

The murmur inside the community gathering spot—the place where the people of the Monte shared a *café* or croissant or world-class *bocadillo*—swelled as he and Roxanne stepped inside.

"She's been waiting for you, *Príncipe*," the good-looking kid behind the counter called in Spanish, his hands busy sliding slices of *jamón* into a just-cut baguette and wrapping the *bocadillo* in white butcher paper. Wiping his hands on his apron, he leaned over the counter to grasp Mateo's hand.

"Gracias, Javi," Mateo said. "Could you wrap up a couple of those with…"

Javi, the grandson of Mateo's *niñera*, grinned big. "*Tortilla y tomate*. Of course. Would your wife like anything else?"

Roxanne answered in Spanish. "No. *Tortilla y tomate* sounds perfect. Thank you, Javi." The twenty-two-year-old kid, big and burly with floppy black hair, looked a little awestruck with his eyes on Roxanne. Mateo got it; he felt a little awestruck as he watched his native-born language emerge from those lush, bare lips in her throaty voice. Yes, right. She spoke fluent Spanish. Last night's dinner party had all been in English, his parents' standard protocol of rejecting their culture and country in favor of appearing more continental.

"*Por supuesto, Alteza,*" Javi replied, and Roxanne looked a little startled at hearing herself called "highness." Mateo smiled as he led her through the swinging door to the back, nodding at a couple of growers as they went.

He kept his hands to himself as he passed through the cramped quarters of ovens and prep tables and the large mixing machine for the fresh-made baguettes. She didn't need a hand on the curve of her waist to get where she was going. He knocked on a door in the far wall.

"*Ven,*" his *niñera* called.

He opened it to see the tiny lady, sitting erect in her office chair, looking at him with a placid welcome as they stepped into the room. She was trim, her skin a weathered shade of brown and still tight around her cheekbones, her hair cut, permed and dyed black once a month, making it appear a soft helmet around her head. He came around the desk to stand next to her chair, Roxanne beside him.

Titi's face was his first memory, the one adult who'd been a constant, daily presence in his life until he'd stepped away from her hug, lip trembling, to walk with a six-year-old's determination into boarding school. She'd been the one to soothe him during the summers home, to rub his back as he cried angry, powerless tears into his pillow, humiliated and horrified by the base, spineless, selfish creatures his parents were. She'd been the one to urge him to do better, to be better, and to punish him with reasonable consequences when he failed. She'd been his shelter, but when he didn't live up to her expectations of him, expectations he should have for himself, she'd also been the storm.

He leaned down to kiss Titi's violet-scented cheek and she let him, tilting up her face. "I see you've finally decided to let me meet your wife," she said, coolly.

Oh no. Titi was in a mood.

"It's my fault," Roxanne jumped in with her flawless Spanish. "I've kept him very busy."

Mateo stepped back. "Roxanne Medina," he said formally. "Please let me introduce Señora Loretta Hernandez, maker of the finest *bocadillo* in Spain."

"Medina," his Titi said, all of her steel keeping her back straight in the chair. "Not Esperanza? I understand in America it is common for a wife to take her husband's last name."

It was a tradition they did not follow in Spain. Mateo sighed at her. "Titi, come on…"

Roxanne merely folded her hands in front of her. "I'm sorry, *señora*," she said. "There are so many buildings I'd have to rename."

Mateo watched his Titi for her reaction to Roxanne's outrageous statement. She narrowed her soft brown eyes at her, just a flicker, before she nodded. "*Es así.*"

Mateo bit back his smile. Titi loved her little fiefdom here at the sandwich shop, the place she opened after Mateo and Sofia outgrew their need for a nanny. She could certainly respect a woman who had skyscrapers named after her. He grabbed a couple of folded chairs from the neat jumble of Titi's office—she hoarded recipes and family photos and the printed weekly announcements from mass in precise stacks—and opened them to the side of her desk. He refused to sit in front of it like schoolchildren sent to the principal's office.

"What do you think of our little village?" Titi asked, not yet unbending, as Roxanne sat.

Roxanne smiled. "It's beautiful. Like a fairy tale. Everyone has been kinder than I expected them to be."

Mateo shot her a look as Titi said, "Oh?"

"I implied some not very nice things about the Monte in the beginning."

Mateo stared at her. Roxanne could be so twisty—her devious plans had devious plans—and yet she could be so nakedly honest that it knocked him silly. He had learned since birth that to lie, hide, deter, and inveigle were the most important habits a person in power could have. He'd never known honesty like hers.

He realized he was staring. When he turned, he found Titi's eyes on him, not Roxanne. "And what do you think of our Mateo?" his *niñera* asked.

"Titi—" Mateo murmured, refusing to squirm in his seat.

"As a person who had a hand in making him, you should be very proud." Roxanne's voice seemed quiet in the tiny office. She leaned back in her seat and raised a hand to lightly pinch her lip before dropping it back into her lap. "He's a wonderful friend and lover. I'm lucky to be married to him."

Jesus fucking Christ.

Mateo looked at Roxanne as his heart thundered. Was this... What was this? Mateo thought he was going to be the one playacting for his Titi. But Roxanne didn't look like she was playacting. Not with her steady eyes, her calm hands, and relaxed body. Roxanne Medina, a woman who made him laugh louder and think faster and come harder than he thought was possible, just said she was lucky to be married to him. And god, god, god, the id of him—that little, ninety-six-pound, soaking-wet princeling with daddy issues—wanted it to be true.

"FRIENDS!" his brain bellowed. "FRIENDS!"

His Titi's long, slow chuckle interrupted his runaway brain.

"*Vale*," she said, pushing up from her seat. If it was possible, she'd gotten even tinier since Mateo had seen her last. "*Vale*," she said, smiling and still chuckling as she took Roxanne's face into her soft, wrinkled hands, and kissed both cheeks. She straightened, squeezing Roxanne's shoulder, and leaned to pat Mateo's face, giving him her beautiful rosy-cheeked smile, that smile that could silent crying babies and stun grown men and make the forlorn feel that everything was going to be okay. "*Mi hijito*," she said. And Mateo smiled at her and used every one of his deterring and inveigling powers to hide that he was lying. That his marriage wasn't real. That it was all pretend.

As Titi settled back into her seat and chatted with them about the next night's banquet and events around the Monte with all her warmth and heart restored, Mateo worked hard not to dwell on how easy it had been to convince her.

April: Day Two
Part Two

They said goodbye to Titi with hugs and kisses and a promise to come to her home after Sunday mass for lunch. Mateo escorted Roxanne through the market in the middle of the plaza, introducing her to whoever crossed their path, on the way to the centuries-old church at the other end. Father Paulo, a young priest who said he preferred the Monte's quiet to his hometown of Madrid, nevertheless chatted excitedly with Roxanne in a pew about current events in the big city. As Roxanne had the man laughing uproariously at one moment and then saying a quick prayer over them for the success of their marriage the next, Mateo was once again startled by how much of a chameleon she was.

He'd once thought of it as her manipulation. Now he believed that all of her faces—the lush siren, the brilliant businesswoman, the empathetic friend, the quiet worshipper—were all truly Roxanne.

He couldn't tell what her face was saying now behind her mirrored aviator sunglasses as Mateo shook out a blanket and spread it under the massive oak tree in the middle of the test vineyard for his *Tempranillo Vino Real*. The day had turned blue and warm, but there was cool here in the shade. On his knees, he pulled the two *bocadillos* and a bottle of wine out of his knapsack and tossed them onto the blanket.

"What?" he asked, pushing up his sunglasses to look at her.

She pointed at him and did a swirl with her finger. "In what way is this not romantic?" she asked blandly.

"I..." He looked down and around, at the blanket, the wine, the shade under the mammoth tree limbs, the way his newly mature vines islanded them in this cool and, indeed, romantic spot. He'd envisioned showing her this place, one of his favorite hideaways in the Monte, before the "friends" talk and hadn't thought to recalibrate his plans. He looked back at her and smiled helplessly. "I promise to stay on this side of the blanket?" Her lenses reflected back the dark of the tree. "You've got to eat. We'll only talk about...non-sexy things."

Her lips—sexy, sexy lips free of paint and gloss—curved and gave a sexy huff of a laugh. She stepped into the shade and pushed her sunglasses onto her head, pulling back her thick, sexy fall of hair, giving him the begrudging humor in her sexy eyes.

He tossed her *bocadillo* to the opposite corner of the blanket. "Here is your sandwich, buddy. Don't hold back on the burping and farting."

She rolled her eyes at him as she settled cross-legged on the blanket, throwing her sunglasses to the side. She pulled her hair over her shoulder, revealing a tiny love bite he'd sucked just under her jaw.

Mateo put the wine bottle in his lap, using it as camouflage, and handed her a thick glass tumbler half-full of wine.

They unwrapped their sandwiches and ate, washed them down with good red wine. Mateo stretched out his legs, staying on his half of the blanket, and Roxanne wound her hair into a knot, getting it off her neck. The only sounds besides the crunch of the baguettes were birds chittering far off in the vineyard.

"This wine is amazing," Roxanne said, her elbows resting

on her knees as she gripped the tumbler in both hands, her nose in the glass.

"Yeah?" Mateo said, warmth flooding his belly that had nothing to do with the delicious *bocadillo* he'd just bolted down. "It's made from Monte grapes. I'm glad you think your investment is worth it."

She pierced him with her eyes. "Even if I hated Monte del Vino Real wines," she said, her voice throaty and muffled by the glass, "I'd still think the investment was worth it."

Mateo sat up and crushed his empty sandwich wrapper into a ball, needing something to do with his hands.

"It has Tempranillo grapes from one of our newer vineyards," he said, tossing the wrapper to the side and picking up his own glass. "The family, the Machados, are on the east side of the Monte, so they get a lot of the morning sun. From them, you get the hot grapes. You know, high alcohol." He watched her lean back on one hand, swirl her glass with the other while she kept her full attention on him. "Their *abuela* was the one who suggested that the winemaker add Grenacha grapes to the blend—she said grandmothers need a siesta wine that they can drink and still do the dishes after." He grinned. "Though *Abuela* Machado could drink her weight in wine and still outthink me."

She sat up, reaching for him, and Mateo nearly choked on a gulp of wine before he realized she was reaching for the bottle at his hip.

"That says the vineyard was established in 1850?" she said, motioning with her glass.

"*Sí.*"

"And that's a new vineyard?"

"We began growing grapes in 880. We were rebels, hiding in the mountains from the Moors and their laws against alcohol."

Roxanne set the bottle down. "Rebels? It sounds like you were drunks."

Mateo quirked a brow. "It's called liquid courage and it's a tried-and-true method for rebellion." Roxanne slumped over onto her elbow, rested her head on her hand as she stretched out her legs.

"Anyway, in 1482, Queen Isabella 'discovered'..." He drew quotes in the air with his fingers. "...a document that she'd forged a day earlier. The document said our ancestors had been blessed in the third century by San Vicente de Zaragoza, the patron saint of wine. This allowed her to give our *alcalde* a crown and to have first pick of the finest wines in her kingdom."

He watched her kick off her sandals—her toenails were a ruby red—and twine her long legs together.

"So yes," he murmured. "A 160-year-old vineyard is one of our newer ones."

She closed her eyes as she enjoyed the breeze under the tree. "It's so weird that you have queens and saints and drunken rebels in your background. My history only goes as far back as the shoulder of the country road I was born on."

"You weren't born in a hospital?" Mateo asked, quietly setting aside his glass. He stretched out, too, facing her with his head on his hand, separated by a couple feet of plaid blanket.

With her long, dark lashes still resting against her pale cheeks, she shook her head.

"Mama had to wait and see if Bo and Hope were going to get back together." She lifted her glass and opened her eyes and Mateo watched them stutter wide when she saw him echoing her position. She pulled her glass of wine against her chest. "They did, in case you were wondering."

He smiled softly. "Your mother watched soap operas. My parents acted them out on a daily basis. Trust me, there are worse things than country roads. Castles get crowded with the demands of queens and saints and drunken rebels."

"And the demands of your people," she added. He liked the way she watched him, relaxed in the shade. "I assume the call that we *'Plantan las vidas'* yesterday had nothing to do with planting vines?"

He smiled at her arched brow, at the memory of the joyous chant of his people at the airport.

"It's one of our fables," he said. He shoved his free hand into his hair, pushed it back from his face. He loved this story. "It's said that one of our early queens couldn't get pregnant. The king and queen were known for their modesty, their temperate natures, their obedience to duty, and night after night, with the room dark and the queen's thighs politely spread, the king would perform his duty in their royal bed."

Head still in his hand, Mateo watched the soft flush of color on her cheeks. "But nothing happened. The king and queen loved each other in their own quiet, temperate way. But they were aging; he needed an heir and she wanted a child. So they began to fight. At first, it was just quiet bickering in the bed chamber. But soon, they began to have loud, heaving rows in the dining hall and throne room and village plaza. Their fights were so loud and endless that they echoed throughout the Monte and no one could find peace."

He loved her soft, engaged smile, the intensity of being held in her eyes.

"Finally, the worst fight ever, a roaring match that cracked the church bell and shook the snow off the Picos, rolled the king and queen out the castle and right into the vineyard rows. The servants were afraid to follow them because no one wanted to witness regicide. The couple's screams were swallowed up as they disappeared into the leaves and for the first time in months, the Monte was quiet. The people's ears stopped bleeding, but not a soul could breathe—everyone quaked at what would happen to the Monte without their king or queen or heir to lead them. People waited at the edge of the vineyard, torches in hand, throughout the night."

He stopped, reached for the glass that she still held against her chest so that he could take a sip of it. No one milked the dramatic pause better than a Spaniard. She watched him with absorbed interest. "In the morning, the exhausted, terrified townsfolk roused when they heard the vines rustle. They held their breaths to see who emerged, who survived. It was their king…with his arm around his queen. The men immediately turned around when they realized the queen's dress had been torn in indelicate places. The women rushed to her side. But shirtless and shoeless, with twigs in his hair and mud coating his back, the king shooed them away, and swung his grinning, giggling wife into his arms and carried her into the castle. Nine months later, she gave him twin sons, an heir and a spare. And from that day on, the people knew that if their once-staid king said he was going to '*Plantar las vides*,' as he chased his once-timid queen into the vineyards, another prince or princess would soon be on the way."

Roxanne tugged on her bottom lip with her top teeth, her eyes dreamy in the cool shade, the knot of her hair drooping heavily near her hand.

"You're going to be wonderful at telling bedtime stories to our daughter," she said, surprising him.

He'd never, not once, thought about telling that story to his child, about how he would pass it along the way Titi had shared it with him. For the first time in twenty-nine years of existence, he had a vision of it, of leaning back against the pillows, a little boy or girl tucked up against him, looking out at the vines from his child's bedroom window and sharing all the stories the Monte had stored up in its thousand-year history. It was his duty to tell the tales, and that child would tell them to their children and then to their children and then to their children, the fire of Roxanne racing through their veins alongside their Esperanza blood.

Our daughter, she'd said.

Mateo fought twin impulses: to run away and to pounce on her. Only the hesitation in her voice, her eyes lowered to his chest, kept him from doing either. "We might need to try it in the vineyard if something doesn't happen soon," she said quietly.

He pulled closer so he could smooth his hand over her shoulder. "Does it bother you that you're not pregnant yet?"

She rolled onto her back and looked up at him, her body beautiful against the red plaid blanket, her hair a soft rope coming loose from its knot. "There's still time," she said, softly licking her lips so they shined.

He wanted her to say that it hadn't bothered her. He wanted her to be glad she wasn't pregnant yet. He wanted her to want him for months and months more. If it was up to Mateo, he wouldn't impregnate his "friend" until the last day of the contract.

Mateo dropped to his elbow, hovering over her. She didn't look away. He lifted his hand and stroked his thumb across her silken cheek, over her lush lips. Her tongue touched his thumb like a kitten's lick. He began to lean close to her.

The sound of voices in the leaves stopped him. He looked at Roxanne. She blinked back, realizing where they were and what they were about to do.

He rolled away and onto his knees just as the voices broke through the clearing.

"*Entonces si las vides necesitan mas agua podemos...*" Carmen Louisa, his friend and grower overseeing the test vineyard, stopped talking when she saw Mateo lurch to his feet and Roxanne push up to sitting. Carmen Louisa smiled wide, pushing her chin-length caramel-colored hair behind her ear as the two crew guys looked anywhere but at Mateo.

"I'm sorry, *Príncipe*," Carmen Louisa said in Spanish as she strode to them in jeans and worn Blundstones, the guys trailing behind her. Mateo helped Roxanne to her feet. "We didn't know you were here."

"And if you'd known we were here?" Mateo asked, taking her into his arms and kissing both cheeks.

She kissed his cheek with a smack. "We would have approached more quietly."

"*Joder*," Mateo cursed comically as he pushed her back from him. "Roxanne Medina, I'd like to introduce you to one of our most talented and impertinent growers, Carmen Louisa de Vega. Carmen Louisa, my wife and savior, Roxanne Medina."

Carmen Louisa pulled a stiff Roxanne into her arms and kissed her on the cheek as well. "It is a pleasure, *Alteza*." Mateo also introduced Roxanne to the crew guys who restrained themselves from Carmen Louisa's enthusiasm and then excused themselves to do some pruning in the vineyard.

Roxanne smiled at Carmen Louisa. "Are you a neighbor of Mateo's?" she asked.

"*Sí*, my family's vineyard is next door to the Castillo."

"I understand I have you to thank for much of his…expertise." Although Roxanne's expression didn't change, Carmen Louisa's did, her smile stuttering, her eyes going wide and then shooting to Mateo.

Confused, Mateo didn't get it—and then he realized he needed to return immediately to El Castillo to commit fratricide. His sister must have told Roxanne about that summer, that long hot summer as an eighteen-year-old that he spent in Carmen Louisa's bed. She'd been thirty, unmarried, and wise enough to say "no" when Mateo had tried to keep something going after that summer. Now the woman was just a dear friend.

But he understood what Roxanne saw: Carmen Louisa, now in her early forties, was beautiful, strong, and athletic in her white button-up shirt, faded jeans, and work boots. She'd lost none of the appeal she'd had when Mateo lusted her after her; she was perhaps even more appealing now with her confidence, her wisdom, the humor and understanding that never left her light brown eyes with their feather of lines. Mateo simply didn't lust after her anymore. But Roxanne knew exactly who this chic, gorgeous, confident woman was and knew what she'd meant and done to Mateo.

"*Sí, señora.*" Carmen Louisa took a step closer to Roxanne and looked her in the eyes. Carmen Louisa had a few inches over his wife. "But that was a very long time ago."

"And now?" Roxanne asked.

Mateo stayed silent, cautious, ready to step in if…if what? Did he really think his brilliant billionaire CEO wife was going to claw his former lover's eyes out? Over him? Questions knocked around his brain: Why did she care, if their relationship was temporary? Why was she staking her claim if they were only "friends"? He resisted letting a very male, primal sensation puff out his chest.

"Now, Mateo is my friend, my prince…" Carmen Louisa nodded at the vines. "My boss." Her expression sobered. "And the one person I believe can bring the Monte back from ruin."

"With your help, it seems," Roxanne said, her shoulders relaxing.

"And others," Carmen Louisa said. "Not all of us have lost faith."

That caught Mateo's attention. "What? Who has lost faith?"

Carmen Louisa's brows quirked as her light eyes settled on him. "This comes as a surprise to you?"

"Why would they lose faith?" he huffed.

Her mouth slowly fell open, no words coming out as her fists settled on her hips. Finally, she said, "Because you're never here. Because they haven't seen you in months." "Months" popped out of her mouth sharply. "Because your father buys furs for porn stars and your mother drips Tiffany diamonds while trash is piling up outside your people's homes. And where is their prince?"

"I… That was a hiccup that I solved," he said.

"You solved it!?" Carmen Louisa's eyes went wide and angry. "Were you here, loading the stinking, dripping bags into your truck? No, I did that. Your growers did that. Your growers who tell the townspeople, '*No, your príncipe loves you. No, the príncipe will be here any day.*'"

He was astonished by her mocking voice. "I organized it," he said, furious. How dare she! In front of Roxanne. "I got the funding that would have lasted us until we could get the vines planted if my father hadn't…"

"Funding?!" Carmen Louisa's outburst startled a couple of birds from the top of the tree. "Funding does not build faith. Faith is built by seeing you. Trust is built by being here."

"I can't be here all the time," he said around gritted teeth. He felt like he was suffering whiplash, the quick emotional turn from his contentment with Roxanne to this from-out-of-nowhere attack from Carmen Louisa. "They have to see the blood dripping from my vein to know that I'm bleeding it for the Monte?"

She flung out her arms and scoffed at him. She actually scoffed at her friend and her prince.

"I've never heard you sound more like your father."

The gut punch left him stunned and sickened. His most-trusted friend had been keeping her opinions to herself during the month that they'd been working together to shepherd his test vineyard through the growing season.

"What good does your 'blood' do as we watch the children get frustrated at the Monte's careless decline? As we watch them decide that a life lived *anywhere* else is better than a life in the Monte?"

"I'm trying to fix it."

"How? By *proving* to them that life is better lived someplace else?" She straightened and looked out to the vines for the calm they provided. "If you hadn't come back for the growing season and only sent those twigs for your Tempranillo, *joder*, maybe I would have packed my bags, too."

The weight of shame bent his head, had him staring at the dirt. "It's not *my* Tempranillo. It's *our* Tempranillo, to save the Monte." He heard the petulance in his voice. "Of course I was coming back."

"Of course?" she echoed. "Was it the growing season that brought you here? Or the surveyors barging into everyone's fields?"

Mateo didn't raise his eyes. He'd had a hazy plan to return for some part of the growing season. At least a week or two. But with Roxanne and his work at the lab and…well, his sister had talked about taking classes at UC Davis…and the crew here was so dependable….

Carmen Louisa's voice was almost too quiet to be heard over the breeze. "When the threat of your father's latest scheme goes away, will you go away, too?"

"Is that what everyone thinks?"

"They don't know what to think. You finally brought your bride to see us. And that is good." Mateo resisted looking at "his bride." Christ, what must be going through her head? "But your father is still in control. And that is bad. You hate him more than you love the Monte."

Mateo wanted to howl. "That's bullshit."

"You know your father and mother are still demanding the same tithe while all of our services have declined and people's incomes have shrunk?"

"I can't stop my parents from—"

"You don't even try!" Although he wouldn't look at her, Carmen Louisa couldn't be stopped. "You let your hatred for him keep you away. You let your disgust for him make you silent. You keep your distance and ignore your responsibilities." Every word was a cut, stabbing far deeper than his parents could. "Mateo, I believe in you. I know you have the *ganas*. I'm sorry to say this to you, I am, but you have to hear it: You're a good man and a bad prince."

"That's enough." Roxanne's voice was soft but implacable.

"But he needs to…"

"I know." Mateo kept his eyes on the dirt between his boots as she spoke. "But that's about all the honesty anyone can handle. He needs a break."

"*Vale, señora.*"

Steeped in shame, turning his back on his friend and his wife to walk to the car, Mateo took a second from his misery to recognize that it was the first time he heard Roxanne sound like a queen.

April: Day Two
Part Three

They had other appointments that day, people he'd promised to bring his wife to meet, dinner with the town's *alcalde* and council at the local tavern, and they kept all of them. The art of faking it was one of the first skills Mateo learned. But he had nothing left by the time they returned to his home that evening. He felt as drained as a flat balloon.

He walked straight into his great room and poured himself and Roxanne a bad-idea amount of bourbon. He handed her a glass as she passed him to settle into a nearby chair, but he stayed standing, leaning back against the bar. Best not to be too far away from the alcohol.

He took a long deep drink then pressed the glass against his gut. Kept his eyes on the amber light shining in it. "Do you think I'm a bad prince?"

"Never." Her simple, instant answer helped him draw his first deep breath in hours.

He raised his eyes to look at her. She'd pulled off her sandals and curled into the oversized chair like a cat. Her glass was in her lap, but she hadn't drunk from it, if her soft, velvety lips were any indication. She looked back at him steadily.

"But you do think I've let my father...push me away from this place. You said as much last night."

She smiled gently, paused as if gathering her thoughts first.

"I...don't think your father cares where you are. Just as long as you stay in line or out of his way. You have made it easier on him by living on a different continent."

Mateo stared at her open, calm, nonjudgmental face. "Fuck," he breathed. He raised the glass and emptied it. Clutched it back against his stomach. "I'm the last one to figure out how badly I've fucked up, aren't I?"

Roxanne's beautiful blue eyes, eyes he'd seen snap with anger and sneer with superiority and flash in moments of lust-driven delight, softened with sadness for him. She looked young and vulnerable and endless, like an ocean of understanding and forgiveness that would wash him clean. Without taking his eyes off of her, he carefully put down his empty glass and stepped toward her.

Roxanne dropped her legs to the floor and stood, putting the chair between them. She put her full glass down on a nearby table and said to it, "I'm exhausted. I'm going to take a shower and turn in early."

When she glanced up at him, her eyes were timid. Almost scared. It was the first time he'd ever seen them that way. She turned from him, and Mateo watched her hurry to her room.

He leaned to touch her glass and stroked where her lips had never been. He picked it up and finished it in deep thirsty gulps.

But this tepid replacement for her cleansing kiss couldn't burn away the reality: he'd become everything he feared being.

He was weak, selfish, unworthy, self-absorbed. Everything he'd wanted to avoid—his father manipulating him, his kingdom falling victim to his father's greed—he'd let happen. His ideals had been dust in the face of his spinelessness. He'd abandoned his people to his father's dictates, and now they'd lost all hope that he could save them.

You're a good man and a bad prince.

He resisted shattering the empty rocks glass against the endless view of the valley. It would only be another petulant, useless act among so many.

He needed to make amends. He needed to talk to the grower's council and let them air out their grievances. Then he needed to gather what support he could to confront his father. He needed to figure out how he could take a real sabbatical from the Davis lab, discuss it with his partners and graduate assistants—spend some real time in the Monte.

The idea of doing any of it made him slide down the bar until his ass was on the hardwood floor.

Mateo had convinced himself that the miles away from his father were to preserve himself and his sanity. He'd apparently convinced Roxanne and Carmen Louisa of the same. "*You let your hatred for him keep you away.*" But the problem, at the end of the day, wasn't his father. Ultimately, the problem was Mateo.

He'd spent very little time as prince under the eyes of his people. Boarding school in the States, undergrad at Cornell, and graduate work and a professional life at Davis had allowed him to fake the role of prince from afar quite adequately. He'd never been forced to confront what he'd always suspected: That in his home, he couldn't fulfill the role.

It was the dark secret he'd hidden in the dark cloud of his father. Mateo feared—and now, all but knew—that he wasn't fit to play the role that his blood and legacy and family assigned him. Mateo wasn't equipped for or worthy of being the Prince of the Monte del Vino Real—and soon his people, his friend, his sister, and his lover would all realize it.

He stood and filled another glass when he sensed that two wouldn't hold off the threatening wave of recrimination and self-loathing; opened Roxanne's bedroom door and walked in when he realized three glasses wouldn't do it either. He needed just a touch. Just a taste. When he heard the shower running, saw steam billowing from the just-cracked door, he shed his clothes and walked to the bathroom.

When he opened the door of the large shower stall, she didn't react. He stood and stared, shamelessly, as the overhead shower cascaded streams down the flexing muscles of her shoulders, the crease of her strong spine, the bend of her hips, and the heartbreaking curves of her gorgeous, soft ass. This first look at her completely naked was the touch of grace he knew it would be.

He stepped in and pressed against her, let the water soothe him as well.

"Mateo, I—"

"I won't make love to you," he murmured, stroking her warm, sleek hips. "Just let me touch you." He tongued the wet off her shoulder, gloried when her head fell back against him. "Please. I need to touch you."

He tipped her chin up to him and tasted her lips, showed her his desperation in gentle pleading touches, seeking absolution in her gorgeous, pleasure-giving mouth. He groaned into it when her hand reached up to stroke his jaw, to hold him to her. His fingers traced that tender tendon in her neck before sliding down and enfolding one perfect breast. He was a boob man, base and objectifying, but there'd been too much between them, too much rush, too many clothes, too much of her on top or of him from behind, to give her gorgeous, full breasts the attention they deserved. He held them lightly now, watched as he stroked from underneath over her beaded nipples up to her collarbones with featherlight fingertips as hot water pattered against her, making her shiver and her perfect skin pebble against his hands. Dragging his teeth over her neck, he returned to her nipples, rolled and pinched those rose-brown tips, soft then hard, relentless until she twisted her hips and moaned, rubbing the satiny skin of her ass against his cock. Fuck, he wanted to turn her around and shove her against the tile, suck the water off her breasts, tease her nipples with his teeth, prop her thigh on his shoulder and forget his name. Forget his duty.

But he couldn't. He couldn't keep his promise if he let go.

He gave her nipple another loving rub before letting his nails drag down her stunning torso.

The dark hair around her pussy lips was wet and silky. He loved that she had hair here; didn't understand why grown men wanted women to look like little girls. He stroked through her hair, humming against the lobe of her ear as he did it, then spread her lips with his thumb and middle finger and pushed inside with his index finger.

She gasped, and he caught her lobe with his teeth to keep her still. She was as wet and warm inside as the shower had made her on the outside.

Her body gave and gave and Mateo took, took the pleasure of her skin rubbing and thrumming against him, took the satisfaction of her pearly clit crying against his finger, took the magnificence of being able to make this superior creature moan with want. He began to pulse his finger inside of her, first one, then two, then faster, making his arm muscles burn, fucking her good and fast and deep as his thumb worked her because he was good at this. He could make her happy. He needed to make her happy.

"Say my name," he implored, soft. "Say my name, say my name, fuck, God, Roxanne, please say my name."

His name—"Mateo!"—cracked high and joyous and pleasure-soaked off the bathroom tile. He held her up as she sagged back and shuddered against him, glorying in the feel of her pussy hugging his hand.

With slow movements, he pulled his hand from between her legs. Squeezed her hip. Curled so he could press his forehead between her shoulder blades and give her spine a long, loving kiss. "Thank you," he breathed against it.

Then he left. The pain of his erection helped him keep his sanity. Words, crazy fucking words played on the tip of his tongue, words he couldn't even know were true in his current emotional storm, and he escaped her bathroom before he babbled them and destroyed one more thing that meant everything to him.

April: Night Three
Part One

As Roxanne stood near the door of the Castillo's long ball-room with her husband's hand burning a brand into her back through her red Marchesa ball gown, she realized she might have found herself, for the first time in her adult life, driving down a road without firm control of the wheel.

She tried to blink away the heat of his touch and focus on the frail lady in widow's black standing in front of her. Tears caught in the woman's wrinkles as she pulled Roxanne's face toward her and kissed her on both cheeks.

"*Eres la respuesta a nuestra oraciones, Alteza,*" the woman whispered against Roxanne's skin. "*Gracias por amar a nuestro Príncipe.*" Being called the "answer to our prayers" actually happened on a semi-regular basis for Roxanne. But she'd never been thanked for loving someone.

She'd never had someone rub his thumb against her back in reaction.

The people of the Monte del Vino Real attending this ball to meet their new *princesa* greeted Roxanne like she was the penny they'd thrown into the well, a prayer and a promise for the Monte's revival. She'd learned from Helen that the majority of the townspeople had viewed the initial unflattering stories after the marriage was announced as a wife taking the upper hand, a proudly Spanish move. The fact that she had her European headquarters in Madrid had actually raised the town's hope that Mateo would be returning to them.

Bathing in the gleam of the townspeople's hopes as they came to her in the receiving line, supported by that hand that never fell away or left her, she felt claimed as part of this family, village, and kingdom. Roxanne had never felt more needed. She'd never felt more wanted.

She'd never felt more desperately confused and out of control.

Mateo leaned over and pressed a monogrammed handkerchief into the elderly woman's hands, a kind smile on his face and a twinkle in his eye as he glanced at Roxanne. As the woman, still crying, moved forward to greet Sofia next in line, Mateo leaned to tease into Roxanne's ear, "You know Spaniards. *Apasionada*." When he met her eyes again, it was a private look, declaring that the "passionate" natures of Spaniards weren't reserved just for tears.

Mateo straightened to greet another townsperson, and Roxanne surreptitiously admired the look of him, tall and lean and perfect in his three-piece tux, his hair shining beneath the twinkle of chandcliers, his clean jaw set off by his white collar and the thick Windsor knot of his black tie. She now knew what hid beneath his shirt—gleaming, golden-colored skin pulled taut over muscle and tendon, tawny chest hair that was soft, divots between the muscles of his stomach, the muscles of his hips. When she'd met him this morning in his kitchen, wearing her nightgown and robe, he'd been shirtless in soft, cotton pajama pants. He'd wordlessly opened his arms. She'd carelessly walked into them.

The embrace had been comfort and relief, and as she'd rubbed her nose against his chest, he'd murmured about their itinerary for the day. He didn't mention the day, or the night, before. And she didn't mention their pact to behave as friends.

She'd held his hand and rested in his arms as they saw more of the Monte, she'd stroked fingernails into his hair when he turned morose, and she'd kept her mind thoughtlessly, blissfully blank as she soaked in his constant touches.

His need for her compelled her like nothing else.

She knew he was hurt. She knew Carmen Louisa's revelations had left him aching.

Throughout the day, as they'd paid calls to the Monte's most prominent growers, she'd watched him apologize and make promises, declaring he would be better, do better, be more present for the Monte, but she could see the strain on him. The doubt. Worse, she could understand that doubt. If she had to stand in the toxic presence of her mother to have what she wanted most—she wasn't sure she could do it.

While he stroked her palm or held her against his side or absently ran his fingertips up and down her arm, Mateo declared that he could.

The melodious strings of the quartet playing in the corner seemed to bend sour when Roxanne realized that, without her permission, her emotions were slipping out of her control.

She pressed a trembling hand to her silk-covered stomach.

Mateo's arm was instantly around her. "The crowd is slowing," he murmured in English against her upswept hair. "Take a break. It's hard to be the queen."

She closed her eyes against the sweetness of his concern. "No, I'm…"

She felt Sofia's slim hand on her arm as the woman stepped out of line to face her. "Yes. I'll keep track of who comes and reassure them you'll meet them later. Go take a *descansito*," his sister said, gorgeous in an ivory-and-bronze sheath that hugged her from wrist to ankles. She gave Roxanne a grin. "You're doing so good; the Monte is already in love with you."

Sofia had slipped into Roxanne's room once again as she'd

been getting ready, but this time, the woman launched into village gossip as if they'd always been the best of friends. Roxanne told her what Carmen Louisa had said, figuring that this was the one person in the Monte that needed to know about that horrible but necessary conversation, and Sofia had nodded, a troubled frown on her face.

Right now, Roxanne could barely stand their touches. Here she had a sister and a husband; family when she'd spent most of her life alone.

"Yes, okay," she said, nodding, feeling more fragile than she'd felt since she was a tiny girl. Mateo held her jaw in his hand, tipped her head up for a kiss before letting her go, and Roxanne felt like weeping. She stepped back from them both. "Just for a few minutes."

She turned away from them and used every drop of her billionaire training to walk slowly, to smile kindly, to nod confidently when all she wanted to do was pick up her ballroom skirt and sprint away from the saints looking down at her knowingly from the stained-glass windows. In the retiring room reserved just for the family, Roxanne sat on a tufted stool and stared at her reflection in the gold-framed mirror, deep breathing and repeating to herself over and over again that she was not falling love with her perfect husband.

More minutes later than she would have liked, Roxanne stepped back into the medieval ballroom with its arched, mosaic-tiled ceiling and finely carved balcony circling the interior of the space. She felt no calmer, but Mateo needed her. She refused to think about how that need bolstered her.

Restless to return to his side, she aimed her path along the wall. She came to an abrupt halt when a tall, square-jawed man stepped in her way, cutting her off from the rest of the room.

"Roxanne Medina, it's a pleasure to meet you."

Roxanne took two steps back in shock. His smile gleamed in reaction.

With everything she'd learned about Easton Fuller, the CEO of CML Resorts Incorporated, the company trying to turn the Monte into an amusement park, she wasn't surprised the man enjoyed drawing a negative reaction.

"Does Mateo know you're here?" she asked, dismissing any pleasantries. No way her husband approved this man for the guest list.

His Ivy League blue eyes narrowed at her. "I'm a guest of his parents."

"Of course you are." She didn't hide her disgust.

"Since only one of us seems to know their manners, let me introduce you to my acquaintance." He stepped back and raised his manicured hand to a handsome, dark-haired man standing just behind him. The man nodded at Roxanne without comment, his hands remaining in the pockets of his suit. But his forest-green eyes seemed to take in and assess all of Roxanne in an instant. "This is Roman Sheppard."

Fuller watched her for a reaction. She refused to give him one.

But she hadn't been able to find any information about the dark-haired man named Roman that Mateo's father had been introducing around the Monte. Mateo and his sister assumed the man and the surveyors were lying low until Mateo left again.

Sheppard's gaze—unflinching, analyzing—forced Roxanne to raise her hand and offer it to him. She wouldn't be intimidated by him. "Mr. Sheppard," she said.

The man continued watching her for a moment before he slid his hand out of his pocket. His hand was calloused, his shake firm and brief. "Ms. Medina."

In those four syllables, she could tell he was American. "And are you a guest of the king as well?" she asked.

Sheppard made to open his mouth, but Fuller put a hand up. "I think it's best if we allow the king to explain his presence here."

Well, hell. That sounded ominous.

She needed to get back to her husband. She smiled brittlely at the two men. "Well, this has been... Yeah." She attempted to move around them when Fuller stepped in her path again.

Only the packed ballroom of her husband's people kept her from breaking the man's knee.

"I sought you out to give some advice. CEO to CEO." He oozed the confidence of spoon-fed wealth. "Stay out of the way of what we're trying to do here."

"We?" Roxanne asked. "As in you and the king? Mateo will never agree to sell his heritage."

Fuller's smile was full of teeth. "Mateo might not have a choice."

"Mateo is married to a billionaire." Roxanne smiled as well. "He's got all the choices in the world."

"That's one way to look at it." Fuller leaned close. Roxanne jolted back then realized he'd maneuvered her right where he wanted her: She was almost against the wall, cut off from the rest of the room. She gritted her teeth as he spoke close to her ear. "Another way is that the great-and-principled Mateo de Esperanza sold his body, jizz, and kid to you. The king showed me your contract. You rented a royal whore for three days a month."

Roxanne's blood turned to ice.

"You're paying a stranger to fuck and impregnate you." The overwhelming odor of his cologne was choking her. "What a blow it would be to your empire if it got out that Roxanne Medina had to buy herself a good-looking pro."

Roxanne's eyes flew up to see the dark-haired man just behind Fuller, his lurking presence and wide shoulders unintentionally shielding her from partygoers. Sheppard's jaw was rigid, his eyes steady. He was a wonderfully blank canvas for Roxanne to hide behind while she schooled her expression.

Her empire would suffer if the contract was revealed. The stockholders and board members of Medina Now Enterprises were accustomed to the unconventional antics that had made her a billionaire before she was thirty and made them very, very rich. But this... The press would have a fucking field day. The headlines would force traditional board members to question her morality, her decency, and—most damaging—it would cast a pall over the women and businesses she'd worked with. She could just see the hysterical jumps to conclusions: all powerful businesswomen must want to disavow traditional families in favor of buying babies. She'd go from being a well-respected pioneer to being seen as a man-hating control freak.

And Mateo... Roxanne felt a roll of nausea at the thought of what it would do to Mateo. He was a leader and future king. He was a scientific genius respected worldwide. It would reduce him to exactly what he'd accused her of making him: a gigolo. The coldness of the contract made him out to be a mercenary so desperate for money that he would sell his heir to get it. Roxanne would be toxic, but Mateo...he would be a laughingstock.

So would her daughter.

Roxanne's heart began to race with panic. This reveal would destroy the fairy-tale life Roxanne was building for her; she wouldn't even have a chance of a normal life. Instead, she'd be mocked as the princess who was bought and sold, the daughter of a woman so wealthy and dysfunctional she couldn't have a family like a regular person, the heir of a man so poor and weak he gave it up for money. None of it would be true. But the world was cruel, and Roxanne would unleash it on the girl before she was even born. Her daughter, the one person she'd thought would be a companion in her life, the little zygote she might already be pregnant with, would have cause to hate her before she'd even left the womb.

Roxanne would have failed her before she drew her first breath.

"If you don't want me to reveal your contract, you're going to let tonight play out," Fuller said smugly. Roxanne's skin crawled as she felt his eyes travel over her face, down her neck to where the bare tops of her breasts showed in her dress. "You're going to encourage Mateo that signing our contract is in his best interests. I know your resources are vast, but if you try to stand in my way, my response will be simple and devastating. It's effortless to press 'send' to every tabloid."

She was mortified to say that she was shocked. She'd completely misread the king. The confidentiality requirements of their agreement were ironclad; the king knew that showing the contract to a third party would nullify it. She'd thought that money, simple money, would guarantee his silence. She now understood how much he was driven by the opportunity to destroy his son. And what were Roxanne's options truly? Would she really pull out of the agreement now, deny the Monte the funds it desperately needed to survive? Would she turn her back on Mateo, halt their three nights a month and any chance of a daughter with him, as the contract stipulated?

Would she, could she, give up Mateo?

She pushed away from Easton Fuller, and this time he let her go. She smiled and nodded, half-blind as she crossed the ballroom, but let no one stop her. She needed to get to her husband.

She needed to tell him that Easton Fuller and Roman Sheppard were here. She needed to warn him that his father had something malicious planned for tonight.

She needed time, some space, a blank room, and some spare moments to consider Fuller's threat to reveal the contract. She'd defied all expectations, obliterated all barriers in her life by clearly seeing the best course of action and devising mind-bending solutions to achieve her goal. Fuller's seemingly no-way-out threat was just one more impossible challenge in a lifetime of them. She could figure this out, too. To burden Mateo with it when he already had so much on his plate, so much working against him, seemed...harsh. Seemed unnecessary. She could figure out a way to protect him and her reputation and their daughter and the Monte and their relationship...and then she would tell him how deeply his own father had betrayed him. She would let him know how the contract she'd devised now threatened everything he valued.

She just needed a little time.

But one path became blindingly clear: even if Mateo only had a chance to rebuild half the Monte, it would be better than no Monte at all.

April: Night Three
Part Two

Mateo sat at the long opulent table up on the dais, smiling as he stabbed the food of his homeland off the delicate Sevres porcelain, feeling the hopeful eyes of his people like lead weights against his chest. Each bite stuck in his throat. He picked up his wine to choke it down.

They were only on the third course; there were so many more to come under his kingdom's expectant gaze. So many more as his mother, the queen, ignored him on his right side. So many as he waited for his father, with his loud flatulent laugh nearest the podium, to make his move.

Mateo leaned back in his seat, a movie-set smile on his face, and surreptitiously breathed in the calm provided by the rose-scented woman on his left.

Roxanne was chatting with his sister. She was all at ease, up on this dais, under the watchful gaze of so many, with the ticking time bomb of his father prepped to blow any second. She never pinched those lush red lips, a move he now knew was her nerves getting the better of her. Instead, she was smiling and eating and chatting, her voice a throaty amused murmur that kept his blood humming.

It was soothing just to lay eyes on her. The vibrant red gown made her shoulders and clavicles glow. Her hair was swept up into a braid-circled puff, and although he understood there was an elaborate framework under that dress keeping the bodice tight and the skirt full—his sister had once berated and schooled him when he implied that she just "threw on" gowns—Roxanne looked so soft. The silk of the bodice, the tendrils of her hair, the warmth of her skin; left to his own devices, Mateo would have wrapped himself in her and ignored everything else.

Roxanne turned her head and caught him staring. She smiled, slow and full, and for the first time since they'd sat down, Mateo felt at ease.

She leaned close to him and slid her fingers around his knuckles where they gripped the wineglass. "How are you doing?"

He turned his head so he could nuzzle against her ear. He breathed in her scent of heat-drenched roses, wild and thorny. "Better now," he murmured against her earlobe.

He could hear her swallow. "Everyone's watching you."

He gave her velvet lobe a kiss. "Of course they are. We're newlyweds. We're supposed to behave like this. They'd applaud if I swept you up in my arms and carried you out of the room. In fact, I just might."

"As soon as the king makes his announcement, I'll race you to the door," she said, her voice breathy.

Slowly, he pulled his face away from her and met her eyes. They were deep ocean-blue and beautiful; they asked him to hold on.

He'd gone to his growers, swallowed his pride and admitted his wrongs, and—to a person—they'd looked to his billionaire for reassurance. She was the backbone they were coming to believe Mateo didn't have. Her money gave them a future. Her confidence gave them hope. And yet, for Mateo, she was as ephemeral as the smoke drifting from the tiny flames that shimmered atop the many candelabras. Once he'd successfully planted a baby in her, she'd be gone. She'd no longer want anything from Mateo. Their interactions would be primarily digital; even the handoffs of their shared child would probably involve nannies.

She wouldn't be around to watch him fail in every way that mattered. The weightlessness of her demands made him grateful as much as they made him grieve; he would forever savor the unrealistic fantasy of holding on to this playful, brilliant, sensual woman. Like the king he could only pretend to be, he caught her chin as if he had the right and gave his wife a brief, hot, thorough kiss before leaning back in his seat.

The room suddenly quieted. He looked to his right past the queen and saw that his father was standing where the man liked to be: in the glow of everyone's attention.

"Welcome, my many loyal subjects," his father began, voice booming throughout the ancient hall. The king was deigning to speak to his "many loyal subjects" in Spanish. "Welcome to my home, your Castillo. Welcome to the family seat of a thousand years of Esperanzas who have guided and protected you, who have worked tirelessly to ensure the productivity of our grapes and the prosperity of our people."

King Felipe laid it on thick while wearing a steel-gray Armani tux, his dyed black hair slicked back, his impressive gut leading the way as he spoke with arms and hands. Despite it all, Mateo's father still had a magnetism that held sway over the ballroom.

It had been one of the things that tormented Mateo growing up. He had so wanted to believe in his father.

"For over a thousand years," the king continued, "our kingdom has banded together as one heart." He paused as he let his dark eyes pass over the ballroom. "One soul. We huddled together as we crossed the mighty Picos to find shelter in our sun-drenched valley. We fought together as we protected this land from infidels and raiders, from French wine smugglers and American McDonald's." That earned him a cheap laugh.

It also had Mateo straightening his already tense spine. He could hear the silken slide of Roxanne's skirts as she rearranged herself in her seat. This was supposed to be a banquet introducing Mateo's bride to the Monte; tired anti-American jokes were in poor taste on this night even for his father. Perhaps it was now, with so many courses to go, that his father and Fuller were going to unleash whatever they were wielding.

After Roxanne had told him that Fuller and the dark-haired man were here, that Fuller had insinuated something was going to happen tonight, Mateo had been prepared to be the recipient. He hadn't thought through what he would do if they made Roxanne a target. He took a steadying drink of wine as he felt his temper struggling with his restraint.

"When the phylloxera bug infected our vineyards, we stood together. When the policies of Franco destroyed our markets, we stood together." The king's voice was growing; the gesturing with his hands becoming more dramatic. "Whenever an invader from our own shores or distant lands has sought to end us, to change us, to embroil us and pit neighbor against neighbor, brother against brother, son against father..." The king paused and turned his eyes on Mateo; the queen had the gall to raise a napkin to her eye and pat Mateo's hand. "...We have stood together.

"Why?" the king thundered, up to the rafters, weaving a spell. Every eye in the room was locked on him. "Because we are family. Because Queen Isabella entrusted the Esperanzas to care for the Monte like..." His father cradled his hands together and gave the audience his empathetic eyes. "...Like a baby bird. Like a lost lamb. And generation after generation, your king has cared for you, has protected and sheltered the family of the Monte while preserving its glorious traditions."

Mateo kept his face placid, letting the cool ease of it cover the boiling, ravaging anger in his gut. The only thing his father had ever protected and sheltered was the latest twenty-year-old he was fucking behind his wife's back.

The king straightened and picked up his wine goblet. "Today, we welcome a new family member to our Monte." Dinner guests picked up their own wineglasses as the king's eyes slipped over them. Mateo looked to Roxanne; she stared back. They both picked up their glasses and returned their attention to the king. "This new family member will bring many benefits to the Monte. This member will work hard to make the best decisions for the Monte. This member will maintain the best traditions from our past, while having an open mind about innovations to guarantee a successful future."

The king raised his glass high into the air. The guests did the same. Mateo raised his glass with tension riding down his spine.

"As some of you know, I have a new daughter."

A soft murmur of approval went through the crowd, and smiles spread across the tables.

"But what you don't know is that I also have a new son."

The smiles froze. Shock like frigid ocean air blew across Mateo's skin. With a proud, kingly demeanor, his father motioned toward a nearby table. The dark-haired, green-eyed man who Roxanne had surreptitiously pointed out pushed back his chair and stood slowly, smoothing down his tie. His face told nothing.

"I would like to introduce you to Roman Sheppard, my son and your prince."

A dropped pin would have sounded like a cymbal crash in the deathly quiet ballroom.

"Let us raise our glass to our newest Esperanza." The king's voice boomed. "May his addition make our Monte even more fertile."

Mateo saw his people glance at each other in confusion. But no one could resist the edict of their king. They raised their glasses tentatively, looking while trying not to look at the head table: at the king gulping down his wine; at the queen, who smiled and drank along although she'd just been presented with living proof of her husband's infidelity; at Mateo, whose glass still hung in the air. He met Roman Sheppard's eyes; they were dark and hard as they stared back. With the barest nod, the man retook his seat, drawing Mateo's attention to the other man who sat at the table.

Easton Fuller winked at Mateo as the grin of wolves spread across his face.

Roxanne's foot lightly tapped his under the table. Mateo lowered his glass without drinking.

"Son." His father still stood. He nodded at Mateo expectantly. "Wouldn't you like to welcome your brother to the Monte?"

Mateo fought back a wild laugh. The man was playing "daddy" to the hilt, all while digging the knife in. Mateo wanted to stand, sneer, grab Roxanne, and march out. The man his father had been introducing around the Monte was his supposed brother, a man he was somehow going to use to usurp Mateo's position and give Easton Fuller what he wanted. Mateo wouldn't play acquiescing lapdog for his father.

He relaxed his clenched fists on the banquet table and met the king's eyes. "You've caught us all by surprise, Father," he said simply. "But yes, I look forward to discovering more about my brother."

The king smiled at the challenge and intent in Mateo's words.

Mateo grabbed his glass again and abruptly stood, matching

his father's position. "I hope all of you have enjoyed meeting my wife and your *princesa*." This time, when the glasses rose and lips lifted into smiles, it was with an enthusiasm the king couldn't hope for. He turned to the beautiful woman sitting next to him. "To Roxanne."

She looked up at him, her warm rich smile camouflaging the obvious concern for him in her eyes. She gave a nod, a smile to his people, and Mateo drank her in as he took a hefty pull on his wine.

The rest of the meal stuck in his throat like concrete. The flan, his favorite, tasted like sawdust. He gulped down his port and, the moment people began to depart, swept up Roxanne and headed for the door.

Easton Fuller stepped into his path.

"Don't you want to thank me for finding your long-lost brother?" the man jeered.

Jaw clinched, Mateo moved to step around him. Fuller pulled a manila envelope from behind his back and slapped it against Mateo's chest.

"He's real," Fuller said. "And you might want to check out his birth date. I think you'll find it interesting."

Mateo grabbed the envelope and resolutely kept walking. Only Roxanne's steady presence at his side kept him from spilling blood.

Fists planted on his dining room table, still in his tux pants and shirt with the sleeves folded up his forearms, Mateo stared down at the birth certificate, the light from the chandelier reflecting off the document's gold seal. Roxanne, who'd hurried out of her dress when they'd gotten home, leaned against his side in the seafoam robe he'd held her in this morning.

"Holy fucking Christ," Mateo muttered, disbelieving as he

did the time change in his head. He raised his eyes, met Roxanne's. "He was born two hours before me."

Roxanne's blue eyes widened. Mateo felt the crater expand inside him. His father's final bomb had been a successful hit.

Roxanne snatched up the paper. "It's a forgery," she said, peering at the time. "It's got to be."

"Doubtful." Mateo sucked air between his teeth as he flung his hand at the rest of the papers from the envelope, now spread across his dining room table. "They're way too proud of their proof."

According to the papers, Roman Sheppard was the son of an American stewardess who'd been working the international flights to Madrid and, proven by DNA tests, King Felipe Miguel de Esperanza y Santos. The mother had tried to contact the king several times throughout the years and even unsuccessfully tried to sue the man for child support payments. All of those court documents had been included as well. But it was this simple government document, with its fancy scroll and gold seal and calligraphy naming the great state of Texas, the county of Ector, the town of Odessa, that had truly been the warhead.

The man's birth date was the same as Mateo's, October 12. But the birth time is what had given his father and Easton Fuller their belligerent, shit-eating grins. Roman Sheppard was older than Mateo.

His father could name Roman his successor. It would take no small number of promises and well-placed bribes with government officials in Madrid. But here in the Monte, Mateo had already accomplished much of the work for them by making himself absent, by letting villagers think the kingdom came second for him. He'd all but handed the succession to Sheppard. He'd helped his father and Fuller make a stranger the Monte's next king.

Mateo slowly gripped the back of a dining table chair as a sudden wave of nausea hit him. Roxanne's eyes traced over the birth certificate like lasers.

"Our lawyers will tear this apart."

Of course he'd have his attorneys check and double check every point. He should be heartened by the fact that Roxanne planned to sic her attorneys on it as well. But, in his heart, Mateo knew his father had him by the balls.

"By introducing a new heir, the king risks invalidating the contract with you," Mateo said through gritted teeth. "He wouldn't risk your fortune unless he was confident he had another one waiting in the wings."

Roxanne gestured at the papers, the chandelier's light shining in the silky hair she'd pulled over her shoulder. "An American with no understanding of the Monte or the wine industry is a sure thing?"

"He is if he will do what my father wants. My father wants to sell half the Monte to Easton Fuller. He needs the heir's agreement to do that."

Mateo swung around suddenly, turned his back to the papers and the room. He stared sightlessly out the window, at the view and the dark village beyond. "They're going to take it all away from me." Panic like wild horses charged through his chest. He'd worried today he couldn't lead. But to not even have the choice...

"No." Roxanne touched his bicep. Gripped. "No they won't. We won't let them."

His eyes traced over the mountain peaks, the vineyards, every detail he knew was there but was dark to him right now. "*We* may not have any choice." He kept his hands at his sides, kept them from clawing at the rising lump in his throat. Everything he'd done, every decision he'd ever made, they'd all been in service to one day leading the Monte, worthy or not. There was a sickening siren call at the thought of lifting the burden off his shoulders. But what defined him if he was not to be their leader? "What use am I if I am not the king?"

"Stop that," Roxanne scolded, her grip turning into a small fist that socked him in the arm. "You will be king. Your people need you. Maybe...maybe ruling half the Monte is better than ruling none at all."

He turned on her, astonished. "What are you saying?"

She stared up at him, eyes wide, as if she too was surprised at her words. "I'm...thinking through the options. One of them is conceding to your father. Agree to the deal with Fuller before the king usurps you."

Pain raked through him, clawed him into ribbons. Even his precious billionaire, the woman who could move mountains, was losing hope. He wrapped his anger, his blessed, blessed temper, around him like bandages.

"You want me to be Fuller's puppet?" he growled into her beautiful face, before he jerked back, resisting the urge to grab her, to shake her. "You want to watch my people become the paper dolls he dresses up and sends out on a stage? Watch our heritage and traditions become the backdrop for a royal farce? Oh wait, you won't be around to watch anything, so why would you care about the outcome?" His sense of betrayal wouldn't soften to the hurt marking her brow. "If you want me to become my father, there is no better way to it. The only way I could be king of Fuller's amusement park is if you drowned me daily in liquor and nightly in pussy." He spat the last word. "Are you willing to stick around and help with that?"

"I'm sorry," she pleaded instantly. He stalked farther back, holding his arms away from her as she reached for him. "I'm sorry, I'm sorry." He was stunned by the tears filling her eyes, the impassioned pain in her voice. "I want you to get what you want. You want to be king so I…" She wrapped her arms over her robe tie, looking around as lost and floundering as he felt. "I've never felt this way before. It hurts; it scares me. At the banquet, I wanted to shoot them for what they were doing to you. I wanted to beat them."

Mateo took two steps and grabbed Roxanne, pulled her against him, buried her head against his chest before she could say anything else, before those naked lips could speak one more terrifying, time-stopping word. Mateo's heart thundered in disbelief. He knew the shock was plain on his face.

He didn't want to hear anything else. He was terrified to hear anything more. *Lies*, a part of him beat out. The part that didn't believe he deserved her. *More lies and manipulation, she wants a princess, she needs a king.*

He buried his fingers at her nape and tugged her head back. He cupped her jaw with his free hand and forced her to look up at him, stared into the stormy blue sky of her eyes.

"I am useless to you if I am not the king," he accused, softly and seductively as his thumb ran across her jaw.

Her head shook, pulling against the hands trying to restrain her. "No, you are Mateo," she demanded. Truth rang in her voice. "My Mateo."

He couldn't believe what he was hearing. Seeing. So he closed his eyes to it. Closed his eyes and buried his disbelief against her mouth, swallowed her moan to stop her words.

He shoved her robe to the wood floor. His tux shirt and tie were lost on the steps leading out of the sunken room. Her nightgown was abandoned, one of its ties snapped, in the hallway outside of Mateo's room.

He pushed her down, naked, on his bed and she scrambled up to his pillows willingly, not breaking his kiss as he stalked over her on his knees. She spread her thighs for him and shoved her hands into the open waistband of his tux pants, scraped her nails against hard ass muscle as she pushed down his pants and silk boxers. Pulled him tight against the soft, welcoming wetness between her open legs.

He fell against her, groaning as he felt her body, her breasts and belly and hips and thighs, the first soft give of her like this, cushioning him, inviting him. She was so warm, so soft and silky, and he moved against her, luxuriated in the Roxanne scent and feel while he licked at her shoulder. She tasted cinnamon-sugar sprinkled. Still not quite able to believe it, he pushed up on his fists to look down at her. In the low light of his bedside lamp, she glowed. Full breasts and curving waist and trembling tummy, mind-blowingly naked in his bed. Her fine fingers skated down his arms, restless, and her gorgeous dark hair rioted over his pillows. And her eyes... Jesus, her eyes swallowed him whole, ocean deep and desperate, surrounded by thick, long lashes. Her tears gathered her lashes into black, delicate spikes, made her eyes deadly. Spikes to his heart as he looked into them.

"Like this?" he murmured, shifting his hips, brushing his hard cock against her.

Those lips, that fucking unbelievable mouth, fell open as her head tilted back and she nodded.

He rolled his hips again. "You're not going to turn over?" he growled, pressing and teasing. "You're not going to push me away?" She was quivering beneath him, unbearably open and vulnerable. He couldn't stop himself from punishing her for it.

"No," she begged, trailing her nails up his muscles to his shoulders as she gripped his hips with her thighs. "No, Mateo. *Por favor...*" She pulled herself up by her strong arms and kissed the cords of his neck, her hair trailing back down to the pillows like dark silk. Jesus... She blinded him. Gooseflesh and heat spread out from her kiss like he was a fourteen-year-old boy. He gathered her against him with one arm and settled them both down against the pillows.

"*Bueno, mi hermosa*," he soothed, brushing his lips over her temple, her cheek, her ear. "*Mi reina. Mi amor.*" Pressing against her again was like coming home.

He pulled out of her arms and stood on the side of the bed. Her sob of regret and need thrilled the ancient kings in him, the men who'd conquered and kept. "Shhh, *mi reina.* Just let me get out of my pants." He shucked them and then returned to her, gloried in the eager grab of her hands, the ready spread of her thighs. As he pulled her body into his arms and kissed her, her powerful leg hooked around his, her foot anchoring under his calf, as if locking him to her to prevent him from getting away again. Lust roared through him at her demand and made him snag her by the nape so he could dominate her mouth, grip her close so he could lick and taste at the mysterious power she had to make him lose his mind. She groaned, openmouthed, and went even wilder. Her hips wove a frantic rhythm, stroking her wet bush and swollen hot cunt against his shaft. Her free leg jerked up, anchored itself around the small of Mateo's back like a hot, silken belt, angling her pelvis so that the tip of Mateo's penis caught at her entrance. She wriggled her hips, as if she needed Mateo deep and desperately and now. She panted, making tiny pained female noises into his mouth.

Mateo slid his hand to her hip and held her down. "Shhhh, Roxanne, beauty, feel this. Let me feel this," he urged, his lips still pressed to her. Breaking from her kiss, he looked down at her from his position on his elbow, looked down as he repositioned his hips, and looked at her—at the gleam of sweat on her forehead and her electric eyes and her erotic mouth slowly dropping open—as the tip of his cock found her entrance and pushed inside. He did it gently, almost casually, a slow rocking as his penis breached her then crept a centimeter deeper with every push. He did it as he bit his tongue inside his mouth and sparks shot down his legs and the need to fuck hard screamed in his lower back and wet hot plush tight pleasure crawled up his cock.

All the way in, tight against her, over her and inside her and caught in the silken cage of her gorgeous legs, Mateo looked down at Roxanne, his wife, and bit his tongue harder as his cock gave a desperate lurch and released a hot shot of liquid.

"Mateo…"

Oh fuck. That throaty voice, moaning his name. "Shhh…" Mateo said, squeezing his eyes tight. "Just…" He lowered his head, pressed his forehead to hers. "*Un minuto, mi amor.*"

And she tried to give him a minute, he could tell she was trying, but her soft breasts thrust against his chest with her gasps, and her powerful silken legs trembled around his body, and her velvet-glove pussy pulsed over his cock involuntarily, the muscles at the depth of her pulling at his head like a hungry little mouth.

Fuck it. This wasn't going to last long. But it was going to be earth-shattering.

He said that all to her without words with the groan at her ear, his hand sliding down to trap her nipple between his fingers, and a sinuous pull out of her body so he could push back in.

Roxanne's head arched back in relief. "Yes, Mateo," she moaned, moving her hips with him. "*Mi* Mateo."

God, he could give it to her good and that was all he wanted right now as he moved his hips in the trap of her legs, sliding his happy cock in and out of wet pulsing heat, he just wanted to give it to her good and watch the pleasure play all over her heart-stopping face. He bent to her big breasts, bit and sucked at her skin and hard nipples because he could, he could pleasure her gorgeous chest as he buried himself inside her, as her legs moved and flailed around him but never let him go. She was demanding, his demanding billionaire, as she clung to his biceps or sucked on his tongue or drove her nails into his ass, spurring him on to go faster and harder and deeper. And she could take it, take it when he sucked his brand into the side of her breast and buried his teeth into her collarbone. Take it when he lifted her into his arms, held her ass cheeks in his hands, and teased at her hole, fondling it until it was soft and wet and he could push in the tip of his finger from behind.

Holding her, surrounding, and filling her with tongue, finger and cock, Mateo pistoned in and out of his wife with the single-minded desire to enter her body and never leave. Deeper with tongue and finger and cock until she absorbed him in and surrounded him, kept him forever engulfed in the gift of her.

His cock spurted, hot and sharp and surprising, at the thought of never having to stop making love to her.

He kept pounding at her, coming so hard, as he let go of an ass cheek to bring his hand to her front, to find and—Jesus, Jesus—pinch her swollen clit, rolling it in his fingers and stroking it with his thumb.

Thank God, Roxanne went off like a shot.

"Mateo," she screamed, her hips shooting up, lifting Mateo up with her arch so he had to abandon her clit to slap a hand down on the mattress, holding his weight as his finger still pulsed into her from behind, as his cock moved to stroke at her orgasm. "Mateo, Mateo, Mateo."

Roxanne crying his name almost had Mateo going off again.

He pulled his finger from her when her hips began to sag back to the bed. Her hips still rolled there, still enjoyed the pulse of Mateo's flagging cock. He stroked his hand over her moist, hot side as she settled back to the mattress and he scooped her up against him, settling his weight on his forearms. She was luxurious silk and warmth beneath him, and he didn't want to move. He buried his face into her hair spread across the pillow.

When he woke up thirty minutes later, it was with a jerk.

"*Joder*," he muttered, Roxanne still pressed beneath him. He was still barely inside her. "Am I crushing you?"

"No," she murmured, as if she'd been dozing, too. "But your arms are going to ache if you sleep in that position much longer."

He pushed up, slipping out of her with a warm tingly pull, and she was right; his arms already felt a little kinked. He moved to her side, fell on his back, and immediately missed the warmth and cushion of her body.

They both lay there in the lamplight, Roxanne's breathing soft and measured.

"Are you going to sleep in your room?" he asked, staring up at the ceiling.

"I should." He heard her hair slide across the pillow as she turned to look at him. "Shouldn't I?"

The hesitation in her sex-racked voice was equal parts thrilling and terrifying. It was a bad idea for her to sleep in his room, spend the night in his bed. A horrible idea. Her boundaries had saved them both so many times. What had he truly wanted when he'd worked so hard to beat them down? What had he really been offering? Certainly not something as worthless as himself. And still, he found himself pulling her delicate hand off his comforter—they hadn't even kicked down the bedding—and squeezing it flat between his larger hands.

"I would very much like you to stay," he said gently, foolishly, as he tilted their hands toward his mouth and kissed her fingertips.

Roxanne pulled her hand from his, and Mateo steeled himself for the lifesaving rejection; readied himself for the breath-stealing blow.

She pushed his arm to the bed and then nestled her warm, womanly body against his side, resting her head against his chest, laying her arm loosely over his waist and sliding her thigh over his, nestling her toes between his calves. "I'd like to stay," she said simply, her lips brushing his skin.

She couldn't have surprised him more if she'd stabbed him in the heart. She must have stabbed him in the heart because warmth bloomed at his side where she was pressed, as thick and rich as blood. He brought his arm down to surround her and press her close as he looked down at her, her beautiful blue eyes shining up at him.

He leaned down to kiss her, slow, with terror and without desperation for the very first time. They had all night.

That night was shattered by a 3 a.m. phone call. Mateo ignored the cell phone ringing in his tux pants the first time the call came through, too mesmerized by the sight of Roxanne on top of him, riding him with her siren's smile.

But when the house phone began ringing moments after the cell phone went quiet, Roxanne stopped, eyebrows quirked as she looked down at him. Mateo listened to the phone ring, wondered, before he finally squeezed her thighs. "Yeah, I better..."

She pulled off of him and sat on the bed and Mateo sat up and reached for the phone on his bedside table.

"*Diga*," he said. Late-night phone calls were never good.

His brow furrowed deeper as he listened to the person speak in English. "Okay, one second," he said finally. He pulled the phone from his ear and handed it to Roxanne, who stared at it, wide-eyed.

"It's your attorney, William," Mateo explained. "He couldn't get a hold of you on our cells, so he called this number."

"And he couldn't wait 'til morning?" Roxanne was staring at the phone like it was a rat.

Mateo shrugged. "He said it was a personal matter."

Roxanne nodded slowly, straightened her shoulders, and took the phone from Mateo. She pulled the sheet up, covering her body, as she said, "William? It's me." Slowly, she turned away from Mateo, showing him her smooth, pretty back.

It was a fair move; she deserved her privacy. It was also a punch in the gut after the intimacy of their last few hours. Wounded and not wanting her to see it, Mateo stood, planned on grabbing his robe and letting her have the room.

He was knotting the robe tie when he heard her gasp.

Thoughts of privacy and separate lives flew away as he rounded the bed to sit next to her.

Roxanne's trembling hand was over her mouth and her eyes were welling with tears. He could hear William's voice trying to offer calm over the phone.

"What are his chances?" Roxanne asked, her voice urgent. William answered and Roxanne covered her eyes. Mateo put a hand on her back.

"Yes… Okay… Yes, immediately. I want to see him before the surgery," she said, her voice husky. William said a few more soothing words. "Yes, that would be great. Thank you, William. I'll see you in a few hours."

Roxanne clicked the phone off and held it in her lap. She stared down at it. "I'm sorry," she said, her voice monotone. "I'm going to have to leave for a few days."

"Okay," Mateo said, expecting more explanation. But then Roxanne stood and, naked, began to move toward the door.

He snagged her hand before she got out of reach. "Wait," he said, tugging her back down beside him. "What's going on?"

"Right. Sorry." Roxanne pulled the sheet back over herself. "It's...kind of a family emergency."

"Your father?"

Roxanne scowled. "No!"

Mateo hoped the man never tried to turn up in Roxanne's life. He was not in for a pleasant welcome. "Then who?" he asked.

Roxanne stared down at her lap like the world's secrets could be found there. "Just...just a man. A priest. He..." She fidgeted with her fingers and looked twelve years old. "He helped me out whenever my mom...whenever our relationship wasn't at its best."

"And what's happened to him?"

She took a deep breath. "He's been in an acc—" She broke off and pressed her hand against her mouth, which had started to quiver.

Fuck this, Mateo thought, and he swung a leg behind her, pulled her back into the V of his thighs, surrounded her chest with his arms, and pressed her back against him. Rather than fighting him, Roxanne gripped his forearms tight and clung to him, turning her head to press her temple against his chin.

She started again, not fighting the tears in her voice. "He's been in an accident. They're waiting for the swelling in his brain to go down before they can operate. They're not...they don't think his chances are very good."

"Then I'll go with you," Mateo said into the warm silk of her hair. The words flowed out of his mouth. He didn't want her to leave. He didn't want to be separated from her. He wanted to give her the comfort she'd given him.

It was now that Roxanne tried to pull out of his arms. "No. You can't go." When Mateo's hold didn't ease, she stopped struggling. "You can't leave now," she implored softly. "People will think you're running away again."

Her words hit him hard, like a fist. She was right. He'd spoken like a babbling child, without considering his duties here. Without thinking about the massive, crushing weight of his responsibilities. But he let his voice ooze the confidence he'd perfected in his decade of faking it. "I can't do anything to fight my father until the lawyers have had time to look at the documents." She was silk and atonement in his arms. He ran his big hands soothingly over her biceps and shoulders. "And I'll inform everyone we're leaving for a family matter and that we'll... I'll be back shortly. I'll ask Sofia and Carmen Louisa to, quietly and privately, let the right people know the severity of why we left. A week away, for this reason, won't make them lose their confidence. You're their *multimillionaria*. They want me to take good care of you."

Roxanne's quiet hinted at the depth of her despair. The fact that she was considering this after so little convincing...

She ran a hand over the hair of his forearm. "You sitting at the side of a hospital bed with me wasn't in our contract," she said softly.

"Neither was you helping to convince my people to trust me again."

She turned her face up to look at him and Mateo met her eyes, considered her as intently as she was studying him. They were strangers at the beginning of the year, enemies three months ago. Now they were stumbling into something neither of them had planned or wanted. The decisions they were making now wouldn't make their eventual separation any easier. It certainly wouldn't help them maintain a "distant but cordial" relationship as they shared a child.

She was the first to break their silence. "Kiss me," she whispered.

"Happily," Mateo said as he began to lower his lips.

"And then we've got to pack," she breathed against his mouth.

Mateo kissed her with the knowledge that even if she'd denied him access to her plane, he would have made his own way to that hospital bed to support her. And he kissed her glorying in the knowledge that, even as she considered not letting him come, she'd never let go of her tight grip on his arms.

May: Day One

When Roxanne pulled out of the parking lot of her hometown's tiny airstrip, the only thing waving behind her was wheat. There were no cheering crowds like there had been when she'd arrived in the Monte. The dusty, two-lane highway in front of her was empty, and farmland stretched out endlessly with only a couple of silos and some barbed-wire fence to interrupt its flat expanse.

Freedom, Kansas. She'd made sure her hometown greeted her with all the hostile unwelcome she was accustomed to.

She'd chartered a noisy, two-propeller plane out of Kansas City so no one could identify her sleek air jet, and William had met her on the Freedom airstrip with a big hug, a motel keycard, and the keys to a 1996 Ford Bronco that was in good condition but banged up enough to keep them under the radar. Word would eventually get out that Roxanne Medina was back in town, at least among the locals. She'd pumped too much money into the local economy for anyone to contact the media; it had been the bribe she and the town of Freedom had agreed on long ago to keep her secrets hidden.

Roxanne loosened her grip on the tape-wrapped steering wheel and leaned back in her seat, checked the speedometer and let the pressure off the gas until the Bronco was chugging along at a comfortable 60 mph, hot wind pouring through the open windows. William had assured her, on the runway and during the many phone calls as her plane had rocketed across the Atlantic, that Father Juan was stable. He wouldn't die in the twenty minutes it took Roxanne to drive from the airstrip to the Freedom Medical Center.

She let the speed creep back up to 64 mph.

She glanced at Mateo, feeling his eyes on her like a finger sweep down her neck. "What?"

"I've never seen you drive before," he said, grinning ruefully. "I've never seen you dressed…like that." He made a motion at her clothes. "My libido hasn't gotten the message that lusting after you right now is inappropriate."

Roxanne was doing everything in her power to control her panic; she'd spent the last twelve hours meandering from anxiety to tears to not-all-there disbelief. That Mateo could still crave her after seeing her in such a weakened state, after he spent their long flight alternating between holding her, urging her to get some rest, and giving her the space she needed, pushed back the panic a bit. Even in this life and death struggle, he made her feel like she still had power.

Roxanne gave him a small smile before she looked back on the road. "I can hide behind a baseball cap, too." They'd changed on the plane into clothes that would stand out less in a small Kansas town, and Roxanne had put on Levi's, a black tank top, sandals, and a baseball cap pulled down low, her long braid trailing down her back. "Though I don't look as good in it as you do." She glanced at him again, let herself store up the look of him in the afternoon sun, the hot wind whipping his white t-shirt against his muscles and ruffling the golden waves peeking out of the back of his faded Yankees cap.

It was ironic that her princely husband naturally wore the same uniform of every male in Kansas.

He put a big hand on her jeans-covered thigh, more comfort than pleasure. "I don't know how we're going to stay undercover with *that* following behind us," he said.

Roxanne huffed as she looked in her rearview mirror, caught William in the bright red '60s-era classic Cadillac roaring behind them. "He's going to break off before we get to the hospital. He'll let us in through a side door. But he couldn't miss an opportunity to drive his baby."

"That's his?" Mateo asked.

Roxanne nodded. "It's his retirement plan. He's going to move to Freedom and rebuild classic cars. He's already got a house on Main Street and everything."

"A wealthy African-American West Coast lawyer is going to retire in Kansas? Is he from here?"

"Nope, born and bred in Oakland," she said. "He started traveling to Freedom to take care of some personal issues for me and he says he loves the place." As she raced past an abandoned diner with boarded-over windows, Roxanne heard the snarkiness in her voice.

"But you don't," Mateo said.

Roxanne adjusted in her seat, pressed the gas a little harder. "The man lying in the hospital who barely missed being pancaked on these fucking farm roads is the only reason I give a shit about this town," she said. "Without him, I would have buried it years ago."

Father Juan Daniels had been traveling from Freedom to the nearby town of Cherrydale when an oncoming eighteen-wheeler, trying to pass other cars, had stayed in his lane too long. Father Juan missed the head-on collision but careened off the road into a tree. The rescue crew needed hydraulics to extract him from his car.

Doctors had already taken care of the two broken ribs, his broken leg, and his other cuts and contusions, but they were waiting for the swelling of the fifty-five-year-old man's brain to go down before they attempted surgery. There had already been discussion of cracking his skull to relieve the intracranial pressure.

Mateo stroked Roxanne's thigh. "You said that Father Juan had 'helped you out' when things were bad with your mom?"

Roxanne restrained herself from grabbing the folder of lies, obfuscations, and subject changers she'd pulled out her whole life when someone crept close to the story of her origins. This was Mateo. Mateo had left the code-red state of his kingdom to stay with her. He'd been pulled through his own emotional wringer over the last few days, and yet he'd offered only comfort, no questions, on that endless jail-like flight from Spain to Kansas City. This proud, intelligent, and noble man who'd looked to her and leaned on her and *trusted* her was now asking her to trust him.

With the hot wild wind whipping a loose lank of hair against her cheek, Roxanne took a deep breath, knowing her next words would have her inching toward another first with her *príncipe*.

"Yes, he..." Roxanne tucked the hair behind her ear. "He runs a... I guess, for lack of a better word, he runs a youth shelter? An orphanage?" She shrugged. "I don't know, it's a place for the kids of Freedom to go and stay, no questions asked. He runs it under the auspices of the church, St. Paul's, but really it's just him and volunteers."

She squeezed the steering wheel when she saw a hauling truck on the horizon, coming toward them in the opposite lane. "I guess he first found me when I was about...four? Five? I was sleeping in Hansel and Gretel's house at the park... Freedom's municipal park has a Fairy Tale Land...anyway..." She waved off those truly unimportant facts. "He convinced me to come back to the shelter and got me enrolled in kindergarten at St. Paul's school—so I guess I was five..."

The truck was barreling closer. "My mom always came for me eventually—she kept saying she was going to sue him or call the cops for 'stealing' her daughter—but..." There was a pain in her chest. "But he made sure I got to continue at the Catholic school, regardless of whether I was living with him or with her or...wherever I was sleeping...and, you know, little things—like making sure I had a winter coat, or had somewhere to spend Christmas—and when I got older, I helped with the other kids, especially the little girls who needed me, and I'd help him with his rounds, taking care of people who couldn't get to church, and he wrote a really nice recommendation for Princeton..."

The truck tore past them, rattling the Bronco and battering them with sulfurous exhaust, and for a second, Roxanne was afraid she was going to be sick.

"Hey." Mateo took off his seat belt and slid close, gripped her thigh with one hand and her white-knuckled fist on the steering wheel with the other. "Hey, *mi hermosa, mi vida*, it's okay. It's okay, I got you." His beautiful, rich voice soothed like satin against her skin.

She breathed deeply, working to calm her racing heart, and glanced at the speedometer. She was approaching 80 mph. She eased her straining thigh under Mateo's comforting hand, lessened the pressure on the gas.

Mateo's hand slipped from her fist to her tummy, his spread hand covering her from the bottom of her bra to her waistband.

"It was bad," he said succinctly.

Roxanne swallowed, couldn't look at him. "It was real bad."

"And Father Juan saved you."

Tears popped into Roxanne's eyes; she blinked against them. She couldn't talk so she just nodded as the first buildings of Freedom appeared in the distance.

Mateo belted his arm across her waist and gripped her like she was precious. "Then I'm not leaving his side until I get to tell him thank you."

Roxanne looked out her driver's side window and bit her lip. Mateo had just obliterated her wall of denial. She'd been resisting the knowledge, but now there was no doubt. She was in love with Mateo.

It was as stupidly Oedipal as it could be. As a little girl, she'd actually fantasized that her father was a prince, a man on a giant white steed who was going to pull her off whatever torn sleeping bag or paper-thin mattress in a corner she was sleeping on and gallop her away to a kingdom of security and safety. The reality of the Golden Prince burned away all childish daydreams. Her perfect prince, her Mateo, was kind and funny, idealistic and wicked smart, driven and loyal to the point of misery. Falling in love with him, needing him, was the most reckless and irresponsible thing she'd ever done. But there was nothing she could do to stop her runaway-truck-of-a-heart.

"I…" She hesitated, terrified. "You now know more than anyone else." She glanced at him, hoping he understood.

His eyes shone like the sun from under his baseball cap as he looked unhesitatingly back. Still pressed against her, he nodded. "Your secrets, whatever you want to share, they're safe with me. *Me lo prometo.*"

She relaxed against him, giving in to her idiot heart just the tiniest bit, as she tapped the brake in honor of the speed limit drop from forty-five to twenty-five as they crossed the Freedom city limit.

She was home.

Freedom, Kansas, current population 9,456, was the county seat and was proud of its pretty Main Street, its nine stoplights, its annual Halloween festival, and its newly renovated hospital. Roxanne didn't demand that the good works she funded use her name, but if she had, the Freedom Medical Center could easily have been called the Medina Medical Center. They'd certainly used more of her money than taxpayers' to pay for the expanded hospital with its updated equipment. It had occurred to her, even when she'd been authorizing checks, that one day Father Juan would depend on its services.

But as she looked down at the man in his hospital bed, encased in tubes and braces and casts, she realized she'd never imagined that the fit-and-healthy man would need the hospital's services so soon. She gripped her small gold cross in two fingers and gave a silent prayer of thanks that the hospital was properly equipped to care for him.

As promised, William had snuck Roxanne and Mateo in through a little-used staff entrance. Acting as Roxanne's intermediary, he'd made sure that Father Juan was set up in the best room in the hospital. Now, he was off fetching the doctor as Roxanne stared down at the only father she'd ever known.

"He's really a very handsome man," Roxanne said absently. Right now, Father Juan's face was a mass of bruises and cuts, his eyes swollen shut and bulging.

"I look forward to squaring off with him," Mateo said. He stood just behind her, supporting her without touching her. "We'll see who wins your affections."

"You know he's half Mexican like me?"

"I see," Mateo said. "He's already won."

"Probably," Roxanne said, reaching down to stroke Father Juan's lax, dark-hued hand. Two of his fingers were wrapped in a bulky splint. "He's the one who taught me Spanish."

"Okay, well now I just feel pathetic." Mateo's soft words, comforting silliness like pink cotton candy, drifted away when the door to the room opened. William walked in with two doctors.

The neurosurgeon who'd flown in from Kansas City on another plane chartered by Roxanne explained that they'd seen some minor reduction in swelling, but it was still too soon to perform a surgery, too soon to determine whether a surgery would even be possible. His condition was stable, but still critical. The concern was that his swollen brain, inhibited by his skull, would stop performing the functions necessary to keep his body alive. Cracking his skull could relieve the pressure, but could also make a bad situation worse in his fragile state.

Freedom's lead surgeon stepped in. "I want you to think positively," the middle-aged woman said. "We are. But as Father Juan's healthcare proxy, you need to be aware that there could be a variety of outcomes. I want you to be prepared if you have to make some end-of-life decisions."

Mateo fit his big hand against her waist. The surgeon's voice *wah-wahed* in Roxanne's ears. She'd had that talk with Father Juan, had everything written up and notarized by William. But for the life of her, she couldn't remember what Father Juan wanted if he could no longer make decisions for himself.

William's deep voice sounded like it was coming out of a cavern. "Father Juan provided clear direction on his wishes. We'll have no problem getting those to you if needed."

"Wonderful." The surgeon took a look at Roxanne's face and seemed to decide she'd had about all she could handle for now. "We'll be closely monitoring him, and we'll let you know immediately of any changes. It's going to be a long haul; make sure to rest when you can."

Roxanne dully watched the doctors as they left the room and closed the door behind them. Rest would be a good idea. She hadn't slept in…well, she didn't know how long. She'd calmed her fear that he was going to die before she saw him again, and Father Juan wasn't going to wake up soon. She believed the doctors' assurances that they would call her if anything changed. Their jobs essentially depended on it.

She went to the side of the room and began wrestling a heavy hospital chair to the side of Father Juan's bed, the cumbersome thing squeaking and groaning against the tile. Mateo touched her arm. She looked up and willed him to argue with her and give her something to swing at. Instead, he picked up the chair and placed it near Father Juan's head. Then he grabbed another chair, placed it as close as the armrests would allow, and sat down. He took off his baseball cap, tossed it to a side table, and stretched his arm across the back of Roxanne's chair.

Roxanne smoothed down her hair as she took off her cap and placed it next to Mateo's. Then she took a seat and rested her head against Mateo's shoulder.

William came up behind them and patted her head. "I'm going to grab a nap. I'll be back in a few hours."

"Take your time," Mateo said, soft and deep. "We're not going anywhere."

May: Night Five
Part One

Over the next five days, the initial boil of panic, fear, and activity settled down into a simmer of anxious tedium as they waited for Father Juan's swelling to go down. His condition didn't deteriorate, for which Roxanne was grateful, but his swelling declined at an incremental rate.

As a woman of action, control, and power, Roxanne felt she was crawling the hospital's rose-colored walls. Left to her own devices, she probably would have been crawling them and making life a living hell for herself, William, and every staff member in shouting range. But after eight hours on their first night, when William returned after a good nap and a shower, Mateo had physically manhandled her out of the hospital, into the Bronco, and through the door of their cheap-but-clean motel room, although Roxanne had stubbornly refused to tell him where the motel was located and he'd had to call William for directions. When she'd woken up alone sprawled across the king-sized mattress sixteen hours later, it was with a note from Mateo that he was already back at the hospital and an understanding that, maybe, to survive all this, she needed to let her capable husband carry a bit of the load.

One of them was always by Father Juan's side. It was a demand Mateo and William had agreed to without Roxanne asking. The staff was wonderful and St. Paul's many parishioners wanted to help, but the doctors recommended minimizing Father Juan's exposure to possible infections and overexcited stimuli, and Roxanne couldn't stomach the idea of him waking up or slipping away without herself or someone she trusted by his side. Father Juan had been the one person who'd wanted her around before she was rich; she wasn't going to abandon him now when he needed her most.

So they shared the watch duties. William played endless rounds of solitaire, read seven daily newspapers including *The Freedom Gazette*, and became best friends with every patient and staff member on the floor. Roxanne worked on her laptop when she could concentrate, but more often than not, she was pacing or overthinking or doing some light, tap-only sparring with Mateo, the room's furniture pushed to the side walls.

Too often, Mateo stayed with her when he should have taken the opportunity to sleep. But it was on one of those long nights in Father Juan's room, stretched out on opposite ends of an uncomfortable loveseat, her feet in Mateo's lap as the muted TV flickered over them, that he discovered that she was an amateur kickboxer. He'd looked both amused and amazed as he'd rubbed his thumbs into her arch.

"How do you think I put you down in the back of that restaurant?" she asked, reminding them of a time when the last thing he would have done was blissfully rub her feet.

"With the power of your mind?" He'd shrugged before he bit her little toe and then stood, his hand out to her. "You've got to show me some moves."

When he did sleep and shower back at the hotel, he always returned with her favorite: a nickel-thin burger from Johnny's, extra pickles. She always brought him a large black coffee and a ginormous maple bar from Freedom's only doughnut shop; Mateo, she was beginning to learn, had a weakness for sweets.

When William showed up to spell them both, they played hooky and took a guilty but much needed break.

Time away from the antiseptic cling of the hospital sometimes felt too good to waste on sleep. Which was why, five days after arriving in her hometown, Roxanne found herself at midnight sitting on a swing in the municipal park, enjoying the chirp of the crickets and the song of the cicadas as she sipped on a bottle of beer. Mateo's swing creaked as he leaned over, placed his empty bottle in the carton and grabbed another, twisting it open.

She watched him tilt back as he drank, the bright glow of the prairie moon licking at the tips of his hair. He looked up and up. "These are really tall swings," he commented, the moon highlighting his perfect profile.

"Yeah," Roxanne commented, not having to look up to see the eighteen-foot tall swing poles. "Jumping out of them made me feel like I could fly. I used to bet other kids that I could jump out higher than they could."

She drank her beer as he shook his head, still looking up. "You could have killed yourself."

"Hey, it was a great way to make lunch money."

He dropped his chin to lean his forehead on the chain and stare at her. His dimple poked into his cheek, but there was no smile in his eyes. "I act like I had it so hard as a kid," he murmured. "But I was a pampered and overprotected child."

Roxanne dropped her eyes and drank her beer. There'd been no additional discussion about her past, no time for it in the rush and crawl of caring for Father Juan. Part of her liked it that way; part of her was preparing to eventually tell him more. It was the bipolar state of her love for Mateo, something she found herself shrieking away from and scrambling toward, depending on what minute of the day it was. There'd been no one, ever, that she'd trusted enough to even consider disarming herself that way. Did she trust Mateo?

"You had your own nightmares," Roxanne mumbled against her beer bottle.

"I never had to commit death-defying acts for my next meal." When Roxanne said nothing else, Mateo let her off the hook and leaned back in his seat, looking out to the large, moonlit playground. "This playground would have scared the shit out of me."

Planting her beer between her thighs, Roxanne held on to the chains and also leaned back, although she didn't have to look around to know the exact locations of the two-story tall slides, the uber-tall fireman's pole, the slick four-person-wide slide that sent children shooting off of it, exhilarated and squealing.

"We'd discussed removing the old-fashioned equipment when we renovated a few years ago and making the park less of a liability." She relaxed into the soft non-temperature of the seventy-two-degree night. "We decided to add more ADA-compliant equipment and restore the old stuff. The ancient equipment is still the park's most popular draw."

"'We?'" Mateo asked.

Roxanne pushed with her heels, set the swing to moving and let the ground slide away beneath her. "We, they, them," she said, gripping the chain with one hand while she sipped from her beer with the other. "'They' make a lot of decisions with 'my' money. The more of my money they use, the more they want me to weigh in."

One of the park commissioners still sent Roxanne invites to her family's annual pig roast on the lake. Brandon always took care of the replies.

"Huh," Mateo said, stretching out his long legs, his Wellies anchored on the ground as she glided past him. "Why do you give this town so much money if you hate it so much?"

"Why do you think we're not being stalked by paparazzi right now?" she answered, pushing off again to add a little more steam to her swing. The chains squealed against the pole overhead. "I fund this dying town, and the locals don't share information about me." It was a little awkward to drink her beer now, but she managed it.

"Is that an agreement you came to with someone?"

She swooped past Mateo. "Essentially."

"Essentially? So you didn't sign a contract or shake hands and say..."

She planted her flip-flops in the soft dust and stopped herself on a dime. "Say what, Mateo? Say, 'I will give you millions of dollars to prevent you from exposing me to the world? I agree to be blackmailed so you will protect my secrets?'" She shoved her hair behind her ear and stared at him. "No, nothing as mercenary as that was ever said. But I know. And they *certainly* know."

She felt foolish and exposed.

The man she loved now knew that tycoon Roxanne Medina never got anything for free.

She'd paid off a town. Her only support system were her employees—who she paid. And she'd bought herself a husband and a baby.

He stood, grabbed the chains of her swing, and pulled her back until she was off the ground and wrapped in his arms. "Hey, hey, *belleza*," he said into her hair, against her struggles. He'd immobilized her so fast it infuriated her. "I'm sorry. I wasn't trying to upset you."

"You did," she said, wanting to bristle up and protect her soft parts. "Put me down."

Instead, he nuzzled into her neck and the tenderness of it

soothed her with a surprising surge of lust. There'd been no lovemaking, honestly no desire for sex over the last five days. Every touch had been about comfort and reassurance. The rare moments that they'd slept together in the motel bed, they'd been out the instant their heads had hit the pillows. But now he held her effortlessly, powerfully, in his strong arms and his lips feathered his words against sensitive skin.

"No one behaves like you're paying them off," he murmured, words for only her. "They seem to be grateful. When I go into Johnny's, he starts frying a fresh patty, just for you. The grocery store won't let me pay for anything. The other day, I had an elderly lady insist on holding the door open for *me* so she could tell me how lucky I was to have caught you."

While Roxanne was physically still, she struggled internally against the soft seduction of his voice. She'd noticed it, too: the doughnut shop always started a new pot of coffee when she walked in, the nurses at the hospital checked on her and asked about her well-being as often as they checked on Father Juan.

"Let me go," Roxanne said, her skin pebbling under his lips. "I can't...think when you're doing that."

Gently, he slid his arms to the chains and lowered her swing until she could get her feet under her.

She stood and faced him. An equal even though, in her flip-flops, he towered over her. "Greed can look like gratefulness if you're doing it right," she said. "They'll stay in line as long as I give them what they need—but if that well dried up, they'd sell me for the cost of the bucket."

"Okay," Mateo said, nodding slowly, looking down at her from under his gorgeous tousle of hair. "I just thought, wouldn't it be interesting if you also had a kingdom that needed you?"

"Don't get any romantic ideas here, Mateo," she said, shaking her head. "This town holds nothing but misery for me. I'm leaving it behind the instant my mo—the instant I can."

There'd been one person Roxanne dreaded seeing; one person who had yet to make an appearance. Roxanne girded herself for the possibility every morning and said a prayer of thanks every night when it didn't occur.

She took a deep gulp on the beer she was still holding and wrinkled her nose; it had gone flat and warm. Mateo took it from her, slid it into the carton, and grabbed two new beers, twisting the caps off of them both. He held a sweating bottle out to her.

"*¿Paz, mi reina?*" he asked. His eyes were soulful and intense. He'd pushed out that lickable bottom lip just the tiniest bit.

Okay, this guy was just as adept at using his looks to manipulate people as she was. Was it wrong that she felt that just made him more perfect for her?

She snatched the beer from his hand and pointed it at him. "Don't think that calling me your queen and looking at me with your puppy dog eyes is always going to get you off the hook."

Always? As if their relationship had a shelf life beyond her first positive pregnancy test. She'd peed on a stick this morning and when only one line had appeared in the window, she'd tried to feel disappointment. Tried real hard. But she'd wrapped the stick and box in toilet paper and shoved it into the bottom of the trash can with a stupid, exhilarated joy. She was guaranteed another month with Mateo. Another month without having to explain to him this thing happening in her, without having to wonder and worry and ultimately ask if it was happening in him, too. The contract bound him to her, and right now, with so many other emotional fault lines around her, she would relax into the false relationship it created. She could kiss him and care for him and lean on him and use the contract as camouflage.

She stuck a hand into the back pocket of her jeans. "Anyway, I think we have *plenty* of kingdoms to worry about right now. What's the word from the Monte?"

Mateo gave her his placating smile before he took a deep drink of his beer. "We don't need to discuss that right—"

"Mateo," she said, cutting him off. "I am aware that Father Juan smashing himself into a tree does not stop the rest of the world from turning. What's going on?"

Mateo leaned back on a heel and picked at his beer label with his thumb. "My lawyers got my father to agree not to discuss or try to change the succession while they were verifying all the documents. That should give us a few weeks—but again, the king wouldn't be so conciliatory if he didn't have me by the short hairs."

Roxanne saw the sigh of his beautiful Atlas shoulders in his black t-shirt. "In the meantime, my father has had more contact with our people than he's had in years. He's zipping his long-lost son all over and introducing him to everyone. Sofia tried to assure me that everyone is skeptical, that they think our 'brother' is just another one of my father's tricks. But Carmen Louisa is concerned. She said my father's newfound enthusiasm for the Monte along with my absence has made more people willing to listen."

"He's definitely your brother and not a trick," Roxanne said. "I don't need my investigators to tell me that."

Mateo looked at her. "Why do you say that?"

Roxanne took a thoughtful sip on her beer. "He just reminded me of you. Something in his shoulders. He can be still, take it all in without giving anything away. He reminded me of you when I met you in the bar, when you were so angry with me but were covering it up in the guise of the cool European."

"He's a Texan!"

"Yeah…" She waved her hand over her face. "Manly facade."

"The initial report we received from your investigators says he's ex-military, an Army Ranger," he said. She hadn't had the time or concentration to read the cursory report.

"He works now as a professional bodyguard. Do you remember Trujillo's daughter, the girl who was kidnapped a few years ago?"

Roxanne nodded, remembering the teenaged heiress's world-famous abduction and recovery.

"He was the one who found her."

Roxanne's elite investigators were uncovering details about Mateo's brother while staying under Easton Fuller's radar. She didn't want to trigger his itchy "send" finger. She still hadn't told Mateo about the CEO's threat to reveal the contract. She'd had no bandwidth to work on Fuller's trap, and the last thing Mateo needed was more pressure. She would wait until Father Juan was better, and then she would tell him.

The beer burbled uncomfortably in her stomach at her continued silence.

Mateo tipped back his beer again and looked to the black velvet sky. "If my father is going around telling *that* story, of the heroic, child-saving bodyguard, then I am well and truly fucked."

Roxanne put a hand on his wrist. "Which is why you should go home."

He didn't look down. "I am not having this conversation again."

While Roxanne hadn't asked for many details of the Monte—there was only so much the human psyche could handle—she had repeatedly and daily insisted that she was fine, that she had plenty of help, and that Mateo should go back to Spain. Each time she said it, she meant it. And repeatedly and daily, when he insisted he was staying, she snuggled into the comfort of having him by her side.

But she did not want to be the reason he lost his kingdom.

"Mateo, we don't know how long Father Juan is going to be this way."

He looked down at her. "We'll give it another week. If nothing's changed, we'll figure something out."

The way he kept saying "we" had her toes curling in her flip-flops. "Is that smart?" she asked, fighting herself to put his needs ahead of her own. "Waiting a week?"

He snatched her hand off his wrist and pulled it up to his neck, pulled her close with his beer-bottle-holding hand at the small of her back. "Since when has anything we've done been 'smart,' *mi hermosa*," he said, his eyes flashing golden devilment down at her. "Why should we start now?"

The sudden press of his long, hard body against her, the wicked grin so close to her mouth, had Roxanne breathless in a way she hadn't been since the night of the phone call, in a way she'd had no capacity for when she was overwhelmed with fear and worry. When Mateo looked down at her like this, when he needed her like this, the fear of death and endings seemed very far away.

Her desire to jump up onto her toes and press that mouth down on hers was interrupted by her cell phone ring.

With her hand still on Mateo's neck, his hand still pressed to her back, she took the call. "William?"

"Father Juan's swelling has gone down. They're prepping him for surgery now."

"Now?" she asked a little wildly, her hand digging into Mateo's neck. "But I didn't get to say goodbye."

It was such a stupid, fatalistic, exposing thing to say. Mateo put down his beer and wrapped her in his arms as William continued talking in her ear. "Roxanne, there's a good chance you won't have to. Come back to the hospital, and we'll all wait together."

"Right, sorry," she gasped against Mateo's shoulder into the phone. "Okay, we're coming right now."

She ended the call. Mateo surrounded her in his arms and hugged her close.

"Lie to me and tell me he's going to be okay," she murmured.

"It wouldn't be a lie." He was heat and strength, surrounding her. "I believe he's going to be okay. But if he's not, we'll get through this. You're not alone. You have so many people who love you."

Roxanne closed her eyes and put his words in her pocket, saved them for a time when she needed them as fortification or when she could take them out and look at them, press them to her lips. He was wrong; he obviously hadn't been paying attention. Very few people loved her.

But she prayed, along with the other prayers she was sending up right now, that if she only had one person's love, that it would be his.

May: Night Five
Part Two

They'd already started the surgery by the time Roxanne and Mateo rushed into the private waiting room. She was sure she smelled like cheap beer in the antiseptic space; over the next several hours, as the walls begin to close in on her, she wished she'd picked up another six pack.

She imagined William wished he had something stronger to pour down her throat as he had to intercede—again—to keep her from biting off the head of another nervous nurse who stepped in to give an update.

The doctors had tried to warn her: The surgery to repair tissue and eliminate a large clot was going to be slow and intricate. They'd hesitated to give her a time frame. But as the clock ticked on, the increasing sense of doom made her want to flee the hospital and leave it burning behind her.

William joined her as she made her twelve-thousandth circuit of the room. "You know," he said, falling into step beside her as her flip-flops slapped the floor. "You're going to have to get it together. I hear that kids are in and out of the hospital all the time. How are you going to react when young Timmy breaks his arm falling out of a tree?"

"Tammy," Roxanne growled, still pacing. "She will be a young *Tammy*. And she will never break her arm."

William laughed, big and hearty and irritating. "Indeed. What kind of velvet-lined bubble will this child live in?"

"She just…" Roxanne stopped and tossed her hands up at William in exasperation. Her attorney had been a tireless companion on this nightmare ride. But right now, he was a pain in her ass. "She'll be protected. She'll be safe."

"So she won't ever climb a tree? She won't learn to ride a bike? She won't, I don't know, take up kickboxing and end up with a cracked rib every now and then?"

Roxanne looked up at his annoyingly wise face. Of *course* she was going to teach her daughter to defend herself. But among all the ideals and aspirations she'd considered for her daughter, she hadn't spent a lot of time thinking about the day-to-day: the diaper changing and nightmare soothing and grit-your-teeth teen years.

William clasped his hands over his well-earned belly. "I'm merely recommending that you work on your game face now. If this child is anything like you, visits to the doctor's office will be a common occurrence."

The world was large and Roxanne had never considered the reality that she couldn't protect her daughter from every inch of it. She took a seat on the waiting room couch, rested her elbows on her knees, and studied her dusty pedicure as Mateo sat next to her. As she heard the room door click shut—William liked to play chess with the security guard down the hall—she realized how effectively she'd just been managed by her attorney. Her friend.

"You ever think about that stuff?" Mateo asked, stretching his arm along the back of the couch. She was conscious, even in her mental state, of his physical closeness. Of the appeal of his body. "Do you think about what our kid will be like? What he'll be into?"

She shook her head, clasped her hands, and looked back

down to her toes without looking up. "Not really." She breathed, deep and slow, letting her concern for Father Juan simmer on the back burner as the thoughts of a little girl with her socks pulled up to her knees, running across a green field chasing a soccer ball, filled her mind. "I think I've spent all my time thinking about what she *won't* be. She won't be scared, she won't be humiliated, she won't be subject to others' whims. She won't wonder where she came from or if anyone loves her."

She was too exhausted and worried to filter the words falling out of her mouth. When his warm hand fell on her nape, she didn't shrug it off. She turned to look at him. "Have you thought about her?"

Mateo nodded, surprising her. He bent his big body to mimic her position, elbows on his knees. "Ever since you said I would be good at telling him bedtime stories."

"I'm pretty sure I said 'her.'"

He ignored her. "This child will bear the weight of a legacy and the responsibility of a kingdom. But..." His voice went far away. "I can also teach him how to parasail. Or maybe he'll be into superheroes and I can share my comic collection with him."

"You have a comic collection?" she asked.

Mateo grinned and shrugged. "Each issue is in plastic. There's a very specific packing methodology."

A breeze of joy, warm and precious, flitted through her.

"Maybe he'll want to be an industrialist, like his mama." He folded his hands together between his knees and shrugged. "But maybe the vines will speak to him the way they speak to me."

Roxanne watched him. "You always saw the reality of this child more clearly than I did," she found herself saying. "It's one of the things I admire about you."

His golden eyes, as weary as hers around the corners, widened in surprise. "Thank you," he said. It took so little to give him her admiration. And she admired him so much. She'd have to give him more regular doses.

"Why, really, did you want a child this way? Now?"

She rested her cheek on her fingertips as she looked at him. Why, really? It had been enough at the time to decide in a flash that she wanted a daughter and then put into motion the scenario that would make her ideal child possible. But now her well-compensated sperm donor had become the husband she loved. He wanted her truth. How much could she give him? "Twenty-nine is an ideal age to have a child, I'm young and healthy, I have all the resources I need, and it's not like I'm ever going to get married." Roxanne startled, realizing what she was saying. She looked into his half-smiling face. "I mean…"

He nodded. "I know what you mean."

She crinkled her eyes at him, not unkindly. "Maybe you do. When a man has the wealth and power, everyone understands and respects that power dynamic. A man can say, 'I want things the way I want them because I have the power and I've earned the right.' But we all know what a woman is called when she says those exact words."

She waited, forcing Mateo to fill in the blank. "Domineering? Pushy?"

She shook her head. "You can do better than that."

Mateo visibly cringed as he opened his mouth again. "A… bitch."

"Right," Roxanne said, nodding. "We as a society have been taught to resent powerful women. I knew when I started down this path that I would never have a traditional relationship with a man. So I wasn't going to wait to meet Mr. Right to have a daughter."

"But why get married at all? Why not buy the world's best sperm? I mean, the world's best sperm coming out of a jar."

Aw, this. She could soapbox for days about the harsh realities faced by a woman in a traditionally male role. But Mateo wasn't asking about billionaire Roxanne Medina. Mateo wanted to know about his wife.

She pulled her legs up on the couch and turned to face him. "Because I don't want her daddy to be a jar." She looked down at her hands in her lap and straightened her lopsided wedding ring. "I didn't know my father." The tiniest of white lies, just a shade from *I don't know who my father is.* "I hated that. I felt… unwanted. Unnecessary." An unprotected, barely conscious mistake. "Not having a father in my life felt so shameful. I never want that for our daughter."

Although if Easton Fuller leaked the secret of their contract, her daughter would have a far worse scandal than an unknown father to deal with. She would grow up under the cloud that her mother had bought her father. Bought the world's best sperm and a princess crown.

Unknowingly, Mateo echoed her darkening thoughts. "Even a title and a fortune won't shield our child from hardship. We're proof of that." Mateo took her hand and tugged it against his chest, brought her attention back up to his face. "But it's not the Hallmark moments that make a person," he said, his heavy brows highlighting his eyes. "Look at you. Look at all you've done. It's the fire that tempered the steel."

Roxanne tried to pull away from him. "But I don't want—"

"I know," he said, keeping a strong hold. "Of course, I know, neither of us wants our child to go through what we've been through. But I'm saying, whatever happens, when life isn't a perfect fairy tale, our kid will be fine. We'll be there for her. She'll be fine."

Roxanne's stomach trembled with joy and devastation at

Mateo's words. He was destroying her, breaking her apart with his words and assurances: *our child...we'll be there for her... she'll be fine.* She wanted to weep, press up against his chest and crumble into pieces as she told him she loved him, that she never wanted him to leave, that she wanted to make this marriage real and raise their child together. Would he gather up the pieces and make her whole again? Or would he look at the mess and walk away? Just because he wanted her body and respected her help, because he was a truly decent human being who was going to be a spectacular father, didn't mean he had to love her.

She gave in to the smallest of her desires and leaned forward, pressing her forehead to his comforting chest. He smelled delicious and she inhaled him in as he wrapped his arms around her shoulders.

She felt him squeeze tighter the moment before she heard the waiting room door open.

Roxanne stood as a young intern hustled into the room, William on her heels. Mateo stood also, placing a hand on Roxanne's lower back. She straightened her spine, ready for anything with Mateo there to support her.

"Ms. Medina, the doctor wanted me to let you know right away—the surgery went well." The woman was all business in her blue scrubs, with blue-rimmed glasses and her black hair trimmed close to her head. "He was able to repair all the damaged tissue and remove the clot. Father Juan handled the procedure just fine. They're finishing up now."

Mateo slipped his arm around her waist as Roxanne felt herself inadvertently slump back against him. "And when will we know whether the accident affected his abilities?"

"We'll start testing him for responses in about twelve hours." The intern surprised Roxanne by leaning forward, as if telling her a secret. "I don't want to get your hopes up, but between you and me, things looked far better in there than we expected. I think Father Juan will be back cracking people up at mass in a couple of months."

Roxanne peered at her. "Do you go to St. Paul's?"

"All my life," the woman declared. "In fact, one of your scholarships through the church paid for my medical school tuition. I wrote you a letter but..." With a sudden shyness, the woman hesitated. "I'm glad to have the opportunity to thank you in person."

Surprising tears popped up in Roxanne's eyes. Or maybe, not so surprising, considering the emotional roller coaster she was riding. She put a hand on the woman's scrub-covered arm. "It was money very well spent. Thank *you* for taking such good care of him. I'm sure he was glad to have one of his flock by his side." She gave the intern an impulsive and quick hug before she stepped back.

The woman's apple-round cheeks plumped up before she straightened and put back on her doctor's mantle. "We don't expect there to be any additional news until we're able to run our tests. But if there are any changes, we will contact you immediately."

Roxanne nodded sedately and said, "Thank you, doctor," before the two women smiled at each other goofily. William had a few more questions and asked them as he followed the doctor out of the room.

She turned to Mateo, who smiled warmly. "So..." he said.

"So..." She could barely get her head around it. "It looks like he might be okay."

Saying the words out loud made her feel dazed, like all the blood was rushing from her head. Thank God Mateo opened his arms; she fell into them.

"Oh my God," she said into his shoulder, gripping him around the waist. "He might be okay."

Mateo rubbed her back.

"I just… I just can't believe it." Roxanne realized she was starting to tremble. "I expected it to turn out so bad. In my life, when I can't control it, it always turns out so bad."

She was trembling hard enough now that she actually had to hold on to him.

"Let's get you home," he murmured against her hair.

"Home?"

"Home. Hotel. Whatever." His mouth slipped to her ear, which he kissed softly. "Let's get you to bed."

The sun was already high by the time they got back to their motel room—Roxanne's body clock was completely screwed up—but Mateo went around the room closing their light-blocking curtains tight, sealing them up in darkness while Roxanne sat on the slippery, polyester comforter covering their king-sized bed. Her legs still weren't working quite right.

He flipped on the tiny lamp on the bedside table. "And now, my favorite part of every day," he said, pulling her up by her hand and reaching for the bottom of her t-shirt. "Getting you naked."

"Mateo," she said, muffled in the fabric as he pulled it over her head and off. "I don't think—"

"Don't think," he murmured, his voice suddenly low and urgent in her ear as he tucked her against him with a hand at the small of her back. His other hand reached for her jeans button. "Let me take care of you. I can take care of you." He said it like a secret, meant just for the two of them, and Roxanne felt the trembling harder, in her spine, down to her tiniest bones.

"Anyway, *belleza*," he said, louder, as if he was were performing. "Not even you can get away with the perfume of hospital disinfectant." He unzipped her jeans and gently tugged them down her legs and off her feet, kissing her knees as if he was healing her boo-boos before he pushed back to standing. He turned her around and marched her in her bra and underwear to the bathroom with his hands on her shoulders.

He was all no-nonsense as he turned on the water in the tub, fiddled with the temperature when he flipped on the shower head, and then quickly undressed before slipping off her bra and panties. He pushed back the plastic shower curtain, stepped in first, and then held his hand out to her.

She stared at his muscle-wrapped body, at the big, tanned hand reaching out for her. "I…"

"If you don't get in, I WILL make you sleep on the floor," he promised.

She took his hand and demurely stepped into the tub, her heart pounding as the hot water sluiced down her side. She wasn't averse to showering and washing away the chemical smell of the hospital. But why, oh why, was he making her shower with him? Why was he turning her to face him and then gently maneuvering her backward until the water was cascading down her hair and back? Why was he tilting her head back and running his hands through her hair, making sure the water soaked it? She caught his eyes, sure that astonishment and terror were screaming in hers. He could probably see her heart pounding in her chest, like some Bugs Bunny cartoon.

When he turned her around and pulled her back against him, making sure the water hit her body and not her face, she buried her chin against her chest. When she heard the *snick* of the shampoo bottle and then felt his hands sink into her hair, she was so glad for the water dripping over her. She hoped her chest didn't shudder as she cried.

As his long capable fingers slowly massaged her scalp and neck and shoulders, rubbing and stroking, a week's worth of suppressed emotion dripped off Roxanne's chin and swirled down the drain.

"It's been a while since either of us have had a good scrub," he said when her hair was a mass of suds. His voice was rough.

She nodded, unable to speak. Misery and pleasure misted over her like the water.

He cleared his throat. "I need to rinse your hair. Can you… Are you okay to turn around now?"

She sniffed and nodded again. She turned to him and lifted her face. Of course, he had known she was crying. But rather than commenting on her tear trails, he smiled gently and then swirled her long hair on top of her head like whipped topping.

She swiped at a drip of suds that fell on her nose. "What are you, ten?" she croaked, still sniffing.

He eyed his masterpiece. "I think I used too much shampoo." He tilted his head the other direction. "This is the first time I've washed a woman's hair."

Roxanne bit her lip to keep the waterworks from starting up again. But Mateo seemed to notice anyway, because he once again backed her up into the warm water and tilted her head back into its spray.

"Close your eyes." His command was a canyon echo in the brown-tiled space. Roxanne did close her eyes and focused on the pleasure: his hard front barely skimming her body, his big hands gently combing into her hair, tilting her this way and that. He worked conditioner in from scalp to tip, slow, long strokes, and then Roxanne felt nothing but the hot blast of the water for a few moments. She jumped and opened her eyes when she felt a wet cloth stroke down her arm.

With suds in his hair and soap dripping from his just-washed golden body, Mateo ran the washcloth up the inside of her arm, giving a little extra scrub to her armpit, and down her side. She watched his quick, efficient movements, watched his eyes trace over her body as he ran the washcloth over it, over her breasts and tummy, down her hips, kneeling to get at the long length of her legs and her feet, and then back up to wash her back, her ass and between her legs. He did slow then, gave a swirl to her pubic hair and then spread her to gently clean the tender pink flesh. He watched intently as he did it. He absently licked his perfect, bitable upper lip as he looked at her pussy.

His pussy. He made her feel owned and needed and valuable and beautiful.

"Mateo…" she whispered.

But she was interrupted by his "All clean!" announcement, loud and jarring against the tile. "Now rinse." His hands swept over her as he rinsed her, turning her as he wished and working through her hair. She felt dizzy with his care, unsure of it, unfamiliar with it, wanting the more stable ground of mutual lust but craven for the tender way he was seeing to her needs. He kept a steadying arm around her hips as he rinsed his own body and hair, making sure she stayed in the warm spray with him, and then he grabbed one of the motel's towels, turning off the water so he could dry her off while she stayed in the steam-filled enclosure.

With the thin towel tucked around her and anchored between her breasts, Mateo quickly dried himself off, wrapped the towel around his hips, and then led her out of the bathroom.

"Are you hungry?" Mateo asked as he looked around the dim room, still only lit by the bedside lamp.

Roxanne made a small grunt of disgust.

He smiled absently as he continued to look around. "We'll sleep then get you a burger. Where's your brush? And that lotion? Right. In the bathroom. *Por supuesto.*" Although he held her hand, she could have been in another room. "I'll brush your hair and then tuck you into..."

He turned to glance at her, his eyes almost sliding past her. But he stopped. Mateo's grasp on her hand was suddenly hard, almost painful, as his golden eyes focused on her face, free of makeup; her wet hair coiled in a rope and trailing over her shoulder; and her body, barely covered by the too-tiny, too-thin white motel towel.

His dark brows furrowed over his beautiful eyes. "*Joder*," he breathed.

Roxanne's mouth trembled open. "Mateo..."

He halved the distance between them, his eyes burning over her face and body. "I'm sorry." His low voice was a hot wind over her skin. "I... I just want to take care of you."

"Yes," she moaned, swaying into his hard, naked chest. Pinprick sensation raced across every inch of her.

"No, I mean..." He ran a calloused finger over her jaw like he couldn't help it. "You need your rest." He brushed against the bruises of sleeplessness under her eyes.

The joking, his overloud voice belying his tender touches, they'd all been in avoidance of this—this intimacy, this intensity that had built up between them over this last week. He'd tried to build up a wall. Now he was tearing it down and Roxanne wanted to pulverize every last brick.

"I need *you*," she pleaded, pressing up against him, stroking her hands over his beautiful face and into his wet, curling hair. "Please, Mateo. Please take care of me."

"Yes," he said, without pause, without hesitation as he bent to kiss her. "Yes, *mi vida, mi mujer*. Whatever you need." The kiss she expected to be desperate was soft and thorough, an exploration of her lips and her tongue, her own mouth answering and kissing, kissing. Her towel dropped to the floor and he molded his hands to her breasts, took their heavy weight, slid over her skin like he was enjoying its silk and then feathering over her nipples. His mouth slid from her mouth, down her neck, over her chest for soft bites to her skin before licking to her nipple, bending low to take it into his mouth and bite, suck, and stroke at her like it was one of the chocolate truffles he liked to savor.

His position made his towel slip off his body, and Roxanne ran her hands down the sleek muscles that stood out against his back. She pushed against his shoulder and as he stood, she burrowed against him, wanting to feel him against every inch of her.

"Sweet silk," he breathed into her ear as he surrounded her in his arms and turned her toward the bed. "My sweet silky *mujer.*"

He pulled her down with him and, seeming to understand her need for his skin, kept her pressed against him as he arranged them on the bed. He buried his arms beneath her, holding her close, as she held him between her thighs and twined her legs around his. He felt so good, so big and warm and grounding as he held her against the cool slippery comforter, that she rocked them with the pleasure of it, joy bubbling up inside her like champagne, fighting a laugh that was as unexpected now as the crying in the shower.

"Make love to me, Mateo," she begged into his ear, running her hands down his back and over his ass, his skin still hot and damp from the shower. She rocked and rolled beneath him. "Please, please, *mi esposo.* Please, *mi Mateo.*"

"Yes, yes," he said, pulsing against her, kissing her neck and her ear. "Just…" He bit at her jaw and pulled back only slightly, just enough to meet her eyes. He was so beautiful and careful in the weak lamplight that he made her want to cry. "Just, Roxanne, you're not ovulating now. You know that, right? It's less likely I can make you pregnant now?"

She met his eyes, the intensity in them, saw both the question and the demand. Saw his tenderness and the clear line he was drawing in the sand.

She stroked her hands over his hard jaw, pushed back his wet hair against his skull, and tilted up her hips so that his penis swept against her entrance. "Yes, Mateo. I…" She wouldn't say the word. She couldn't. Not right now. Not yet. "I…want you. I need you." His eyes were so brilliant as he looked into hers she wondered how she ever held herself away from him. "You. Not just the baby you can give me."

Wrapping herself around him, holding him close, Roxanne adjusted her hips and kept her eyes open as her husband slowly, achingly pulsed into her until he was as deep as he could go. She gripped him close as he moved against her, arched into his hands as she squeezed around him. She stroked wherever she could and let him kiss whatever he could reach. They muttered senselessness into each other's skin and their cells recorded every word.

For the first time in her life, Roxanne Medina made love.

May: Day Seven

"Faster," Roxanne urged, gripping Mateo's arm.

Mateo bore down and went faster.

"Harder," she demanded.

He whipped his head to look at her. "How much harder do you think I can push?"

"Put some muscle behind it, *Príncipe*," she ordered. She gave a thump to the ancient dashboard. "Why are you driving anyway?"

Mateo jammed the pedal down on the dirty mat, making the Bronco squeal around a rusted Toyota Tercel that honked its horn at him. "Because you barely know your own name before coffee," he said as he spotted the top of the Freedom Medical Center over the trees. "And you can afford to bail me out of jail when I get arrested for breaking the sound barrier."

Father Juan was awake and responsive.

Roxanne's phone had jarred them upright with the news this morning. They'd been dead to the world in their dark womb of a cheap motel room, as exhausted by the week's tension as they were by yesterday's revolutionary lovemaking, a lovemaking interrupted only when pizza was delivered at sunset and sleep dragged them down to its depths.

As Mateo flew over the sun-soaked, small-town streets, the blue Kansas sky stretching out all around them and Roxanne shifting in her seat like a little girl eager for the bell on her last day of school, he felt fucked in all of the best and worst ways.

She was astonishing. She needed him.

She was vulnerable. She could pulverize him.

He was her husband. He could give her comfort and support, a good time, and a hard shagging.

He could give her little else. He was a temporary husband and a worthless prince on the verge of losing his kingdom, his legacy for their child, his pride, his life's work, and any hope that he could control his destiny.

He never should have fought the contract. He should have relaxed into its depths and let it create three perfect nights to kiss and stroke and adore Roxanne Medina, nights free of the emotional turmoil and what-ifs and chances for mind–heart–soul rending disappointment and disillusionment. What if some day in the near future, when Father Juan was on the mend and Roxanne had her bearings again, his wife looked up from his shoulder and decided that it wasn't that strong of a shoulder to lean on?

She'd not asked for anything outside of the terms of their contract. And why would she? What, honestly, could Mateo even offer her when she offered so much: wisdom, beauty, security for so many people (including his own), a soft place for Mateo to lay his pathetic head. What were the chances, if he was honest with himself, that he could hang on to a woman like Roxanne Medina? His own father hadn't found much to recommend him; it was an old wound that wasn't supposed to smart anymore. But the idea of seeing his father's bored disdain in Roxanne's eyes was enough to make Mateo wish that he'd simply met her in any number of luxury hotel beds and fucked her until neither of them could speak.

I need you, she'd told him as she'd gripped him tight. *You. Not just the baby you can give me.* Christ, he'd forced the words out of her, made her say them after she'd faced the possible loss of her father figure, after Mateo had primed her with his hands and teased her with his body. He could have gotten her to admit to being a spotted mare at that moment. A beautiful, iridescent, rainbow-winged unicorn.

He squeezed the steering wheel and gritted his teeth into what he hoped looked like a smile as they screeched into the hospital parking lot.

William, Freedom Medical Center's head doctor, and the intern from yesterday met them at the hospital entrance. He and Roxanne had given up using side doors or trying to remain anonymous, although Mateo had shoved on a baseball cap as a matter of habit. Everyone in Freedom seemed to know they were in town, and if they'd wanted to reveal their resident billionaire and prince to the press, they would have done it already. With her perfect face free of makeup and her hair pulled back into a braid that trailed down her pale blue t-shirt dress, Roxanne was as naked and exposed as he'd ever seen her.

"How is he?" Roxanne asked without slowing her step as she walked through the sunlit lobby. Mateo became part of the orbit that circled around her.

"He's groggy," the doctor said. "He may fade in and out easily and not everything is going to be coherent. But that's okay. We're pleased with his responses considering what he's been through."

"Are there any concerns?" Roxanne asked once they were in the elevator.

"He's had massive brain trauma, so he's not out of the woods yet," she said honestly, watching Roxanne. "We're going to continue monitoring him. But all indications are that he's going to continue improving."

The intern spoke up. "When you see him…" She stopped for a moment, choosing her words as the elevator doors opened. "He's foggy, he's on pain meds, he may fall asleep in the middle of a sentence. He won't be the Father Juan we're used to."

Roxanne stepped out of the elevator, giving the women a troubled frown. She absently wrapped her fingers around her small, rose-gold cross. "Will he be that man again one day?"

The intern smiled, that full smile of a spiritual person who'd found peace in a world with their God at the helm. Mateo was always envious of those people. "I'm praying for it."

The doctor and intern left them outside Father Juan's room with reassurances that they would keep Roxanne informed of the man's progress. William quickly mentioned that parishioners from St. Paul's were desperate to help out.

"I've set up a schedule to allow people to come and sit with him," he said. "You two need a break and more sleep."

It was a measure of how distracted and desperate to see Father Juan she was when Roxanne just nodded in agreement. As she grabbed the handle, William unfolded the newspaper he'd been holding under his arm and leaned back on the doorjamb.

"What are you doing?" she asked him.

"Giving you some privacy."

"Absolutely not," she demanded. William smiled, lifting his bushy gray brows. "You've been at his bedside as much as we have and you're a dear friend to all of us. C'mon!"

Mateo bit back a smile at her annoyance at having to state what to her was obvious. For a woman who described herself as cold, Roxanne Medina was one of the most openhearted people he'd ever met.

Roxanne opened the door gently, and Mateo and William followed her inside. The room was dim, all the blinds tilted just enough to add a dusky glow to the room. In his white bed, with a white cast encasing an arm and a leg and a white bandage wrapped around his head, Father Juan was easy to see. The three of them paused as one when Father Juan turned his head toward them, his brown eyes blinking open groggily. It was shocking to see the still, small form they'd kept watch over for a week move and react.

"*Mija,*" he croaked, the voice that apparently boomed at Sunday mass now barely a whisper.

Roxanne moved forward quickly and wrapped her hands over the bed railing. She said nothing as Mateo and William hung back.

"*Mija?*" the man whispered again. "Why are you crying?" Only then did Mateo notice her tremors in the shoulder blades pressed against the thin t-shirt material. He stepped closer, put his hand against the small of her back.

"I'm crying because…" Roxanne stopped, trying to clear the heartbroken huskiness from her voice. She put a hand against her chest. "I'm crying because I was afraid I'd never get to hear you call me 'your daughter' again. I'm so…" She turned her head away, and they were all quiet as they gave this strong woman a moment to compose herself. Mateo rubbed small soothing circles with the flat of his palm.

The frail man in the bed looked so different than the vibrant priest Roxanne had described in small slips and bursts, little details of her past she hadn't even realized she was surrendering. Father Juan who'd crocheted mangled and ugly Christmas stockings for all the shelter kids, who drove a Prius and bullied the whole town into energy-efficient streetlights, who taught Roxanne Spanish by speaking it to her exclusively for days on end—driving her insane—and who gave her a rosary and taught her its prayers as a form of meditation, as a way to center herself and think beyond herself when life was at its worst.

Mateo had much to thank the man for even though he didn't know him: Father Juan had been a stalwart wall in the storm of Roxanne's life, the one resolute protector who'd sheltered her with kindness and intelligence. Now, it looked like the weight of Father Juan's casts were the only thing keeping him from blowing away.

"William, *hermano*, you're here?" the man asked, as if unsure of his vision.

William stepped closer to the bed. "Of course, Father Juan. I wouldn't be anywhere else."

"If you're here and Roxanne is here, who is running the company?"

William smiled. "Roxanne has created a company that runs pretty well on its own for a time. How are you feeling?"

"Tired," the man croaked. "The doctors said I ran into a tree?"

Roxanne gently touched the hand that was free of a cast, although two of Father Juan's fingers were splinted. "You were forced into a tree. When I find that trucker…"

"*Mija*, forgiveness is divine."

"And revenge is sweet," she declared.

Father Juan's dazed smile and slow-blinking eyes were an indication of the meds he was on. "I've missed you," he said. His voice was unaccented except when he spoke Spanish.

Mateo watched his wife bite her lower lip as she looked down at the priest, her long braid trailing over her shoulder. "I've missed you, too."

"Why didn't you tell me you were getting married?"

Mateo felt her stiffen under his hand. Her teeth sank deeper into her lip. "I…"

Mateo stepped up to the bed's rails. "I rushed her into it," he said, slipping an arm around her waist. "*Perdóname, Padre.* I had to have her."

But instantly, Roxanne was elbowing him away. "No," she said. She met Mateo's eyes. "No. I don't lie to him."

She looked down at Father Juan. "I didn't tell you and

I haven't called you back because...because I was ashamed. Not of him..." Her voice lowered when her lovely blue eyes touched on Mateo. "Not of you," she promised. "But of what I did to get what I want. I was afraid..." Her voice lowered to a whisper as her fingers white-knuckled the railing. "I was afraid you'd be disappointed in me."

Father Juan's bruised brow furrowed further. Mateo was unsure how many of Roxanne's words were slipping through. "Never, *mi hija*," the man murmured. "How many times do I have to tell you? I could never be disappointed in you. Stop trying to prove your worth. Your value is beyond measure."

Silent tears tracked down Roxanne's cheeks. Mateo felt a little misty-eyed himself.

Then the priest suddenly focused his gaze on Mateo. "*Príncipe*, I want to share one piece of advice with you."

"Yes, *Padre*?"

"Don't hurt her. My grandmother was a *bruja* in Mexico and taught me some curses."

"Father Juan!" Roxanne scolded.

"Don't forget." The man, who up until this moment Mateo had thought of as frail, turned his bandaged head and snuggled into his pillow. "I already have the holy water and consecrated earth," he murmured. "All I need are the chicken feet..."

With a heavy, satisfied breath, Father Juan fell asleep while William chuckled, Roxanne adjusted his blankets, and Mateo tried to maintain his cynicism as a lapsed Catholic while the former altar boy in him sweated at the idea of a priest aiming curses in his direction.

Roxanne finally relented to leave two hours later when Father Juan still hadn't woken up and the first of the parishioners scheduled to watch over the sleeping priest showed up. The parishioners, a mustached, tattooed and chaps-wearing man and his petite wife, lugging her motorcycle helmet and also wearing chaps, had thrown their arms around Mateo's stiff billionaire, thanking her for her donation to the Southeast Kansas chapter of Bikers Against Child Abuse.

"We never coulda made it to the national rally in Austin without your help," the wife told Roxanne, looking up through tears and a pile of eye makeup. "Half of the chapter woulda had to stay home."

The husband, who seemed to finally understand who he was gripping, stepped back from Roxanne, his sweaty palms leaving trails on his leather chaps. "Darnell, Honey, and Johnny Ray were real, real grateful."

The large, muscular man bumped into Mateo as Roxanne tried to extricate herself from his wife. "You work for 'er?" the man asked.

Mateo, who'd been a lifelong favorite of the international paparazzi and who'd gotten into the habit of wearing baseball caps partly to shield his face, merely nodded. "Yep."

"Then take real good care of her. That's one special lady." He crossed mammoth arms over his "Live to Ride, Ride to Live" t-shirt. "Y'all need anything, you just call over t'the salvage yard and ask for Bulldog."

"Will do," Mateo affirmed.

Roxanne scolded him on their ride down in the elevator.

"Don't let people think you work for me," she said. "Tell them who you are."

Mateo shrugged. "I'm glad to meet people who don't know who I am. People have more to do with their time than worry about the comings and goings of the Golden Prince."

She trailed her hand down her long braid. "You can tell them you're my husband."

Mateo nodded slowly. "I can. But...it's an impermanent state. If they don't know already, why should I tell them just so one more person can be titillated by our divorce in a few months."

Roxanne looked up at the descending numbers and Mateo would have assumed that everything was fine if she hadn't pinched her full bottom lip, just for a moment, before she dropped her hands and clasped them in front of her baby-blue skirt. She kept her eyes on the elevator panel.

A frisson of awareness buzzed up Mateo's spine.

"Don't you agree?" he asked, watching her face. "We don't need to promote this 'wedded bliss' story line while we're in town. I'll probably never see these people again, you know, since our marriage has an end date."

He tilted closer for an answer and let the silence brew up around them in the confines of the elevator car. "Maybe..." she finally said, her beautiful eyes still on the numbers. "Maybe we can just see how it goes."

That buzz rattled down his legs, his arms, almost shaking his teeth in surprise. "See how what goes?"

The elevator dinged and the doors opened. Roxanne strode out—she always walked like it was a game of Follow the Leader—and Mateo was right on her heels.

"We can see how what goes, Roxanne?" he demanded as they strode down the hospital hallway, careless of the people in their vicinity.

She looked around and shushed him. "Just...us," she said quietly but without slowing down as she headed to the hospital exit, a bright sun and blue sky showing beyond the glass door. "Maybe we can see how 'us' goes. We don't have to rush into a divorce." Beyond stunned, beyond shocked, Mateo bit back an urge to laugh and shrug off her words. Was she fucking with him? "And what about your contract?" he asked, more demanding than he needed to be.

"We didn't know we'd like each other when we signed

that contract," she said, chin high and shoulders back as she walked through the glass doors into a blazing summer day. "We didn't know we would support each other." She glanced at him and Mateo felt the quick hot stroke of those blue eyes. "There is a lot that contract doesn't cover."

Panic threatened to choke him like a garrote. "But why do you want to—"

"Well, it's about goddamned time!" Underneath the shade of the overhang that protected patients being picked up or dropped off, a harsh female voice called out. Mateo blinked, his eyes still adjusting to the bright light. Out of the shadows, a blonde woman in jeans and high heels came clacking up to them. "You're in town a week and you can't take a second to come see your mother?"

Mateo straightened in surprise.

"D'you know I had to hear it from the bartender at the country club that you're in town?" The woman had a long, bedazzled talon pointed at Roxanne. On spindly heels, she was taller than his flip-flop-wearing wife. "You know how embarrassing that was for me? Just when I got all those bitches kissing my ass for money for their social clubs, you give 'em an excuse to laugh at me."

The woman seemed to have no care for the filth spewing out of her mouth, or the people coming and going who could hear it. Mateo tilted his head at her in wonder.

"Mateo," Roxanne said quietly, looking down. "This is my mother, Tonya Medina."

Inside of a blink, he was pulled into the woman's tight embrace. Rock-hard breasts poked into his chest and he was engulfed in the scent of menthols and musk, an acrid and overwhelming odor. "You poor thing," Tonya said into his ear. She had the harsh rasp of a lifelong smoker, a bastardized echo of Roxanne's throatiness. "What you gotta put up with to be married to this one." She stroked his back. "But we can put up with anything for the right price, am I right?"

Mateo jolted back from her and Tonya smiled, her full lips sticky and shiny.

Well-done plastic surgery made it look improbable that the woman was Roxanne's mother, but Mateo could see hints of resemblance in the mouth and the shape of her eyes, even though those eyes were green. Whatever her hair color had originally been, she was now a blonde, big curls cut at her shoulders and frosted at the tips. She was...attractive; Mateo imagined that she'd been beautiful once, with those lips and the carriage of a woman who'd always known that men looked. What had worked then, what Mateo found so off-putting now, was the way she looked back. She stared at a man, even her son-in-law, like she was starving. And he was her feast.

He had no idea how to respond.

"Mom, I've been busy with Father Juan." Roxanne had put on her sunglasses and she seemed to be looking somewhere beyond Tonya's left shoulder. "I planned on coming by when he was better."

Tonya *tsked*, crossing her arms in her silk tank top and plumping her breasts up high. "That man's still got his grip on you. You're a full-grown woman but you act like you've got Stockholm Syndrome or something." She cocked her hip toward Mateo. "You're not buying into her bullshit, are you? That man practically kidnapped her when she was little. He should be rotting in jail; he's lucky he had the chance to be hit by a truck!"

Mateo straightened, ready to hold back his wife, but she just kept that still, sunglass-covered gaze aimed over her mother's shoulder.

Tonya raised the back of her hand to her mouth, leaning

closer to Mateo. "I mean, we all know what priests get up to," she fake whispered. "It's revoltin'."

Mateo finally noticed the people around him through his shock, the way they hustled past, eyes pointed at the ground. Everything he'd ever learned about small-town nosiness was defied by the way the people of Freedom were actively trying to give Roxanne privacy for this very public humiliation.

"I've asked you not to talk about him that way," Roxanne said, dispassionately. Where had she gone?

Her mother rolled her eyes. "You never could take a joke. At least I knew where to track you down. It's about time I met this looker."

She took a step closer and hooked her sharp fingernails into the edge of his t-shirt sleeve. "She's gonna tell you a lot of nonsense," the woman murmured near Mateo's shoulder. "Don't listen to her. You wanna know the truth, you come talk to me. My door is open anytime."

She turned her head and gave Roxanne a predator's smile. She'd positioned them so anyone glancing over would assume Mateo was with her. "So when y'all coming by the house?"

"Soon." Roxanne was far away.

"Don't make me wait too long. You gotta see the new pool I put in. It's got a waterfall and everything. And we should probably talk terms." Mateo flinched as her nail tapped at his elbow. "Looks like there's going to be a few more people eating into the pie. I'm gonna need to protect my cut."

With a final nail stroke down his arm, Tonya Medina grinned at her daughter and then turned, her hips rolling in her low-slung jeans as she walked away. Mateo laced his fingers through his wife's and tugged her to get her moving, glad he'd parked their SUV in the opposite direction. He walked fast, let the Kansas sunshine burn away that woman's touch and presence.

He pushed Roxanne into the passenger side, slammed his door on the driver side, and cranked the air conditioning. They sat in the turbo engine roar as the ancient AC filled the interior with hot air.

"You should head back," he heard Roxanne say quietly.

"What?"

Roxanne was looking out the passenger window, her chin in her hand and her sunglasses still on. "I'm going to stay at least another week, make sure Father Juan is on the mend. But you should go back to the Monte and start—"

"*Joder*, like hell I will!" Mateo burst out. "I'm not leaving you alone with that viper!"

Roxanne slipped her head down so her hand fully covered her mouth.

"Hey, hey," he said, turning her to face him. He took his ball cap off and then reached up to slide her oversized sunglasses off her face. The coolness in her eyes… She might as well have still been wearing the glasses.

"Hey!" he said, shaking that sleek arm in his grip. "She's the worst. She's a fucking nightmare. She needs to meet the king, they'd be a match made in heaven. All this time, I thought I had it so fucking bad. But she…" He jabbed his finger toward the window. "Your mother is a goddamned sociopath." He leaned close to make her see. "And you still turned into this brilliant, ambitious, kind, generous creature. She uses her body like a…guillotine, and yet you…" Mateo closed his eyes and pulled Roxanne toward him, burying his head against her neck. "You're a gift. You're a fucking gift."

Father Juan was right. Her value was beyond measure.

Mateo kept his eyes closed, kept her pressed against him with his grip on her biceps, and only began to relax when he felt one of her hands curl into his hair. "She's not a sociopath." He could feel her throaty words vibrate against his forehead.

"She's a narcissist with tendencies toward a histrionic personality disorder."

He huffed against her neck. "My therapist won't diagnose the king."

"I'll give you my therapist's number. She's brilliant."

He stayed where he was, finding comfort in the silk of her skin and the brush of her hair, letting her warmed rose scent wash away the stench of Tonya.

"I'm not going anywhere," he said against her skin. "You're stuck with me. Show me the joys of a Kansas summer."

May: Day Eight

Their lives settled into a surreal, all-American summer camp, which neither of them had attended as kids. They'd wake up early to go on a jog before the May sun heated up, or they'd walk the two blocks to the high school, passing lawns full of tiny grasshoppers popping out of the dewy grass, to work out in the gym until the football team came crashing in. After a big diner breakfast (Roxanne liked to "carb load" every couple of days; Mateo generally only had coffee and toast unless Roxanne ordered waffles with chocolate chips and whipped cream), they'd head to the hospital where they'd spend a couple of hours with the steadily improving Father Juan.

Sitting at the side of his bed, Mateo discovered that Father Juan was fiercely intelligent, endlessly compassionate, and definitely the source of Roxanne's smart-ass sense of humor. Father Juan treated him kindly and inquired about his life and background outside of what had been reported in the media, but Mateo understood that the jury was still out on him, as far as the priest was concerned. Mateo didn't mind. He recognized the contradictory impulse to protect the fiercely strong Roxanne; the more her spine stiffened, the more Mateo wanted to massage it and tempt her to lean back against him.

Once she ceded Father Juan to the parishioner or townsperson who'd come in to spend the day with him, she'd check in with William, who was keeping tabs on Medina Now Enterprises, and then turn off her phone, turn to Mateo, and ask, "What do you want to do today?"

As requested, she was showing him the joys of a Kansas summer. One day, she drove down dusty farm roads until she pulled over into a ditch and led him to a thorny patch of blackberries that were so sweet and juicy they made him want to cry. Sticky and stained, they'd barreled through the brambles to a secluded farm pond, where'd they'd stripped down to their underwear and swam themselves clean. Another day, they'd wandered through room after room of a dilapidated Victorian mansion, tall and stately through its peeling paint, that had been transformed into a used book store. Books were crammed floor-to-tall-ceiling in rooms titled "Steamy Romance," "Cozy Mystery," and "Books Your Professor Made You Read" and decorated thematically. Mateo's favorite was the "Fantasies Like *Lord of the Rings*" room, painted in rainbows and populated with weathered garden gnomes.

What was so crazy about their days was how normal they were. For the first time in their five months together, he had a sense of life not as a prince and a billionaire, but as two regular people, Mateo and Roxanne. They wore jeans and t-shirts, they drove a car that had a suspicious rattle, they went to the drug store for antacids, and washed their clothes at a laundromat. This Roxanne, this "normal" Roxanne, liked to keep a schedule, liked her hair off her neck in high ponytails or thick, top-of-her-head buns, used the *Wall Street Journal* as the bookmark for her tome-like fashion magazines, and was considerate in a way that surprised him. When she made a point of keeping their mini-fridge stocked with fruits and veggies for him, or grabbed him a Freedom Community College ball cap when he'd mentioned days before that he liked the logo, he was out-of-proportionally touched. When he kissed her and told her thank you, she'd kissed him back and thanked him for never expecting conversation first thing in the morning.

In that summer camp time, all that separated them from every other citizen in Freedom was the number of times they were hugged, back-slapped, and arm-pumped. Roxanne, and Mateo by extension, received thanks everywhere she went. It was during their fourth or fifth incident, when Roxanne was resisting a second free chocolate malt from the owner of the local drug store, who was thanking her for purchasing and preserving the old movie theater, that Mateo realized how genuinely surprised she was by all the gratefulness.

"Doesn't this happen every time you're here?" Mateo asked as they walked down Main Street, looking for children to give the ice cream treats that had been forced upon them.

Roxanne wiggled her head and shrugged her shoulders. "I don't really get into town often. I come to visit Father Juan; I mostly stick to the parish."

It was another Freedom resident who finally helped Roxanne clearly see her place and reputation in her hometown. They'd been at a local bar, playing pool and drinking cheap beer, when a gorgeous, opulent woman in her mid-thirties strolled up to his wife. Rather than stiffening up, as Roxanne usually did when approached by a citizen, she had relaxed and beamed, shaking the woman's hand in her own. Roxanne introduced her: Cynthia Madsen was the heir and owner of Freedom's largest employer, Liberty Manufacturing, an auto parts manufacturing plant. Mateo immediately understood why the two women got along.

As he stepped back and allowed the two gorgeous women to play against each other, he sipped his beer and tried very, very hard not to get fuzzy headed by the view.

His wife's quiet murmur under the blare of country honky-tonk snapped him back to attention.

"They don't make fun of me?" Roxanne had asked, her blue eyes focused on the cue ball.

Leaning on her cue stick, Cynthia Madsen threw back her thick head of black hair and laughed. "Are you kiddin'?" she said in her slow Kansas drawl. "Do you know how annoying it is to be in this town, every day, working your ass off to keep it alive, and still be outdone by someone who's never here? I'm queen but you're the patron saint. Anyone who tried to badmouth you would be run out of town on a rail."

Roxanne straightened slowly, her eyes still on the felt. "But…what about my mother?"

Cynthia's full mouth smiled sympathetically. "Sweetie, no one holds her sins against you. If she's the cross we gotta bear for you, we're more than happy to take its weight." She picked up her stick and leaned over the table. "Now move over. I'm not going to win your donation for the youth center if you keep yappin'."

Roxanne won, even after Cynthia teased her into making it the best of three, and yet she still promised the woman a check the following morning. With a barely civil goodbye to Cynthia, Mateo had paid their tab, rushed Roxanne to the Bronco, and pulled off on the shoulder of the first dark road he encountered to take his wife, hard and fast and sweaty, on the long bench of the front seat.

Their sex life was…enthusiastic. And constant and energetic and not really restrained to their hotel room, although that's where Mateo liked it best, giving him the room to stretch her out and the light to see her fully and the time to touch and lick and kiss all that delicious skin. Freed from the restraints of the contract, their sex seemed less compulsive, more fun, so when he made love to his wife in that pond, holding on to the deck while she twined those heart-stopping legs around him, they'd both grinned at each other like fools as she pulled him into her hot, tight depths. She'd pounced on him one morning after his shower, deep-throating him as she pressed him against the metallic wallpaper and following him down when he lost his knees. He'd loved her, long and slow, one evening after a couple had stopped them at dinner to tell them how her $500 prize for a local art contest had positively affected their daughter's depression. He'd made her orgasm, again and again, as soft as a sigh.

Neither of them discussed the future, the contract, or Roxanne's startling suggestion that, perhaps, they didn't need to plan on divorcing. Mateo didn't ask; Roxanne didn't tell. He recognized the avoidance bubble he was floating in; did he really want to start poking at it? If he asked her about staying together and she declared it an impulse—or worse, if she said "yes" now but then later changed her mind—his fall would shatter him. Why risk it right now when so much teetered on the brink? He had to preserve what little worth he had for the people of the Monte. She liked his company, she liked his cock, she liked his supportive hand at the small of her back. He could give her those things and preserve the bulk of himself, the mass of his heart, for the people who truly needed him. Who were right now waiting for his return.

His plan made perfect sense.

It was the mantra he repeated over and over to himself now—*My plan makes perfect sense, don't fuck it up, I have a plan and it makes sense*—as he watched his wife grab on to a rope, move back several steps, and then go running full tilt and screaming to fling herself in a high arc over a twenty-foot drop. As the rope began to swing back, she let go, tucked up, and made an impressive cannonball puncture into the quarry pond below, splashing the kids laughing and yelling on the bank. When a nine-year-old boy extended his hand to help Roxanne out, she grabbed on…and jerked him into the navy-blue water with her. The other five kids and teens they'd brought to the quarry pond, a crystal-cold pool created by a hidden water flow and a fifty-year abandoned mine carved into the stone, used that as an excuse to clamber in and splash, dunk, and essentially try to drown his wife.

Sitting on a beach towel on a flat, wide ledge cut about ten feet up into the stone, Mateo physically relaxed when he saw her laughing, sputtering, and giving as good as she got. Emotionally, he was a fucking wreck.

He'd been surprised when they'd picked up a van at the local rent-a-car site after saying goodbye to Father Juan, his wife being cagey about their plans for the day although she'd told him to wear his swimming trunks. He'd been more surprised when they'd pulled up to the neat, two-story home behind St. Paul's Catholic Church, walked into a living room furnished in soft couches and bean bags, and met six kids who, in swim clothes and towels, seemed to know more about his day than he did. He'd been shell-shocked when a teenage girl and the nine-year-old boy greeted Roxanne with hugs, hugs she returned with hard squeezes and back rubs. They introduced her to the other four kids and Roxanne introduced Mateo to all of them.

Ranging from nine to sixteen, these were the kids currently making their home at St. Paul's Shelter for Children and Youth, Roxanne's safe place as a girl.

He couldn't figure out what left him the most dumbfounded and misty-eyed: that she had such a strong relationship with the shelter, that she *wanted* to take the kids on an outing, that she knew kids and had a close-enough relationship with some of them that they trusted and relied on her. He felt stupid, the way he was set so far back on his heels by this new insight into her as he watched her impressive aim with the squirt gun she made with her joined hands. He'd assumed her knowledge of children was as theoretical as his own. He'd never fathomed she could be like this: playing, rough-housing, laughing, and shrieking, shielding an eleven-year-old girl with her body and then conspiring with the girl to launch a counterattack.

He never imagined her as a mother. And Jesus fucking Christ, what a mother she would be.

He had to look away, up into the ring of trees that circled the quarry. He felt light-headed.

"You okay?"

He turned to see his wife toweling herself off as she climbed up the path toward him. She'd managed to extricate herself from the kids, who continued to splash and thrash in the water. He scooched back, made room for her on the wide ledge as he sat cross-legged on his towel. She snapped her towel out and placed it next to his, stretched out long on her side and propped her head on her hand, watching him.

She was wearing a demure, navy, one-piece suit, her full breasts restrained by the high-neck halter top. Her body was still heartbreaking in it.

"I'm fine," he said, making a lame gesture at his stomach. "Just...all the fried food."

She smirked, her beautiful, naked face resting on her palm. "I told you those fried Twinkies were a bad idea."

"So..." he began. He steepled his fingers in his lap and nodded at the kids. "You do this often?"

She nodded and pulled her heavy rope of wet hair over her shoulder with her free hand. "I visit Father Juan two or three times a year. When I do, I hang out with the kids." She played with the wet ends of her hair. "Is it weird?"

"Not weird, just unexpected." He ran a hand back through his hair and then leaned back on his arm, studying her. He'd taken off his shirt and felt the Kansas sun all over his torso.

He wished he had his sunglasses. "I thought your desire to have a child was based on daydreams."

She smiled softly at him instead of sputtering. "I guess the daydream is to create a child whose life isn't defined by nightmares; I'm excited to see what that looks like." Her smile flattened along with her voice. "Josie was abused by her uncle for years." She was referring to the teenaged girl who watched over the rest of the children like a mother hen. "When she told her mother, her mother kicked her out. And Nathan..." That was the boy. "Nathan is swimming in his shirt to hide the cigarette burns on his chest." She met Mateo's gaze. "I'd like to balance all this darkness with a little light."

Without thought, with only heedless impulse, Mateo leaned forward, captured Roxanne's head in his hand, and kissed her. The kiss created enough light to power the sun. Just as abruptly, he pulled back from her lips before the kiss became more dangerous. With his forehead pressed against hers, he said, "Tell me what happened."

He sat up, leaned back on his hands, and tried to give the impression that his heart hadn't just exploded in his chest. *I'd like to balance all this darkness with a little light.* If she had said *that* from her laptop on that fateful day in January, he would have flown to the Bahamas or wherever the hell she'd been to impregnate her.

"I just suffered from good ol' fashioned neglect and humiliation," Roxanne said, combing her fingers through the ends of her hair. "It probably occurred to my mom to hit me a few times, but in the end, she just couldn't be bothered." She looked up at Mateo and saw by the set of his face that she wasn't going to be let off the hook that easy. She sighed heavily as she understood that it was time. She settled her cheek onto her hand, the kids' laughter acting as background music.

"My mother wasn't officially the town whore—I mean, she

didn't set up a shingle or anything—but husbands and truckers knew that if she was around and bored and if they tossed a few bucks her way, she was open for pretty much anything. For my mom, it's always been about…ease of effort. That's why she didn't abort me when she got knocked up at a bonfire by a farm worker. Or, at least, she thinks that's when it happened. She isn't sure. She likes to say she got pregnant during her 'bandito' phase. She listed his name as Daniel Medina on my birth certificate but, honestly, she doesn't know who my father is."

"I thought they were married," Mateo said quietly. "Her last name is Medina, too."

"She changed it to match mine when I made my first million."

"Of course she did."

"And a tale of an absentee husband and father is a much easier story to tell than this one."

Mateo nodded, understanding and accepting the need for Roxanne Medina lore.

"I was useful to my mother when I was pretty or adoring or the guys she was with admired me." She quickly shook her head when Mateo stiffened. "No, they never got the chance to admire me *that* much. The one thing my mother could never stand was competition. And as a malnourished, unwashed, and disregarded kid, I wasn't that pretty or adoring either. So I got left a lot. My mom would come back to our crappy apartment after a couple of days and just sigh at me like, 'Oh yeah, *you're* still here.' The best thing she ever did for me was abandon me at the playground. I kid you not, it probably wasn't even intentional; she probably had an itch for a beer or a man and just wandered off. Someone called Father Juan and my whole life changed. I'd be dead if it wasn't for him."

She said it with a surety that made Mateo want to lay her

flat and cover her completely, protect her from anything that ever tried to hurt her again. But he stayed upright and tried to keep the discomfort of her story from showing in his shoulders.

"Why did she fight Father Juan so much?" he asked. "Wouldn't it have been easier on her to surrender you to the foster system?"

"Her delusion is that she's an okay mother. Father Juan's involvement gave that fairy tale added spice. Now she was an avenging mother protecting her daughter from an overly interested priest. She always lost interest in that story the second I was home again. But it was drama, and I gave her leverage over him." Roxanne smirked. "My mama always likes leverage."

Mateo let his eyes wander over her delicately sculpted face, the straight nose and the naked lips and the tanned olive skin, showing its Latino influence under the constant barrage of Kansas sun. Her roots revealed a deep chestnut, still dark but lighter than the glossy black she colored her hair with. Even during a time of so much anxiety, she'd let so much of herself relax during their weeks here in Freedom. He wondered how Tonya Medina slept at night.

"So you pay her to keep quiet," he asked.

Roxanne nodded, her eyes on the rock beneath her hand. "I was made of shame when I was younger. My classmates, the teachers, the other moms—everyone knew who she was. The kids were cruel. The parents were embarrassed. Probably ashamed that this thing was going on in their community. All that kept me going sometimes was the thought of getting away from here, getting away from her, and being shed of all of it. Of being free. My money walls her away from me, but I'll never be fully free of her."

God, he knew that feeling. He knew the weight of your family's bad decisions. He knew how that weight made you make bad decisions all your own. By paying her mother for her silence, Roxanne exposed a tender spot that Tonya Medina could stab at for the rest of her life.

"You know," he said gently, "the shame is hers, not yours."

"So my therapist tells me."

"You give her power with the secrets you keep."

She huffed a laugh. "Secrets... They're our stock in trade, aren't they? All these secrets we keep to pretend to be something we're not." She watched him from under her full dark lashes.

Suddenly she pushed up, swung her legs around so she could sit cross-legged and face him. "Do you want to know a really good secret?"

Unsure what to expect, Mateo nodded slowly.

Without hesitation, his gorgeous blue-eyed wife lifted her hand to her face, gently pulled down her eyelid with one finger, and touched her eyeball with another. Then she lifted her fingertip to Mateo.

Hovering on the end of her fingertip was a blue-colored contact.

Startled, Mateo looked up, leaned in to get a better look at her face. Roxanne opened her eyes wide. Her iris was the soft, glossy brown of chocolate mousse, of hot cocoa cooled with a splash of heavy cream. He leaned back and looked at her blue eye and then her brown one, her blue eye then her brown one. His eyes traveled to her hair, took in the way the sun was shining in those chestnut roots, and then back to her face, to that gorgeous sugar-cookie tan making her skin glow, freckles beginning to dust her cheeks and nose like sprinkles.

Mateo realized he was mentally describing his wife like a dessert because he wanted to eat her up. He had never been more viscerally attracted to her than he was right now, when she was as naked with him as she could possibly be, when he could see the elemental being that she was, this smart indomitable girl growing up Latina and parentless in a conservative small town. That girl roared in this beautiful billionaire sitting in front of him.

He just had one question before he threw her down and made love to her in front of six children. "Why?"

She pinched her lip as she looked down at the contact at the end of her finger, her hand resting in her lap. "At first, it felt like a smart business move. I was already facing a massive barrier to entry; looking more white would help me jump at least one hurdle." The contact had grown shriveled and tacky on her finger, and Roxanne flicked it away. "Now, it serves as armor. The head of Medina Now Enterprises is a pale-skinned, black-haired, blue-eyed Amazon."

"She's Wonder Woman," Mateo teased.

Roxanne grinned at him shyly. "Exactly. She has nothing to do with the scared Mexican-American girl who wakes up drenched in sweat that a decision she'd made will sink her company and destroy the livelihoods of thousands of people."

Mateo reached out and wrapped his hands around both of her knees. It felt like the only safe place he could touch her while the kids were still around. What do you say when a woman like Roxanne Medina shows you her soft underbelly? What do you say when you're doing everything in your power to keep yourself rolled up into a tight ball? He was glad his hands didn't tremble on her knees.

"Now I know all of your secrets," he intoned in the hokey voice of a movie announcer.

He was fucking this up, but he was still surprised when she ducked her head away.

"Not really," she said, rubbing her palms together in her lap. "I've been wanting to mention that—*AAAHHH!!*"

Roxanne arched up as water shot her square in the back. Mateo glimpsed the massive Nerf squirt gun being aimed at them from the quarry below before he caught a faceful of water. He sputtered, waving his arms. Roxanne grabbed his hand and pulled him to standing as the kids shrieked with laughter.

"This cannot stand, *Príncipe*," she grinned at him. "We attack!"

She turned and took off at top speed down the treacherous pathway. Mateo watched her run, prayed she wouldn't crack her head open, and then took off after her, glad to have something—even drowning—to distract him from the growing understanding that he was a worthless little shit. He was everything his father accused him of being.

Roxanne was in a mood when they got back to their room that afternoon.

When a freshly showered Mateo stepped out of the bathroom, she ripped away his towel, manhandled him onto the bed, and instructed him to "Stay!" before she hurried into the bathroom. At the bang of the bathroom door, he glanced up and saw that she'd shoved him down on the edge of the bed where the long mirror on the opposite wall could catch him. He looked at himself: long bare feet on the red-orange carpet, leg hair turned that blond it got in the sun, good strong thighs and stomach and chest and shoulders, cock lying shy but interested against his thigh. He met his own gaze. "Golden" they called it. He saw the flush of anticipation high up on his cheekbones.

Was this wrapping enough to sustain the interest of Roxanne Medina if the stuff inside proved to be more cotton than steel? Minutes passed as Mateo examined his own self-worth like a jeweler with a magnifying glass, searching for the flaws. His erection seemed to only be aware that his naked wife was on the other side of the door.

But his wife wasn't naked when she came out of the bathroom. Somehow she'd managed to sneak in his white dress shirt and tie, and when she walked toward him, hair flowing over his low-buttoned shirt, the tie loosely framing her cleavage as the hem fluttered at the top of her thighs, Mateo had to clench his jaw to keep his tongue from lolling out.

He moved to stand.

"Your billionaire told you to 'stay,' *Príncipe*," she commanded. She raised her imperious nose at him and tugged her hand slowly, suggestively, down the red silk of his tie.

That "stay" was an erotic spike in Mateo's blood. She hadn't given him a sexual command since their first night together, when she'd ordered him onto the couch. Now he trusted her with the same intensity that he scorned her then. And he wanted her—this stunning, accomplished woman—with an ocean of desire that had only been a drop in January.

He relaxed back on his arms and gripped the sheets in his fists.

"Face the mirror."

He smirked at her, covering up the panting he'd rather do, and slowly turned to face his reflection. In it, he watched her get on the bed and then slowly crawl up behind him, the muscles of her tanned, powerful legs flexing. She pressed against him, the tie slippery and cool against his back, her breasts soft and warm through the starched shirt. She reached around him and carefully scored her nails down his torso.

"*Qué bien, Príncipe*," she said almost absently, like he was a particularly fine statue she was assessing. "So perfect," she said as her fingers traced the muscles of his chest. "So beautiful," she said as her nails dragged across his clenched stomach. And then her elegant hand with her giant glittering ring wrapped around his blood-filled cock.

"And all mine," she crooned.

He grunted as she bit his earlobe, and then he squeezed his eyes shut as she began to pump his cock.

She ran her thumb over the tip, causing his hips to arch up, and she grabbed his hair in her free hand, tilting his head up and licking into his mouth. When he let go of the sheets to turn toward her, she bit into his bottom lip and raked those nails over his balls. "*Príncipe*," she growled against his mouth, making his balls tighten up in her hand. "It's a one-word instruction. Don't make me tie you up. You won't be able to bury your hands in my hair when I'm swallowing your cock."

"Fuck, Roxanne," he gasped, jerking up against the inside of her wrist, trying to get some friction.

"Soon, *mi rey*." She grinned against his mouth, her lips wide and soft. "Soon. But first, relax and let your billionaire worship her king's perfect, beautiful body."

And he did. As her lush tongue slid into his mouth and her hair slid over his face and her hot hand surrounded his cock, Mateo just leaned back and relaxed into it, let her tongue pick out the pleasure in his mouth, let her free hand play along his torso, let her other hand jack him slow then fast, hard then whisper soft, strumming at that tender spot just under his head and then stroking flat palmed across his balls. He was chained to the bed by her touch, her hot rose scent, and the delicate links of her desire. He craved to give her whatever she wanted.

"God, look at you, *mi amor*," she purred as she licked into his ear. Mateo lowered his head because she allowed it to see himself, heat-flushed, sweat-sheened, muscles tight and jumping as he gripped the carpet with his toes to keep from pouncing on her. He looked at her with a lazy, half-mast look—caught her soft caramel eyes, free of artifice—and let his knees fall open just that little bit more, let his cock bob and his balls stretch in offering to her.

She made a pleased moan in her throat—he'd pleased her—

before swiveling around his body, kissing his shoulders and chest, testing the muscles of his bicep with her teeth, swirling that thick silky hair over his stomach and letting it fall into his lap, across his weeping dick. She ended up on the floor, between his knees, wrestling out from under her hair and pushing her hands out of the oversized cuffs to wrap them around his penis.

"Watch me," she panted, and he did, he watched her as his billionaire slowly swirled the wet tip of his dick around her luscious lips, poked out her pink tongue to lick at his slit, and then surrounded the angry-red head with her mouth, pushing him into heat and wet and spine-racking suction. She took him down deep as she stared up at him, ate him alive with honest, open, beautiful brown eyes. Eyes gone dark chocolate with desire for him. Eyes she'd hidden from everyone but him.

He scrambled to grab the bottom of his cock, knocking her loose, squeezing hard to stave off his orgasm as he closed his own eyes tight.

"No," she moaned, sulky and sultry, "that was mine." She sounded as lost in desire as he felt. "Come for me. I'll make you do it again and again. Put your hands in my hair; pull me down on your cock." Her tongue licked at his tip. "Touch me. Show me what you want."

And he did. He leaned forward to grab her by the waist and lifted her struggling body until he could lie back on the bed and pull her over his face. "This was not what I meant," she gasped, laughing and wriggling above him as he clamped his arms around her thighs and arched his neck to flick up into the wet beautiful heat of her pussy, stilling her.

"Please, *mi reina*," he said, muffled by her thighs, under his shirt, in this dark, humid, Roxanne place that was the only place he wanted to be. He turned his head and kissed her thigh. "Please. You still have control here. You own me completely. Let me worship you. Let me…" But his words were forgotten as he pushed his tongue up into her, past the muscle and into her taste.

Thank God for her, for her ability to forget her agenda and just start fucking her body onto his tongue.

Underneath his shirt, he was all but blind. But there was a universe to explore here. He tasted her sweet, swollen clit, sucked on it, while his hands slid over her stomach and then took on the weight of her full breasts. He squeezed her nipples as his tongue vibrated against her clit, mixing the delicate sting of nails or teeth with soothing rubs or licks. He counted her ribs and fitted his hands to her silky waist as he swept the whole of her cunt over his tongue, back and forth, and then petted at the small of her back while he fucked her deep, his thumb frigging at her clit as fast as he could get it. She was a vibration of uncontrollable sex sounds around his head, a soundtrack he'd remember and replay during the lonely years that stretched after her.

Suddenly there was light and coolness washing over his face as she wrenched herself off of him. He blinked, grabbed for her. She was on her hands and knees, looking back at him in supplication. "Take me," she begged, her eyes dark and lust blown. "Now, Mateo, *mi amor*. Please. Now."

He reared up, got on his knees behind her and clamped his hands on her hips as he recorded the sight: his hard cock, her beautiful ass, and sinking into her wriggling, desperate body. He fell forward onto her back as she groaned, and he felt his own fucking shirt. "*Joder*," he cursed, getting his hands under her, into the plackets, and ripping it open, buttons flying. The tie caught at her neck and he jerked at that, too, slid the silk loose enough to get it over her head, her laughing and gasping as he tugged off all the offending clothing, everything that separated her precious skin from him. Finally—fuck, *fi-*

nally—she was naked beneath him, and he ran his hands over her gorgeous back, squeezed her perfect ass, planted his left fist on the bed so he could run his right hand over the front of her, from her soaking wet cunt up her belly and breasts to cup her delicate neck. He stroked that fragile skin with his fingers and thumb, felt her life-giving pulse in his hold. He wanted to squeeze, to claim, to own. She was his. *His.*

He shifted his left hand to cover hers, entwining their fingers, pressing wedding ring to wedding ring as he arched his hips and pushed deep into her. She moaned and tilted her hips to take him deeper. He gripped his eyes closed as he began to move, pressed his forehead against her rolling spine, feathered kisses against the trembling skin of her back. She was everywhere inside him, in his arms and against his chest and around his thighs, the essential heat and scent and silk of her surrounding him and sheltered by him. He opened his eyes and caught her face in the mirror, her lips pursed in a moan, her eyes gripped in painful pleasure as her forehead leaned against her fist, as if she could barely stand it.

When his hips began to pick up desperate speed, she tilted her head, resting her temple on her hand and opened her eyes slowly, dreamily. She stared at him in the mirror as if she knew he'd been watching. As her body jolted beneath him, she looked at him like he was the world.

"I love you." He watched her mouth shape the words in the mirror. Heard the whisper from the body beneath him. Saw the tears filling her eyes. "I love you," she gasped again.

He hooked his arms across her chest, grabbed her by the shoulders, and roared his orgasm into her skin. The pulse and drench of her own orgasm sent him deeper, higher. He kept going until he had nothing else to give. He collapsed them both to their sides, not letting a millimeter of space between them, and wrestled the blankets over them, cocooning them inside until there was nothing but darkness and their recovering breaths. He pressed his face into her hair, her skin, trying to inhale her.

Perhaps if he did, he thought as he began to drift off, holding her sleep-lazy body, he would inhale some of her courage. Perhaps he would wake up knowing how to respond.

Mid-May

God, god, god, god, god, god. God!

As Roxanne drove to her mother's house the next day, she white-knuckled the steering and fought the urge to bang her head against its fake pleather wrap.

Only Mateo sitting next to her, blithely humming along to the pop song on the radio, kept her from doing it.

Why?!?!?!?! Why had she said it at *that* moment? Face-down, ass up, seconds from an earthquaking orgasm with Mateo touching every inch of her. Who wouldn't have said, "I love you," in that position? How many thousands of times had Mateo heard it then, some woman over him or under him gasping "I love you," as she gazed at his golden beauty and enjoyed his princely penis? He probably just assumed it was some quirk of his undeniable magic and had decided eons ago to let women off the hook and avoid questioning them about the undying devotion they declared when he was blowing their minds.

Billionaire Roxanne Medina, offering the same dime-a-dozen love every woman gave him.

Or, holy shit, what if he hadn't heard her at all? What if, in all the gasping and moaning and mind-blowing, he simply hadn't heard the once-in-a-lifetime phrase she'd never uttered to another man? What could she do now? Should she ask, "Hey, did you hear that thing I ripped out my chest to say to you? Did you catch that statement that was the biggest leap I've ever taken in my life?"

She looked out her side window and took a sip of air. She was effortlessly working herself into a panic attack.

She'd woken up fine, quite dandy, actually, wrapped up in Mateo. It was only over the course of the slow lovemaking in the shower and the long breakfast with coffee and waffles, when Mateo continued to be his sweet and solicitous self but said *nothing* about loving her back, that Roxanne began to get nervous. To worry. To sweat.

Because what if he *had* heard her? What if he knew she meant it?

What if he just didn't feel the same way?

Roxanne cranked the window handle, letting the ninety-degree heat *whoosh* into the interior of the car and beat against her.

The possibility that she'd misread all of his happiness and lust and devotion was too big to comprehend. What if she'd begun to believe in a reciprocal emotion that just wasn't there? If he didn't return her feelings—well, she would be like the world's most nightmarish sexual harasser, wouldn't she? She had a contract with him to bear his child; she'd promised him a fortune to save his kingdom. Maybe he was searching for a polite way to say, "Thanks but no thanks," to the woman who held his future in her hands.

He wouldn't fake it, would he, until he got her pregnant and got his hands on her money?

Oh God.

The possibility that she read him all wrong throbbed inside her skull. Her instincts were her foundation and her temple. They were the one aspect of herself that she could depend on when she had nothing else. That her intuition could betray her now, when she was the most exposed, was unfathomable.

It would call into question every certainty she'd ever had, every judgment call she made in the future.

Her long, lonely future without Mateo. That's the what-if that truly terrified her. What if Mateo didn't love her? What if Mateo didn't want her? Intellectually, she knew why her mother didn't love her: the woman was incapable of the emotion. Thousands of dollars in therapy had helped her understand the damage that had wreaked, the cracks in her foundation that let her believe she wasn't worth loving, no matter how much she spackled over them. But if she could swing and miss like this, again, didn't it call into question whether it was a "them" problem? Maybe it really was a "her" problem.

She looked out the driver-side window and let the coarse, hot wind beat at her sudden tears.

What a horribly perfect time to go see her mother. She couldn't cancel their appointment; like a shark, her mother could always smell the blood in the water, and the woman would do something that would make Roxanne's already shitty day that much worse. No, she would suck it up, wrap herself in the emotional Kevlar that was the only way she could interact with her mother, and pay whatever bill Tonya Medina believed she was owed.

Mateo had insisted on accompanying her. "*Shut up. You going solo is not an option. Just let me grab my bullwhip.*" She glanced over at him now and was distracted by the consternation on his face, his heavy brows in a frown as he read his phone.

"What is it?" she asked, clicking off the radio.

With a start, he dropped his phone into his lap and smiled at her. A smile that didn't reach his eyes. "*Nada.* How much longer until—"

"Mateo," she insisted.

He'd left his ball cap off, and he ruffled his hand through

his hair as he leaned back into the worn seat. "It's nothing. Stupid. There's a story in *El País* that my sister forwarded. They think they came up with a clever title."

"What is it?"

"*¿Dónde en el mundo está el príncipe del multimillonario?*" he said dryly.

"*Where in the world is the billionaire's prince?*" Roxanne parroted back. "What's going on?"

"It's more of Fuller's *mierda*," Mateo said, trying to appear at ease but failing. "The story is implying that, faced with a challenging growing season and the economic hardships of the Monte and the emergence of a more handsome and intelligent brother, I've decided to abandon ship."

Roxanne shook her head in disbelief as she stared out the windshield. "Not a drop of that is true! Even the growing season is amazing."

"It appears the reporter doesn't care. Especially when he can pair it with some lurid conjecture about where I'm spending my time. It's the one detail he got right."

"Where?" she asked, glancing at him.

Mateo leaned close and slipped a big hand around her jeans-covered thigh. "In the heaven between my wife's legs." He meant the words to be teasing, but Roxanne heard his frustration and disgust. She felt it, too. She didn't want anyone talking about their sex life.

"So he's saying you're hiding between my legs."

"It doesn't matter," Mateo said, sliding his hand off of her.

"It does," she said, already feeling the loss. "Fuller's going to encourage doubts in the Monte with stories like this. And your sister and Carmen Louisa can only fill in so much. You have to go back."

For the first time in the two weeks that Roxanne had been insisting he return to the Monte, he didn't argue with her. The silence grew in the cab like a black hole. She felt its edges press against her heart, wondered if she'd just provided him the escape hatch he'd been looking for since her declaration of love.

"I'll wait a couple of days," Mateo said, finally. "I'm not going to let Fuller think he's making me panic."

"I'll join you in the Monte as soon as I... I..." She stammered to a stop. "I mean, when it's time for..." She stopped again. *This* is what she'd been avoiding when she'd insisted on sticking to the terms of their contract. What were their boundaries now?

"Yeah, of course. Come when you're...ready. Or before. If you want to. I'd stay if I..."

"Of course," Roxanne cut in. "No worries."

No worries?

For the first time in five months, an awkward silence descended between them. In it, she could feel the weight of her panic. She could feel her fear that Mateo was pulling away. She could feel her desire for the normalcy of the contract... which wasn't normal at all.

As she took the turn into the subdivision of high-end homes near the country club, she said, "I'm really sorry about all of this."

"All of what?"

"All of...everything. I'm sorry I introduced so much chaos into your life."

"My life was speeding toward chaotic before you got involved."

"But this arrangement made it much worse." Especially since Fuller and the king were threatening to reveal the contract if they didn't get what they wanted out of Mateo. He could either agree to Fuller's deal and lose half of his kingdom, or be outed as a penis-for-hire and potentially lose all of his kingdom, his reputation, and his self-respect. After this meeting with her mother, she planned on telling him everything. "I'm sorry I forced you into this. I wanted what I wanted and I didn't care about the consequences. And that was wrong. Really wrong. It was wrong of me to coerce you and to arrange this with your father without your consent and to manipulate you…"

As she ticked through her sins against him, she felt any chance of keeping him slip through her fingers. Of course he didn't love her. Why would he? But he needed to know that she was sorry, regardless of how little good it did. She respected him more than any other person in her life. All she wanted were bright and beautiful things for him. She fell silent as she turned into the long driveway leading to her mother's mansion.

"Thank you," he murmured. She glanced at him, at his beautiful golden eyes taking her in. "I didn't believe your apologies in the beginning. And then your help and your friendship and all the stunning sex covered up how angry I was with you. But I needed to hear those words. Thank you for giving them to me."

She parked the SUV behind the overblown marble fountain in front of her mother's home. Four water-spouting dolphins cavorted around an Aphrodite that looked like Tonya Medina and blocked the view of them from the front door.

"You've always been upfront with me," he said. Her guilty conscience fluttered. "So I'll be upfront with you. I wouldn't have chosen this course, Roxanne. But I don't regret where we've ended up."

Roxanne had to breathe through her nose as her heart rate sped up, as she met his eyes underneath the fall of his summer-kissed hair. What did he mean, she wanted to demand in her upfront way. Which part did he not regret? The friendship? The stunning sex? The undying love that he was going to profess any moment now? Roxanne felt like she was still on thin ground, but it was just enough for a tiny bloom of hope.

"And where have we ended up?" she asked quietly. Mateo dropped his eyes to his lap, which wasn't the best sign. But this was hard. So hard. And Roxanne was the queen of confronting hard situations and coming out victorious, wasn't she? She was a fucking billionaire, for God's sake. She would tell him, the instant they were away from the cloud of her mother, about his father's betrayal and Fuller's threat and her own guilt-ridden quiet. She would tell him, while still clothed, that she loved him. And they would figure it all out together. Together.

Mateo opened his mouth, and Roxanne crossed her fingers.

A bang on the front of the SUV startled them both. They looked to see her mother standing in front of the truck, both hands on the hood and an annoyed squint wrinkling her manicured face.

"Y'all coming in or what?" The woman scowled. "I got more important things to do than watching y'all diddle each other in front of my house."

Roxanne kept her eyes on her mother as she clutched the door handle, slowly pushed the door open, and stepped out onto the sparkling granite roundabout that she'd paid for, shoving deep her worry and love for Mateo and putting on the armor that buffeted her from Tonya Medina.

Putting people through an excruciating tour of her thirty-five-room home, a caricature of a Beverly Hills mansion, was Tonya's favorite activity. For Roxanne, her mother made sure to point out every update and change, including the new, gold-flecked marble in the eighth bathroom, the updated naked gladiators in the breakfast room's ceiling fresco, and the recently installed rock-faced waterfall that emptied into the pool Tonya never swam in. She listed the cost of every change with relish.

"So you like to have work done on the house?" Mateo asked blandly.

"I like the workmen that come with the work," Tonya said, smiling as she licked her front teeth.

Roxanne pictured herself floating in the air, seeing all the clouds approaching—storm clouds and rain clouds and wispy clouds—and letting them slip past without touching her.

Finally, Tonya led them into her "living room." A mammoth chandelier twinkled in the mirrors that lined the left and right walls, where twin fireplaces crackled with fire on this ninety-degree day. Air-conditioning and a cloying flower scent were pumped noiselessly into the room. Tonya perched herself in the middle of a gargantuan white couch piled with white fur pillows. She patted the cushion next to her with a sly, under-her-fake-lashes look at Mateo. He elected to take a seat on the leopard-print armchair on one side of the couch. Roxanne sat in its twin opposite from him.

They looked at each other across acres of antique Aubusson carpet before they looked at Tonya. She was wearing a low-plunging spangly gold top, ripped jean shorts, and gold heels. Objectively, Roxanne could see that the woman still had a fantastic figure.

Tonya clasped her hands in her lap and raised her shoulders to her ears, looking as pleased as punch. "Let's talk terms," she said with glee.

Ready and expecting this, Roxanne still felt a rumble in her stomach.

Mateo made a move to stand. "I'll go…"

"Uh-uh. You sit," Tonya commanded, waving a long fingernail at him. "You're an important part of my negotiations."

Roxanne let her words sigh out like fog. "We don't need to negotiate. Just name a number."

Tonya slapped her hands down on her tanned thighs. "You see, that's the problem. You think you can just buy me off." She pressed a hand to her abundant cleavage and looked mournfully at Roxanne. "A woman's got her self-respect. I'm tired of being your dirty little secret."

The hair on Roxanne's arms stood up. "What do you mean?"

Tonya leaned back, draping her arms over the fur pillows and crossing her toned legs. Her bobbing gold heel reflected the chandelier light. "I don't wanna hide no more," she said smugly. "I want the world to know I'm the one who made Roxanne Medina. I mean, if I'd decided differently, you would have ended up just a little scrape on a doctor's knife."

Mateo flinched, but her mother's accusation that Roxanne should be more appreciative that she wasn't aborted was an old and tired one.

"I want you to introduce me to everybody," Tonya continued. "You know, at one of those press conferences. You and the prince here." She flicked a finger at him. "And I want to go to Spain. Rub up against some royalty. I'm ready to live the good life. It's boring here; this town ain't got no class."

She flicked a frosted curl behind her shoulder before her smile grew to its full, greedy width. "But most importantly, I want to be part of the little tyke's life." Tonya pointed a talon at Roxanne's belly. And even though her womb was currently unoccupied, Roxanne fought the urge to wrap her arms around herself to protect it. "I want to see him every quarter. You come to me or I'll come to you, I don't care, I'm flexible. But I wanna be grandma to a prince." Tonya's smile took on the gleam of a predator. "Can't you just see the spread in

People? Me, the devoted grandma, holding a future king. Shit. That'll make the people in this town spin on their heads."

Roxanne fought to maintain her calm as alarm bells shrieked in her head. "No," she bit out quickly before she took a breath. "No," she said, firmer, placing her hands on her jeans to cover up how sweaty they'd become. "You take the money. And you be quiet. Or you'll get no money."

Looking at the triumph on Tonya's face was like looking into the cold, dead eyes of an oncoming shark.

"Oh, sweetie," she grinned. "That dog ain't gonna hunt no more."

Tonya uncrossed her legs and slid to the edge of the couch, coming in for the kill. "You're gonna keep paying," she purred, nodding. "And you're gonna do whatever I tell you to." Then she turned those evil eyes on Mateo. "And you, your highness, you're gonna sign the papers that turn your kingdom into the next Disneyland. 'Cause if you don't, your daddy and I will tell everybody about the fake marriage you two dreamed up so she could get herself a kid and you could get yourself some fuckin' money."

Tonya's eyes went wide. "Fuckin' money," she repeated, startling herself with her accuracy. "That's perfect, ain't it?"

Mateo stood with a growl, his body long and tall and furious. "How do you know about that?"

"That guy, Fuller, told me. He put together this whole little plan."

"Fuller? He knows about the contract?" Mateo looked at Roxanne. And Roxanne felt all of it—her shock at what was transpiring, her horror at her mother's demands, and her own guilty conscience at not telling Mateo sooner—on her naked, naked face.

Mateo's eyes narrowed on her as his mouth dropped open in disbelief. "Roxanne, he knows the details of the contract?"

Unable to look away from her husband's shocked face, she could hear the joy in her mother's voice when the woman said, "She didn't tell you? He told her he knew all about it before you left Spain. Told her to stand down or he'd get y'all."

"Roxanne," he demanded in a voice more horrible than she'd ever heard. His fists were clenched. "What is she talking about? *¡Digame!*"

Roxanne felt her lower lip trembling, a horrible show of weakness in front of a woman she hadn't shown a weakness to since she was twelve. "I was going to tell you. I was just trying to figure a way out before—"

Tonya butted in, and they were both too shaken to stop her. "He said he was real happy with how she got you out of the way and preoccupied. But now he's ready to start moving things along. You know, break ground before winter and everything."

Fury blazed in his eyes, and Roxanne bolted out of her chair toward him, hands outstretched. "No, it didn't happen that way," she said, panicked. "You know that!"

But the distance away from him gave room for her mother to keep talking. "The man came up with an ironclad plan. Even if you two break up, it won't matter. We can still embarrass the shit out of you. Who's gonna buy the 'big powerful billionaire and noble prince' bullshit when people hear what you've been up to?" As Mateo turned to look at her mother, staring at Tonya with disgust and disbelief, Roxanne stopped moving toward him. Shame filled her to the brim. "I told him why Roxanne takes such good care of me, how popular I am with the gentlemen, but he figured that was a detail we could save for the press later. When we needed something else out of y'all."

Roxanne closed her eyes, drained of every drop of value.

"Prince, if I can give you a little motherly advice, I recommend you protect your own ass. All that girl cares about is her image. She wears fake contacts for fuck's sake. She's gonna do everything she can to come out lookin' squeaky clean, even if it means throwing you in the shitter."

Roxanne heard Mateo storm out of the room. She opened her eyes and turned to face her mother, her limbs heavy with despair. Tonya looked at her like she was an interesting cockroach she'd scraped off her glittery heel.

"My lawyers will be sending over some papers. I'd sign 'em if I were you. Along with everything I've mentioned, there will be an increase in my allowance. You're not the only one with an image to maintain." Her mother sighed heavily as she relaxed back into the couch. "I do feel bad about your situation. It's pretty sad when the only way you can get people to have a relationship with you is if you pay 'em."

Mateo was already behind the wheel when Roxanne stepped outside. She felt flayed, bared to the bone, without tools or armaments or the shield of her own self-worth to process what had just happened and help her see what step to take next. The drive back to the motel was silent; Roxanne's ears felt muffled by shock, self-disgust, and Mateo's vibrating anger. She couldn't believe how stupid she was; to be outplayed by Easton Fuller, the king. And her mother. The variety of Tonya's demands kept pinging around in Roxanne's head, one demand glowing red hot and tearing through flesh: that her mother wanted to play grandma. That she expected to be in the same room with Roxanne's child, that she expected to hold her child. That that horrible, abusive, disgusting woman, a woman she spent her whole life trying to escape, planned on exposing herself to Roxanne's daughter on a regular basis. Roxanne fought the urge to roll down her window and scream into the pummeling wind. Or curl into Mateo's lap and sob.

Emotionally overwhelmed and without a welcome, she stayed blank and silent.

Only the shock of watching Mateo drag his suitcase out of the closet and throw it onto the bed once they got back to the motel room brought her back online.

"What're you doing?" she asked, her skin prickling with returning blood flow as she watched Mateo stalk to the dresser.

"I need to go back." He grabbed an armful of clothes without looking at her.

"That's it?" she asked as he moved across the room. "We're not going to talk?"

He tossed the pile into his suitcase. "What is there to talk about?"

A puff of disbelief came out of her mouth as she watched him cross the room again. He would just walk out on her like she was…nothing? "Everything." She stepped into his path. He stopped, focusing beyond her shoulder. "I'm sorry I didn't tell you that Fuller threatened us with the—"

"Stop it." Now he was looking at her. Glaring, eyes burning her up. "I was such an idiot for believing your apology meant something today."

She felt her mouth soften with hurt. He had every right to be angry, but that was a low blow. After everything they'd been through together, after behaving like partners working toward the same goal, she thought he liked her. She thought he trusted her enough to investigate what had happened and not go straight to contempt. She felt gut-punched by his cruelty, by the face that sneered at her like he had through her laptop screen when they'd first met.

"Are you working with Fuller?" he demanded.

"No!" she declared, stunned by the question, staring into the depths of his eyes to find the Mateo she knew.

"Are you trying to keep me away from the Monte so that he can turn my people against me?"

"No." Now he was starting to piss her off. "That's ridiculous. You know me better than that."

"Do you believe I can save the Monte without signing Fuller's deal?"

She was surprised into silence by the question.

His heavy brows clenched over his eyes. "You think I'm fucking pathetic. You think the only thing worthy on me is my cock."

She gasped against the blow. "That's not true!" she declared, grabbing his bare arm as he moved to turn away from her. "I was… I was afraid. I was afraid you'd hate me. My contract gave Fuller leverage and I was afraid… I was afraid you'd walk away from me." She admitted the truth to herself at the same moment she admitted it to him. Her nails dug desperately into his tense arm. "It was stupid and selfish and I'm so, so… You don't want my apology but please know I didn't do it to hurt you or disable you. I admire you more than anyone I've ever known. You know that. You know me," she begged, searching his face for that spark of recognition. "You know my intentions. You said…you trusted me."

But the eyes that looked at her were blank and cool. "How can I believe anything you say?"

She wanted to reel back in disbelief; her jaw wanted to drop to the floor. She'd just stripped away her last defense and exposed herself to him, told him her greatest fear: that he'd abandon her. And he replied like he was talking to his father.

She realized then that she might be fighting for her life.

"How can you believe what I say?" she echoed back. "Because, besides stupidly and foolishly holding some facts back, I've never lied to you. Because I have done everything in my power to help you." As her disbelief and anger grew, she discovered an ember of self-respect. "Because I'm a good person." As that ember grew into a flame, Roxanne felt the urge to burn down all pretense between them. "Because I have been more nakedly honest with you than I have been with any person in my life. And you know that! In that bed"—she pointed to it fervently—"I told you the most terrifying truth I've ever shared with any man. Why should you believe me?"

She pressed her hands against her heart and looked at him with all of her grief and apology and hope and belief in him in her eyes. "Because I love you."

At that, the word "love," Mateo dropped his eyes to the wiry orange carpet.

Clarity stabbed through her. She pressed her lips together to hold back a mournful gasp. She'd gotten it all wrong.

"Oh," she said, dropping her hands and stumbling two steps back from him. "Okay."

He glanced at her from under his hair. She imagined he wished he had his ball cap right now. "What's okay?"

The AC was suddenly frigid in the room. She felt it flowing through her. "You don't love me, do you?" she said numbly.

"It's a little hard to love someone who thinks you're worthless," he said, again to the carpet.

The careless way he reached in and twisted her heart was the most painful thing she'd ever felt. "I don't think you're worthless," she said, the words falling out like tears. "I think you're perfect."

And he laughed. Ugly. "Perfectly incompetent. I'm the perfect child who'll play in my pen while you clean up my messes." He shook his head, still glaring at the carpet. That beautiful shining hair stroked his high cheekbones and sharp jaw.

"That's not love, *Princesa*. That's pity."

And what else was there to say?

Oh God, she prayed, wrapping her arms around her middle. *Dear God, help me survive the next few minutes.*

She'd risked everything. She'd stepped out from behind every barrier, peeled away every layer, and showed him the naked essence of who she was. And he didn't want what he saw. Maybe it was because of anger. Or distrust. Or simple disinterest. The "why" really didn't matter.

He didn't want her.

She spun her back on him and put her hand over her mouth. But she couldn't hide the tears in her voice. "You should go," she said, tears already dripping down her face.

"Roxanne," he said. And she closed her eyes on the sound of her name in his mouth. Tried to imprint it so she would never ever forget it.

"Please, Mateo, please," she begged him. The words came out with her sobs. Still holding herself, she walked to the motel room door. Placing her hand on the door handle, she said, "I'm so sorry for everything. But, please, if you ever had a drop of care for me, please don't be here when I get back." She shook with her weakness, trembled in her nakedness as she pulled open the door, stepped outside, and walked blindly into the hot Kansas night.

June: Day One

The Monte was enjoying one of its most perfect Junes on record.

Mateo marveled at it as he sat in his office in the Castillo, his leather desk chair turned so he could look out one of the arched medieval windows, tapping a stiff slip of paper—a check—against his knee. A rich Caribbean-blue sky arced over the vineyards; the vineyards' green leaves fluttered with health. The vines that stretched to the foothills were bursting with fruit; seamless sun-filled days were plumping the grapes with juice, while cool nights slowed down the process, allowing the juice to grow rich with flavor.

The fruit from his *Tempranillo Vino Real*, still at least three months from being picked, was already showing incredible balance. It was responding well to the heat, could take even more as the Monte turned inevitably warmer over the years with the effects of climate change. Back at his greenhouse at UC Davis, several of his research assistants were putting the *Vino Real* through stress tests, exposing them to wet, cold, heat, and reporting the same excited results to Mateo—the vine could take it.

The Vino Real *can save the Monte*, Roxanne wrote in the letter that accompanied the check. He glanced at the letter he'd thrown onto his desk, at the roll of blue ink across the page. Still tapping the check against his knee, he forcefully returned his eyes to the view out the window before he did something stupid. Before he pressed his face to the page to see if he could feel her hand against it.

A dark hawk swooped down into the vines, snaring something innocent out of the fruit.

His sister had taken over most of the day-to-day watch on the *Vino Real*, checking the sugars with a focused intensity that surprised him. They'd brought in a top Riojan winemaker whose name would ensure the varietal received the most press when they released the wine, but Sofia had made it immensely clear to Mateo and the ever-patient winemaker that she'd be overseeing the fruit's transformation from grape to wine.

She was no longer his little rebellious sister. Sofia had declared it when she'd dragged his ass out of the Castillo's wine cellars—endless tunnels under the castle that he'd retreated to the first four nights he'd been home—and he believed it when he acknowledged how capable she'd been as his emissary when he'd been gone. The remaining shreds of hope his people had that his family could save them were based solely on his sister's efforts. With gritted-teeth optimism, she was one of the few in the Monte enjoying the sun-soaked, blue-skied, crystal-mountain-air days.

Everyone else was watching the sky for steel clouds and a mood-matching storm.

Mateo had now shown all the growers the *Vino Real*. They were positive about the results, but it was impossible to be enthusiastic about a vine that wouldn't be mature in their own plots for three years when they lacked confidence that they would be in charge of those plots for another year. No one, including Mateo, knew what the future of the Monte held, and townspeople and growers alike walked around with their own private rain clouds over their heads.

Mateo sneered at the perfect day and spun his chair on it, flinging the check next to the letter.

He could find no way clear of his father's threats. His lawyers had looked. Mateo had gone over and over it with Sofia and Carmen Louisa. But the blackmail was simple and irrefutable: Sign or his father would name Roman Sheppard his heir. Sign or he would expose Mateo and Roxanne's contract to the world. His father, cold and sneering, had presented him his options and a deadline the night Mateo had returned from Kansas. Then both the king and Easton Fuller had made themselves remarkably absent. It was a sign of their confidence that Mateo was 100 percent fucked.

He had one more week to decide.

When a tap came on the ancient oak of the office doorway, Mateo looked up to see the one person who unfortunately hadn't made himself absent.

Roman Sheppard liked to lurk.

"Got a minute?" the man said in his low, gruff voice. His voice and those lines that winged away from his green eyes made him seem older than their twenty-nine years.

Mateo leaned back in his chair. "Don't you have a life to get back to, Sheppard? I'm sure there are children in burning buildings that need saving."

Roman just walked in with that relentless but expressionless manner he had, the way Mateo had seen him walking through vineyards and talking to townspeople and even having dinner with Sofia a few times. The man certainly wasn't trying to smile his way into anyone's heart, and no one, from what he'd heard from his growers and Sofia, trusted him yet or had a bead on his intentions. But no one *not* trusted him either. With a military and security background, he seemed really good at keeping his thoughts under wrap while getting people to open up more than they'd like. And faced with the king's and queen's histrionics—and, hell, even Mateo's drama over the last few months—he imagined his people were unwittingly drawn to the solid, Texas-lawman image that Sheppard seemed to effortlessly project.

The fact that he'd rescued the teenaged daughter of Mexican tycoon Daniel Trujillo several years earlier, an abduction and rescue that made international headlines, didn't hurt his image either. Even grudgingly and slowly, Mateo could tell his people were coming to respect the man.

With a fervency coming to define his existence, Mateo wished for the slap of rain against the window.

Roman dropped into the heavy, straight-backed chair in front of Mateo's desk. "You hear from your wife?" he asked without hesitation.

Mateo stiffened. Sheppard apparently had warmed up the Castillo staff enough that people were letting him know when Mateo got courier-delivered packages. "That's none of your fucking business," he shot back.

But Roman's eyes were already tracking the check, letter, and thick packet of stapled documents on Mateo's desk. Mateo imagined those light green eyes had lasers in them, that they'd been souped-up by some secret military agency to scan, store, and process information to most elegantly flay the enemy. With his dark hair cut almost military short and his tendency to wear black, Roman Sheppard looked like a highly trained soldier, albeit with a bit of hair gel and decent fashion sense.

He'd make an excellent king.

Roman nodded at the stapled papers. "If you let her go, you're going to become the piece of shit you already think you are."

His delivery in the Texas drawl was so soft and casual that it took Mateo a moment to process the content. He turned a granite face on the man. "You get the fuck out of my office."

But Roman kept on like Mateo hadn't spoken. "Not that I'd mind if you were more of a dumbass. I'd love to get my hands on that woman."

Fury like a forest fire roared through Mateo as he bolted to his feet. "You keep your goddamn hands off of her!"

"Since you're just rolling over and giving your kingdom to me, I guess I can take care of your queen, too."

Mateo was around his desk and pulling back his fist as red filled his vision.

Sheppard looked supremely unconcerned. "There he is…" the man murmured as Mateo let his right fist fly…and saw it wing off into air.

Only slightly tilted in his seat, Roman said, "It's about time you stopped being such an emo princess and tried to kick my a—"

Mateo connected with a cross from his left. "I can do more than try, *hombre*," he purred as Roman shook his rung bell and stood up from the chair. Roman backed away from the desk, fists ready and smirking. It was the first time Mateo had seen anything approaching a smile on the stern man's face.

"Wondering how long you were going to offer up your ass for their boot, *Príncipe*." Roman said the honorific with a drawn-out twang. "You got your people wonderin', too."

"I'll make sure to toss your bloody carcass out on the lawn so they'll know," Mateo jeered back.

Mateo's jab was a test, and Roman reacted as such, dodging and smiling wider as he paced back into the office's open space. Mateo's next three shots were a miss, but he connected on the fourth, getting a satisfying "*oof*" out of Roman when his fist hit the man's solid side. Quickly, though, Mateo felt himself on the defense, raising his forearms to protect his head and torso from Roman's fast taps. As sweat began to bead and roll down his sides, he wished he'd taken off his goddamned suit jacket.

He hadn't been in a fistfight since college. He was winded and starting to ache. It felt fucking incredible, movement when everything else was stuck in tar.

Roman dropped his shoulder. Triumph roared through Mateo at the opening; he leaned in to deliver a victorious uppercut. And found his hand captured, the momentum of his own body sending him forward and turned around, that once-victorious arm now a bound captive behind his back. Roman slung a restraining arm around Mateo's neck and said in heavy breaths against his shoulder, "You can keep slapping at me until one of us gets hurt or you can—"

Mateo lifted his heel, slammed it down on Roman's toes, and then leaned his head forward to jam it back into Roman's face. Roman grunted and let go of Mateo, stumbling back. Mateo whirled, and found the man down on one knee, holding his nose as he blinked away tears.

"Ha, tough guy, I learned that from my wife!" Mateo jeered, blood racing. "She's gonna love it when I tell her how her moves took down the big, bad Army Ranger."

Still holding his nose, Roman looked up at Mateo. And kept looking, his green eyes steady.

Mateo panted around his rabid smile, big exhausted breaths like he didn't regularly jog miles. His shirt stuck to his chest. He swallowed, his throat suddenly dry.

His smile slipped a notch.

He took a couple of steps back, weirdly light-headed like there wasn't enough oxygen in the high-ceilinged room, and felt behind him for the wooden chair that he'd punched Roman out of. Its solidity, when he smacked his hand against it, was soothing and cool. He circled around, dropped onto its hard, carved seat, rested his elbows on his knees. He hid his face in his hands and felt the weight of the ring he hadn't earned but hadn't taken off.

He wouldn't be talking to Roxanne. He couldn't call his partner, his friend, his best sparring buddy, to let her know that her grabbed-in-a-parking-garage self-defense moves helped him score one on his brother. He couldn't call his Aphrodite-shaped bundle of spontaneity and laughter and joy because he'd turned his back on her and let her walk out, crying, into a dark Kansas night.

He couldn't call his wife because on his desk was a letter that said in a few simple sentences that she was letting him go, a check that would see the Monte through until the *Vino Real* was profitable and he could pay back her low-interest loan, and a document nullifying their contract and requesting a divorce.

He groaned into his hands. "I've lost her."

Roman Sheppard's voice was an amorphous weight in his office. "Then get her back."

"She doesn't want me."

"You know that's not true."

"I'm not good enough for her." That was the truth, at its barest.

"Be better." The man was a tried-and-true American, always with an answer for everything. Always with that confidence that the worst can be fixed.

"It's too fucking late," he said, swiping his hands away from his face, swiping at the tears and the misery. Roman was sitting on the edge of his desk, looking at him with those intense eyes. "Fuller threatened her and she didn't tell me. She thought I was too weak to handle it."

He'd wrapped her betrayal around himself like cold comfort during the weeks he'd been home, repeated to himself over and over again that she hadn't believed in him, that she'd seen into the core of him and thought he was worthless as a man, husband, and ruler. The looping mantra that he'd been right, even justified to leave her, had gotten him through his days. However, at night, he hadn't found the amount of alcohol that would drown out her throaty, heartbroken sobs.

"I saw the way she looked at you," Roman said. "No way a powerful woman looks at a weak man like that. More likely, she's a take-charge woman who was just taking charge."

Jesus fucking Christ, billionaire Roxanne Medina was just supposed to be his temporary wife. His baby mama. And that was easy and good and emotionless...until it wasn't. Until being with her was hard and fantastic and filled every cell of him with terror and exhilaration and so much fucking love.

Every cell screamed with love and terror.

Noble or worthless, brave or such a fucking coward, he loved Roxanne Medina. It didn't matter if he was prince or pauper. It didn't matter what she thought of him. The sky was blue, the vines were green, and he loved his wife. There was no hiding or shielding himself from a reality that was as inescapable as the wall of his mountains, the needs of his people, and the mocha brown of Roxanne's beautiful eyes.

Beautiful eyes that had shined naked truth at him when she told him she loved him. *I don't think you're worthless. I think you're perfect.*

Mateo shoved his knuckles against his teeth.

"Get her back," he heard his brother say again.

"How?"

"If I knew I'd be sitting on a porch behind a white picket fence somewhere."

"It's too far gone," Mateo said. He rested his forehead against his fists, breathing through his mouth. His stomach rolled. "I fucked up."

She'd overcome so much to love him. She'd climbed mountains of toxic waste to become the woman she was, topped that mountain with her empathy intact, her sense of self firmly held, her commitment to her responsibilities unshakable. And when this tough-as-nails, brilliant, perfect-for-him woman had opened her hand and offered him her tender, terrified heart, a heart violated by her mother...he'd slapped it away. Ignored her. Denied her. Let his hurt and fear lash at her. And then crossed an ocean to hide.

Of all the transgressions he'd committed, this had been the worst.

"Picking up the phone would be a good start," Roman said.

"Fuck." Mateo dropped his fists and leaned back in his chair. "What would I say? I've got nothing to offer her but 'Sorry. I'm the piece of shit I always thought I was.'"

Roman gave a quick shrug. "Sure, use my line if you want. Sometimes a good grovel is all a woman needs."

And Mateo could maybe picture it working, throwing himself repeatedly at the wall he'd created around Roxanne until he reached her big generous heart. He'd weasel under or try to scale high, chain himself to her desk until she heard him out, bribe the shelter kids with trips to the Monte if they'd plead his case. Tie her to his bed so he could whisper a million "sorrys" into her skin. He would match Roxanne for insanity to get what he wanted.

But if he could lure her back into his arms, if, by some miracle, she let their lives once again wind together... Then what?

Then they'd just be where they were in her mother's living room, their dark secrets being shaken and teased in front of them by the worst human beings on the planet. Mateo's home and people would still be in jeopardy. Roxanne would still be victimized by a horrible woman, still fearful that everything she'd worked to overcome would be used to humiliate her in the press. And their child, that son or daughter that Mateo felt a glimmer of hope that he'd still be able to make with her, would still be threatened by the stigma of being a product of a signature on a dotted line.

Another failing Mateo had to hold himself accountable for: in the midst of his righteous indignation, he hadn't reassured Roxanne that Tonya Medina would never step within a thousand feet of their child, no matter what it cost. No matter if Mateo had to give up his legacy to a brother he didn't know.

He narrowed gritty eyes at Roman Sheppard, perched on the edge of his desk. Already making himself at home.

"What are you doing here, Sheppard?" he asked. "What do you want?"

Roman pushed off the desk and took a seat in the matching wooden chair next to Mateo's. He leaned forward and clasped his hands together. Mateo hadn't noticed it before, but saw then that the man was missing the tip of his right ring finger. The second knuckle and nail were gone. On his left hand, an inch-wide burn scar left a stripe of shiny skin across the back.

"My mother never had more kids," Roman said, looking at his hands. "Having a brother might be nice. Having a sister is already growing on me." He saw Roman's jaw firm. "I think I'll skip the dad thing."

"I thought you were making nice with the king," Mateo said. "You've let him prance you all around the village, let him introduce you as his long-lost son."

Roman rubbed his hand over his jawline. He was one of those guys that had a five o'clock shadow at 10 a.m. Rugged. Mateo hated those fucking guys.

"The first thing they teach you when you join the Rangers isn't weaponry or victim extraction or secret ninja moves," Roman said. "The first thing they teach you is patience. They make you wait and wait and wait. In cold. In heat. Standing on a beam a hundred feet in the air. Because you have to assess the situation. Hold your horses and gather your intel. You watch. And you wait."

He leaned back in his chair but kept his eyes steady on Mateo. "Reading people is all I'm good for. I read that woman and knew she was in love with you. I read the way you fight and knew you were going to try to take me down with a girl move."

"There was no 'trying' about it," Mateo smirked.

The humor in Roman's eyes slipped away as he said, "I was told I had a father and that he might want to give me a kingdom. I had to assess what was going on."

"And what do you think is going on?"

Those steady green eyes narrowed on Mateo. After a beat, like this warrior-spy was assessing whether Mateo was worth the intel he'd gathered, he said, "You're a decent guy. Your heart's in the right place. But you pay way too much attention to the worst voices in your head." There was something about being stripped down as methodical as a gun that made it easier to bear. "So now you've got a million things working against you. And one thing still on your side. You don't deserve it and you've done everything in your power to fuck it up, but people still love you. Your sister loves you. Your kingdom loves you. And by some unfair miracle, that gorgeous woman loves you.

"If all these good people are willing to risk themselves on you, well I've got to back them up."

Mateo's brain was spinning. "I thought you wanted to take over."

Roman scoffed. "I don't want your kingdom, man. I'm a soldier, not a king. I had to pick a side and I pick yours."

Dumbfounded by his brother's analysis and choice, Mateo shook his head. "I hope you do a better job of picking sides when you go to war," he ground out. "If you don't, you're not gonna survive long."

Mateo was exactly where he'd always feared being: on the lost side with his cowardice exposed to his family, his people, his stranger brother, and the love of his life. Every ditch he'd dug in the last six months, every time he walked the trench thinking the absolute worst had happened, he'd found a deeper hole to trip into. But now, right now, he'd actually hit bottom. Every horror he feared was coming true. Everything he tried to protect he was losing. He was truly as worthless as he'd always thought he was, and now everyone knew it.

There was nothing else to lose, nothing else to protect. Nothing else to hide.

Nowhere to go but up.

Mateo felt a tug, a lightness, like a tiny helium balloon set free in the darkest, dankest pit of himself. He'd lost everything. So there was nothing to cling to anymore. His ego, his fear, his nobility, his worthlessness, those useless weights, he could just let them go and fly. Everyone had already seen him, naked and exposed.

And yet they still had hope. His sister still had hope. His brother, this terse American offering his sword, still had hope. And his wife, while she may no longer believe that he was wise enough to care for her heart, she still believed he could care for his kingdom.

The Vino Real *can save the Monte. You can save the Monte. I never doubted it; not then and not now,* she'd written in her letter. Her words had been spare beats of emotion in her otherwise all-business packet. But they'd stabbed at him.

Now they could set him free.

He had no need to save anything for himself since he was a self-professed and actualized piece of shit. But he could save them. He could save his sister's inheritance. He could save the future of every person of the Monte del Vino Real. He could save his wife's reputation and legacy, protect the majesty of her creation and its beneficiaries from the greed of their parents. And he could save their future child—that little girl or boy—from ever thinking for a second they weren't wanted and loved by their mom and dad.

All he had to do was sacrifice himself.

"Fuck it," Mateo said, popping to standing, almost cracking heads with Roman. "Okay." His shirt was clammy against his body. His hands shook with possibility as he circled around his desk. "Then we've got work to do."

His brother looked at him like he was cracking up. "Work?" Roman said, dark brows raised. "What?"

Mateo leaned his fingertips on his desk and smiled the bloodlust smile of their ancestors. "Welcome to the losing side, brother."

June: Day Two

Sofia waited anxiously by the sleek marble-and-chrome security desk in the lobby of the Medina Building, trying to wrap her pure-bred stubbornness around herself to stem her nerves. She straightened her shoulders and flicked up the oversized faux fur lapels of her sweater, closer to her face. Damn these San Francisco summers.

What was she doing here? She could have been in the Monte, soaking up the sun and shine, enjoying the evening in the arms of Farid, one of the grower's handy-dandy interns, and spending the night among the dirt and green and creatures of the vineyards. She had that crystal-cool world to herself when she checked the sugars.

Instead she was here, in the fog and the damp, while a blond man the size of a bull bore down on her like she was the matador he was going to impale against the wall.

She touched the folded-up sheaf of documents in her sweater coat and allowed them to give her strength.

The man stopped just short of looming. "Come with me," he said tersely. He was handsome if you liked men carved in granite. His width more than doubled hers and as they approached the elevators, Sofia realized she would be stuck in a tiny box for fifty-five floors with those shoulders. And lots and lots of aggression.

He let it hiss out the second the elevator doors closed,

which made Sofia white-knuckle the documents. "What are you doing here?" he asked, jaw clenched as he stared at the ascending numbers.

She could become quite princessy and tell him it was none of his business. But this was Henry, the head of Roxanne's security, so *who* came to visit his employer and *why* was very much his business. Secondly, she'd never quite recovered from the cold-blooded way he'd looked at her at their first meeting, when she'd tried to attack Roxanne. She'd stared certain death in the eyes. Lastly, she'd come to suspect in her brief observations over the last insane months that Henry might care for his employer slightly beyond the bounds of a standard employer-employee relationship. She didn't blame him; everyone who spent time with her sister-in-law seemed to fall in love with her. Sofia was half in love with her herself.

His massive biceps, revealed in his short-sleeved black polo shirt, skipped and jumped as he kept his face tilted up toward the numbers. He wasn't angry. He was scared. For Roxanne.

Sofia wondered what he'd seen from Roxanne in the last three weeks. She wondered if it was anywhere near as heart-breaking as what she'd seen from her brother.

She decided to tell him the truth. "I'm here to see if she'll take Mateo back."

And so quick that her brain couldn't keep up with the movement of her body, Sofia found herself pressed up against the elevator wall, her shoulders delicately but implacably pinned.

"Leave," Henry growled into her face, his quarterback good looks transformed into something snarling and terrifying.

Shocked frozen, Sofia stammered, "I—I—"

Her shoulders were squeezed infinitesimally more in his massive hands. "Leave. I'll make an excuse for you. Don't show your face—"

Outrage bloomed larger than her fear. "No!" Sofia de-manded, wriggling against his hold. "I've got to—"

"You don't know what it was like."

Suddenly, his bulk was leaning toward her, as if she could help hold him up. He leaned the top of his head against the elevator wall, kept his mouth close to her hair. He seemed to be...wilting. Sofia had the outrageous impulse to put shelter-ing arms around him.

"You don't know what it was like," he said again, almost whispering, keeping close dark secrets. "When we... William got to her first. A family from town had seen her walking the highway, had taken her home and called the sheriff. William got to her first and then called me and Helen. We got there as soon as we could. But you don't understand how bad..." His breath was soft in her hair. "She couldn't stop crying. She was like a little girl. Just crying and crying." Then his voice did drop to a whisper. "She used to cry like that. That's what Father Juan said. When she was little, when she'd been left somewhere, she'd cry until she made herself sick."

During one endless, liquor-soaked night, Mateo had ranted about the woman who'd birthed Roxanne Medina. As Henry pushed himself away, Sofia wiped at her eyes before putting a hand on his arm. "Please don't compare that horrible woman to my brother," she said. "He's devastated, too. He knows he did wrong. He's trying to make it right."

Henry shook her off by crossing those massive arms over his chest. "Then why isn't he here instead of you?"

"He...he doesn't know I'm here..." Though if the three un-listened-to voice mails on her phone signified anything, he suspected. "He's working right now to save their marriage. I'm trying to save...everything else."

Henry continued to stare without comment. Sofia glanced

over his head and realized she had eight floors to convince him.

"Roxanne Medina is the only woman for my brother," she implored. "And my brother is the only man for Roxanne. And if we let them screw this up, they'll settle into the worst part of themselves and tell themselves they're okay." She glanced at the numbers and talked faster. "They'll tell themselves they're better off: Mateo, scrounging around in the dirt and trying to save everyone but himself. Roxanne, icy and impenetrable and so, so alone in her tower."

The elevator gave a delicate ding as they reached the fifty-fifth floor. The doors slid open. She panted out, "If we let them screw this up, that's on us."

As impenetrable as a brick wall, Henry stood in front of her blocking her way into the pale woods and glass of the executive floor. Sofia straightened her spine and put on the mantle of the implacable princess. In truth, as the seconds ticked down to the doors closing and the elevator descending back to the lobby, she fought the urge to shove, kick, and bite him aside.

With a simple step back, Henry prevented the doors from closing.

"I don't disagree with you," he finally said. It was something. "But you're going to find this harder than you realize."

"Then help me."

After another twenty thousand years of staring at her, Henry finally turned to the side. "Okay. If I get fired, I'm using you as a reference."

Sofia smiled as she slipped past his bulk onto the creamy white carpet. "If you get fired, I'll hire you myself."

As Sofia continued to stare at the part in her sister-in-law's hair, she began to sweat. How much was it to hire a personal bodyguard? She hoped her dwindling trust fund could take it.

Because Henry was definitely getting fired.

Roxanne already looked half frozen in ice—she was wearing a gorgeous-yet-cruel white leather dress that slicked over every one of her curves, and her liquid-red lips had pulled into a terrifying smile when she greeted Sofia without coming out from behind her desk. She wasn't wearing her ring. When she noticed that Henry had stationed himself beside the door, when she told him, "That will be all, Henry," like a queen of the ice castle and not at all like the bold-yet-kind Roxanne, she'd noticeably stiffened at his reply: "I'll stay put until you hear what Sofia has to say."

Now Roxanne ignored them both as she had her head bent to her desk, reviewing and annotating a document, tiny red reading glasses pinched on her nose. Her hair, perfectly parted in the middle and swept stick straight down her back, was a rich glossy black down to the roots. Which Sofia were getting to know intimately.

Sofia grabbed on to her patience, reminded herself of the woman sobbing on a Kansas highway and the man shattering his bourbon glass against the castle wall, and flipped her thumb across the papers in her sweater pocket. She could wait her much-beloved sister-in-law out.

Finally, Roxanne leaned back in her office chair and took the reading glasses off. She flipped them haphazardly onto her desk. "Now," she purred, eyeing Sofia and Henry. "What are you two up to?"

Sofia took a deep breath and tried to remember the words she'd cobbled together on the plane flight here. Although the memory had barbs, she tried to remember what she'd felt like at this moment, heartbroken, betrayed, every warm-and-soft emotion scooped out by a man who'd said he loved her. That man, or his emissary, had never tried to make amends. But what if he had? What combination of words could make her forgive him?

"My brother doesn't know I'm here," she began. "He wanted to come to you after."

Roxanne's expression of bored patience didn't change. She certainly didn't react to the obvious question: *After what?* She was playing it as closed off as Sofia would. *Don't give them an opening. Not even a sliver.*

"But he's making choices now that you'll both regret later," Sofia said, trying to meet her sister-in-law's eye. Trying to connect with the woman she'd grown so fond of. She took a deep breath. "He's so very sorry. He regrets completely how he treated you. Once he's done, he will be here on his knees begging for another chance. You can't imagine how he's been—he's end-of-the-world depressed one moment and then barking out plans the next. I've seen him drunk and raving and an hour later he's slurping down espresso and strategizing his attack. He's haunted by how badly he hurt you—"

Roxanne cut her off. "He did us both a favor," she said with an indulgent smile. "How pathetic it would have been if we'd attempted some lifelong effort just because our pelvises bang together well. A week or two away from him finally shook me free of his penis spell."

Sofia hid her flinch.

"Just imagine if we'd kept down that road. He'd be saddled with a wife and child he didn't want. And I'd be saddled with the Monte." Roxanne rested the long red tips of her nails against her exposed cleavage. "I've made my fortune saving failing companies, but I still needed to be cleared of his cock before I could see what was glaringly obvious: Your kingdom is doomed. Trust me, sweetie, we both dodged a bullet."

Sofia felt her lower lip trembling outside of her control. She knew—she hoped—that it was all a facade, Roxanne's lash out after being made vulnerable. But Sofia looked up to her. She believed in her. It was hard to protect herself from punches she hadn't expected.

Roxanne formed those lush lips into a pretty pout. "I'm not trying to be mean. But your brother and I are over. You and I can still be friends, though. Henry can escort you to my assistant's desk, and he'll set up something the next time you're in town. Henry?"

Sofia leaned across the desk and grabbed the elegant finger trying to point her out of the office and out of Roxanne's life.

"Friends?" Sofia spat out, winding her fingers through Roxanne's although the woman tried to tug away. "You're more than *una amiga. Tú eres mi hermana.*"

You are my sister.

For the first time, Sofia saw something warm and dark snap in the icy blue of Roxanne's eyes.

"I don't know how you did it, but you wriggled under my skin just like you wriggled under my brother's," Sofia said, palm to palm with Roxanne, keeping her close. "So, *joder,* maybe you and my brother don't work out. But you're always going to be a sister to me. And I'm certainly not going to talk to your assistant so I can hang out with you."

Roxanne had stopped struggling. "Your brother refused to make plans through my assistant, too," she said numbly.

Sofia smiled. "I bet."

"My assistant is really a wonderful person."

"Who, Brandon?" Sofia said. "We all love Brandon."

Carefully Roxanne unwound her fingers from Sofia's. She leaned back in her chair, her hands at her waist, and looked out her magnificent windows. The bay was wrapped in fog, but up here, the sky was blue and bright. The top of the Golden Gate Bridge poked up from the fog like a glowing red promise.

"I always wanted a sister," Roxanne said, her eyes still on the view.

She returned her gaze to Sofia, and Sofia realized then how much makeup she was wearing. How exhausted she looked. She wondered how many hours the woman had slept since Mateo broke her heart.

"What are you doing here, Sofia? What message can be so important that you make my best man commit treason to deliver it?" Roxanne leveled retribution eyes on Henry and Sofia hoped that the half-hearted joke meant she wouldn't have to hire the bodyguard.

"He's going to sign," Sofia spat out before she lost her nerve. "They have a press conference scheduled for tomorrow. They're making him sign in front of the world. He's going to sell half the Monte to Fuller and CML Resorts."

Again, Sofia saw that snap of feeling. But Roxanne lowered her eyes to the desk, put her hands on the stack of paper piled in front of her. "That's probably best. He wasn't doing that great with a whole Monte anyway."

"That's not funny," Sofia hissed out.

Roxanne shrugged an apology. But she didn't look up as she half-heartedly fussed with the papers, aligning their edges. It was surreal: watching this supermodel billionaire futz at her desk like a schoolgirl being chastised.

"Do you really think they'll stop there?" Sofia insisted. "Once the king and his minions know they can get an inch, they'll take a mile. They'll keep slicing and slicing at the Monte, and Mateo will bleed at every cut. How long do you think he'll survive watching everything he cares about being stolen away by a man he hates?"

"What other choice does he have?" Roxanne said softly, tapping a stack of papers against the desk. "If he wants to stay prince—"

"He's not doing it for the princedom!" Sofia shouted, slapping at the pale wood, desperately wanting Roxanne to snap out of it. "He's doing it for you!"

Roxanne tapped the papers one last time. Then she sat them directly parallel an inch from the edge and folded her hands in front of her. Finally, she looked at Sofia. "What do you mean?"

If Roxanne truly were her sister, she'd already be grabbing for a handful of hair. "He knows that agreeing to this deal is the beginning of the end. But he's agreeing to it for you. To protect your secrets."

"They're his secrets, too."

"He doesn't…" Sofia huffed in frustration, trying to cling to the patience that came in short supply for her on the best of days. "Do you think he'd trade half of his land and the livelihoods of so many people to protect his *pride*? So he's a prince who married for money. *That's what princes do!* He's making this deal for you, to protect you and everything you've created from our father and your mother. He wants to show you that he chooses you. You're the most important thing in his life. He's willing to sacrifice everything else—even the kingdom he loves—to prove that."

Roxanne stared at Sofia with the befuddlement of a stranger in a strange land. "Why would he… I don't… If…if that's true, why isn't he here telling me that instead of you?"

Was that the tiniest note of hope in Roxanne's voice amid all the skepticism? Sofia grabbed on to it. "Because he wanted it to be a fait accompli," she said, pushing to the front of her seat. "He wanted the act over and done with before he came to you. So you would have no doubt that he valued you over the land and the vines and the kingdom. Over himself."

Sofia then slipped back into her seat, crossed her legs in her skinny jeans, and bobbed her heel. "But I thought that was stupid. You're the most powerful ally the Monte has. Why tie your hands?"

Roxanne narrowed her eyes at her. "Then all of this is conjecture. You can't prove any of it. You mean to drag me back to the Monte simply to save your brother's ass when—"

Sofia was already drawing the folded documents out of her pocket. She threw them on Roxanne's desk, right in front of her.

Recognizing them, Roxanne flinched back. Then, as if unable to help herself, she gingerly spread them flat.

Mateo had slashed his signature to the bottom of the divorce decree. Right next to Roxanne's signature, which she'd had dated and notarized before she sent it.

But in the margins, Mateo had written a note in blue. And he'd attached a small white envelope to the documents with a paper clip. Roxanne lifted the envelope from the page and read the note.

I'm only signing this to get a do-over. I'm going to do it right this time. I'm going to court you then seduce you and then lure you into my bed. I may ask you to marry me every time I see you, but ignore me until I've earned it. I'm going to do everything in my power to earn it.

I didn't think I was worthy of you. I was afraid you'd see that. And my fear made me unworthy. That's not an excuse. There is no excuse for what I did to you.

But I hope you give me a chance to grovel. I pray you give me a chance to do better.

The worst thing I've ever done was make you believe your love was anything less than the rarest and most valuable gift. Better than fertile vineyards and prosperous kingdoms.

You are my kingdom. A lifetime spent loving you is the only legacy I want.

Her jaw clenched, Roxanne looked up and out her window. She wasn't looking at the view. "This doesn't…" She took a quick inhale, trying to steady herself. "I'm still useful to him. My money, my power. This doesn't—"

"Open the envelope," Sofia said quietly.

Roxanne ripped open the paper with trembling hands, a jagged frantic tear. Then she turned it over and shook.

Torn pieces of rigid, light blue paper sprinkled down like confetti. Aghast, she put the envelope down.

The check she'd provided Mateo, the only financial security the Monte had if he didn't take Fuller's deal, lay like inconsequential trash on her desk.

Roxanne looked at Sofia and pinched her bottom lip, marring the sleek red lipstick. "He's going to give away the Monte."

Sofia nodded, a told-you-so look on her face perfected by little sisters all over the world. "He's going to give away the Monte."

Roxanne glanced over Sofia's shoulder. "Henry, what are you still doing here?" she cried, smudging lipstick across her chin as she threw her hands out. "Go get my plane ready. Tell Helen we're leaving. *¡Joder!*"

"I know," Sofia said as she stood, snatched a tissue off a side table, and rounded the desk. Roxanne was already on the phone and clacking at her computer.

Sofia grabbed Roxanne's chin, cutting her off mid-sentence as her sister-in-law barked orders into the phone, and wiped the offending lipstick off her skin. "It's impossible to find good help these days."

June: Day Three

Roxanne Medina might have been the most badass, brilliant, beautiful, billionaire bitch around.

But she was no match for Mother Nature.

That glorious whore socked in SFO with fog—*it was the San Francisco airport; of course there was fog!*—grounding Roxanne's plane for hours. And then she pummeled Newark with a surprising summer squall and what was supposed to be a refueling stop turned into another hours-long delay.

So by the time Roxanne's plane finally screeched onto the Monte's airstrip, the press conference was minutes from starting. Roxanne, Sofia, Henry, and Helen raced from the airplane to the waiting limo while Carmen Louisa held the door open, imploring: "*¡Rápidamente!*" Henry terrified the poor driver by shoving him over to the passenger seat and taking the wheel.

As he rocketed them out of the parking lot, the rest of them kept their eyes on the limo's television screen, tuned to a livestream of the press conference. A stage decorated like a renaissance fair had been set up on the Castillo del Monte's lawn, with the castle's ancient brick walls as a backdrop. Flashy gold and red velvet fabric covered every inch of the stage in swags and bows and banners, and honest-to-God, men in livery and holding bugles stood at each side of the platform. The camera focused on a reporter, who gave useless commentary as her peers and competitors jostled and moved around her. The sale of the Monte would have gone unnoticed without the notoriety Roxanne had brought to it. With her help, Easton Fuller had created the ideal media circus to announce his new amusement park to the world.

Roxanne pressed her heel to the floor as if her will could make the limo go faster.

Her sister-in-law cursed in the seat next to her. Sofia pulled the phone from her ear. "He won't pick up," she said, stabbing at her phone in frustration.

Carmen Louisa had reported the same thing when they'd leapt into the car: "He wouldn't listen. He locked me out of his office once he knew what I was there for."

Sofia had called Mateo once they realized they might not get to him before the press conference. And he'd been furious. Roxanne hadn't heard his exact words, but she could hear his shouts above the plane engine noise. He'd refused to talk to Roxanne. But he'd texted her: Let me do this for you. I'll see you when it's done. He'd ignored the rest of their calls and texts and, apparently, locked their emissary out of his office.

Roxanne pinched her lip and wrapped her arm around her jumping, burbling, coffee-coated stomach as she anxiously watched the screen.

She didn't want this from him.

He thought he was handing her gift-wrapped proof of his love, trading the Monte to protect her, choosing her over the Monte. But she never wanted or needed him to choose. She would *never* ask him to give up something that gave him joy and purpose, just as he would never ask her to give up her empire. That was one of the reasons she'd fallen in love with him, because they mutually enjoyed, respected, and supported each other's dreams.

Yes, it might have taken Mateo a little longer to get back

into her good graces if he hadn't taken such extreme measures (*okay, it might have taken a few years, a kidnapping, and bondage to get her to ever speak to him again*). But she couldn't imagine that romantic gestures that robbed you of everything important to you were the best foundation for a lifelong love.

Because that's what she wanted with Mateo: forever. How could they start on the first day of forever when he'd sacrificed everything for her? How could he not come to resent her? How could he not come to *hate* her? She didn't want to be the cause of diminishing him and forcing his capitulation to his father. She wanted him full and fighting, and she wanted to stand by his side and fight right along with him.

So they *had* to get to the press conference before—

Roxanne's heart sank as bugles trumpeted in the limo's speaker. On the screen, a procession of people made their way up onto the stage. First, King Felipe, belly tightly encased in his shiny Italian suit, dark hair slicked back, smug smile on his fat face. Then Roman Sheppard, with that still and steady way he had of moving. The traitor.

Next was her husband. Still her husband, regardless that they'd both signed the divorce decree and she'd left that truly atrocious ring at home. With his rigid jaw and steely gray suit, Mateo looked like a sharp blade of determination. His beautiful dark-and-light hair, touched with gold, waved back over his collar as he kept his chin up. He would take whatever punch his father wanted to give.

Behind Mateo, Easton Fuller walked onto the stage.

Roxanne gasped. Clinging to Fuller's arm, her blond hair in an updo and her body sheathed in a tight purple dress suit, was her mother. Tonya Medina grinned at the cameras like she'd won the lottery. Fuller smiled down at her and patted her hand reassuringly as he leaned down to whisper in her ear.

Her mother was the knife Fuller was holding to Mateo's

throat. She was his insurance that Mateo would attempt no last-minute maneuvering.

"Faster, Henry!" Roxanne urged. The stately vehicle gave a lurch, trying to answer Henry's lead foot.

As the others took their seats on ancient, carved wooden chairs set to one side of the stage, the king walked up to a swag-covered podium, smiling and waving and pointing at various members of the press. He clenched both sides of the podium with thick, bejeweled fingers like he finally had his hands on the world he wanted. Roxanne had never hated a man more.

After a welcome and some platitudes, the king said, "This is an historic day for me, your king, and a new beginning for the Monte del Vino Real." He leaned on one side of the podium and gave the camera what Roxanne assumed was supposed to be an endearing look. "It's been tough. Being a king in the twentieth century isn't all wine and serving wenches," he chuckled. "But I single-handedly held the Monte together with the sweat of my brow, the love for my family, the commitment to my people, and the dignity of my royal blood. Now, at last, I have *compadres* to share my burden. I want to thank them."

He swept his hand toward the people seated in the chairs. "First, my son, Roman." He said it in the Spanish way, *Ro-MAN*, and the man tilted his head in acknowledgment. "*Mi hijo*, without your help, I never could have gotten your little brother to think more practically.

"Next, CEO Easton Fuller." He'd purposefully drawn attention to Mateo and then skipped over him. Mateo didn't react. "*Mi amigo. Hermano.*" The king clapped his hand over his heart and Fuller copied "his brother" with exaggeration, making the crowd titter. "You have helped make my dreams, and thus every dream of the Monte del Vino Real, come true."

In the limo, Carmen Louisa groaned in disbelief.

"Finally, we have a new friend to the Monte. Tonya, come here, please." Roxanne fought the urge to cover her eyes as her mother stood up, shimmied down the tight purple skirt that had ridden up scandalously high, and slinked her way across the stage toward the king. She took the arm he offered her and pressed it against the hard edges of breasts that revealed themselves in the deep V of her suit coat. "Ladies and gentlemen, I would like to introduce Tonya Medina, mother of my daughter-in-law, Roxanne Medina."

A sudden blast of urgent noise from the press and a sparkle of camera flashes indicated what a shocking reveal this was. The king and Tonya gave matching, hungry smiles.

Her mother leaned into the microphone. "Hey, y'all," she called.

"Can you imagine hiding this jewel away in Kansas?" the king said.

Tonya leaned into the praise and looked directly into the camera, arching her back like a swimsuit model. Roxanne felt the hit of that gaze deep in her trembling gut. Tonya was teasing her, walking the tightrope of everything she'd reveal if Roxanne didn't stay in line.

"I look forward to showing you the plans for the Yes, Your Majesty Resort and Theme Park. I'll give you our timeline—we'll be taking reservations in six months—and I'll even discuss the advantages of signing up for His Most Royal Highness vacation package. But first, we need to handle some paperwork."

The king turned and motioned an impatient finger at Mateo, the son who had done everything in his power to keep the Monte afloat, even selling his body to a stranger.

Mateo stood, tall and dignified, and took the time to smooth down his tie and button his elegant suit coat. Then he walked toward the king. Roxanne saw in him the resilient gait of every wrongly convicted man who kept his head high while walking to the gallows.

Roxanne dug into the collar of her shirtdress to find her cross, wrapped her fist around it, and banged it against her chest in prayer. "Faster!" she cried.

"We're close," Helen urged, trying to calm her. Roxanne glanced out the window and could see the tall tower of the Castillo like a beacon in the distance. But it was still too far. For all of his skills, Henry couldn't shrink the distance from the airport to the castle. They weren't going to make it.

A shorter, bedazzled podium had been set up near the speaking podium. On it was a document stand, a leather-bound set of documents, and the ridiculous plume of a feather-tipped pen leaning out of an inkwell. Mateo walked past it and forced Tonya and the king to move back as he took his place in front of the microphone.

Roxanne saw the king glance at Fuller. They hadn't expected this.

Mateo took a breath in front of the podium and then looked past the cameras, most likely toward the people of the Monte del Vino Real that had gathered to discover what their future held.

With a sudden, grim smile, Mateo said, "With a thousand years of history behind us, we here in the Monte have never accepted change well." Reluctant chuckles came from the crowd.

"Today, we must change." That line appeared between his dark, expressive eyebrows. "But we will weather this storm together. And while what I do today may not initially make sense, trust that I believe it is the best solution for all of us."

Mateo then looked directly into the camera. Roxanne felt those sunrise eyes in her chest as Sofia reached across the seat to grip her hand. "I know it is a lot to ask for your trust. I know I have not yet earned it. I did not treat my home with the care it deserved, and I almost let it slip through my hands. Today when I sign, although it may not seem like it, I'm holding on tight. I love my home, and I swear to you, I will protect it."

Roxanne jumped at the unexpected blare of the limo's horn. She realized she could hear a tiny echo of it on the screen. She jolted to look out the window and realized they'd just rocketed through the castle gates. They just might make it.

"Again, Henry!" she cried, and her bodyguard began to jam wildly at the limo's horn as they raced down the long, winding drive toward the press conference. On the screen, the increasing frantic tooting sounding like a child's antics. The camera jostled and Roxanne realized the media was reacting to the noise.

But Mateo had moved to the shorter podium. Immune to the growing pandemonium, he picked up the feather pen.

"Nooooo," Roxanne keened, digging her hands in her hair. All of her money, all of her power, and she was absolutely powerless to stop her one true love from making the one mistake that would destroy him. Would destroy them.

The limo raced past the media vans and toward the stage. The echo of the horn coming from the screen was almost as loud as the actual horn inside the limo.

The king shoved close to Mateo and said something tight and threatening in his ear. But Mateo ignored him as he leaned over, pressed his tie against his chest to prevent it from dragging through the ink, and signed his name to the document. The king snatched the pen from his hand and pushed in front of Mateo to hurriedly scratch his name across the paper.

The limo screeched to a stop, almost sending Roxanne into Helen's lap. Roxanne straightened, shoved her hair out of her eyes, and looked back up to the screen.

The king stabbed the feather pen back into the inkwell with a triumphant flourish and a gloating grin.

It was done.

Stunned disbelief began to cement Roxanne to the seat.

But her sister-in-law threw open the limo door. "Let's go!" Sofia urged, grabbing her arm. "*¡Vamos!*" Momentum alone had her scooching across the seat, stepping out into the blindingly blue day, and racing with Sofia across the lawn, swerving around camera guys and jumping over cables, until they both clattered up the steps to the stage. Roxanne stood there at the top, next to the idiot bugle guy, who was definitely a paid actor and not a Monte resident, gripping Sofia's hand and smoothing back her messy hair and panting in her simple, rose-colored shirtwaist dress. For a moment, she sensed the explosion of light and noise to her left, sensed Sofia letting go and stepping away.

Then she could see nothing, could feel nothing but the impact of Mateo's golden eyes. He crossed the stage toward her with the force of a bomb blast, knocking out her senses to everything else as he came closer. She was deaf, dumb, and blind to all but Mateo when he buried his hands in her hair.

He cradled her skull. "Let me see you," he whispered, his frantic breath on her face, his gaze burning as he stared into her eyes. His thumbs stroked velvet soft at the corners, like he was touching something precious in them. "I was so scared you'd never let me see you again."

And then he was kissing her, pulling her up onto her toes and taking her mouth, licking in like a man who'd been battered by rain and wind but suddenly discovered refuge. He kissed her like she was everything warm and safe to him. He kissed her like she was his world.

He pulled back as a cacophony of shouted questions and camera clicks exploded around them, his life-giving hands still on her face. He looked directly into her eyes. "I love you," he said over the noise, loud but deliberate. "I love you, and I'm sorry I was afraid to say it. I'm sorry I hurt you. I was a coward and a fool. You're stronger than I am."

With tears filling her eyes, Roxanne began to shake her head, her face still safely held by his big, demanding hands.

Mateo just nodded. "Yes. You're a better leader than I am. You're a better person than I am. But I can learn. Give me a second chance and I will spend the rest of my life making myself the kind of man who is worthy of you."

Tears were freely running down her cheeks, gathering against his palms. She clenched the back of his hands and felt the cracks in her heart begin to heal at the warmth of the gold ring he still wore. "You already are," she sobbed. "*Mi querido*, I love you. But, Mateo…" She tried to stifle her cries but couldn't. "What did you do?"

Instead of crying like she was, instead of mourning all he'd given up, Mateo shocked her. He winked. Then he smiled. "Trust me, Roxanne." He leaned in and gave her a soft kiss on her tear-sheened lips. "Trust me, my wife." He tilted her head and kissed her again. "Trust me, my perfect…" Another kiss. "Brilliant…" And another. "Beautiful…" Multitudes and multitudes of kisses. "Queen."

As he tilted his gorgeous head for yet another kiss, Roxanne caught a flurry of movement behind him. She clenched his wrists, stilling him, and saw Fuller bending over the pretentiously leather-bound set of documents, flipping through the pages as he jabbed his finger at them and spoke with barely restrained fury to the king. The king's eyes flew wide, and then he was inspecting the documents, too.

He gave an involuntary shout.

Roxanne felt the glare of the cameras swing away. She

looked at Mateo. A smile with just a touch of gloat was spreading across those gorgeous sulky lips.

"What did you do?" she asked again, this time with wonder.

"*Espere. Y ver,*" he said, wiping her tears away but leaning in for one more leisurely kiss before he turned around to face the unfolding drama, wrapping an arm around her shoulders and pulling her against his side so she could "wait and see."

The heads of both Easton Fuller and the king swung around to glare at Roman Sheppard, who still sat in his seat, knees spread, arms crossed over his chest, as Tonya sat close and cooed in his ear. With her threat established, she'd already grown bored of the spectacle. Roxanne wondered if the woman even realized her daughter was on the stage.

Without even glancing at Tonya, Roman stood in his summer navy suit and strolled toward the two fuming men. He walked with a contained power that must have made alarm bells go off in the psyches of most men whenever he walked into a room. He walked like a warrior. Her husband, even with the loose-limbed sway he gained from working in the dirt, walked like a king. The bone-deep surety of both of their walks is why, Roxanne realized, she never doubted that they were brothers.

Roman looked down at the document over their shoulders as both men gestured and jabbed angrily. He looked back up at both of them. Their shoulders were heaving. After a moment, he simply nodded.

King Felipe exploded. He jabbed a finger in Roman's face and yelled expletives, his face an instant tomato red as he called his *mijo* "trailer trash who isn't fit to lick my asshole." The world's press recorded every second of this sweaty-browed man's "love for his family" and "dignity of his royal blood." Some play on his earlier sanctimonious words would be the next day's favorite headlines.

Easton Fuller took it one step further. This Ivy League-educated CEO, whose only experience with fighting had been ganging up on landowners who didn't want to sell, thought it would be a good idea to take a swing at an ex-Army Ranger. With the graceful ease of a dancer, Roman grabbed his punching arm, swept it around his back, and shoved the man facedown against the documents that had been his undoing.

"Roman's gotten better at that since the last time he tried it," Mateo muttered to Roxanne. Her jaw had dropped somewhere below her hemline.

CML Resorts' termination of their CEO would be announced before the end of the business day.

"That's our cue," Mateo said to Roxanne. Sofia had appeared on his left side. He offered them both an arm and then glanced to Roxanne's right. Henry had taken the spot on the other side of her when the yelling started.

"Henry," Mateo nodded.

"Sir." It was the first time her bodyguard had called him that.

"If you could make sure no one leaves the stage."

"Of course, *Príncipe.*"

Henry gave a shrill whistle and was joined by a couple of palace security guards. They crossed the stage as a group, and by the time they'd reached the podium, Roman had stared the king back into his seat and manhandled Easton into his. Tonya sat between them with an impatient scowl of disapproval. She seldom found herself on the losing side, and when she did, she didn't stay there for long. Roxanne met her mother's eyes and saw the steam of her gears already turning.

Henry and the palace guards stationed themselves on each side of the chairs while Mateo, Roxanne, Sofia, and Roman moved to the podium. Roman picked up the ponderous book and handed it to Mateo, who laid it on the lectern in front of him. Standing in between them, Roxanne looked out onto the small village of cameras, and the larger mass of Monte del Vino Real residents gathered on the lawn. Even though the residents were far away, with the king having made no special arrangements to accommodate them, she could feel their stress from here. She shared it.

What the hell had just happened?

She felt her husband take a deep breath as he surveyed the crowd. Hidden by the podium, she took his hand.

He laid his free hand on the book. "We've gathered you here under false pretenses." His voice rang out over the lawn, deep and sure. "The document the king and I just signed does *not* sell half of the Monte to CML Resorts for the development of a theme park. Instead, it verifies that I abdicate my claim to the throne in favor of my brother, Roman Sheppard."

Roxanne kept her face still, set, instead of letting it crumble into tears as the media rumbled in shock and shouts of denial came from the villagers. She wanted to shout, too.

"It also declares that *Príncipe* Roman Sheppard can sell no part of the Monte for thirty years or until the death of King Felipe Miguel de Esperanza y Santos."

The crowd grew silent as people put together what this meant.

Roxanne tried to sort it out: Mateo and Roman must have pulled off some kind of switch with matching bound documents, and then relied on the pompousness of the proceedings, the determination to rub Mateo's face in it, to guarantee that Fuller or King Felipe wouldn't review the documents before signing.

"Any attempt to coerce, blackmail, or intimidate me for a different outcome will be futile." Roxanne could feel the tension in Mateo's arm. "I will no longer allow myself to be used as a tool to harm the Monte. I cede control to my extremely capable brother and sister. My brother is a military strategist who has saved people's lives. My sister is an expert of the vine with the wisdom of the world's best rulers."

Mateo paused, just for a second, for just a sip of a breath. But in that second, she could tell what all of this was costing him.

"I have not been the prince you deserve. But I swear to you, I will be your most loyal servant. I will continue my work here in the Monte on an innovative new vine whose results we will unveil at the end of the growing season. Any involvement outside of that will only be at the request of my brother and sister. Should anyone try to reveal information out of spite or malice that discredits me, mine, or the Monte, they will find themselves facing lengthy criminal and civil court battles that they cannot afford. With our new partnership with Trujillo Industries, we can fight for a long, long time."

Roxanne's head spun. Trujillo Industries, as in Daniel Trujillo, the billionaire whose daughter had been rescued by Roman Sheppard? *That's* why tearing up that check hadn't been recklessly daring or ceding to Fuller's plan. Mateo had found a way to see the Monte through until the *Tempranillo Vino Real* was profitable while still proving to Roxanne that his love wasn't based on her money.

He had done it. He had saved the Monte. He'd kept it whole, kept it solvent, and kept Roxanne's secrets.

And all he'd had to do was give up everything.

Sofia had known that this was his plan all along. Roxanne didn't care that her sister-in-law had lied to her, made her believe that he was getting in bed with Fuller, to compel her here. *How long do you think he'll survive watching everything he cares about being stolen away by a man he hates?* The Monte was safe, but the net result was the same: Mateo was forced to give up his heritage by the worst, weakest sort of men. And woman.

He wants to show you that he chooses you. He's willing to sacrifice everything else, even the kingdom he loves, to prove that.

It was a sacrifice Roxanne never wanted him to make. Sofia was right to rush her here to try to stop him. There was still something she could do.

She tugged on his hand.

Mateo glanced at her but kept speaking.

She leaned against him toward the microphone. "Excuse me," she said, interrupting him, her voice jarringly loud over the speakers. "I just need one minute with my husband. I'm sure you'd love to hear from your new *príncipe*."

She looked at Roman Sheppard and was surprised by the man's wide green eyes. Apparently podium speaking was not one of the things he enjoyed. As she dragged her husband away, she watched Roman grab Sofia and tug her next to him.

She felt the death glares of her mother, his father, and Fuller as they crossed the stage. She pulled Mateo behind an over-sized banner near the back corner of the stage and put his broad back to the crowd. Then she told him what she wanted to do.

Minutes later, Roxanne stood in front of the podium, her husband standing at her side.

She took a moment to look at the citizens of the Monte, the mass of press, the bank of microphones that would carry her words to the world. What she was about to say would undermine twenty-nine years of effort and make her a laughingstock to everyone who knew her.

But for the first time in her life, she would truly be free.

"I'm sorry to interrupt," she said, the microphone carrying her words away. "But I have a story to tell, and it's going to make a difference to what happens here." She smiled tremulously at the crowd. "I've worked hard my whole life to make it a fairy tale. I wanted to be the Midas of money, the Snow

White of beauty, and the Fairy Godmother of motherhood." She paused and forced a backbone into her shaking voice. "But recently, I've found something better than fairy tales. I've discovered real life. I've found a real husband, prince though he may be, and a real partner. A real friend. And I don't want to cling to stories anymore.

"My brilliant partner and friend once told me that I give people power with the secrets I keep. And he was right. To live in my fairy-tale world, I gave bad people too much power. I let them take things they hadn't earned, let them punish good people. Today, I'm taking that power away."

Roxanne looked down and took a deep breath. She felt Mateo step close. Felt his hand at her lower back.

When she'd told him behind the banner of her plan, he'd taken some convincing. *I'm not worried about me*, he'd told her. *But about you. And our child.*

She knew, without him saying a word, that if she decided to step away now, decided to abort this plan and leave the fairy tale intact, he would stand by her. Knew, left to his own devices, he'd already be tugging her away.

She raised her head and let the world see her.

"In January, I orchestrated an arrangement with King Felipe to compel *Príncipe* Mateo to impregnate me in exchange for funding for the financially struggling Monte del Vino Real." Her voice echoed loud and clear over the lawn, over people's stunned murmurs. "I thought I wanted a royal baby without the hassles of a royal husband. I was wrong. *Príncipe* Mateo, who was adamantly against the arrangement, agreed only because he is a good leader. His father had pushed the Monte into financial difficulties, and Mateo had no other options if the Monte was going to survive. At the close of this press conference, my PR people will send out a copy of our contract." She jabbed a finger over her shoulder. "If I don't send it, Easton Fuller will, and I won't give him the satisfaction. He attempted to use the contract to blackmail my husband into selling half the Monte. As of today, I am not pregnant, there is a signed divorce decree already in San Francisco district court to terminate this arrangement, and *Príncipe* Mateo and I are very much in love." She bit her lip, unable to hold back her grin. "A wedding date will be announced soon."

She glanced over her shoulder and caught the dazzling smile of a gloriously in love man.

But they were not free yet, and Roxanne still had more to tell. She faced the stunned audience again.

"The other detail I must disclose is my arrangement with my mother." She felt that same dark shadow on her heart, that same cold shroud she felt whenever she had to refer to the woman. "You've met her today. People of the media, perhaps you'll track her down. Perhaps you'll ask her invasive questions about her life and mine, and perhaps you'll pay her oodles and oodles of money to answer them. I hope you do. Because she is never getting one more red cent from me."

She took a shuddering breath. "She was a bad mother. She left me alone for days or abandoned me at random places when I was too young to care for myself. She slept with men for money because it was convenient, and she didn't care if her child was in the room or not. She didn't care *where* her child was. And she didn't care that it made her child's already miserable life more difficult in a tiny, conservative town. Once I became wealthy, she determined to keep making my life difficult by threatening to reveal her past unless I paid. So I paid, with my checkbook and my dignity and my self-worth. And I will continue to pay, as will my husband and our future children, if I don't stop her now."

As her words soared away over the crowd, to her surprise,

so did that shadow. The weight of that shroud lifted up and the Monte sun warmed her bare skin.

"That scared little girl didn't do anything wrong." She looked back at her husband. "It's not my shame to bear anymore."

She wouldn't turn to look at her mother. There was no need. The woman, without conscience or heart or love, was a void on the stage. And Roxanne's world, her real life, was so full. She had brawn and brains. She had a sister and, apparently, a brother. She had a Father. She had an empire and two small towns that adored her and needed her.

And she had her love. She smiled at him now. "Does that cover everything?"

He smiled back. "I think so."

"Oh, thank the Lord," she heard Roman groan on her opposite side. She turned to grin at him. "Does that mean I don't have to be prince anymore? I don't even speak Spanish."

Roxanne smiled at Sofia, who gave her a tear-glittering grin, before she shrugged at Roman. "If you don't mind..."

He immediately leaned over and lugged the book off the podium. "Let's find a shredder."

The crowd slowly began to comprehend what had just occurred. A buzz of questions from the press quickly became a shout. The platform rumbled as Henry and the security guards escorted Fuller, Tonya Medina, and King Felipe, all hiding their faces from the cameras, off the stage. From the back of the lawn, rising like a wave, came a roar.

"*¡Viva la multimillionaria!*"

"*¡Viva el príncipe!*"

"*¡Viven a nuestro próximo rey y reina!*"

Mateo stepped next to her and pulled her against his side. He leaned down to murmur in her ear, "Wave at your people, *mi reina de ojos marrones.*"

My brown-eyed queen. Roxanne had left her contacts at home. When the people shouted, "Long live our next king and queen," they were referring to her. This was real. This was permanent. These were her people. And she would one day be their queen.

Because Mateo, their king, would be her real and forever husband.

Feeling like she was actually in a fairy tale, Roxanne watched her husband for cues and then raised her hand. She began to wave. The shouts from the residents became exultant. She waved harder, her hair in her face. Mateo roared, "*¡Viven el Monte!*" and squeezed her against his side.

Screw fairy tales. Real life was awesome.

December
Two Years Later

Roxanne stared at Mateo over the glistening bump of her belly.

"I hate you," she said.

Mateo just smiled back. "You once were willing to pay me an impressive amount of money to do this to you," he said as he squeaked closer on the rolling stool and traced a heart into the gel.

Reclining on the obstetrics bed, she slapped at his hand. "I was an idiot. I didn't know what I was doing. I'll pay you even more if you take over the remaining six months of this pregnancy. 'Kay? Great!"

He protected his hand by grabbing hers, running his thumb over the simple diamond-and-emerald spiraled ring that they'd discovered together in the Monte's vault. He raised her hand and kissed it, looking down at her with sympathetic eyes. "It doesn't work that way. How're you feeling?"

"Nauseous," she grumped. "Starving."

Her 24/7 "morning" sickness, paired with an unreasonable amount of heartburn and an impressive belly considering she was only twelve weeks along, was why she was laid out for this unscheduled ultrasound, stomach slick and waiting for her doctor to get back from an emergency phone call.

"*Pobrecita*," he murmured, his thick, gold-tipped hair hanging in his face, his eyes shining honey down at her. *"Mi reina gloriosa."*

My glorious queen.

Okay, how was a woman supposed to stay mad at that?

It was infuriating, the number of weapons her husband could use against her. The hair, the eyes, that body, those hands, and his deep purring voice were bad enough. But his kindness, loyalty, empathy, dedication, and perseverance were devastating. His humor slayed her, his intellect made her his slave; when he combined his humor and intellect into horrible jokes that had her rolling on the floor—well, she'd follow him to the ends of the earth just to share a quip that no one else in the world would think was funny.

His weapons had only gotten more powerful since their marriage two years ago. Just three months after that chaotic press conference in the Monte, she'd said "I do" in the village's small chapel, with Father Juan giving her away and the children of the shelter acting as her wedding party, and had honestly thought that she couldn't love Mateo any more than she had at that moment.

Just two days later, he'd proved her wrong. When he'd danced with every single woman and a few young men at their reception after they renewed their two-day-old vows at St. Paul's Catholic Church, when he'd drunk beer and slapped backs with most of the men while Sofia and Roman and Carmen Louisa and his Titi dazzled the townspeople like exotic birds, when he full-heartedly embraced the small town that had provided her foundations, she realized she might have only dipped her toe into the ocean that could be her love for Mateo.

As she grabbed the front of his t-shirt, she inhaled the stomach-soothing smell of soil coming off of him. He'd been at his lab before the appointment; he traded his ball cap for a blazer. She dragged him down toward her.

"Distract me," she said against his mouth.

"Gladly." But instead of the smooth slide of his lips, Roxanne felt the cool press of paper. She snatched at it…and discovered that it was a check made out for half the amount she'd loaned the Monte after she and Mateo were married.

She stared at him, stunned. His grin spread itself beautifully wide. "We sold next season's *Tempranillo Vino Real* fruit for three times what we offered it for. Once they tasted Sofia's wine, some of the winery holdouts started a bidding war."

She wished she could blame her sudden tears on her pregnancy, but she'd grown embarrassingly emotional since marrying Mateo. "That's wonderful," she breathed. "But, Mateo, you know you can wait to pay this back until…"

He nipped her nose. "It's okay, my lovely Midas." Calling herself that was the only thing she regretted about the press conference; it had become one of Mateo's favorite teases, especially as Medina Now Enterprises continued to grow and thrive. They now had a headquarters in Buenos Aires and were making a significant impact bolstering female-owned South American businesses. Mateo even had begun his own project, helping female Chilean growers select the best grapes for their land.

"I wouldn't repay it if we didn't have it," he continued, tucking the check into her purse before straightening on his stool. "The rest of your money is an investment and you and Trujillo will begin seeing dividends faster than we'd hoped. But I'm more comfortable with you as my partner than my banker."

The sum he'd allowed her to loan him was paltry compared to the amount she'd offered in their original contract. Daniel Trujillo's surprising investment had eliminated the need, and Mateo wanted the royal family and the Monte to live within reasonable means. The Monte's longtime treasurer had been replaced with a seven-person panel of Monte citizens and financial experts. King Felipe and Queen Valentina could withdraw nothing beyond their monthly stipends without the signatures of Mateo and at least two members of the panel.

His father had agreed to it to avoid blackmail charges. The blackmail case against Easton Fuller, however, was moving forward.

People magazine had lost their gone-to-the-highest-bidder interview with Tonya Medina when they'd informed her of the charges against Fuller.

"You can go to jail for that?" she'd asked.

She'd run out on her million-dollar interview and fled Freedom. Roxanne never intended to press charges, but now she was glad that she'd kept a lifetime's worth of threatening letters, emails, and voice mails.

Eventually, she'd had her investigators track Tonya to Tennessee. She sent her a modest monthly check, enough to handle rent, food, and healthcare. She would never again interact with her or refer to her as her mother, but she didn't want her to be society's burden.

Her stomach's loud and uncomfortable gurgle brought her back to the present and she grimaced at Mateo.

He shot out that sulky bottom lip she loved. "Want me to grab the trash can?"

"Yes…no? Maybe I just need a burger." She clutched her non-gooey sides. "God, I wish your son would just make up his mind."

He rolled over to fetch the small trash can just in case. "I hope you keep calling her 'my' daughter when she's not causing you misery."

She no longer cared whether it was a girl or a boy; she simply yearned for a healthy child. So, of course, now he always referred to the child as a girl and she always referred to it as a boy. Just to be contrary.

"I'm so sorry about the delay," said Dr. Wan as she came back into the room.

Mateo got off her stool and stood on Roxanne's other side. Dr. Wan refreshed the jelly on Roxanne's belly, turned on the ultrasound screen, and pressed the transducer against Roxanne's skin.

"So do you have any names picked out yet?" Dr. Wan asked as Roxanne squinted her eyes at the white fuzz on the black screen.

"No first names yet," Mateo said, tilting his head to the side as he looked at the screen. "Her middle name will be Sofia."

"His middle name will be Roman," Roxanne echoed.

They'd made a drunken promise after their elegant "premarriage dinner" at Joël Robuchon in Vegas with his siblings turned into a twelve-hour "bachelor party." Over tequila shots during a sunrise breakfast at a strip club, they'd toasted Sofia and Roman for their help bringing them together and swore to name their firstborn after one of them. They still thought it was a good idea the next day, nursing massive hangovers by the hotel pool.

Sofia was now a certified winemaker and had invented a winemaking chemical that could revolutionize the industry; Medina Now Enterprises was providing seed money for development and production. Roman had bought a home in the Monte and spent several months a year there between security jobs.

The Monte and Mateo's reputation had, thank God, escaped the negative repercussions of Roxanne's revelations. She'd taken a hit; there had been several "exposés" on her as reporters tried to uncover ways she'd lied or manipulated in order to hide her "scandalous" past. Fortunately, the most morally compromising thing she'd ever done was force Mateo to have sex with her, and the world already knew about that.

She lost some business contacts, and a few deals stalled, but she could barely look at them as losses.

Considering all she had gained.

They now split their time between their homes in Black-hawk—conveniently located between San Francisco and Davis—and in the Monte. They also built a lakeside home outside of Freedom, where they spent a few weekends a year. After a long recovery, Father Juan was once again healthy and back in his pulpit and whenever Roxanne and Mateo were in town, parishioners always made sure to save them seats in the front pew.

She was so glad she hadn't gotten pregnant during those first six months with Mateo. This baby, made three months ago during the hyper-sexed days that always accompanied harvest in the Monte, when Mateo would come home to her, dirty and sweaty, fuck her into the mattress like she was the earth and he was the plow, and then pass out for a few hours until he staggered into the fields again, was made with love. This baby was made with ferocity and sweat, with understanding and empathy. This baby was earned through hard choices and truth telling, by standing up to a world that was no fairy tale.

This baby was going to be able to take on the world and win.

Dr. Wan narrowed her eyes at this baby on the ultrasound screen. "Oh!" she said sharply. She peered closer at the screen as she moved the transducer on Roxanne's belly. "Oh."

"Oh?" Roxanne asked, mildly panicked. All she could see were white mountains of fuzz. She was going to invest in improving ultrasound technology ASAP.

"We've discovered the reason for your nausea. And why you're the size you are." A smile grew on Dr. Wan's face as she pressed a button on the screen. A frozen still replaced the moving image.

"We have?" Mateo asked. Her genius husband was as clueless as she was.

"Yes. Morning sickness is caused by high levels of HCG and when you're carrying twins, you're dealing with twice the normal amounts."

"Twins?" Roxanne squeaked.

"Yes! Twins!" Dr. Wan was jubilant as she pointed at one fuzzy lump, and then another.

Roxanne looked up at Mateo. He looked down at her, beautiful mouth hanging open in the same shock she felt, and shrugged his shoulders. Oh thank God. She hadn't just failed Parent Test 101: deciphering your twins on an ultrasound screen.

"And…" Dr. Wan was like a game show host, building up what was behind the curtain. "You won't have to pick which middle name you'll use."

"We won't?" Mateo asked, lovely and deep and befuddled.

"No. You'll get to use *both* names. You're having a girl *and* a boy."

This time, when Mateo looked down at her, she could see it, the humor playing at the corner of his shock. She felt it, too. His girl. Her boy. His son. Her daughter.

As a billionaire and her prince, they always demanded perfection. And this was perfect.

★ ★ ★ ★ ★

Author's Note

My writing used to be paralyzed by facts. I once took three days trying to find whether 1920s Mexico City had electric streetlights. Now, after some initial research, I let the muse fly free and lean on Google to save me.

I gave myself the freedom of a pretend place and people. But the place and people are set in the beautiful country of Spain with a nod to the Riojan wine region. I wrote with great respect for the country but leaned into the fantasy.

Please forgive any inaccuracies.

—Angelina

Acknowledgments

I never liked acknowledgments. They felt too much like Oscar speeches. But it was a long, difficult walk to get to this podium, and I did not make it alone.

Thank you, Kerri Buckley, Angela James, and everyone at Carina Press for responding to this book with immediacy and fervor, for behaving like this baby was as beautiful as I thought it was. Thank you Anna Sullivan for the spectacular title.

Thank you, my brilliant agent Sara Megibow, for thinking this book was magic, and for knowing exactly the tweak it needed to create fire.

Thank you, Washington Romance Writers DC, for consistently providing the training, access to industry professionals, and enthusiasm that made me believe I could succeed at this lightning-strike of a dream.

Thank you, Peter, Gabriel, and Simon. Every time I opened my mouth about writing or this book or the journey, you looked at me like I was a writer. Not mom. Not wife. But a writer. Your faith helped me believe.

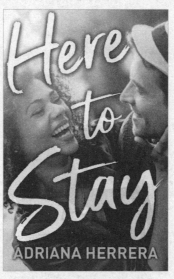
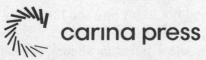

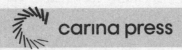
At Dallas's iconic luxury department store, you can feel good about indulging a little...or a lot. The staff is proud of their store. If you're one of them, you're three things: brilliant, boss and bomb.

Julia del Mar Ortiz moved to Texas with her boyfriend, who ended up ditching her and running back to New York after only a few weeks. Left with a massive—by NYC standards, anyway—apartment and the job opportunity of a lifetime, Julia is struggling...except that's not completely true...

Read on for a sneak preview of
Here to Stay
by Adriana Herrera,
available now from Carina Press.

He brought his cat to dinner.

I opened the door to my apartment and found Rocco holding the little carrier we'd bought for Pulga at the pet store in one hand and in the other he had a reusable shopping bag with what looked like his contribution for dinner.

"Hey, I know you said she was uninvited." His eyebrows dipped, obviously worried I'd be pissed at this plus-one situation. I wanted to kiss him so bad, I was dizzy. "But whenever I tried to leave the house, she started mewling really loud. I think she's still dehydrated."

Boy, was I in over my head.

I smiled and tried not to let him see how his words had actually turned me into a puddle of goo. "It's fine, since she's convalescent and all, but once she's back in shape, she's banned from this apartment."

He gave a terse nod, still looking embarrassed. "Promise."

I waved him on, but before I could get another word in, my mom came out of my room in full "Dia de Fiesta" hair and makeup. Holidays that involved a meal meant my mother had to look like she was going to a red carpet somewhere. She was wearing an orange sheath dress with her long brown hair cascading over her shoulders and three-inch heels on her feet.

To have dinner in my cramped two-bedroom apartment.

"Rocco, you're here. *Qué bueno.*" She leaned over and kissed him on the cheek, then gestured toward the living room. "Julita, I'm so glad you invited him. We have too much food."

"Thank you for letting me join you." Rocco gave me the look that I'd been getting from my friends my entire life, that said, *Damn, your mom is hot.* It was not easy to shine whenever my mother was around, but we were still obligated to try.

I'd complied with a dark green wrap dress and a little bit of mascara and lip stain, but I was nowhere near as made-up as she was. Except now I wished I'd made more of an effort, and why was I comparing myself to my mom and why did I care what Rocco thought?

I was about to say something, anything, to get myself out of this mindfucky headspace when he walked into my living room and, as he'd done with my mom, bent his head and brushed a kiss against my cheek. As he pulled back, he looked at me appreciatively, his gaze caressing me from head to toe.

"You look beautiful." There was fluttering occurring inside me again, and for a second I really wished I could just push up and kiss him. Or punch him. God, I was a mess.

Don't miss what happens next…
Here to Stay *by Adriana Herrera,*
available wherever Carina Press books
and ebooks are sold.

CarinaPress.com